The
Rattlesnake
Master

The
Rattlesnake
Master

BEAUFORT CRANFORD

AVAILABLE
PRESS

BALLANTINE BOOKS · NEW YORK

Every one of the characters in this novel is fictional. There is no Talmadge County in the state of Georgia, and no town named Alachua. For purposes of this book, both have been plonked down roughly northwest of Savannah, incorporating parts of the real-life counties of Screven and Effingham. Nothing in Talmadge County is real except the town of Brooklet, which is actually across the Ogeechee River in Bulloch County and bears little resemblance to its namesake here.

An Available Press Book
Published by Ballantine Books

Copyright © 1990 by Beaufort Cranford

Library of Congress Catalog Card Number: 89-92108

ISBN: 0-345-36319-1

Cover design by William Geller
Text design by Holly Johnson

Manufactured in the United States of America

First Edition: January 1990
10 9 8 7 6 5 4 3 2 1

To Mother and Daddy and Lannis

ACKNOWLEDGMENTS

First I want to thank Bobbie Williams, who believed before anyone else that I might someday write a book and so not only encouraged me but also gave me a place in which to practice writing when I didn't have a dime to contribute to that place's upkeep. I hope she thinks it was worth it.

Others to whom I'm indebted include Ruth Pollack Coughlin, for telling me what to do; Ralph Finch and Sean Keenan, for coming through; Elmore Leonard, for advice; Dan Tonsmeire, for hospitality; and Cliff Ridley and Bob Wyatt, for the things writers appreciate from their editors past and present.

I'd also like to thank Sharon Smith for her patience and especially for making sure she was nearby whenever I needed a friend or a fan.

ONE

I was sitting on Wilbur Bonniwell's feet, or at least where his feet would have been if Wilbur Bonniwell hadn't been under a slab of granite with his name on it. I had a peanut butter and jelly sandwich in one hand and a Pabst Blue Ribbon in the other. It was early for a beer, but it was Saturday, too.

Buddy Crittenden was sitting on a headstone off to my left. On the other side of him a cherub was poised as if to leap off its pedestal and fly home to heaven. The bright, still day was hot as a bonfire and muggy, too, but the noontime of it was almost pleasant under the live oaks that stood around the little cemetery. Cicadas were buzzing in the treetops, and somewhere a single vireo was singing the same thing over and over again.

But the loudest sounds besides Buddy and me eating and making small talk came from a pair of squirrels exploring a pile of dead leaves and from the faraway whine of a car coming up the county road that passed in front of us and turned north and ran out of sight into the haze.

It had been Buddy's idea to pull into the churchyard. "I ain't gone drink a beer on the road," he'd said, "and I really do want a beer. Besides, if we don't eat them sandwiches before we get home, they'll just go to waste."

"That's admirable," I said.

"What's admirable?" Buddy said. He was driving, I was watching the swampland go by. Most of it was cypress, sweetbay, sweetgum and blackgum, with lily pads and pickerelweed in the ditches.

"What's admirable is that you don't want to drive around with

1

a beer in your hand, for one. That wouldn't look good. For somebody that practically everybody in the county knows is a deputy
sheriff, I mean. And it's admirable that you want to stop, because
I'm hungry, too. Besides, I ain't particularly ready to go home yet."

A pair of cardinals rose up from the shoulder of the road ahead
of the car and flew toward the deep green woods.

"Uh-huh," Buddy said, and looked at his watch. "Ain't neither
of us got any place to be, I reckon, at least for a while. Maybe if we
had any fish to clean, it'd be different."

"Yep," I said, and put my hand over my mouth.

"Thank you," Buddy said.

"For what?" I looked at him as innocently as I could.

He turned his head a little and gave me a rueful grin. "For not
making some smart remark. I'm the one that was talking so loud
about all the fish we was gonna catch down there."

"We caught a few."

Buddy grunted. "Minnows," he said. "A bunch of tadpoles."

"I don't care. Not much, anyway. It was pretty on the river in
the early morning. Cool, too."

"Uh-huh. But next time I'll pick a better spot."

My stomach growled and I looked down at it. "You were also
gonna pick a spot for us to stop at and eat," I said, and stifled a
yawn and tried to stretch.

"I've picked it already," Buddy said, taking his foot off the
accelerator. "That's it up yonder in the clearing."

Which is how we came to be sitting in the little cemetery next
to a faded white building that a sign said was home to the Pine
Chapel Assembly of God, drinking beer and eating sandwiches.
Buddy had one made of egg salad that I could smell from ten feet
away. The tiny church was dappled with shadows from the great
oaks around it.

Between bites I could hear that car getting closer. Buddy heard
it, too, and cocked his head to listen.

"Car coming," he said.

"Uh-huh," I said. "So how come this here's the Pine Chapel
Assembly of God when I haven't seen a pine tree for two miles? And

where's the assembly? We haven't passed a lot of houses, either."

"I dunno," Buddy said, through a mouthful of sandwich. "Maybe Swamp Chapel didn't sound right. And it don't mean nothin' that we ain't seen a lot of houses. There's more people living out here than you can shake a stick at."

The car was almost to us now, and its tires were roaring on the old tar and gravel pavement.

"You know any of them?" I said.

"Some of them, and some of them too well," Buddy said, and looked out at the road. "Hold on a minute. Let's see who this is that's gone fly by."

He was watching the hedge of bayberry and privet that ended on the roadside at the churchyard, and I looked, too, and a light green Pontiac with two men in it and rust on the quarter panels came ripping along and rounded the curve in front of the church and headed north. As it sped up I looked down for some reason and saw a fat blob of grape jelly on the leg of my jeans.

"Wait a second," Buddy said. I was busy scraping at the jelly with a fingernail but looked up again, and he seemed to be still watching the back of the car that was now going straight away from us. "There's a great big . . . Well, goddammit."

Buddy threw the remains of his sandwich over his shoulder, bouncing yellow bits of egg salad off the ground. While I was watching it, I saw the two squirrels run up the trunk of a tree and look at us. I looked at them, too. Their tails were twitching.

"What's the matter?" I said.

"Those sorry bastards swerved all the way over to the other side of the road so they could run over the biggest dern snake I ever saw," Buddy said hotly.

"A snake?" I said. I hadn't seen anything, I'd been preoccupied with eating and minding my own business.

"They ran over a snake," Buddy said. "The biggest damn—"

"Yeah, I've seen people do things like that," I said, working on the blob of jelly again, wishing I had a little water to dilute it with so it wouldn't get sticky and aggravating.

"So have I," Buddy said. "And I don't like it."

I took my last swallow of beer. It was warm and bubbly and tasted like dirt.

"I don't like it, either," I said. "But lots of people hate snakes and some people just like to run over things." It's true.

Buddy didn't say anything to that, and he didn't really seem to be looking at anything but his feet, but then he looked up at the highway again and at the Pontiac, which was tiny in the distance by then, and his jaws were tight.

Buddy stood up. "Come on," he said, "get in the car."

He was already walking, pouring his beer on the ground.

"Hold on," I said, getting up and trying to collect my junk.

"Come on," he said again, and I took account of his voice and came on, and in nothing flat we were back in his Cutlass, peeling rubber out of the churchyard and passing the snake, and then the bridge over what a sign said was Hard Labor Creek came at us and went by very fast. The snake was a canebrake rattler as big around as my forearm, the sort of snake that properly belongs in a picture book and not abroad in the green countryside where innocent people can blunder into it; in fact, we passed it so fast and my angle of view was such that it looked perfectly and disturbingly healthy to me, coiled back on itself in what seemed to be less a posture of death than of defense, maybe even defiance. The Pontiac Buddy had accused of killing it was an indistinct shape far ahead of us in the rippling heat.

But we gained ground on it in a hurry and Buddy was leaning on the horn. Then just as it looked as though we might not simply catch the Pontiac but engulf and devour it as well, the driver looked in his rearview mirror and a puff of black smoke came out of the Pontiac's tailpipe and the distance between us increased again.

"Shoot," Buddy said, and put the accelerator to the floor. I was petrified and consternated and starting to be afraid I was going to die in a car wreck without any clear idea of just what I had gotten in a car to die for.

Pretty soon the straightaway ended and we began taking a series of tight curves, which meant that every so often the Pontiac was out of sight. Then finally there was a curve on which the Pontiac stayed in sight and then a straightaway again and a little bridge, and suddenly the Pontiac was pulling over and Buddy was pumping his brakes and we were pulling in behind it.

We were still rocking when Buddy opened his door and fairly leaped out. A tremendous cloud of fine dust was blowing all around us.

I could hear my heart beating in my ears, but I couldn't hear what Buddy was shouting as he ran up to the Pontiac and jerked open the driver's door. Then he said something to the driver, and I could see the driver's head moving as though he was saying something back. Neither of them looked very happy from where I sat.

Suddenly Buddy reached both arms into the car and pulled the driver all the way out by his collar and stood him up and threw him against the side of the Pontiac so hard that beads of spit flew out of the driver's mouth. The driver was as tall as Buddy but not as big, a man with lots of curly red hair and freckles and a face that got redder while I watched. Buddy was bouncing him lightly against the Pontiac with one hand and pointing with the other at another man who had gotten out of the passenger's side looking a bit apprehensive, holding on to the door of the Pontiac with his left hand and the roof with his right.

My mouth was open and I closed it. Now Buddy was shouting at the man on the other side of the Pontiac, then saying something into the face of the driver. The driver said something of his own and grabbed Buddy's right arm in his left hand and drew back his own right, and Buddy hit him quickly with his left fist and threw him against the car again. When Buddy took his hand away, the redheaded man slid down the side of the car and sat on the ground and bowed his head.

I was sweating like a pig. The windows of the Cutlass were rolled up, so I never knew what Buddy had shouted at either the driver or the passenger, but when he pounded on the roof of the Pontiac three times, I heard that, and the passenger came around to Buddy's side of the car with his hands out as though he was about to draw pistols. As he went by between the Pontiac and the Cutlass he looked at me, but there was nothing in his face that I could understand. His hair was black and unkempt and he needed a shave; he was wearing dark blue pants and a dirty white undershirt with a green shirt unbuttoned over it. Like his friend on the ground, he was in his early thirties.

When the passenger got around the car, Buddy pointed down at the driver and he and the passenger picked up the redheaded man and pushed him through the open door into the front seat. Then Buddy said something and pointed into the car, and the passenger got in behind the wheel. Buddy slammed the door and backed up a step or two as the Pontiac was started up and driven away.

I didn't do anything but sit still until Buddy had come back to the Cutlass, gotten in, closed the door, and put his hands on the steering wheel. "Whew," he said, and sighed.

"What the hell?" I said. It was hard to talk. My tongue was as dry and tough as an old sponge.

Buddy looked at me, then started the Cutlass and eased it out onto the highway.

"Okay," he said, "so you had to sit here and watch it, you had to sit here and maybe find out something about me that you didn't know—hell, maybe I didn't even know it—and maybe something you don't like, either. I'm sorry. But you didn't see me being part of the county law back there. You saw me telling a couple of badasses something I wanted them to hear, and I reckon I thought I had to tell them in a language they'd understand."

Buddy sighed again. "I don't think I'd have hit that guy, though, except he said somethin' nasty about my mama."

"All right," I said. My heart was slowing down. "So what'd you tell them?"

Buddy was staring at the bright road ahead of us. "I told them," he said, and gritted his teeth. "Aw, hell. I reckon I just told them they'd better not run over no more snakes."

———————

As it happens, Buddy Crittenden also told the passenger, whose name was Sperry Bissell, that he knew who he was and that if he ever saw another snake or turtle or possum or anything else run over on any road in the county, he'd come over to Sperry Bissell's house and give him some of what he'd just given Sperry Bissell's friend.

His friend's name was Jerry Spivey, and Buddy knew that, too.

Both Sperry Bissell and Buddy knew Buddy was exaggerating, though, since this county is so full of animals and cars that run over them on purpose or by accident that if Buddy had kept his promise, he would have worn a path to Sperry Bissell's door just to collect some more of whatever he had already collected a piece of on that hot, brilliant Saturday when he threw an ugly redheaded man named Jerry Spivey around for running over a snake. Or trying to, at least; I'm still not sure he did it.

Sperry Bissell, who rented a room from his mama and daddy in the house he grew up in, had always been a fairly invisible sort of person except to those people he infuriated or at least antagonized in one or more of the myriad ways a man with so many rough edges and so little sense just naturally infuriates or antagonizes people. But Jerry Spivey was as hard as Sperry Bissell was limp as a dishrag, and he was also strong and shrewd enough to attract the company of dishrags like Sperry Bissell so his own peculiar brands of mayhem and offense would have the spectators a man like Jerry Spivey so silently and passionately craves.

And what those spectators, of whom Sperry Bissell was simply the latest if not in fact the most docile, were to be present for was pretty much nothing more than Jerry Spivey going to and fro in the world tormenting the weak, taking advantage of the gullible, insulting the righteous, and generally making of himself a nuisance and a misery.

The woman who might have saved this part of Georgia from the depredations of Jerry Spivey, had she had a little foresight on her side or even a condom in her bedside table, owned a little house on Savannah Boulevard here in town that she had inherited from her husband. The husband's name was Carl Spivey, and he never did find out that he was in fact not Jerry Spivey's real father, and so he raised him, more or less, as his son. The man whose illicit collision with Dorothy Spivey actually resulted in her boy Jerry was a bachelor named Hoyt Flowers, who came by the Spiveys' house to fix the floor furnace and caught Dorothy Spivey in a weak moment, which is to say 1955.

That same house is where Sperry Bissell drove Jerry Spivey's Pontiac on Saturday afternoon after watching his pal and mentor get punched out on a deserted highway by Deputy Sheriff Buddy Crittenden. Apparently it is also where, once Jerry Spivey could see straight and had quit sulking, the two men had an argument that went from words to shouting and then to pushing and shoving because Jerry Spivey not only had a headache that would stun a buffalo, he was also embarrassed to his guts by having been punched out in front of his handpicked spectator and because Sperry Bissell was equally embarrassed to have been present.

Deliberations closed only when Jerry Spivey finally had enough of being in the same room with Sperry Bissell, which served to remind him that someone who had seen him receive his comeuppance not only lived and breathed but also might very well decide to spread the word about it. So while emphasizing some point or another of argument, he gave Sperry Bissell a good hard push that sent him backward over a coffee table and onto the floor, turning over the coffee table and spilling a glass canister of hard candy all over the place.

Very soon after Sperry Bissell picked himself up and retrieved nearly all the little hard candies from the floor, along with a fair amount of fibers and hair from the cheap carpet, he was on his way out the front door while Dorothy Spivey stood by waving a poker at his back. Hers was a stance and attitude the late Carl Spivey had come to know well.

But Dorothy Spivey wasn't finished just because Sperry Bissell was out of her living room and hotfooting it down Savannah Street. She had a toothache that was already well on the way toward ruining her weekend all by itself, and she was damned, she thought, if she was about to put up with any carrying on in her house. "And you," she said to her son, who already was thinking that this might be the worst day of his life, "I'd rather have had to give birth to a porcupine than say I'm the mama of such as you. You oughta be ashamed, comin' in here and fightin' with yo best friend. Hell, yo only friend—even if he's just as shiftless as you are."

At that point Jerry Spivey said a couple of things that were so disrespectful that they even made his mama forget her toothache for a few furious minutes. So pretty soon her son went out the front door, too, just like Sperry Bissell, and drove his Pontiac to the Knight Club, where he had some Budweiser and told the other regulars about how he'd gotten the red blotch on his face in a fight, which he'd won, with a marine from over at Parris Island.

The argument that Jerry Spivey and Sperry Bissell had, and which they continued loudly over the next several days, was just how come that deputy sheriff was to pull them over in the middle of nowhere and bust the living shit out of Jerry Spivey if he really didn't know anything about the bag full of silver dollars that Sperry Bissell had between his feet.

"And don't give me none of that crap about runnin' over no snake," Jerry Spivey said. "Ain't nobody gone pull you and me over for runnin' over no damn snake. So how come he was chasin' us if he didn't know we had that money? And how come he didn't say anything about it? What the hell was he tryin' to prove?"

"Maybe he was tellin' the truth," Sperry Bissell said. "Maybe he's some kind of animal lover."

And Jerry Spivey said again, "Don't gimme none of that shit about no snake, the son of a bitch must of known somethin'. But what I really want to know is, how come he was onto that bag of money? Tell me that. Nobody knew about it but me and you and old man Hutto, and God damn his soul, old man Hutto ain't gone never tell nobody.

"I swear I believe somebody's got it in for me. Dern that old man, if he'd of stayed alive maybe just one more week, I'd of got him to tell me where the rest of them silver dollars were."

"Maybe we can still find them," Sperry Bissell said meekly.

"Shit, we ain't even got that one bag of them no more," Jerry Spivey retorted. "Thanks to you."

"But we can go back out there and get them," Sperry Bissell said.

"If that deputy ain't done beat us to them already," Jerry Spivey said. "I just cain't understand it."

But Buddy Crittenden didn't know anything about a sack of silver dollars, and neither did I, then. I hadn't really done anything yet but sit in Buddy's Cutlass with my mouth open and my heart pounding while Buddy hit Jerry Spivey in the face for running over a rattlesnake. An action—the hitting, not the running over—of which I entirely approved once I had time to think about it.

I had been in town barely six months, and had maybe three friends, of which Buddy Crittenden was one. I had reached the point at which I no longer thought of him as a deputy sheriff every time I thought of him, but when I met him the first time he was wearing a uniform and I was glad to see it.

A woman who works part-time for me lives way out in the country over in Bulloch County, and late one night after visiting her and her husband and their two pestilential collies I had a flat tire about a mile this side of the county line. I was immediately worried, but I was outraged, too. It was a steel-belted radial, I thought stupidly. It's not supposed to go flat so fast.

The night was as black as the inside of a trunk, and the dark, monstrous trees on both sides of the road came almost to the edge of the pavement. All I had was a good dose of adrenaline, a flashlight, and a determination to change my tire and get out of there as fast as I could, and those three things had me well on the way to finishing the job when I saw headlights coming my way from up ahead.

Even though I bloodied my knuckles, I still wasn't done when the oncoming car slowed down to pull over on the other side of the road from me. I got a good grip on my lug wrench and hoped for the best.

But it was a car belonging to the sheriff's department, with a county seal on the door and a rack of colored lights on top and a spotlight. It's a wonder I didn't pee on myself with relief.

A big guy with a mustache and light brown hair that fell over his forehead got out of the cruiser and said, "Funny place to be at this time of night. You need some help?"

And I smiled politely and croaked something at him that sounded like no, thanks, and then cleared my throat and said I'd appreciate him hanging around till I was through if he didn't mind and didn't have anywhere urgent to go. He said "Sho," and came over to watch, which naturally made me self-conscious and meant that I took longer to finish.

In the next few minutes he found out who I was and where I lived, and I found out who and what he was. We also established that he had seen me eating in the Ogeechee Grille here in Alachua and we agreed that the coffee was terrific but the scrambled eggs were awful. That was about it.

After I drove home I pretty much forgot about Buddy Crittenden the deputy sheriff—except once, when I remembered to thank God it was him that pulled over rather than some psycho pervert just escaped from the prison in Reidsville—until we both happened to be going through the door at that very same Ogeechee Grille a week or so later and ended up sitting down to supper together. The place was packed; in Alachua, things like going a half block down the street to have a waitress serve you fried perch can carry a lot of weight. There's not a lot else to do that you probably already don't do every day.

Between our opening and closing cups of coffee I found out that he'd graduated from the college in town, the one I worked for (which at the time seemed to me to be an odd thing for a deputy sheriff to have done), that he lived by himself in a tan brick house on Hancock Street, and that he had a longtime girlfriend named Karen Wheeler who was half owner of a flower shop.

Along the way, he found out I was born in Georgia, too, though I'd lived in two other states besides. When Buddy asked why I came back to Georgia, I said, "Because I like it here."

I do like it, although it stays too hot too long every year and I left a lot of friends where I was. Alachua's best recommendation is that it's a small town, despite the college, and it's nice to live where people speak to you on the street without asking for a dollar or demanding your watch. It's quiet, too, and not much more than an hour from the ocean. But what I didn't tell Buddy Crittenden was that the only reason I moved to this particular place in this particular state was because our little college was the first to offer me a job and a fast way out of Minnesota, which is where for a long time I thought I was going to stay.

But I didn't stay there; I got a nasty surprise instead and so I left and came down here, where surprises are normally few and far between. In Alachua I saw the same people in the same places doing the same things every day, just as I did. It was comfortable to live like that, though people who had done the same things in the same places every day for a long time had told me it could drive you crazy, too. Even so, for a while, at least, Alachua was a good place in which to go to ground.

This town is also full of good-looking women, as you might expect, what with it having a college and being in the South, to boot. There were so many that sometimes I actually felt as though I was somehow neglecting my responsibility by leaving them all alone. I wouldn't have had to leave them all alone; a few of them had already made it plain that they could use a little attention. But I wasn't ready to think about entangling alliances, even the undemanding kind that entangle no more than a Friday or a Saturday here and there. I still wasn't unentangled from a very demanding alliance, the effects of whose demolition I had come here to get away from.

On that hot Saturday afternoon I had been in town barely six months and had maybe three friends and I had just watched the biggest and strongest of them hit a redheaded man after chasing him down and yelling at him for crossing the center line to run over a snake.

TWO

I reckon you think I ought to be ashamed of myself," Buddy Crittenden said.

This was later that same Saturday afternoon, when we'd gotten back to Alachua after our adventure on the high road with the two guys in the Pontiac. We were in Buddy's kitchen, which was straight out of 1959—white appliances, real wooden cabinets, and counters of yellow Formica with curlicues on it. I had just remembered the glob of jelly on my jeans and had tried to wash it out, but it was still sticky on the inside against my leg.

"What?" I said.

Buddy was sitting at the table, using a finger to draw pictures on the tabletop with the water left in a ring around his glass of iced tea.

"I mean," he said, "those two guys didn't really break any laws to speak of, and here I am, the stupid macho south Georgia deputy sheriff, runnin' them down and bustin' one of them in the face mostly because they pissed me off. But—"

"I don't care," I said. "I've always wanted to do something like that. To people who do things like what they did, I mean. I know what you're talking about, but I think they got what they deserve."

"Yeah," Buddy said, and took out a cigarette. "But I did it and I know better than to do something like that, just like you do. What's worse, I'm a cop, too."

"But you weren't wearing your uniform."

Buddy pulled an orange lighter from his left pants pocket and lit his cigarette with it. The lighter had a picture of an armadillo on it.

"No," he said, "but that guy I hit, he knows I'm the deputy sheriff. Me 'n' him have met before."

"Oh yeah?"

"His name's Jerry Spivey," Buddy said, "and he has a bad habit of pickin' fights with people he can beat and then gettin' the best of them and not knowin' when to quit. He's one of them that just likes to hurt people."

"So that's how he knows you?" I said. "From hurting people?"

"Well, for one thing, I'm the one his mother-in-law called to come get his wife the last time Spivey came home with a snootful lookin' to punch her around a little and ended up just about beatin' her to death," Buddy said. "He come up to the hospital about the time they got her in a room and was gettin' ready to do some X rays to see if he'd broke anything. Shoot, he wanted to fight me right there for havin' taken her to the emergency room."

"So did she go back to him?"

Buddy took a long drag from his cigarette and blew smoke. "Lord, no," he said. "She'd done it before and like as not would have been crazy enough to've done it again, him comin' up there and spreadin' sweet talk around after I left, but her mama got tough with both of them and run him out of there. Later on, she made Joy Beth—that was her daughter, this Jerry Spivey's wife—go see a lawyer and then pack up and move to Columbia."

Buddy stubbed out his cigarette in a blue ashtray that had *Caesar's Palace, Las Vegas* printed on it. I knew for a fact that Buddy Crittenden had never been to Las Vegas.

"So is that it? Is that the real reason we ran down this Jerry Spivey guy? Forgettin' about that snake, I mean. Was it so you could bash him around for beatin' up his wife?"

"No," Buddy said. He was standing at the refrigerator, staring into it. I could smell the cold coming out. "You want a tomato sandwich? Karen near 'bout inundated me in ripe tomatoes yesterday."

"No, thanks," I said. "This tea's enough. After that business

14

this morning, that peanut butter hasn't moved out of my stomach yet. I'm not cut out to be a cop, not even on the snake patrol."

Buddy grunted. I heard a snap, then a drawer closed inside the refrigerator.

"But look," I said. "How come you ain't finished answering my question?"

"What question?" Buddy said, shutting the refrigerator door and sitting down at the table with more iced tea and a piece of carrot.

"The question of whether we scared the daylights out of me and you beat on this Jerry Spivey just because you had to clean up after him abusing his wife," I said, trying to sound peevish. "Or maybe we did all that just because you were pissed off that we got up at six o'clock and drove all the way to Fort McAllister and didn't catch any fish to speak of."

Buddy seemed mesmerized by the sight of his carrot, but he gave that up and looked at me instead.

"No," he said. "It ain't that at all. It's a lot stupider than that." He put down the piece of carrot and began to pull at his right index finger with his left hand. His hands were big, but his arms were like a blacksmith's.

"Okay. So it's stupid. Stupider, I mean. What is it?"

Buddy pulled out another cigarette and went through all the rituals associated with lighting it and taking the first puff.

"All right," he said, and put his cigarette in the ashtray. "When I was in high school, eleventh grade, maybe, I was drivin' my daddy's truck into town one afternoon to get a motor for somethin' or 'nother repaired."

"How old were you?"

"Not old enough to have a license, if that's what you mean," Buddy said, "but I was the only one with time to do it." He took a sip of tea and a little belch puffed out his cheeks. A clock in the shape of a chicken was hanging on the wall over the toaster; it said three o'clock sharp.

" 'Scuse me. Anyway, I was coming into town out yonder by the heater factory, and I passed a snapping turtle the size of a washtub that was comin' out of the grass to cross from the creek side over to what back then was an empty field, old man Whittaker's place—you heard of him? old man Joe Whittaker whose fifteen-year-old boy ran off with Alvin Tucker's fourteen-year-old daughter and nobody ever heard another peep outa them for ten years until they come back to town with money? No, I reckon there's no way you could've. Anyhow, I'd seen some big turtles, but that one was big enough for me to try and get a better look. And I was just a kid, y'know.

"So I whipped the truck around and went back and pulled off the road and got out. What I was gone do was put him across on the other side, if he didn't seem bent on takin' a plug out of me. Actually, I even thought about throwin' him in the truck and haulin' him back to our place and puttin' him in the pond, but he'd've run everything else off, what he didn't eat."

Buddy turned and looked at the chicken clock. "I got to be at Karen's in a little while," he said apologetically.

"So I'll go home," I said. "But first you've got to finish the story. Wait a minute—those kids had come into some money?"

"What?" Buddy said. "What kids?"

"That Whittaker kid," I said. "And his sweetie, whatshername. Tucker."

"Oh," Buddy said. "Oh yeah. They not only stayed together and stayed alive, which is at least one thing and pretty generally two that nobody around here figured they'd do, but they got their hands on some money, too. And a big Buick."

"I give up," I said. "How?"

"Well," Buddy said, "it's been done before, but it went something like this: The girl, Reba, would put the move on some older guy in a hotel bar or something, a guy who looked like he had money on him, and long about the time they got together in a room and he got his pants down, in prances Joey Whittaker with the camera and there's nothing the guy can do but shell out everything he's got on him or consider that he can get busted for contributing to the delinquency of a minor or something. A good-lookin' minor, by the way, with very big tits."

Buddy took a drag from his cigarette and blew smoke.

" 'Course, none of this is what they told everybody when they come home, they said Joey won a pile of money gamblin' or some such crap. But anyhow, they played that dodge till Reba was seventeen or so and then they graduated right on into pure old robbery. There'd be the guy, and Reba, and the motel room in Charlotte or Jacksonville or New Orleans, but they added a pistol in Joey Whittaker's hand or even a crack on the head if that's what they thought was necessary to do the job.

"How they messed up was decidin' after they'd moved back here that they needed a new sofa or something, or maybe it was even the rent by then, and hadn't neither of them seen fit to get a job, y'know. So they drove up to Atlanta one weekend to relieve some salesmen or some Shriners of their ready cash. But Joey pulled a gun on what turned out to be an FBI man and somehow the gun ended up on the floor of the hotel room and the two of them made a run for it back down this way.

"That's right after Ed Lundquist was elected sheriff, and the FBI let him make the arrests when the time came. 'Course, there was the fact that the FBI man had gone up to that room with Reba, and of course he claimed he was just going along, that he'd smelled a rat all the time. And then he was down to his shorts, too, the kids said, when Joey came in and they tried to put the bite on him. It don't matter now why he was up there, though; he got a promotion out of it and Big Ed's been in high cotton ever since."

"Okay," I said. "I appreciate the crime report. Sorry to interrupt your story."

Buddy scratched his right ear, then pulled on the lobe a few times. "Well," he said, "there I am, gettin' set to go pick up that turtle, when out of nowhere comes this great big ol' ten-wheeler dump truck and just smashes him to pieces—*blam!*" Buddy's hands came together and flew apart.

"There was snapping turtle all over the doggone highway. I couldn't believe it, I just stood there on the shoulder, gawpin' like an imbecile. What really got me was that this guy had come all the way over to my side of the road to get that turtle, just like those guys this morning did to get that snake, and when he went by me, he was laughin' his goddamned head off. It still makes me mad to think about it."

Buddy looked less mad, though, than sheepish, and took a sip of iced tea. His lighter was still on the table beside his glass.

"So where'd you get the lighter?" I said, pointing at it. "I've never seen one like that. With an armadillo on it, I mean."

"No," Buddy said, "me, either. Gus Dixon had a dozen of them over at his store and I bought 'em all."

"Ah," I said. "So what?"

"What?" Buddy said, and looked at his lighter, then at me. "Oh. So that's when I decided to become a cop."

"To stop people from running over animals on the highway?" I said incredulously, and yawned even though I didn't mean to.

"Hah," Buddy said, and scratched the back of his neck. "No, can't nobody stop people from being cruel and stupid, whether it's to animals or other people. Back then I didn't think of it quite the same way I do now, y'know. But maybe you could say I've got an exalted sense of injustice. There's just so much meanness around, I guess I just came to figure that by being a cop of some sort, I could do something about some of it, maybe do something to fend off some of the bad stuff that people do to each other."

"Or to snapping turtles or snakes," I said.

"Are you making fun of me?" Buddy said.

"No sir," I said. "I'm just leading you on."

Buddy sighed and put his chin in his hand.

Later on, after supper, I went over to Sam Campbell's house to shoot a few games of eight ball, at which I am no good. Sam works down the hall from me at the college and sells some real estate on the side. While we played, Sam and April's little girl giggled and squealed and tumbled around the table and over our feet. Sam and I were high as kites; it was Saturday night.

"You and Crittenden are a couple of morons," Sam said, chalking his cue. "Buddy ought to know better, anyhow, than to go waltzing up to a car with two guys in it out in the middle of nowhere with no gun or anything and not even a radio in the Cutlass, for Chrissake."

"And nothing much legal to back him up, either," I said, sort of agreeing with Sam in spite of myself.

Sam laughed, but crouched and shot and the nine ball went into the side pocket, *whock!*

"Yeah," he said, and laughed again. "Nothing to back him up but you."

"I appreciate the vote of confidence," I said, though at the same time I felt less righteous sarcasm than something like fear, having already wondered what I would have done if something had happened to Buddy and I'd been left out in never-never-land up against the two guys in the Pontiac with neither hope of rescue nor even a way to acquit myself with dignity.

Sam straightened up and moved around me. His eyes were gleaming and fixed on the table. He bent down and sighted past the cue ball and said, "And what if one of those two fellers had had a sawed-off shotgun? Then what? You guys lyin' out there dead because of some snake?" *Whock!*

But Jerry Spivey and Sperry Bissell didn't have a sawed-off shotgun, and they didn't have a bag full of silver dollars, either, when Buddy and I pulled up behind them. And it wasn't long before the two of them had quit wondering about whether Buddy Crittenden had had suspicions about them carrying silver dollars and had moved on to wondering about something that Jerry Spivey considered more urgent.

What puzzled Sperry Bissell, and what utterly infuriated Jerry Spivey, was the question of just where in the world that bag full of silver dollars went when Sperry Bissell threw it out the window of the Pontiac.

"I couldn't of slung it far," Sperry Bissell said, "it was too heavy. I just tried to heave it off over the bank into the bushes."

"Maybe you threw it in the creek," Jerry Spivey said disgustedly.

"No," Sperry Bissell said, "it was just after one of them curves when the bastard couldn't see us. It's down the bank or just inside them bushes and stuff, or something. It's got to be."

"It'd better be," said Jerry Spivey.

But even though Jerry Spivey and Sperry Bissell tromped through the bushes and slogged through the slimy water off every curve on the route along which Buddy Crittenden and I were behind them, they didn't find a sack of silver dollars but found only some whiskey bottles and beer cans and an old stove and a dead dog instead.

So here they are. It's Tuesday, three days and a couple of hours from the moment at which Sperry Bissell threw the bag out the window of Jerry Spivey's car. Tuesday is even hotter than Saturday was, the kind of heat that makes babies fret and cry and older people think of killing each other. Jerry Spivey is cussing as he stomps up a bank toward his Pontiac, which is parked on the shoulder of county road 263. He has cockleburrs in his socks and beggar lice on his pants and two ticks are embedded in the soft white skin of his abdomen just below his belt. He is sweating steadily and smells bad and is in a terrible mood.

Sperry Bissell, meanwhile, is sitting on a cinder block at the bottom of the bank, putting on his shoes. He has been wading through what looked to him to be a rainwater ditch, poking around with a stick, hoping and praying that he'd find those damned silver dollars that he never should have had anything to do with anyway, and all he was trying to do was save him and Jerry Spivey from having to explain to a deputy sheriff why he had a bag full of hard money on the floorboard between his feet.

And now Sperry Bissell hears Jerry Spivey say stupid asshole in a way he knows is supposed to make him think that Jerry Spivey is talking to himself but send him a message all the same. At practically the same time, Sperry Bissell notices that he has a thin speckled leech about a half inch long stuck to the arch of his foot.

Here Sperry Bissell has an epiphany of sorts, too, the kind of revelation generally not rapidly forthcoming to a man with barely the insight of a sturgeon: he realizes that although it is mostly what he wants to do, jumping around and hollering won't get that leech off his foot. So he tries to grab it and pull, and can't hold it. He tries scraping it off with his fingernail, listening to Jerry Spivey muttering as he opens the door of the Pontiac behind and above him. He looks at the leech, trying not to think about what it's doing to him, then lets go of his right foot and puts a sock and a shoe on his left foot and then looks at his right foot again and the leech is still there.

"Are you coming with me?" Jerry Spivey hollers.

"In a minute," Sperry Bissell hollers back. If he had known then how mad Jerry Spivey really was, and how hot his friend was and how gritty his neck was in his collar, Sperry Bissell might have put his remaining sock and shoe on his foot over that little speckled leech and gotten the hell up the hill. But he didn't know that, of course, and even if he had, there's still no guarantee that it would have been enough to get him to walk around with a leech.

The sun is bright, the birds are singing. "What's the god damned hell the matter with you?", shouts Jerry Spivey.

Sperry Bissell sighs, then takes a quick breath and hollers back to Jerry Spivey that he has a leech on his foot, but that serves only to make Jerry Spivey cuss a little more and hit the steering wheel with the palm of his hand. Now Sperry Bissell can smell his own sweat, and this makes him desperate; so he tries his fingernail on the leech again. To his astonishment and relief, the butt end of the leech raises a little and Sperry Bissell gets a sort of grip between his thumb and forefinger, but as he begins to pull he feels the leech's hold on his foot and immediately has a pure clear burst of panic in which he imagines his insides being sucked out through the hole in his arch and into the leech. He lets go of his grip as Jerry Spivey starts the Pontiac and blows the horn twice and loud.

So what can Sperry Bissell do? He thinks Jerry Spivey would drive away and leave him, and he doesn't know what to do about the leech except that he doesn't want to walk on it. But maybe it's a choice between being left and having somehow to deal successfully with the leech that prompts Sperry Bissell to take out his knife and slide the blade under the leech from behind. As he does this Jerry Spivey blows the horn of the Pontiac again and yells something that Sperry Bissell can't make out over the noise of the engine.

But Sperry Bissell finally has a plan. He works the blade of the knife toward the leech's head, very slowly, seeming to be transfixed by the drama taking place on his foot. Now the blade is finally at the leech's front end and Sperry Bissell grits his teeth and forces it a little and the leech comes off. A tiny trickle of blood runs down a wrinkle in Sperry Bissell's arch.

Sperry Bissell exhales and flips the leech into the water in front of him and shudders. He then takes out his handkerchief and wipes the blood and water from his foot and puts on his sock and shoe and stands up and adjusts his pants and spits.

But by this time Jerry Spivey has driven away. With nothing else to do, Sperry Bissell climbs the bank to county road 263 and starts walking east toward Brooklet, which he knows is three, maybe four miles up that long, hot highway. By the time he gets to the Amoco station in the middle of town and spends twenty of his thirty-five cents to call his sister Jennifer and persuade her to drive the eight miles from Alachua down to Brooklet to pick him up, he is wilted and wrinkled and his mouth is foul and dry.

This is a good time indeed to get away from this miserable vassal and footstool as he sits on the curb outside the Amoco station, the people who drive by wondering who he is, him wondering if he should put some Mercurochrome on his foot when he gets home. He doesn't even have a cigarette and wants one very badly.

Or a cold beer or a Coca-Cola, something wet and tasty to take the heat out of his throat. Maybe even some watermelon.

THREE

Speaking of watermelons," said Buddy Crittenden, "do either of you know Harold Buckminster?"

Sam Campbell and I looked at each other, and Sam made a
face. Sam had juice all over his chin and some on his shoes, too,
which Buddy said was because Sam was born and raised in Montana
and so never learned how to eat a watermelon with dignity. Sam,
who thought that was a lot of baloney, belched.

"Let me take it," I said. "Harold Buckminster is a watermelon?"

Buddy snorted. "Harold Buckminster is this guy who lives
down in Brooklet," he said, "and he grows the biggest watermelons
you ever saw."

"This one is a fruit of some substance itself," I said, and
belched, too. "Excuse me. Did he grow it?"

"Naw," Buddy said. "It came from the A&P. Up against some
of Harold Buckminster's watermelons, this here is a crabapple."

Sam was making slurping noises with a piece of rind. "All
right," I said. "Who's Harold Buckminster?"

Buddy said Harold Buckminster was pretty much your garden
variety peckerwood, not particularly bright but at least good-
hearted, but he was also a guy who had trouble staying away from
a ferocious substance he distilled in the woods behind his house.
On the other hand, lots of economically disadvantaged people
besides him still made whiskey or wine for themselves and whoever
else would drink it. What set Harold Buckminster apart from his
peers was a collection of blue ribbons from the annual Tri-County

Agricultural Exposition for the size of the watermelons he grew in his backyard.

This Harold Buckminster used to work at Bill Puddy's 7-Eleven store in Statesboro, but now his legal earnings were mostly what he could pick up doing odd jobs around Brooklet, where he had a little clump of house also occupied by his wife, Doris, who called herself a beautician and did other people's heads in the parlor of her home, and by three children of unknown ages and slim promise.

Buddy said Harold Buckminster made his own whiskey even when he worked at the 7-Eleven, and the combination seemed to have sustained his family fairly well in those prewatermelon days. But then one evening Harold Buckminster got to work just drunk enough to feel safe in lighting up a joint in the back room, and when Bill Puddy walked in at 10:29, Harold Buckminster had finished a box of ginger snaps and a quart of chocolate milk and had started in on the Zero bars. Since then, he had never stayed long at any job, mostly because after he was fired from the 7-Eleven he took to making and drinking whiskey the way some dogs take to eating chicken shit, meaning he just couldn't leave it alone.

The only reason Harold Buckminster had a garden was because his daddy had always had one and taught Harold Buckminster that any man who lived in the South and didn't have a garden was somehow violating the natural order of things. As it happened, having a garden also gave Harold Buckminster something at which to make his children labor in what he considered was a way to divert them from the temptations of lassitude. But the kids had to stay clear of the watermelon patch or risk a good whacking.

"So why'd he start growing watermelons in the first place?" Sam said. By now we were done with our own melon and I carried the slices off the porch and set them on the grass where the yellow jackets could crawl on them without getting in our way.

Buddy said that was because Harold Buckminster believed black folks would give him a couple of dollars each for his watermelons, and since black folks also bought most of his whiskey, he figured he'd have a nice sideline to his regular income. But since it is actually a toss-up whether black folks or white folks like watermelon the most, Harold Buckminster did even better in the fruit business than he expected, especially after his fame as a grower began to spread. Now there were people who stopped by Harold Buckminster's house to get a watermelon who didn't even know about the whiskey, and Harold was renting an acre next door to his place just for planting them.

Then about three years ago, Buddy said, he and Sheriff Lundquist happened to be out at Harold Buckminster's place because somebody in Alachua was complaining that her yardman seldom got to work on Monday morning because he spent all weekend drinking Harold Buckminster's liquor. But when they got there, they found Harold Buckminster in the backyard in his garden on his knees, trying to pick up what Sheriff Lundquist said was a watermelon that was probably big enough to hide a still in if Harold Buckminster really had one.

So Sheriff Lundquist and Deputy Sheriff Buddy Crittenden never did get into the woods behind Harold Buckminster's house to look for a still, because Sheriff Lundquist was basically a kindly man and saw in that mammoth watermelon a way for Harold Buckminster to discover some pride in himself and maybe turn aside from the broad avenue of sin on which he had set his feet.

On that revelatory afternoon, Buddy Crittenden and Sheriff Lundquist and Harold Buckminster sat on the porch of Harold Buckminster's house, which Buddy said looked to have been around since the Pilgrims landed and might even have been built from the planks of the boat they came over in, and Sheriff Lundquist told Harold Buckminster that he should enter that big watermelon of his in the Whoppermelon contest at the upcoming Tri-County Agricultural Exposition and win the fifty-dollar first prize.

"If you got any sense, Harold," the sheriff said, "you'll do it." And Buddy says he worried that right there Big Ed Lundquist might have put a qualification on Harold's entering that he couldn't live up to, but sure enough, Harold Buckminster rode to the fairgrounds the next day in the sheriff's car and signed up his melon.

He won the fifty dollars with pounds to spare, which made

Sheriff Lundquist feel very good about himself and about the twenty dollars he had bet John Scroggins of the Merchants and Farmers Bank that Harold Buckminster's watermelon would win. But Harold Buckminster didn't seem to feel any better about himself despite the sheriff's hopes, because he spent most of the fifty dollars on new copper tubing for his main source of income and went right back to his rut in the highway to ruin.

A bluejay hollered from a dogwood tree in the yard. "Well well," Sam Campbell said. "So . . ."

"That ain't all," Buddy said. "Unless you're through listening."

"Go ahead," Sam said. "This is about all I've got to do today, anyhow. April and Anne are down in Savannah to see April's mama, and I've already cut the grass. Only thing I'm going to do later is go over to the gym and pump some steel."

"Iron," I said.

"No," Sam said. "April did that this morning." Sam and I snickered, and Sam belched.

" 'Scuse me," Sam said.

"Are the two of you through playin' Abbott and Costello?" Buddy asked grimly.

"Who?" I said.

"He's on first," Sam said.

Buddy sighed and picked at his front teeth with a thumbnail. "You people ought to know better than to mess with the law," he said.

"While we're on the subject of the law," I said, "how come you know Harold Buckminster's got a still behind his house and you don't take some of your deputy friends and go out there and bust it up?"

Buddy spat a piece of watermelon string into the yard. "Well," he said, "mostly because if it wasn't Harold Buckminster doin' it, it'd be any one of nine or ten other people that don't need the money and attention nearly as much as he does."

"Do you drink his whiskey?" Sam said.

"No," Buddy said. "Aside from the fact that I'd like to keep my guts intact, if I'm gone be deputy sheriff, there's someplace I gotta draw the line. Even if it's a fuzzy one."

A week later I was sitting in the same place on the porch listening to the crows razzing at each other across the road, wondering what the world might be coming to and figuring that if it came to what I thought it would, then I'd just as soon it waited till after I left, when Buddy Crittenden drove up and announced that it was time to go down to Brooklet for a viewing.

So we stopped in town to pick up Sam and then sped out through the green countryside to Harold Buckminster's watermelon patch.

Harold Buckminster's place was about two blocks off Brooklet's main drag, which consists of two filling stations, a little post office, J. B. Barrett's Feed and Seed store, a general store with a lot of dead moths in the windows, and a big furniture store that seemed incongruous until you found out that its clientele came from seven states and that it was Brooklet's primary claim to fame and the fundament of its economy.

The house Harold Buckminster and his family lived in had a long front porch and was set back from the road on a bare dirt yard under three or four red oaks with great thick roots exposed around them. At various angles of repose in the yard were an ancient pickup truck and a '62 Dodge, a Philco refrigerator, a stove, a cast-iron bedstead, a crib, and numerous smaller oddments in assorted states of disrepair or dissolution. Ever so often, Buddy said, a new piece of junk would appear under Harold Buckminster's trees, as though the house periodically got sick of an especially noxious furnishing and so hawked it up through the hall and blew it out into the yard.

Harold Buckminster was waiting for us on his porch, which was fine since none of us showed any signs of wanting to see the innards of the house, though Buddy Crittenden claimed to have been in the parlor at some point and swore that we would have been hard-pressed to tell any difference between it and any of a dozen places visited by wars and plagues and cyclones.

Harold needed a shave, and his sandy brown hair was mashed down on one side as though he'd just been asleep. He had watery eyes, a crust on his lips, and mud on his khaki pants (which he had brought home from the state hospital in Milledgeville, an exile that was meant to dry him out but which served only to give him three weeks' worth of gnawing thirst). He looked fairly dim-witted to me, but Buddy said that was only his breeding coming through, and that some people in the outlying areas of the county claimed Harold Buckminster was a genius at making whiskey, that he possessed a gift that could have been given him only through the definite partiality of Almighty God.

After the usual greetings and introductions, we trooped around back of the house to a cleared space, some of which was taken up with ragged plants of indistinct origin and the rest of which was fairly rolling with watermelons. The ones in front of us were at least double the size of their cousins in the acre next door, where Harold Buckminster grew melons for consumption rather than competition. The stuff of real champions seemed to be scattered on the ground before us.

"This here's it," said Harold Buckminster, pointing to a watermelon a little smaller than a Volkswagen. Sam took off his cap and held it reverently to his chest.

"Glory hallelujah," Buddy Crittenden said.

"I'd of called you last week," Harold Buckminster said to Buddy, "but I was laid up with somethin' or other and just this morning got around to seein' 'bout this thang."

Buddy nodded, but he said later that what Harold Buckminster had been laid up with was a visit from his brother's family from Sevierville, Tennessee, a disorder Harold customarily treated by increasing his intake of liquor.

"So this here's the one," Buddy said quietly. Sam was still looking at the watermelon, holding his hat. Somewhere in the woods a wren was singing and in the weeds all around us the crickets and grasshoppers were sawing away to beat the band.

"Yep," Harold Buckminster said proudly. "It ain't as big as that 'un what won in 1982, but it'll do."

Buddy was still giving the watermelon a good look, but he wasn't wearing the sort of face anybody puts on to show off how happy he is. "How long's it been ripe?" he said.

"Uh, just a couple days, I reckon," Harold Buckminster said.

Buddy flashed him a look bursting with mistrust. "Thunk it," he said, and Harold Buckminster squatted down and thumped the big watermelon with his middle finger, producing a noise that we all recognized and which Sam later said made him think of a tomb slamming shut.

Harold Buckminster looked at his watermelon as though it had said something impolite. For a minute there was general foot shuffling. Sam put his cap back on. Buddy's right hand found something interesting to do along the edge of his belt.

"Harold," Buddy said, "maybe we better turn this thing over and have a look."

So Harold Buckminster crouched down again and turned the watermelon about sixty degrees and from under it came a smell that Buddy later said he was familiar with from the time he cleaned out a birdhouse and found it full of dead baby starlings. Instead of the honest pale underbelly of a healthy melon, this one's was white and mushy and had become the home of several small, multilegged creatures. I tried to remember some of them to look up in my *Field Guide to the Insects* when I got home.

"Harold, you got your knife?" Buddy asked.

I didn't know Harold Buckminster very well, but about then he looked as downhearted as any soul should be able to look, his general dishevelment notwithstanding. But he didn't say anything, just reached in his pants pocket and pulled out a knife with a blade so long that Sam Campbell said it made him want to hand Harold Buckminster his valuables.

Harold put one knee on the ground and stuck his knife into that melon and slit it lengthwise and cracked it open. What was inside it was neither pretty nor appetizing.

Harold Buckminster stood up, and all of us stood for a minute or so and looked down at the two halves of the watermelon lying side by side in the dirt.

"Sic transit gloria mundi," Sam said.

"What?" Harold Buckminster said.

"Nothing, Harold," Buddy said grimly. He was looking around at the other melons. "Looks like you'll have to pick another one, if they ain't all gone to the devil, too."

So we spent a half hour in the hot sun while Buddy and Harold Buckminster thunked and turned and fondled most of the rest of the melon crop looking for another prospect for the Whopper-melon contest. And they did find one, too, though not nearly as big as the one we had come all the way to Brooklet to see.

By the time Buddy and Sam and I were leaving, we had silently decided to be optimistic about Harold Buckminster's declaration that his largest remaining melon would beat anything anybody else in the county had raised. By then, too, Buddy Crittenden had extracted a promise from Harold that he would be sober enough on Monday to make it to the fairgrounds and enter the contest.

Harold Buckminster seemed calm enough at the way things turned out, but Sam said that if Buddy had given him the choice he gave Harold Buckminster, he'd have had himself locked in the icehouse till Monday just to make sure a drink of liquor and his hand never got within shouting distance of each other. For his part, Buddy seemed reassured, if still a little disgruntled at the way his viewing ceremony had turned out, so on the way back to town he didn't drive a hundred miles an hour the way he often does when he's mad. Sam and I appreciated that.

On Monday, Harold Buckminster picked his watermelon and hitched a ride out to the fairgrounds and back with Rodney Winslow, who was taking a coonhound to loan to somebody over in Portal. And thanks largely to what I understand was another visit from Buddy and a pep talk this time instead of a threat, Harold Buckminster was still sober when J. B. Barrett came by in his pickup truck on Thursday evening to take him out to the judging. Harold Buckminster actually had a car in working order then, but his wife steadfastly refused to give him the keys to it just to make certain she'd still have something to drive when she was ready to go somewhere.

I went on out to the fairgrounds about sundown, stopping to eat on the way, and after visiting Sam and April Campbell at the 4-H home-economics exhibits, where April was working as a volunteer, I spent most of my free time looking at pigs and chickens and getting sawdust all over my socks.

The Whoppermelon contest, which was sponsored by the JayCees over in Statesboro, had its own little tent next to the produce barn. As is the case with most agricultural brag festivals, at this one the animals awaiting the scrutiny of judges were kept on display, because most people can't tell a champion duck, for instance, from any other duck. But watermelons competing for honors based on size are bound by their very presence to advertise their relative position among competing fruits, so in the Whoppermelon contest all contestants were kept away from public view until after the judging.

This strategy spared anyone—usually Harold Buckminster—an attack of premature pride, just as it spared pangs of embarrassment to also-rans. The practice of keeping competing melons out of sight started the year after Jack Flemister's boy, Fred, ran away from home after taking his mama into the Whoppermelon tent to see his entry only to find that Big Ben, which is what he called his watermelon, was destined only for the booby prize. In fact, when Sheriff Lundquist and the posse finally found Fred, who had hidden from the sheriff's bloodhounds in a large trash receptacle on the outskirts of Portal, he refused to come out until the sheriff swore that his watermelon had won a ribbon for symmetry, which Buddy says was the only thing the sheriff could think of at the time.

So, faced with awarding ribbons for symmetry or hiding the Whoppermelon judging altogether, the JayCees now advertised keeping the melons out of sight as a way to add suspense to a contest that previously had no suspense at all. But at the same time, hiding the competing melons also produced an interesting sidelight, because it gave people a chance to put a little money on the results.

As Sam and I came across the midway we could see Harold Buckminster standing on the edge of a little crowd outside the Whoppermelon tent, smoking a cigarette. He was wearing khaki pants, maybe the same ones I'd already seen him in, and a gray and wine-colored short-sleeved shirt with two pockets and a pack of cigarettes in each of them. Buddy Crittenden and Sheriff Lundquist were there and looked as though they were talking to him, but when Harold Buckminster looked up and said something, it was to J. B. Barrett, who pointed over Harold Buckminster's shoulder toward the dark edge of the fairgrounds. So by the time we got to where Harold Buckminster had been, he was already halfway to the portable toilets.

Sam and I made our way into the group that was waiting for Harold Buckminster to get back and waiting somewhat more impatiently for it to be seven o'clock, when the tent would be opened and the competing watermelons displayed. Then mostly we all just stood in the dry dust and talked about lots of what amounted to nothing at great length while J. B. Barrett chewed a toothpick and spat out the splinters. Sam later said he tried to think of something clever to say about how both Sheriff Lundquist and J. B. Barrett could be accused of hiding prize watermelons under their shirts, but gave it up since the sheriff didn't know him from Sylvester P. Pussycat and since he depended on the goodwill of J. B. Barrett for cheap firewood.

Pretty soon the crowd around us was fairly substantial, and people kept looking at the corner of the Whoppermelon tent, out of which someone would come and let us in.

By and by, Harold Buckminster came shuffling along.

"Zip up your pants, Harold," Buddy said. "And damn it, you went down yonder and took more than a piss, didn't you? You took a drink, too—right?"

"Jes' a little one," Harold Buckminster said. He got a pack of Marlboros out of his left-hand shirt pocket, saw that it wasn't open, put it back and took the other pack out of his right-hand pocket and pulled out a cigarette. "Jes' a little one to keep the edge off, y'know? Any you boys want a smoke?"

We shook our heads. Sam Campbell stepped back while Harold Buckminster lit his cigarette. "Harold," said Sheriff Lundquist, "that bottle you drank out of better be lyin' at the bottom of that shitjack right now, y'hear?"

"That was the last of it," Harold Buckminster said defensively. "I always get a little nervous waitin' for the judges to get through."

"Well," Sam said, "don't worry over it anymore. I believe this is them now."

Sam was right. Porter Wilkes, who runs the Tasti-Freez in Statesboro, flapped his way out of the Whoppermelon tent and hollered for everybody's attention. Then he said in a voice that wasn't nearly loud enough that the contest had been decided and that all the entries were on display, with appropriate ribbons attached to the first-, second-, and third-prize winners.

So we crowded inside all at once, and soon everybody knew that Harold Buckminster's watermelon was the one with the red ribbon for second place stuck to it, because the blue ribbon was pinned to a regular Annapurna of a watermelon grown by Miss Emily Marie Tuttle, a spinster of indeterminate years who lives with her sister between Portal and Hopeyulikit and previously had never shown any public interest in watermelons or contests, either.

Sam and I didn't stay around long after what April Campbell called the chickens coming home to roost, though we did catch up with Harold Buckminster in the middle of what looked like the onset of a stroke to tell him we had faith he'd be back on top next year. To do that we had to interrupt Sheriff Lundquist, who was saying something to Harold Buckminster about how if he could find J. B. Barrett wherever he had slunk off to, he'd make sure Harold Buckminster had as long to think about where his sorry life was goin' as it would take him to walk the ten miles home to Brooklet. Sam and I were real impressed with the way the sheriff could talk with his teeth clenched.

As it turned out, J. B. Barrett took Harold Buckminster home anyway, and he says Harold Buckminster didn't say anything for the whole ten miles except "Watch out for that possum, J. B.," which J. B. Barrett did. J. B. Barrett also says he missed the possum well enough, but figures that if Harold Buckminster could have had his way, he would have taken that possum's place by the side of the road and laid down in front of the first tractor-trailer that went by.

But what happened at the Tri-County Agricultural Exposition that Saturday night wasn't the last disappointment to be visited upon Harold Buckminster for his neglect of his watermelon crop, since Sheriff Lundquist and Buddy Crittenden had each bet Lewis Stark of the jewelry-store Starks twenty dollars that Harold Buckminster's watermelon would win the contest. So not only was Harold Buckminster at least temporarily deposed as our local prince of watermelon raisers, his primary source of income was also severely curtailed for a while and in fact was spilled over a fair space of woods during a surprise visit from some of Sheriff Lundquist's friends on the federal payroll.

But though the federal men did a great deal of violence to Harold Buckminster's illicit little whiskey operation, they didn't find Harold Buckminster himself, because he had decided the day before the G-men appeared that he needed some time with his sister's family in Jacksonville, and so went there. Sheriff Lundquist told the federales that he'd be sure to take care of Harold Buckminster himself, but Buddy says the sheriff had already done that by giving Harold the $24.65 for his bus ticket.

And not only did the federal men not find Harold Buckminster, they also didn't find the eleven silver dollars he had gotten from a regular customer named Royal Mango when the still was running and he still had something to sell.

In fact, the reason Jerry Spivey and Sperry Bissell couldn't find the sack full of silver dollars that Jerry Spivey had stolen from old man Calvin Hutto's house while old man Hutto's kinfolks and friends were at old man Hutto's funeral was that while they were scouring the malarial right-of-way of county road 263, the sack of silver dollars, the one Sperry Bissell had heaved out the window of Jerry Spivey's Pontiac, was hidden in Royal Mango's chicken coop.

Royal Mango lived in a frowsy three-room tin-roofed house

with his sour and ugly wife, Rita, about thirty yards from his chicken coop and in a cleared space about a hundred and fifty yards back into the woods off county road 263 four miles or so from Brooklet. Now Rita Mango—whom she became in the eyes of the state of Georgia after sharing the bed and board of Royal Mango for seven years, the lack of a formal ceremony notwithstanding— had no idea that her husband had come to possess a sackful of silver dollars. If she had, she would have taken it away from him.

And Rita Mango being the sort of woman she was, and being convinced as she was of the innate and everlasting perfidy of men, her husband in particular, she would never have believed the way in which those silver dollars came to Royal Mango, which is to say out of the clear blue sky in such a way as to hit him square in the middle of the back as he squatted amongst the privet and bay trees off county road 263.

Oh, she would have believed that Royal Mango had decided he never should have eaten all those hot sausages. And she would have believed that Royal Mango realized that thanks to those sausages, he was never going to make it the two miles home from old man Fulton Peters's place in time to avail himself of his dismal outhouse, and that he had better just waltz off into the woods and take care of business right away. But she would never have believed that while he squatted there in the bushes listening to the flies and mosquitoes buzz around him that he heard a car or maybe cars coming his way fast and that about two seconds after the first car went roaring by a bag full of silver dollars had come arcing out of the sky and landed like a thunderbolt in the middle of his back.

Of course, it took a while for Royal Mango to find out that he had been walloped by a sack of money. First he had to lie on his belly on the damp ground with his face in the soft, wet leaves and his pants still around his ankles. He knew only that something had come whizzing through the branches behind him and landed on his person and that when it hit all his breath went away and was taking its own sweet time coming back, and that no matter what had happened he must be lying perilously close to his own feces.

But imagine Royal Mango's joy and surprise to discover what

had come to him out of the sky! For up to and including that Saturday noontime that began so ordinarily and became so thrilling, punctuated by a solid blow from the rear, life had been no bed of posies for Royal Mango. No, he had begun his life at several points of disadvantage and had since steered a course dizzingly close to thorough disappointment if not downright despair.

It wasn't just that he was half-white and half-black, J. B. Barrett says, though that was a situation which almost universally promised a tougher row to hoe than either race could provide on its own; it was also that his mama had worked in a traveling whorehouse and that beyond being an employee of the Seaboard Air Line Railway his daddy was unknown. It was also that Royal Mango had never had anything resembling an education or even supervision until the county took him under its scabrous wing when he was ten years old and sent him to a foster home.

And as if all that wasn't enough, Royal Mango's white foster daddy would regularly whip him just for being what his foster daddy called half a nigger, and Royal Mango's friends and acquaintances were few and far between until he fell in for a while with a bunch of Haitian immigrants living outside of Savannah and somehow managed to convince one of them to leave her squalor for the alternative of life with him in the swamps of Talmadge County.

It is unfortunate but also unquestionable that Royal Mango was ignorant, and he was superstitious, too, but he was nobody's fool. He knew that bag of silver dollars he hid under some filthy straw in his chicken house had somehow come from the first car he heard going by; and he figured that nobody was going to throw a bag of money out of a car on a county road unless they were desperate to get rid of it, which even Royal Mango could reason meant that it was money they were afraid of being caught with. And any fool knew that was a sure sign that money was stolen.

Though he didn't plan to, he finally broke down and spent some of his newfound dollars on whiskey he bought from Harold Buckminster, just a few of them, and Harold was glad to get any money at all so long as it was American. But Royal Mango decided not to tell anybody how he got his cache of cash. In fact, for now he didn't intend to tell a soul anything about what had happened to him or that he had a lot more silver dollars at home stowed away under a mound of straw and dirt and chicken shit, and his expenditures for emergency whiskey made the bag only a little less heavy than when he got it.

Besides, if he did tell somebody, they'd only accuse him of stealing those dollars or take them away from him. He liked having those silver dollars, too, he liked shaking the bag to hear them rattle, and he especially liked having some money Rita didn't know about.

He wouldn't tell anybody right now, but there was one person Royal Mango thought he could let in on his secret if the time came that he needed to. If there was some kind of trouble over those silver dollars, Royal Mango figured he had access to at least one man who'd know what to do.

FOUR

But Royal Mango might never have had anyone to tell about his bounty from the sky if J. B. Barrett and Woody Myers had picked a better time to go fishing.

Talmadge County is a place that sees a lot of warm months. In those months, when he isn't presiding over his store or working in his yard, J. B. Barrett is usually either fishing or at least thinking about it. And while he is a good fifteen years older than Woody Myers and is no more like him than a raccoon is like a strudel, the two men have been fishing pals for years. That's where their friendship begins, and where it stops.

One day in mid-September, J. B. Barrett and Woody Myers decided they were bored stiff with the same old ponds and riverbanks. So they agreed to take off early Friday afternoon and spend the night and the next day at J. B. Barrett's cousin's cabin in Gum Swamp, which is not quite as large as Delaware and only two or three times as dense.

J. B. Barrett's cousin, Randall Pursley, owns 2,200 acres in or around Gum Swamp that he inherited from his daddy, and into which runs a dirt road about six miles long. Most of the acreage is well treed and usually under anywhere from three inches to three feet of water. But Randall Pursley and some cheap labor keep a hog lot plus some corn, soybeans, and citrons going in the dry places.

The plan was that J. B. Barrett would drive to Randall Pursley's house in Salisbury with his boat in the back of his truck, pick up the key to the cabin, then go on and air out the place before Woody Myers arrived. Woody Myers got off from the woolen mill at four o'clock, and by then J. B. Barrett should have been at the cabin for an hour.

Just before J. B. Barrett left home that afternoon, his wife DeeDee warned him that there was rain coming because Hurricane Harriet was going by up the Gulf Stream and soon would probably make our part of the world too wet to be fished in for a week. But J. B. Barrett quit listening to his wife gripe at him about fishing sometime in 1963, and she might have told him she was moving to Tulsa in the middle of her tirade and he'd never have heard it.

When J. B. Barrett turned off the highway and drove four miles or so and rattled over the rickety plank and piling bridge over Gum Creek and pulled up at Randall Pursley's cabin, the weather still looked pretty good. It was about 3:15. Since when he last heard, Hurricane Harriet was two hundred miles away and moving north, J. B. Barrett took a quick snort, wiped up some dust, evicted a mouse from the cupboard, and lay down to take a little nap while he waited for Woody Myers.

But about the same time that J. B. Barrett started down the dirt road to the cabin, Hurricane Harriet—which so far had just been throwing water around out in the Atlantic—turned back northwest toward the coast. And aimed herself directly at Gum Swamp.

Since Gum Swamp is much closer to the coast than Brooklet is, J. B. Barrett's nap was getting rained on considerably even before his wife saw a line of deep black clouds in the east and had time to think that a good dousing and a ruined fishing trip would serve him right.

Around this time, Woody Myers was having troubles of his own, since a pair of union organizers was working the parking lot at the woolen mill that afternoon and he and Hubert Lloyd had to persuade them to leave without actually cracking their skulls, which took longer than Woody Myers expected since the union organizers were unaware that having their skulls cracked was a real possibility and acted very stubborn. So by the time he got home to Alachua to collect his fishing gear and some food, it was already 4:30 and the air was heavy and smelled of rain. By the time he drove down into Effingham County and decided that the map J. B. Barrett had drawn to his cousin's cabin would take him out to sea if he followed it long enough, the wind was snapping power poles and water was coming down in slabs.

So Woody Myers figured his fishing trip was shot to hell and that he was free to make other arrangements. If he had bothered to fix the radio in his Torino, he would have known a terrible hurricane was on the way and would have taken steps to see about his pal J. B. Barrett. But he hadn't, so he didn't.

What he did do, though, was to realize that life had unexpectedly dealt him four aces, so he turned off highway 301 toward Salisbury, which was not far as the crow flies from where J. B. Barrett was sleeping through the early gusts of a thunderstorm.

It was also where Dawn Maddox lived in the left-hand side of a brick duplex on Duval Street.

This Dawn Maddox was mildly attractive even underneath the camouflage of frizzing and perming and pancaking she did to improve her appeal to the truckers in the saloon where she worked. What she saw in Woody Myers besides good looks and a desultory tumble now and again is unknown. But what Woody Myers saw in her was the morals of a tomcat, and that was enough for him.

They had happened on one another some months before, while Woody Myers was in Savannah at a Shriners convention and Dawn Maddox was a waitress at the Pink Owl Lounge downtown. Woody Myers followed up this legitimate trip with a few illegitimate ones to Dawn Maddox's place in Salisbury, but gave it up when Louise, his wife, expressed concern over the purple marks he was bringing home on his neck.

When Dawn Maddox opened her door to see Woody Myers standing in the driving rain with a pint of vodka in each hand, Woody Myers seemed to have been right about his luck because she invited him in and locked the door. Sometime during the evening, Woody Myers was persuaded that with J. B. Barrett down in Gum Swamp for the night and a hurricane in the neighborhood, he had no need even to think of home and Louise Myers until sometime well into Saturday.

About the time Hurricane Harriet came ashore below Salisbury and began to raise pluperfect hell with docks, piers, boats, and weekend cottages, rain began to fall with sufficient force on the tin roof of Randall Pursley's cabin to wake J. B. Barrett from his nap. J. B. Barrett hadn't heard anything like the noise that was going on outside and on the roof since the Korean War, and the first thing he thought was that he had been having a very real dream that the war was over and he had been running a feed and seed store in Brooklet, Georgia. Then he remembered that during the war, he could see his feet when he was lying on his back.

He heaved himself up off the little cot, a bit overwhelmed by the cacophony on the roof, and stood at the window trying to see through the blowing rain. But he couldn't see a thing unless there was a flash of lightning, and then mostly what he saw was water, water everywhere. When he tired of that, he tried to turn on the one bulb hanging from the ceiling, but found hardly to his surprise that he was without electricity.

Since Woody Myers had the propane lantern in his Torino, J. B. Barrett realized he was about to spend what might be several hours or even the night in the dark with nothing but a flashlight that was still outside in his truck. And he certainly wasn't about to try to drive home through what he figured must be an unpleasant surprise visit from that hurricane he'd been hearing about.

But J. B. Barrett wasn't entirely without amenities, because there was a little pile of kindling by the fireplace and the wood at the bottom of the stack on the cabin porch was still dry enough to burn, though he had a hard time coming and going through the door with the wind trying to snatch it out of his hand. He lit a fire, ate a can of cold pork and beans and a bag of potato chips, and puzzled over where Woody Myers was and what he ought to do.

Just about the time he put the potato-chip bag on the fire, the tin roof over his head gave out a long, painful screech and the ceiling began to leak in a half-dozen places. J. B. Barrett began to wonder if perhaps he was in trouble, so he took out his fifth of Rebel Yell and had a little pick-me-up and then another one, and before long he not only had been picked up but toted away as well.

Then suddenly he was waking up in a chair in the pitch-black cabin listening to a knock on the door.

He sat there stiffly for a few seconds hearing the storm, trying to clear his head, wondering for the second time in as many hours if he had been dreaming and hoping that he had been, but then there was another set of knocks, louder this time. If it was Woody Myers, J. B. Barrett thought, the door would have opened and Woody Myers would have walked in. But since it obviously wasn't him, J. B. Barrett got up and sloshed through pools of water over to the door and snatched it open and stepped back out of the way.

"Hello in air," something said, just loud enough to be heard over the fury in the yard. J. B. Barrett didn't say anything, because no matter how hard he looked at where the door was, he couldn't see anything on the other side of it.

"Hello in air," something said again. "That you, Mr. Randall?" And then, J. B. Barrett thought that even though he still couldn't see anything, he knew at least part of what he was dealing with, because no white man would call Randall Pursley Mr. Randall.

"Naw," J. B. Barrett said into the darkness. "Randall ain't here. This is J. B. Barrett from over in Brooklet. Who'm I talkin' to?"

"This here's Sears Ellis," said the darkness. "It's an awful night out here, you mind if I come in?"

"You got anybody with you?" said J. B. Barrett, still unable to see anything but rain drifting in through the open door.

"Nossir," said Sears Ellis. "But I'm 'bout to be blowed away."

"Well, come on in, then," said J. B. Barrett.

So in came what J. B. Barrett figured was the wettest human being he'd ever seen outside of swimming pools and bathtubs, though at first he wasn't even entirely sure that what came in was a man at all since all he could see was something the size and shape of a man that was shedding water like a Labrador retriever. J. B. Barrett hated Labrador retrievers, but once he made sure Sears Ellis wasn't one, he built up the fire again and Sears Ellis took off most of his sopping garments, hung them over a chair to dry, and put on J. B. Barrett's army surplus poncho instead. J. B. Barrett gave his guest a paper cup of Rebel Yell to take away the shivers and the two of them sat in front of the fire listening to the rain and the howling wind and limbs scraping the roof on their way to the ground.

About 10:30 the wind began to die down a little, but about that same time the two men had reason to jump because there was a louder noise than usual from outside, the kind of noise J. B. Barrett knew a truck would make if something heavy fell on it. But J. B. Barrett also thought to himself that the news had been all bad for a long time now and nothing was going to get him out that door just to get him wet and give him another dose of misfortune. So he and Sears Ellis just sat with their feet to the fire. They spent most of their time complaining about the wet and cold until J. B. Barrett asked his guest how come he was abroad on such a night.

Sears Ellis explained that he was staying with his mama and his sister in their little house at the intersection of the highway and the dirt road that led to the cabin, and while his mama and sister were over in Augusta for the week, he figured this was a good time to ride his bicycle down the dirt road through Gum Swamp and see if there was any salvageable tin on an old shack at the end of the road so he could patch the roof on his mama's place. And since Randall Pursley was paying him to look after his hogs, Sears Ellis stopped off at the hog lot and fed them before cycling down past Randall Pursley's cabin, where J. B. Barrett was asleep, to the decrepit shack at the far end of the dirt road next to an Indian mound.

J. B. Barrett wasn't surprised to find out that Sears Ellis had abandoned his bicycle well up the road since the road had become more mud than road by the time he decided he'd better try to get home. And J. B. Barrett wasn't surprised that Sears Ellis thought that whoever had that pickup truck at the cabin would take him in despite his being a mysterious black apparition appearing out of a hurricane. What did surprise J. B. Barrett was that he was spending the night with a man named after a mail-order company.

J. B. Barrett could tell that this was a story Sears Ellis had found it necessary to tell a lot of other people, so he tried to appear even more interested to hear it than he already was, just to give Sears Ellis some encouragement. What Sears Ellis said was that before he was born, his sister kept asking his mama how come she'd been saying there was a little baby on the way to their house and just where did them little babies come from in the first place. So Sears Ellis's mama told Sears Ellis's sister that the new baby was going to be delivered to the door by Sears & Roebuck. When his sister came running into the house after he was born, Sears Ellis said, she hollered, "Is Sears come yet?" and Sears Ellis's daddy thought that was so funny that he agreed that Sears had come, indeed.

About the time Sears Ellis was introducing himself to J. B. Barrett in Gum Swamp, DeeDee Barrett began to worry about her husband being blown away or drowned and so called Louise Myers to see if she had heard anything from Woody. Since Louise Myers hadn't heard anything except Hurricane Harriet, both women began to worry in earnest about their men and DeeDee Barrett even started to feel a little sorry for some of the things she had thought about what J. B. Barrett deserved for going fishing and leaving her at home. She even went so far as to try to call Randall Pursley in Salisbury to see if he had heard anything from the two sportsmen, but the telephone lines were down.

So Louise Myers came and spent the night at DeeDee Barrett's house, and about the same time J. B. Barrett and Sears Ellis killed the last of the Rebel Yell and lay down on their damp cots to try and get some sleep, Louise Myers and DeeDee Barrett were dropping off to restless sleep, too, in the Barretts' master bedroom.

During the waning hours of night, Hurricane Harriet blew off up into the Carolinas out of the way, so in the morning everything in this end of Georgia looked fairly busted up and sodden but did so under a sky that was reasonably free of menace. And as soon as they got up and had eaten breakfast and Louise Myers smoked four cigarettes, the two women set off for Salisbury and Randall Pursley's house.

They had a more difficult time than they expected, because all the people who had cleared out the night before were trying to get back home to see if they had a home left to get back to, but even when they got to Salisbury all they accomplished at first was to wake up Miriam Pursley, Randall Pursley's wife. And all Miriam knew was that her husband was over at the high school passing out coffee and doughnuts to the homeless and the electricityless and that J. B. Barrett had come by and picked up the key to the cabin the day before.

So Louise Myers and DeeDee Barrett started off for the high school to find Randall Pursley and see if he'd go with them down to his log cabin. But they didn't know Salisbury very well, so they made their way less than directly toward the high school and by and by found themselves on Duval Street, where at number 221 they passed Woody Myers's gray Ford Torino, which both of them recognized.

They pulled over to the curb down Duval Street from number 221 and talked over the few possibilities that would have led to Woody Myers's Ford being behind them in front of a brick duplex. Perhaps in other circumstances they would have shared some relief over evidence of the lost fishermen, but not this time. While DeeDee Barrett was somewhat relieved because J. B. Barrett's pickup truck wasn't parked outside 221 Duval Street with Woody Myers's Ford, seeing the Torino out there made her smell trouble coming her way at a pretty good clip.

The two women finally decided that Louise Myers should go and knock at the door of number 221 and check things out, and that DeeDee Barrett would come along for moral support. So they locked DeeDee Barrett's Sunbird since Duval Street had looked a little suspicious even before they saw Woody Myers's car, and walked up to number 221 and knocked on the door. Number 223, next to it, had newspapers all over the porch and was obviously empty.

From inside number 221, somebody female said, "Who is it?"

Louise Myers elbowed DeeDee Barrett in the ribs.

"Red Cross," DeeDee Barrett said, which was what she had practiced saying ever since she left the Sunbird. And then the door opened and Dawn Maddox was standing there in her housecoat.

"Out of my way, cheap trick!" yelled Louise Myers, barging into number 221 and shoving Dawn Maddox sideways against the television. The cable box fell off onto the floor. DeeDee Barrett didn't know what to think, things were happening so fast, and hearing her friend say "cheap trick" threw her, too, because she wasn't entirely sure she knew what it meant and wondered if Louise did, and if so, where she learned it. Just about the time Louise Myers found the bedroom, which didn't take long given the size of number 221, DeeDee Barrett heard somebody in there say "Oh my sweet Jesus" in a truly despairing voice. What followed was mostly a couple of women screaming and hollering, not necessarily at each other.

Meanwhile, J. B. Barrett and Sears Ellis had gotten up at first light, damp and sore and hungry, and built a fire and had half a can of pork and beans and a cup of instant coffee each, which pretty much exhausted the food supply except for a Snickers candy bar that J. B. Barrett was saving for an emergency. While Sears Ellis put on his clothes, which were still wet, J. B. Barrett stood outside in a drizzle wondering how much the insurance company would pay to fix the roof of his truck, on which rested a hickory branch of such size that he and Sears Ellis later sweated like what Sears Ellis called pulpwood niggers getting it off.

There was no question of trying the truck on the road, which was entirely mud and deep, too. That also made it silly for Sears Ellis to try to retrieve his bicycle. So finally they decided to try to walk out together, which as it happens was the best use of their time, since after they'd gone about a quarter mile and started down the long slope toward Gum Creek and the flatlands beyond it, they could tell not only that the road in front of them was under several feet of water as far as they could see but also that the old bridge that had been over Gum Creek was now somewhere else and nowhere close.

The two men stood for a while watching the brown water go by, commiserating with each other for being in such a predicament. They could see a cleared space between the trees up ahead where the road had been, and where it was now under the flood, and nobody needed to say out loud that even if the road was dry it wouldn't do them any good, since there wasn't a bridge anymore to drive the truck over.

So J. B. Barrett and Sears Ellis talked a little and figured they could either wait where they were and hope somebody would come looking for them, or they could think of a way out. Since they didn't have any food left except J. B. Barrett's secret Snickers bar, and since the water was too high and muddy to offer them hope even of catching a fish, they decided that trying to get out was the thing to do.

They walked back up the slope and stood on the porch of the cabin to get out of the mist that was still falling even though the sky had been getting brighter since early morning. J. B. Barrett spat at a mudhole and wished he had a tall cool glass of orange juice to cut the starch in his mouth. He would have been mad at Woody Myers but he was too hungry and his ankles hurt from the damp.

"Well, look here," Sears Ellis said.

"Shoot," J. B. Barrett said.

Sears Ellis's forehead was rippled with thought. "I seen you got a big ol' rope in the back of yo truck, aintcha?"

And J. B. Barrett said yes, whereupon Sears Ellis said he had a way to get them out of the swamp, maybe, if J. B. Barrett was up to a little labor. J. B. Barrett says he wasn't about to let a colored fella think he wasn't up to if not downright eager for some hard work, especially a colored fella that was named after a mail-order company, so he agreed to listen to what Sears Ellis had in mind.

"Back yonder in that old run-down house where I went yesterday," Sears Ellis said, "Mr. Randall keeps a lot of farm junk, y'know, old plow pieces an' boards an' stuff, and there's a grapple hook in there that we can fit to the end of yo rope." Here Sears Ellis looked meaningfully at J. B. Barrett, and though J. B. Barrett didn't understand, he wasn't about to let on, so he just said "Uh-huh" and waited for more information.

Sears Ellis looked into the yard. "So we fixes that rope on that hook," he went on, making tying motions with his hands, "and one of us sits in the back of the boat with the paddle and the othern sits in the front with the hook and thows it round a tree and pulls us up to it. Then we thows the rope again and pulls us up to the nex' one, and that's how we gets out." Sears Ellis smiled and looked hopefully at J. B. Barrett.

J. B. Barrett looked at Sears Ellis, too, and wondered if Sears Ellis could tell by his expression that he thought that was the stupidest idea he had ever heard. He even thought about saying it out loud, but then he realized two things: the mist had stopped, which elevated his mood immediately, and he couldn't think of a better idea than the one Sears Ellis had. So, with his morale boosted and his back against the wall, J. B. Barrett said only, "Well, what if that don't work?"

Sears Ellis waved a hand at the dripping trees. "Then we gets to choose," he said. "We can start swimmin' or we can jest settle in here and go to farmin'."

So they walked over to the truck and gave J. B. Barrett's coil of rope a good look, and pretty soon Sears Ellis started up the road to fetch the grappling hook. J. B. Barrett, understanding that he was fifty-five years old and had a big job in front of him, decided he'd better take it easy till Sears Ellis got back, so he sat on the tailgate of his truck and listened to the birds singing and wished he were home where he belonged.

After a while, Sears Ellis came back into J. B. Barrett's life through the mud and the goo with the grappling hook.

"The eye in that thing ain't big enough for this rope to go through," J. B. Barrett said testily.

"Okay, then we fays it a little," said Sears Ellis, which didn't make any more sense to J. B. Barrett than if Sears Ellis had said "Okay, then we goes to the moon," but J. B. Barrett began to catch on when Sears Ellis took the end of the rope and frayed it enough to get part of it through the eye of the hook.

So they toted J. B. Barrett's boat down to the water's edge, which had once been the middle of the road about fifty yards up the slope from what had once been the bridge, and J. B. Barrett got in the front end with the rope and the hook and Sears Ellis got in the back with the paddle and they pushed off. At first they did just fine with the paddle by itself, since the water they were in had been flowing through a thousand acres of trees before it got to them and wasn't moving too fast. Before they got to where Gum Creek should have been and where the bridge used to be, J. B. Barrett had to throw the hook around a tree only a couple of times to keep them from being carried off into the swamp by the current.

But when they got near what should have been the creek bed, and after J. B. Barrett finally got the hook around a little blackgum, both he and Sears Ellis had to haul hard on that rope to get them up to it. And there they sat and rested, J. B. Barrett holding the hook around the tree so they'd stay in place, with the dirty water rushing past.

Since there weren't any trees in what had been the creek bed, that particular stretch of water was moving lickety-split. Even worse, the closest tree on the far side of the creek bed was somewhat past the limit of J. B. Barrett's ability to pitch a rope and a steel hook. So Sears Ellis took the rope with the hook on the end of it and pitched it toward the trees on the other side of what had been a creek but now looked to J. B. Barrett, at least, to be as wide as the Mississippi River. Sears Ellis threw the rope eleven times and never once came close to getting it to catch on a tree, and in fact never came close to a tree at all. J. B. Barrett was beginning to get tense, because even though the day was cloudy, he could tell that the sun was about where two o'clock ought to be and they weren't making much progress toward saving themselves from another night in the swamp.

Just then a drowned beaver came bobbing along and thumped to rest against the boat.

"That colored fella and I looked at that dead beaver," J. B. Barrett said later, "and then we looked at each other, and I said, 'Let's get the damn hell out of here' and that colored fella says, 'I'm right behind you, Mr. J. B.,' and he commenced to paddle and I grabbed that hook back and commenced to look for someplace to thow it."

While J. B. Barrett and Sears Ellis were sitting on the edge of what had been Gum Creek, about the time the dead beaver came rolling along, DeeDee Barrett was sitting in Louise Myers's kitchen watching Louise Myers smoke a cigarette and sniffle and blow her nose. They had left Woody Myers standing in his boxer shorts in Dawn Maddox's living room, and though Louise Myers had told her husband between screams of outrage that he might as well just stay there because he wasn't ever coming back home, Dawn Maddox had by then tired of the excitement and was hollering for all of them to get clear of her place before she called the police.

But while she felt she should stay near Louise Myers and help her through her time of tribulation, DeeDee Barrett was worrying hard about what her own husband might be up to, wherever he was.

About three o'clock, Woody Myers walked into his house and Louise Myers started wailing again and grabbed her cigarettes and ran into the bathroom and locked the door. Woody Myers looked as though he had been crying, too, and suddenly DeeDee Barrett felt she had had her fill of Myerses for one day, so her only response to this maelstrom of grief and remorse was to sit Woody Myers down and make him tell her what he knew of J. B. Barrett's whereabouts—which was practically nothing—before she got up and left that place and drove back down to Salisbury to find Randall Pursley.

As DeeDee Barrett was crossing the Brooklet city limits, J. B. Barrett and Sears Ellis were booming down the swollen current of Gum Creek in the general direction of Salisbury, too, while Sears Ellis paddled with all his might to swing the boat toward the trees on the other side of the channel. But the current carried them about a half mile back into the swamp from the washed-out road before the water spread out among the trees and slowed up enough for J. B. Barrett to fling the hook around a sapling maple and pull them to a stop. They sat there and blew for a few minutes, then paddled and hooked their way steadily but slowly northward toward the edge of the swamp.

J. B. Barrett kept thinking to himself that all these damn trees looked alike and they could be going around in great big circles and he reckoned he'd never know it. His arms and shoulders were sore from throwing the hook and pulling. He noticed that the boat was a lot lower in the water at his end of it, too, but he didn't say anything about that. What he did finally say to Sears Ellis, and he noticed how happy it made him to do so, was that he could tell the current wasn't moving so fast anymore.

"Uh-huh," Sears Ellis said. "I reckon you can quit thowin' that hook, too. You 'bout to run out of velocity anyhow"—J. B. Barrett blushed but kept his head turned away—"and I oughta be able to paddle us outa here by myself."

"Well," J. B. Barrett said, considering whether he'd feel better if he whacked Sears Ellis upside the head with the grappling hook and deciding he wouldn't, "jest lemme know if you need a hand."

"Sho," Sears Ellis said, but he never did ask for help, even though it took him almost till sundown to paddle them out of the swamp and into the middle of what looked to J. B. Barrett like the low end of the pasture back of Uncle Turk Simmons's place, which is where the water began to run out. They got only within about ten feet of relatively dry land before the boat grounded, though. So Sears Ellis jumped out and sloshed up to the front, where J. B. Barrett sat, and grabbed the gunwale. The two men looked at each other.

"I cain't pull this thing through the mud with you in it," is what Sears Ellis said.

So J. B. Barrett stood up while Sears Ellis held the boat and he stepped out, too, but when he put his foot down, it didn't stop where he thought it would and went into a hole instead. J. B. Barrett said "goddamn" quietly but emphatically and sat down hard in the brown water. His ankle hurt, but not so bad that he didn't look around to see if what he heard was Sears Ellis laughing.

Sears Ellis was looking away, but he was shaking. J. B. Barrett had sudden comforting thoughts of torture and punishment, but then he remembered that if it wasn't for Sears Ellis, he'd still be back at Randall Pursley's cabin, and he was ashamed of himself.

Whether Sears Ellis laughed or not, he did help J. B. Barrett out of the cold water and onto the grass and sat him down on the poncho. Then he waded back into the water and pulled the boat up onto the land high enough so it wouldn't float off right away. At that point Sears Ellis sat down, too, and neither of them said anything for a few minutes. Sears Ellis was breathing hard and J. B. Barrett's ankle that went into the hole was swelling up and felt to him as though it was about to ignite.

After a minute J. B. Barrett pulled his emergency Snickers bar out of his jacket pocket and held it out to Sears Ellis, who took it, broke it in two pieces, and offered one back to J. B. Barrett, who shook his head.

"Thank you," Sears Ellis said.

"Don't mention it," J. B. Barrett said. "You reckon you're up to walking out of here by yourself before it gets dark?"

"If my onliest other choice is totin' you, I know I am," Sears Ellis said.

J. B. Barrett sighed and thought of his wife and his house with its refrigerator full of good things to eat. "You know where you are?" he said.

"I reckon," Sears Ellis said. "I reckon we done gone about a mile and a half east of my mama's place. I know probly where we are, but I don't know none of the people down this way."

"You don't need to," J. B. Barrett said. "If they're who I think they are, their name's Simmons and they're decent people despite not having a whole lot of good sense left in the family now that there ain't no women around. The old one's named Turk and everybody calls him Uncle Turk for some reason and the young one's named Eugene and he's been living there since he got a divorce. You can see the house back up yonder, cain't you?"

"Uh-huh," Sears Ellis said, turning to look. "I see a place with a light on in the winder."

"Then you ain't gone miss it, right?" said J. B. Barrett.

They looked at each other again, neither one of them knowing for sure whether J. B. Barrett was trying to be sarcastic or whether his ankle just hurt and was starting to make him mean. The sun had broken through the clouds to shine a few minutes before going down.

"I be back," Sears Ellis said, and got up and started off up the slope.

After Sears Ellis left, J. B. Barrett found that his ankle was most comfortable if he lay down on the poncho on his back and pulled his knees up and kept his feet flat. He was comfortable that way all over, too, so he closed his eyes and tried to take it easy until Sears Ellis brought some help.

More time went by than he expected before he could hear Sears Ellis coming. It sounded as though he was by himself, too, dammit. But since he had begun to feel better generally, excluding his ankle, J. B. Barrett just lay there with his eyes shut and waited for Sears Ellis to speak to him. Maybe that Ellis would think he was asleep, and that sounded all right, it put J. B. Barrett at an advantage of sorts.

The footsteps stopped, and J. B. Barrett waited. Then something poked him in the ribs, and he opened his eyes.

"Hello, Uncle Turk," J. B. Barrett said, sitting up immediately.

Uncle Turk Simmons pulled the muzzle of the twelve-gauge back from the vicinity of J. B. Barrett's ribs and cradled it in the crook of his elbow. "Hello yourself," he said. "Who're you and what're you doin' takin' a nap in my pasture?"

So J. B. Barrett reminded Uncle Turk Simmons that he was J. B. Barrett from over in Brooklet and that they had met, usually in hunting parties, off and on for the last twenty years. And while he was talking, J. B. Barrett was thinking that pretty much every time he laid down and then opened his eyes again he got an unpleasant surprise, so maybe he just wouldn't do it anymore until he was home in his own bed with the door locked.

"I thought you was a dead man lying down here," Uncle Turk Simmons said.

"When I saw that shotgun, so did I," said J. B. Barrett. "But I ain't dead, I'm just the next best thing to it. Didn't that colored fella talk to you?"

"One come to the door a while ago," Uncle Turk Simmons said, "but I didn't answer it. He looked like a crazy man to me."

"He is a crazy man," J. B. Barrett said. "But he was comin' up there to tell you I was down here. If you didn't talk to him, how'd you know I was here?"

"I seen you out the window," said Uncle Turk Simmons.

J. B. Barrett was pondering the reasonableness of that statement when Uncle Turk Simmons abruptly raised the twelve-gauge and fired it into the air, then pumped it and fired it again.

"Jesus H. Christ, Uncle Turk," said J. B. Barrett, "how come you was to do that? You scared ten years off my life."

"Funny," Uncle Turk Simmons said with a gap-toothed grin, "you don't look no younger to me. Haw-haw. See, Eugene's up yonder, and I tole him if he heard me shoot to come runnin'. If he don't, there ain't no way I can get you off yo campground and into the house."

Meanwhile, Sears Ellis, who had gone east on the main road to see if he could find someone at home somewhere after nobody answered the door at the Simmons's house, had heard the two shotgun blasts and was now running as hard as he could back into the west to see what was going on.

And about the very same time, DeeDee Barrett and Randall Pursley were turning off the main road in Randall Pursley's truck onto the dirt road that led to the cabin. Randall Pursley heard the shots, too, but figured there probably wasn't anything to them except hunters, out of season or not.

Uncle Turk Simmons and his son Eugene were helping J. B. Barrett onto their porch just as Sears Ellis got back close enough to where he had left J. B. Barrett in the pasture to notice that J. B. Barrett wasn't there anymore. The water was a little higher, maybe, but not that much. And by the time Sears Ellis discovered the two empty twelve-gauge shells on the ground in the gathering twilight and was beginning to be upset with gusto, J. B. Barrett was seated at the Simmons's kitchen table with his sore ankle propped up on a chair.

While Sears Ellis was scrabbling around on his hands and knees in Uncle Turk Simmons's pasture looking for the spilled blood of J. B. Barrett, DeeDee Barrett and Randall Pursley were stopped in the middle of the road to the cabin looking at the truck's headlights shining on the place where the road stopped and the floodwaters began.

"I bet the bridge is out, too," Randall Pursley said, at which point DeeDee Barrett began to blubber like a baby, thinking about

J. B. Barrett out there alone in the swamp or maybe even drowned and about all the snide things she had said to him before he left. But Randall Pursley had had five daughters, two wives, a mama, and a grandmama in his day, so he considered himself accustomed to hysterical women and got DeeDee Barrett back into the truck and headed off toward the main road again, most of the way in reverse.

As it happens, the first thing Randall Pursley thought about when they got to the intersection was whether Sears Ellis's mama was at home, but no lights were on in her house. So he and DeeDee Barrett drove up the highway to Uncle Turk Simmons's house and pulled into the yard just as a dark, muddy, bedraggled, and wild-eyed Sears Ellis came tearing through the privet hedge, bounded up onto the front porch, and began beating on the front door.

Randall Pursley pulled his 30.06 off the rack behind his seat and cocked and fired it into the air as he was getting out of the truck and Sears Ellis stopped in midbeat as though he'd been cast in bronze. And while Randall Pursley was surprised to find that the phantom on the porch with its hands in the air wasn't nobody but Sears Ellis, he wasn't nearly as surprised then as he was when Sears Ellis asked him if he'd shot J. B. Barrett. But about that time Eugene Simmons came to the door and soon things began to sort themselves out and DeeDee Barrett had a chance to tell her husband how worried she'd been and how sorry she was to have nagged him, and to ask him if he knew somebody named Dawn Maddox.

J. B. Barrett's truck stayed out in the middle of Gum Swamp next to Randall Pursley's log cabin for two solid months before enough bridge was put back over Gum Creek for him to drive it out. Woody Myers is still living in a rooming house on Pelham Street in Alachua, but he and Louise Myers look as though they might patch things up and have even been talking about a trip to Gatlinburg to get away where they can sort things out.

About a month after J. B. Barrett came home from Gum Swamp, Sam Campbell and I drove down to Brooklet to his feed and seed store to pick up two hundred-pound sacks of sunflower seeds that April Campbell's sister's Girl Scout troop was planning to divide up and sell to people to put in their bird feeders. Like every other feed and seed store in south Georgia, Barrett's smells warmly of chicken feed and chicken shit, but J. B. Barrett's place is different from most in that there's a full-length concrete loading dock out front.

When Sam and I walked into the store, Penny Peavey and one of the Johnson brothers were standing by the counter. J. B. Barrett was behind the cash register, and he was saying, "I tell you the truth, I ain't never heard the wind blow like that in my life," when he interrupted himself to tell us that the bags of seed were already outside on the dock and that if Sam would sign the tab he'd send somebody out there to help us put them in Sam's truck.

So Sam signed the tab, said we'd load the sunflower seeds ourselves, thanks, and he and I went into the back room for a few minutes to look at the baby chicks. When we got outside, the bags were indeed waiting. Sam and I were bending down to pick up at least one of them when a guy in shoes that squeaked came walking toward us down the loading dock.

"Mr. J. B. sent me out here to help y'all with these sacks," he said, and grinned. He was about six-foot-one, the color of a pecan. He had a thin mustache and was wearing new black shoes, a Red Rose Animal Feeds cap, khaki pants, and a dark green uniform shirt with a white patch outlined in red over the left-hand pocket. His name was written in script in the middle of the patch.

Sears, it said.

FIVE

Royal Mango decided he could tell Sears Ellis about the silver dollars he'd gotten from the wild blue yonder after the two of them had spent less than a week on the loading dock together.

First of all, Sears Ellis wasn't just a hero, though he was certainly that for a while after J. B. Barrett told practically everybody within earshot about what he described as Sears Ellis getting him out of the swamp. He was also, at least the way Royal Mango saw it, everything that Royal Mango was not. He was brave, clever, handsome, resourceful, young, and had a future.

Besides that, Royal Mango knew Sears Ellis had graduated from high school, and that he had spent six years in the army but no time at all in jail, all of which was designed to raise Sears Ellis to grand heights of esteem in Royal Mango's mind.

Royal Mango would never have considered the possibility that Sears Ellis might not in fact have taken a considerable step toward making a success of himself, having but lately secured the position of lifter and toter at a feed and seed store. And he could have had no idea that J. B. Barrett was already thinking of making Sears Ellis his number-one assistant when John Crooms moved to Norfolk in November. No, Royal Mango just naturally thought of Sears Ellis as temporary on J. B. Barrett's loading dock, just as he saw himself standing on that dock four days a week until J. B. Barrett told him to get off of it or until he died.

Nobody knows exactly when and where Royal Mango confided in Sears Ellis that he had come to have a bagful of silver dollars, though on the where side J. B. Barrett says he figures it was out back under the big chinaberry tree one day or another at noon while the two of them ate sandwiches of baloney or souse meat or something for lunch and drank mason jars full of sweet tea.

Maybe, sort of on the when side, J. B. Barrett says, it was one day after work before Sears Ellis's sister picked him up on the way home from work at the woolen mill. Maybe it was nothing like that, though.

But some of the when part can probably be pretty well fixed at a point not long after Harold Buckminster got his nose broken.

The official report of the breaking of Harold Buckminster's nose got to Buddy Crittenden from the town police, and it says the assault occurred behind Roberson's Grocery on South Wayne Street. And while it also says that persons unknown ambushed Harold Buckminster as he was getting into his car of the moment, a battered light blue Datsun B-210, which he had been allowed to take to the grocery store only because his wife had a migraine, it's pretty clear now that Harold Buckminster knew the fist he met not just once to break his nose but apparently several times besides for emphasis, belonged and still does belong to Jerry Spivey.

But nobody else knew that at the time, and it might not have even mattered if they had.

Buddy Crittenden had a nose problem of his own about then, in that he had bought a sun lamp at a flea market in Savannah and had gone right home and turned that most prominent part of his face into the color of molten lava. I could tell that it hurt, but it looked sort of funny, too.

Buddy wrinkled his nose a little and grimaced. "All Harold will say is that there was these two guys and one of them kept asking him where he'd gotten those silver dollars they'd seen him spending in Roberson's."

The other one, Buddy went on, didn't do much but hold Harold Buckminster's arms and say "whoa, there," whenever Harold Buckminster took a punch or flinched because he thought one was coming.

"I got to figurin' on it," Buddy said, "and even though it was a town thing, there was something that didn't ring true to me, and I told them I wanted to sniff around in it a little and they said fine. To them it wasn't nothin' but two guys beatin' up on another guy to get his money. What are you starin' at?"

"Won't you guide my sleigh tonight?" I sang in my best falsetto.

"Up yours," Buddy snarled. "Do you want to hear this? One reason I'm tellin' you about this in the first place is because you know Harold Buckminster and I thought you might be interested."

"Don't get your nose out of joint," I sneered. "Of course I'm interested. And besides, who else would know that you figure things out by talking out loud and waving your hands? You're better off doing it in front of me than at home in front of the mirror."

Buddy sighed and made a glum face around his radiant nose. "Okay," he said. "Harold Buckminster didn't tell this to the town cops, probably 'cause he wanted to leave his business out of it, but he told me. He says he got those silver dollars from a fella name of Royal Mango who lives way off down in the sticks. But what I'd really like to know is where Mr. Royal Mango got them silver dollars to give to Harold Buckminster in the first place."

"So how come you're asking me?" I said. We were sitting in my little office at the college, Buddy in the green armchair. The windows were open a little, although the weather was cool, and I could see a mockingbird in the top of one of the little dogwoods that line the sidewalk between the administration building and the cafeteria. "I don't even know anybody named Royal Mango. I don't even know if it's a real name."

"It's a real name, all right," Buddy said. "And the question was rhetorical. So where's your secretary?"

"She's at lunch," I said, and loosened my tie a little. "The show doesn't start again till one-thirty."

Buddy smiled. "Everybody says she's smarter than her husband," he said, "but he has to have something going for him to have gotten her."

We both sat there and thought it over for a minute, but it didn't work. When we finished, Angela Stallings, who might have been the most perfectly beautiful woman I had ever seen, was still

married to somebody and it wasn't either of us. At least she was my
secretary, though. A good one, too.

Buddy and I looked at each other, and then away. His nose was
the color of agony. He cleared his throat.

"Anyhow," he said, "Royal Mango is this black feller—well,
he's half-white, I guess—who lives down yonder off 263 back up
past that church where you and me was eatin' that morning after
we went fishin'."

"And when them two guys ran over that snake, or looked like
they did, anyway," I said.

"Yeah," Buddy said, shifting a little in his seat and giving me
a funny look. "Out that way. So Harold says to me that he got them
dollars from Royal Mango."

"Maybe he did," I said, and yawned.

"I figure that's the truth," Buddy said. "But what I want to
know is where Royal Mango, who normally ain't got a pot to piss
in or a window to throw it out of, gets silver dollars to spend all of
a sudden. And even more than that, how come those two guys who
poked Harold were so interested in them?"

"Maybe he's had them hidden away for a long time," I said.
The telephone rang out in the reception area and I heard Grace
Teal pick it up and start talking and then hang up.

Buddy grunted. "I figure any money Royal Mango comes into
gets processed pretty quick," he said, "unless his wife gets her hands
on it first. Naw, that ain't it."

"Maybe he stole them."

Buddy rubbed his eyes, being careful to miss his nose, and
shifted in the chair again. "I dunno," he said. "But I doubt it. Or
anyway I doubt he'd steal them and then turn right around and
spend some on whiskey."

"Unless that's why he stole them in the first place," I said. The
phone rang again and Grace Teal got it, just the way she's supposed
to. It doesn't always happen that way.

"I'm gone find out, anyhow," Buddy said. "Mango works for
j. B. Barrett, so I'm just gone go down there or maybe even out
yonder to his house if I can remember where it is and ask him myself

where them dollars came from. You think they might have been valuable or something?"

"Depends on where and when they were made," I said, "and what condition they're in. But it's a safe bet that if they were made before 1935, they're worth a hell of a lot more than a dollar apiece."

"Because they're old?" Buddy said. There was the sound of the door from the reception area to the hallway opening, and Buddy's head snapped to the right, aiming his eyes through my office door into the broad bright room in which the two departmental secretaries sat. But he frowned and turned back to me.

I could hear a student talking to Grace Teal. "Because there weren't a lot of them made," I said, "and the ones that were are full of silver. Not this junk they make coins out of now. These old dollars could be worth some real money."

Buddy was thinking. "So maybe those two guys know that?" he said.

"They don't sound like coin collectors to me," I said, trying not to seem sarcastic.

Buddy took a little tube of some kind of lotion out of his shirt pocket and rubbed some of its contents on and around his fiery nose. "No, no," he said. "Ouch. I mean maybe those guys knew them dollars were worth something. Or might be. Bill Roberson says his cashiers made a big to-do about them, and that one of them was made in 1887 and the other in nineteen-oh-something or other."

"So maybe somebody overheard all this going on."

"Yeah," Buddy said, "I thought of that. But okay, did these guys even ask if Harold Buckminster had any more dollars on him? Uh-uh. All they wanted to know was where he got them in the first place."

"You mean maybe they figured there was more of them somewhere."

"Thank you," Buddy said, raising the corners of his mouth. "I was thinking that, too."

"Well, did Harold tell them?" I said. "Did he tell you?"

"He says he didn't tell them guys about Mango," Buddy said,

"and I believe him. Po' folks in this county stick together no matter what color they are, and that's all he woulda been doing, plus looking after a customer he probably wanted to keep. He says he told them two guys he had inherited them dollars a long time ago and just had to spend them now because he didn't have no other money."

"And they believed him?" I was drawing scriggly lines on a pad on my desk.

"I guess so, after a while. Harold says he kept thinking this 'un that was hittin' him was finished, then in a couple minutes he'd throw another punch. It was the last one that broke Harold's nose. Sort of a good-bye shot, Harold says."

"So now . . . "

Buddy sighed. "So now I've got other things to think about," he said. "Harold Buckminster's nose ain't exactly number one on the priority list of local law enforcement. And I got to keep Big Ed happy. He's got a list of things two feet long that he seems to think cain't nobody but me take care of."

"Given the general performance of your peers," I said, "he's probably right."

"I don't like to think about it that way," Buddy said, "but I appreciate you saying it. We got everybody going all out still hunting for them assholes that broke into Mr. Goldstein's jewelry store last week. This is getting to be a regular paradise for criminals."

He looked at his watch. "I got to go," he said. "Look, how about—"

I heard the outer door open again, saw Buddy look, heard Grace Teal say, "Why Angela, you got your hair done!" and saw too that Buddy was transfixed.

Angela Stallings was bustling around her desk, crinkling papers. And then she stuck her spectacularly lovely and innocent face into my office and said, "Hi, I'm back. Did you miss me? Anything going on?"

"Hi there," I said.

"Hello," Buddy said, and got a hi and a glance of his own in return. Angela was standing half in, half out of my office, and I saw her sneak another look at Buddy's nose, but he saw her, too, and she blushed. So did Buddy. His nose stayed a lot redder than the rest of his face.

"No, just the usual," I said. "There's a bunch of stuff on your desk, but none of it's very important. Terrific hairstyle you got there."

Angela beamed. "Thank you," she said, and after another minute or two of talk she left. I heard her sit down at her desk, heard the babble between her and Grace Teal start up the way it always does when one of them comes back from lunch.

"There is a God," Buddy said reverently.

"And She created woman in Her own image," I said.

Buddy shook his head slowly, sighed, and stood up. I stood, too.

"Lord," Buddy said. "I got to go."

Well, I didn't think any more about Harold Buckminster or Royal Mango or silver dollars and maybe not even much about Buddy Crittenden, either, for the next couple of days since there were other things to think about like working and eating and sleeping and finding enough excuses just to keep on going from one day to the next. But then one day later in the week at the instant I got home my telephone rang, which was something of a noteworthy event in itself, and when I picked it up, Buddy was at the other end of the line.

And that's why I took a couple of hours off the next afternoon and how come I was with Buddy Crittenden—who was in uniform but was driving his own car, since I was with him and using the county cruiser was therefore illegal unless I was his prisoner—when he pulled up at J. B. Barrett's store in Brooklet. The person I knew to be Sears Ellis was outside at the other end of the loading dock when we got out of the Cutlass. About the time we got up the steps, J. B. Barrett came toward us through the open bay.

"Well, well," he said, "it's the law." He nodded at me, speaking to Buddy: "This here your new assistant?"

"They wouldn't gimme a dog," Buddy said. Two of us laughed.

"Look here," J. B. Barrett said, "I hate it that you come all the way down here. If you'da called first, I coulda told you Royal ain't here today."

I saw Sears Ellis look up from whatever he was stacking on a pallet, and J. B. Barrett must have seen or felt him look up, too, because before Buddy could say anything but "shit," J. B. Barrett had us inside the store.

What J. B. Barrett called his office when he told John Crooms, who was behind the counter, where we would be was a little room with an old desk, three filing cabinets (two with unlabeled drawers), two straight-backed chairs and a swivel desk chair, a window, and an official presidential photograph of Jimmy Carter on the wall.

"Damn it," Buddy said. He and I were in the straight-backed chairs, J. B. Barrett in the swivel chair on the other side of the desk. "Since it was just Thursday, I figured he'd be at work."

J. B. Barrett looked from me to Buddy. He didn't pause at Buddy's face, and that's when I realized Buddy's nose wasn't so red anymore.

"Well, he ain't," he said. "I could of told you the other day when you first said you might be coming out this way that he wasn't gone be here today."

"All right," Buddy said. "So do you know where he is?"

J. B. Barrett smiled and rubbed his chin. "Yeah, as a matter of fact. He's gone way down in the boondocks. To see the Rattlesnake Master."

"The who?" Buddy said.

"The Rattlesnake Master," J. B. Barrett said, and shook with a little laugh. "He's this old colored man who come here from somewhere a few years, hell, maybe eight or ten years ago, and lives on a little place back in the middle of honest-to-God nowhere down yonder below Turleyville."

"And just who is this snake feller when he's at home?" Buddy said. He sounded a little exasperated.

J. B. Barrett smiled, as if to have something pleasant to do before he answered Buddy's question. The room was lit only by sunlight and my eyelids were heavy. "Well," he said, looking up at us and smiling again, "I reckon you could say he was kind of a witch doctor or something."

I heard Buddy sigh. A dog was barking outside somewhere, and it made me look at the window. The panes were clean on the inside but streaked on the outside, and there were a couple of tiny dead moths on the sill. I could tell the panes would be warm if I touched them; sunshine was sticking to the dust as it came in toward the floor.

"A witch doctor," Buddy said. "Wonderful."

"Ah, maybe not so much a witch doctor," J. B. Barrett said, "as some sort of wise man or something like that. I ain't too sure, really." He leaned back in his chair and put one of his legs across the other. A thick white sock came out of his pants leg and went into his heavy shoe.

"Meaning what?" Buddy said, and picked at a tooth with his thumbnail.

"Meaning I dunno," said J. B. Barrett. He chuckled. "You hear talk from the country people—some of 'em say the old man can do just about anything from healing the sick to casting spells, that sort of thing. He don't seem to be a bad man, I reckon, not one of them root doctors or nothing." He sniffed.

Buddy sighed again. J. B. Barrett uncrossed his legs and sat up straight.

"But I spoze most folks who think he's got something to him just kind of ask him what they should do about one thing or another. Dontcha see? Like whether to get married or have an operation or buy this mule or that goat or something. You know what I mean?"

"Old man, huh?" Buddy said.

"I ain't never seen him," J. B. Barrett said, "and most of the colored people, the black people, around here in Brooklet don't seem to know much about him or else just don't care. It's mostly either people from the backwoods, I guess, since backwoods is all there is to Turleyville, or people from up at your end of the county, from town. Some from overn Savannah, even. They tell me he's old, though, just appeared one day and took up in a little house out there in the bottomland."

"Where's he from?" Buddy said.

"Some island, I think," J. B. Barrett said. "Couldn't say for sure."

Buddy seemed to be thinking, picking his teeth with his thumbnail again. I was watching the sun move slowly across the floor, following bits of dust in the beams coming through the window.

"So how'd you know about him?" Buddy said.

"Like I say, country people, mostly," said J. B. Barrett. "And a few city ones, too, but mostly from people who work on my place or rent from me. I don't know a lot, really, just what I've picked up. Most of these people and even some people like Royal that I've known awhile wouldn't tell me nothing about the Rattlesnake Master even if they knew I was interested. Which until lately, I ain't been."

"All right," Buddy said. "So how'd you find out ol' Mango was going to see this rattlesnake guy? And you know why they call him that?"

"Wait a minute," J. B. Barrett said, and sniffed. "One thing at a time. I found out Royal was going down there 'cause this feller Sears Ellis, who works out yonder on my dock, told me."

"That's the guy you got stuck in the swamp with?" Buddy asked, showing a smile of his own.

"Yep," said J. B. Barrett. "Anyhow, Royal, y'see, come told me the other day that he had to go to the doctor and could he take the day off today and make it up later. 'Course, I figured it was some sort of bullshit; where's a fella like him gone go to a doctor around here? The colored doctors in Alachua wouldn't even let him in the door, and he ain't got the money for a white one. But y'see, I didn't think about that at the time, I had my hands full what with shipments coming in and all.

"So this morning Sears and I were cleanin' out them biddy cages in the back and I asked him sort of nonchalant how come Royal wasn't at work today and what he was really up to." J. B. Barrett sniffed again and cleared his throat.

"And he told you?" I said.

"Not straight off," J. B. Barrett said. "He gimme some song and dance about there bein' this new colored doctor down in Turley-ville, but I think me an' him realized about the same time that that wouldn't wash, Turleyville bein' about the size of a fifty-cent piece and not the sort of place anybody's gone hang out his shingle in. So I kept askin' him things like what was the exact nature of Royal's illness, or whatever, kiddin' around a little bit about Royal havin' a woman stashed away back in the swamp somewhere, and me and Sears wasn't gettin' anywhere at all.

"So about this time I begun to get right interested in just what Royal was up to, and so I told ol' Sears that I didn't mean Royal no harm or nothin', and that wherever he was and whatever he was doin', sick or not, he probably had a good reason to get a day off to do it in. I was really pourin' it on, tryin' to get Sears convinced that I wasn't gone do anything to Royal but that I was just curious."

Buddy stood up and went and looked out the window. The sunlight vanished from the floor. "So that's when?" he said, still looking out.

"No," J. B. Barrett said. "It ain't. I finally had to tell him that look, I knew I was his and Royal's boss, that I was The Man and all, but that Sears ought to know that I was a straight shooter and that I wouldn't ever go to Royal with whatever it was that he told me. I spoze I just had to convince him it was okay to level with me."

"Even though you're white and his employer to boot," Buddy said.

"I spoze so," J. B. Barrett said. He sniffed again.

"Huh," Buddy said, and sat back down. The sun reappeared on the worn planks. My seat was getting hard.

"So anyhow," J. B. Barrett said, "Sears told me Royal had this here problem that he couldn't figure out what to do about and that he needed somebody to tell him what to do. So he talked to Sears about it first, I reckon, and somehow or another Sears knows this old Rattlesnake Master guy or knows about him or something, and I spoze he got ahold of him and told him Royal had a problem and he sent word back up here for Royal to come see him."

J. B. Barrett sniffed a couple more times, then took a white handkerchief out of his back pocket and blew his nose. " 'Scuse me," he said, and Buddy and I responded with vague little noises. J. B. Barrett put his handkerchief back in his pocket and sniffed again.

"Anyway," he continued, "that's how come Royal is down yonder havin' conversation with the old man of the woods or whoever he is. I'd rather he'd gone on a day when he wasn't spozed to be workin', but if a man says he's got to go to the doctor, what can you do?"

J. B. Barrett shrugged and grinned and looked at me and I threw him what I hoped was a sympathetic look in return. He looked down at his desk and picked up a pencil and started rolling it around in his fingers.

"So what's his problem?" Buddy said. "Royal's, I mean." The room was even warmer now and the air seemed thick with dust and sunlight.

J. B. Barrett put down his pencil, and it rolled across the green blotter on his desk and came to rest against a little calendar that said February even though we were sitting there a long time after that.

"I still don't know," he said. "You reckon it might be the same thing you're lookin' for him for?"

"Could be," Buddy said noncommittally.

J. B. Barrett grinned. "So what's that?" he said.

"Nothing real official," Buddy said, "I just want to ask him a couple of questions."

"You're being as cagey as Sears," J. B. Barrett said. "Have I got to go to work on you, too?"

We all smiled and shifted around in our chairs. J. B. Barrett crossed his hands over his belly, and Buddy sat up straight and put his hands on his thighs.

"Look, J. B.," he said. "You know somebody beat up ol' Harold Buckminster the other day?"

J. B. Barrett nodded.

"Well, they beat him up over some silver dollars," Buddy said.

"And Harold says he ain't got no idea who it was that did it, only that there was two of them, but what he can tell me for sure is that he got them dollars from Royal Mango."

"Silver dollars," J. B. Barrett said. "Huh. A lot of them?"

"Naw," Buddy said, "at least not that I know of. Harold says he ain't never had more'n maybe ten or so, but he spent three or four of them at Roberson's grocery store the other evenin', and when he got to his car, these two guys grabbed him and hauled him off in the dark to try and get him to tell them where he'd got them. When he wouldn't tell them, they broke his nose and promised to be back, too."

"How come Harold didn't tell them people where he'd got them dollars?" J. B. Barrett said. "Hell, maybe I already know."

"Sure you do," Buddy said. "Harold says he's got to protect his good customers, and I can understand that, as long as we all know he's also lettin' his customers know he can be trusted. The upshot of it is, he says he didn't tell them guys it was Royal Mango he got them dollars from, and I cain't see any reason not to believe him."

"So how come he told you?" J. B. Barrett said.

Buddy thought for a second or two. "Because I am a good cop," he said lightly. "And because people in this county trust me, just like Harold's customers are spozed to trust him. And because I told Harold that I would personally see to it that he'd never make another fifty cents' worth of liquor anywhere in the United States unless he told me and that I'd serve a warrant on him for using his house for immoral purposes besides. Something like that."

"Well, hah," said J. B. Barrett. "If it ain't two mystery fellers picking on Harold, it's you."

Buddy looked at his hands. "It ain't my fault that Harold Buckminster's got such a weakness right there for me to use when I need to," he said.

"Don't take me the wrong way," J. B. Barrett said. "I reckon I just got a weakness for Harold some way or another."

"And don't you worry about me and him," Buddy said. "Long as everybody's got to trust everybody else, you got to trust me to do right by him."

"Okay," J. B. Barrett said. "We done read all that into the record. Now I reckon what you want to do is ask Royal where he got them silver dollars he gave to Harold. But hell, cain't anybody keep silver dollars if they want to?"

"These are probably valuable," I said. It made me feel useful. "We ain't talking about these old Eisenhower dollars, the ones they made out of pressed Kleenex, and they ain't them crummy little Susan B. Anthony dollars, either. Neither of those has a lick of silver, and the ones Harold Buckminster had probably have a lot. That's the first thing, the silver. Then there's the fact that they didn't make a lot of them. Ain't a one of them old ones worth less'n ten or fifteen dollars apiece, and some of them are worth a lot more than that."

J. B. Barrett raised his eyebrows. "So where'd Royal get them, then?" he said, and sniffed.

"That's what I want to ask him," Buddy said.

We all sat there for a few seconds, nobody saying anything. I yawned and stifled it. People were talking outside in the store, and I heard somebody ask loudly if J. B. was in.

"Just a minute!" J. B. Barrett hollered at the closed door. "John! C'mere!"

John Crooms stuck his head into the little office and J. B. Barrett told him to go back and tell whoever it was that was asking for him that he'd be out in a minute. When the door clicked shut again, Buddy said, "Thanks for your time, J. B., I'll let you know what happens. Just do me a favor and don't say nothin' to Royal or nobody till I can get to him first, okay?"

Buddy stood up, and J. B. Barrett started to.

"Wait a minute," I said. "There was another question back there that we didn't get to."

"Whussat?" said J. B. Barrett, settling back in his chair.

I looked up at Buddy. "How come they call this guy the Rattlesnake Master," I said.

"Oh," J. B. Barrett said. "I dunno. Sears says he ain't sure, either. Got a ring to it, though, dontcha think? Just the kind of thing that would get the attention of people livin' out yonder in the woods."

J. B. Barrett stood up, and so did I, and we all headed for the door.

"So," I said. Buddy and I were pulling out of the gravel lot in front of Barrett's store. "There's a juju man down in Turleyville, wherever that is."

"A what?" Buddy said. "Oh, yeah. For all I know about Turleyville, it might as well be on the moon. Bulloch County, see? Outside my jurisdiction. Outside my everything. A witch doctor. Haw. Ol' Mango's gone to see the witch doctor about his silver dollars, I bet. Which maybe he stole or maybe he got from his grandma to buy whiskey from Harold Buckminster with. And which somebody else is after."

"You reckon he knows they're looking for him?" I said. "And that's really why he went down there to see this old guy?"

Some people had pulled a green Capri off the road and had hopped a barbed-wire fence into a huge field of pecan trees and were picking up pecans and putting them in paper sacks despite the slew of No Trespassing signs nailed to fenceposts. Buddy blew the horn of the Cutlass for about three hundred yards as we went by.

"Shiftless," he said, looking into his rearview mirror. "They went right back to pickin' them things up, and there's probably somebody in that bunch knows this is my car, too. I almost hope old man Torrance comes by and sees 'em. That's his field and them's his pecans. One time he did that, though, surprised some people out here, he shot out two of the tires on their car and after a while when they got into town they come by the office and wanted me to go out there and arrest him."

"What'd you say?"

Buddy grinned and pulled out to pass a log hauler. "God, I hate these ol' trucks," he said. "I'm always afraid them logs are just gone roll right off there and smash me flatter'n a tortilla. Uh, I told them

I wasn't in the arresting business, I was in the justice business, and that it seemed to me that justice had already been served."

"Good thinking," I said. "But do you reckon Royal Mango thinks somebody's on his tail?"

"Who knows?" Buddy said, and shrugged as if he didn't really care. We were slowing down now, coming into town out by the mall. "We'll just have to wait till tomorrow and I'll ask him."

"But tomorrow you'll be back on county time," I said.

"Let Ed Lundquist worry about that," Buddy said. "You want to come by and have a beer before you go home?"

SIX

But Buddy Crittenden didn't ask Royal Mango about those silver dollars the next day or the day after that, either.

"He didn't go to work," Buddy said. He was on the other end of the telephone line, and I was sitting on the floor of the hallway in my little house on Magnolia Street in the dark staring at what I knew to be the wall even though I couldn't see it. I had been home from work about ten minutes and had done nothing but make round trips between funk and gloom all day because the barometer was so low that my head felt like it was always about to explode.

From where he was, Buddy couldn't see me roll my eyes. So he went on undaunted.

"And J. B. Barrett don't know where he is, and Sears Ellis says he hasn't seen him, and neither has his wife. Seems like ain't nobody seen him since he went off to see that rattlesnake guy down in Turleyville, and I don't even know how he got there or if I ought to worry about it or just say to hell with it and let it go."

What happened was that failing to find Royal Mango at J. B. Barrett's store the next day, Buddy drove out to his house to see if he could get any nearer to understanding what was going on, or to see if anything was going on in the first place.

It took him a while to find the turnoff, since he hadn't been out there but once, and that was with Big Ed Lundquist a long time ago when the two of them were cruising around looking for somebody who'd escaped from a road gang. Not Royal Mango. He finally had to stop and get directions from old man Fulton Peters, whom Buddy hadn't seen since Fulton Peters retired from working at Roy

Butts's hardware store in Alachua. Buddy's car was making a funny noise, too, and he and Karen had had a fight that morning and he couldn't even remember all the reasons except that it was somehow supposed to be his fault.

Rita Mango was on the rickety front porch plucking a chicken when Buddy drove up.

"She didn't really want to talk," Buddy said to me, "and I started to make it real plain that I wasn't in no mood to talk to her, either. But I tried to be nice. She said what you said, that Royal had gone to see the juju man down in Turleyville. And he wasn't back yet.

"She was the blackest woman I ever saw in my life, red to the elbows, though, and with chicken feathers stuck all over her. Just sittin' there on the edge of that porch gnawin' snuff and flinging feathers. But she wouldn't tell me nothing about this Rattlesnake Master, and wadden very polite about it, either.

"I told her to tell her husband I was lookin' for him, but she gimme this look like I was some kind of a damn fool for thinkin' she'd deliver him to the law. I guess she was right. Ugly woman. Jesus. But some of them chickens, the live ones peckin' around in the yard, was sho pretty. I'd of hated to kill one, myself."

I could see the wall in front of me now. My eyes were getting used to the dark. "So now what?" I said.

"So now," Buddy said, "I cain't give this stuff any more of the county's time, but I figured I'd go down to Turleyville sometime tomorrow, maybe, it bein' my day off, and have a talk with this rattlesnake fella, maybe he's got a doll made up to look like Royal Mango and it's all stuck full of pins." Buddy laughed.

"Since I'm goin' out there all unofficial and all, as sort of a private citizen checking up on the whereabouts of one of his friends, heh-heh, I reckon I'd like for you to come along, too, if you want to, since you've followed this business this far. You ain't doin' nothing else, are you?"

It bothered me a little that Buddy presumed I wasn't doing anything on Saturday afternoon, but he was right. So I told him I'd go and we said good-bye and he hung up and I sat there another ten minutes or so in the dark hallway and tried to think of a reason to get up and turn on the light and do something else. I wasn't just free on Saturday afternoon; I didn't have anything to do on Friday night, either.

Never mind that. The point is that talking to Buddy Crittenden on the telephone is the reason I got to see Turleyville, Georgia, the next day. It didn't take long, since Turleyville was an old filling station and a dirty little store and three or four visible houses and that was all.

Nobody in the filling station or in the store either claimed to know anything about anybody called the Rattlesnake Master, and all Buddy and I knew was that he lived on a county road somewhere between Turleyville and Manassas, which meant we were looking for one man in one house somewhere off thirty miles of black-patched and pitted highway.

It also meant that I got more discouraged and Buddy got more angry as the day dragged on, us stopping at every little shack and getting nothing for our trouble but downcast eyes and people shaking their heads and saying, "Nawsir, I ain't never hearn of no such man," and Buddy coming back to the Cutlass cussing about how this county full of ignorant yahoos was lying through their teeth at him, every damn one of them, he could see it in their faces. I could, too.

But we got lucky, or we got smarter, maybe, because when Buddy finally took the time to go up on the porch of a little house presided over by a tremendously fat black woman in a gray print dress and explain to her that he was looking for a black feller who'd come down this way to see somebody called the Rattlesnake Master and who hadn't come home yet and whose wife and little chirren were crying for their husband and daddy all day long, suddenly we found out where to go.

"She called him a doctor and a man sanctified of God," Buddy said when he got back to the car. "I half expected her to cross herself or something."

"Who?" I said.

"This Rattlesnake Master, of course," he said, starting the

Cutlass and pulling out onto the road. "One thing Royal Mango definitely ain't is sanctified by God."

"Hah," I said, but I was getting nervous for some reason or other. "So where does he live?"

"Couple more miles," Buddy said. "Look for a dirt track going straight off to the right. Miz Tuttle—that's that fat lady's name back yonder—says you can just see the house from the road."

So we drove on a ways and slowed down and crept along for a while and then saw the narrow dirt road and turned off and went down the bank and through about twenty-five yards of tall cypresses and oaks and blackgums. I could see the house all the way in, all right, an unpainted weather-gray house with a covered front porch the length of it and a tin roof with one chimney. It was just like any of a hundred other houses stuck off in virtually the middle of nowhere around here except that there were no cars in the yard and no TV antenna on the roof.

The house was immaculate, at least the parts I could see, no patching and nothing that looked rotten, every nail seeming to have been driven all the way home and tight. A young dark brown woman in a white sundress was standing in the doorway, holding a broom in one hand and propping open the screen with her other hand, watching us come into the yard.

In front of the porch on both sides of the wide wooden steps were the remains of what had been a thick border of flowers—long rows of zinnias, balsam, and marigolds deteriorating fast now that it was getting well into fall, backed by cleomes that were still bright in spots, and flanked at both ends by stands of tall but bedraggled tithonias, their deep orange flowers turned crinkly and dry.

On one side of the little house was a broad pecan tree. On the other—"I'll be dog," Buddy said, and I knew he was looking at it, too, and thinking just as I was that this house was like no other house either of us had ever seen in the wilder, poorer parts of southeast Georgia, with a flower border and actual grass growing in the front yard, the look of the whole place meaning above a number of other things that whoever kept it could attend to it without being distracted by the usual innumerable small catastrophes accruing to poverty, ignorance, and oppression—were two deep green palm trees about fifteen feet tall.

The pecan tree I expected. The palm trees were a pleasant surprise. "This place looks like it belongs in the West Indies," I said as Buddy stopped the Cutlass and turned off the engine.

"Good-lookin' house, good-lookin' woman," Buddy said. "Not a rattlesnake in sight. No skulls and crossbones, either."

The young brown woman in the white dress frowned at us, walked to the end of the porch, looked around the corner toward the back of the house, then turned, gave us another sharp look and walked back down the porch, opened the door, and went into the shadows.

"Screen door," Buddy said.

"No holes in it that I can tell," I said. "These flowers must have been beautiful—there's stuff here I've never even seen before, and there's stuff here that my mama raises, too. Too bad we didn't come out here in August."

Buddy looked at me.

"Why would we have come out here in August?" he said. He seemed genuinely puzzled.

"Forget it," I said. "So what do we do now?"

Buddy patted the steering wheel with both hands. Huge piles of white clouds lay in the sky behind the house; it was warm for this part of fall and that meant we stood a good chance of rain and thunder later on. "I guess we go see a man about a Mango," he said.

"Clever," I said. "What do you say to a juju man?"

Buddy put a hand on the door handle. "Shit," he said. "I just hope he understands English and doesn't have two heads. I reckon we got to get out to find out, though."

So we got out, having strung along one convention—waiting for someone to come out of the house to greet us, with what that meant by way of if not welcome then at least a neutral curiosity—as far as we could, and went up to the steps on a walkway paved with tiny rocks.

Buddy put one foot on the bottom step. "Hello!" he shouted, and opened his mouth again but didn't say anything else because a tall, thin and very black man with short gray hair and a gray mustache came around the corner of the porch past the palm trees and said, "Gentlemen. What may I do for you?"

We both turned to face him, though Buddy interrupted his turning long enough to look hard at the front door—that's how you know he's good at being a deputy sheriff, I thought—and then Buddy said, "Hey there."

The old man smiled at us. He was dressed in blue cotton pants over black work shoes, and his shirt was as blinding white as the high clouds, a white shirt with white buttons and a high frame for a collar that wasn't clipped on to it.

"My name is Leeman Gant," the old man said. His accent was British, but not from Britain. He looked at Buddy. "You," he said, "would be Crittenden from across the river. And you . . ." He looked at me.

"My name's Leeman, too," I said.

The old man grinned, opening his lips to two racks of shining white teeth broken upper and lower by single gleams of gold somewhere among the molars.

"Yes," he said happily. "There was something about you."

Buddy and I stared. The old man gestured toward the porch with the pruning snips in his left hand. "Would you like to sit down?" he said. "Or would you prefer a walk in the garden?" He nodded behind him at the corner of the house. "Back there. Would you like some tea?"

"The porch'll be fine," Buddy said. "And I'd like a glass of tea."

"Me too," I said.

"Excellent," the old man said, striding down the walk between us. "The porch and tea."

So we followed him up the steps and Buddy and I picked chairs—well, Buddy did, anyway, picking a chair and then motioning to me to sit in another by the door so the old man would have to sit between us—and Leeman Gant went to get our tea. There was a murmur of voices inside the house, English but not quite.

The old man came back without the tea, but with a footstool, and he put the stool on the porch between my chair and the door and sat down. "The stool is good for me," he said. "It forces me to be aware of my posture."

He and Buddy looked at each other and Buddy got up and moved to the empty chair between us. Round one to the old man, I thought.

"The tea will be here shortly," he said. He looked at me. "Leeman," he said. "What is your mother's name?"

"Rose," I said.

He seemed disappointed. "Ah," he said. "Mine was named Esther. I was thinking perhaps the coincidence went a step farther." He shrugged.

"Excuse me," Buddy said. "How'd you know who I am?"

The old man put his hands on his thighs. He had big knuckles and long wrinkled fingers and perfect fingernails. "It is the habit of a black man in some places to know the faces of the law," he said, not without cheer. "It is a habit I nourished and one I have not yet had sufficient reason to break."

Buddy grunted. The old man looked me in the eye, and I looked away. The air was almost as warm as summertime, and that made the brown flowers by the porch all the more sad.

"And Mr. Mango said you might be coming out this way to look for him as well," the old man went on. He was watching Buddy and me very closely, his eyes flitting back and forth and settling and moving again, like butterflies.

"This is Royal Mango that lives over in Brooklet, right?" Buddy said.

"Of course," the old man said, and shrugged again.

"You've seen him, then," Buddy said.

"Oh yes," the old man said, smiling merrily now. "In point of fact, he is my guest."

"So he did get here and he's *still* here?" Buddy said. I turned to look at him, then turned back at Leeman Gant, whose face was as blank as could be. "Mango's still here?"

Just then the screen door opened and the young brown woman in the white dress came out with three wet jelly glasses of iced tea on a metal tray. The odor of hyacinths came out with her.

"Gentlemen," the old man said, standing up. "My daughter Elizabeth."

Buddy and I stood, too. Buddy said his name and then "Elizabeth," and held out his hand and she shook it slightly. I said my name and "pleased to meet you," and shook hands with her and she said, "I'm pleased to meet you both." Her hand was lean and strong and had done some work.

Buddy and the old man and I sat back down and took our tea glasses from the tray, on which was a painting of the island of Barbados and beside it a portrait of Queen Elizabeth. *To commemorate Her Majesty's visit* was written in a semicircle above them both. The glass I took was sitting just offshore of Bridgetown.

"Yes," the old man said, "Elizabeth here is the joy of my fading years. But she sacrifices, and she has sacrificed too much to stay with me and help me."

Elizabeth looked at him, then away. "I choose my life, Papa," she said patiently, and bent down and kissed the old man on the cheek. "Will you need anything else right away?"

We all said no, thanks, we were fine, and Elizabeth went back into the house, trailing the slightest breeze of hyacinth, letting the screen door shut against her so it wouldn't slam.

The old man sat up ramrod straight on the stool and took a sip of tea.

"Would you rather have a chair now?" I said, making moves as though to get up.

The old man looked at me and smiled conspiratorially and said, "Yes, that would be nice," and I stood up and got the empty chair from the other side of Buddy and put it down by the door and the old man got off the stool and sat in it. Buddy pulled his chair toward the middle of the porch so he could see me and Leeman Gant.

"Uh, you . . ." Buddy said, self-consciously.

"Excuse me," Leeman Gant said. "I forgot. We were discussing Mr. Mango, who came to me with trouble. But I suppose you know that."

"Where, uh, is he here?" Buddy asked, nodding sidelong toward the house.

"He is my guest," the old man said. The tea was very cold and tasted of mint. It was delicious. Nobody said anything for a minute; we all sat and looked at the autumn colors in the yard and sipped our tea. A buckeye butterfly that had survived the few cold nights so far flew from stalk to stalk in the withered garden, looking for something he could sip, too. The air was warm and I could hear a mourning dove behind the house. I wanted to go to sleep.

Buddy said, "We came out here looking for him. He hasn't been to work for a while."

The old man was watching the buckeye work its way through the dried flower heads and didn't say anything till it paused on a cleome. "Yes," he said. "Mr. Mango has been here. I'm sorry his absence caused you to worry, but he has been quite safe. He came to me with trouble. I'm afraid many people find me that way."

He paused and cleared his throat, bobbing his Adam's apple up and down, then took a drink of tea. "But he had another sort of trouble, too, and we had to relieve him of that one first." He looked at Buddy and me in turn, without humor. "He has been very drunk, he has been seeing things that are not there."

"Hallucinating," I said, and felt silly for it.

"That's right," the old man said, nodding. "He has been hallucinating. So before he and I could talk about what trouble was there, he's had to stop seeing things that are not there. Mr. Mango has been very sick, but today he is better. We have talked, and we will talk again, and then he will go home. Since you have come, I suppose he will go home with you if you are prepared to wait."

"For what?" Buddy said.

"For him to wake up," the old man said.

"Then what?" Buddy said.

"Then we shall see," Leeman Gant said. And he smiled at us and sipped his tea.

"Wait a minute," Buddy said, and leaned forward a little. "I'm the law. I've got questions to ask."

"No," the old man said kindly, "you are not the law. Not in this county."

Buddy was looking at the porch in front of him. "No," he said.

"I'm not. I'm sorry. It must be automatic. I'm not the law here, I just want to know some things."

"What would you like to know?" said the old man. He raised his eyebrows a little and I saw that his eyes were shining. But they were dark, too, as though they were stones that had been greatly polished or stones that had come to life. In the backyard, a rooster crowed at the late afternoon.

"What's Royal Mango's trouble?" Buddy said.

"Only he can tell you that," the old man said. "It is his trouble, and only he can share it."

I was trying to listen to them, but even as interested as I was in what at some points was beginning to sound like if not a battle then at least a skirmish of wits, and as interested as I also was in knowing more about the old man, I began to get wonderfully drowsy. I felt so good that I wouldn't have been bothered at all if someone had told me I'd have to sit on that porch forever. Warm air, a little breeze, the taste of mint tea in my mouth, the rising and falling drone of voices—I was afraid I might topple over.

"All right," Buddy said, "why did he come to you?"

"I have some small reputation," the old man said. "Many people who have trouble seem to feel I can be of help to them. Maybe you would be surprised. White people, too. Even some from your place, back over the river."

"Can you?" Buddy said, and tilted his last swallow of tea into his mouth. The ice jingled in his glass.

"Would you like more tea?" the old man asked.

"No, thanks," Buddy said. The shadows of the palm trees on our left and the pecan tree on our right were extending into the yard in front of us.

Finally the old man said, "Yes. I can help some of them, those who truly believe."

Buddy shot a glance past me and onto the old man. "Believe in what?" he said.

The old man shrugged. "Why, believe in my power to help

them, of course," he said, and looked at Buddy, and the corners of
his mouth turned up.

Buddy stared back at him. "I'm not sure I know what you
mean," he said.

The old man pursed his lips. He seemed to be watching the
dying garden, all of which was in shadow now. Then he looked at
me out of the corner of his eye and cocked an eyebrow.

What the hell, I thought. "Are we talking about advice?" I said.
"Or maybe what we're really talking about is magic."

The old man laughed from down in his chest, a sort of heh-heh-
heh-heh, then reached into his back pocket and got a white handkerchief and brought it out and patted his lips.

"Sometimes the two are hard to tell apart, aren't they?" he said,
and I thought to myself that he must have misunderstood what I
meant, but then I figured that what had happened was that he had
understood, all right, and had decided to talk about something else.
"To some people"—now he looked at me—"words have a power
of their own."

"Sort of like the power of positive thinking," I said, and felt
silly again.

Leeman Gant opened his mouth and another laugh, a short
bright one this time, came out of it. "My friends," he said, "the day
is dying in the west, as the hymnbook tells us, and I think you have
not yet received what you came for. So let us be direct."

"I'd like that," Buddy said. Too peevishly, I thought.

"You," the old man said, and pointed quickly at Buddy, "you
want to know if I paint myself and bay at the moon, maybe even
if I kill goats and sprinkle chickens' blood over the ground." He
paused, and took off his glasses and rubbed his eyes.

"No, I am not. No, I don't. I dispense herbs that I grow myself.
I dispense advice. And tea. I sit on this porch and drink tea with
people who have trouble and offer them what comfort I can. I am
not what you would probably call a witch doctor. No."

"They call you the Rattlesnake Master," I said.

The old man took a deep breath and let it out. "Yes," he said, nodding. "They do. I have a reputation for being able to cure snakebite. Some people are impressed by that, they have to have something to call me that makes me special. What does it matter to me what they call me as long as they trust me?"

The screen door opened and Elizabeth was standing there. "Excuse me, Papa," she said. "Mr. Mango has awakened."

"Ah," the old man said. "Our Mr. Mango has returned."

"Returned?" Buddy said.

The old man stood up. "Please excuse me," he said. "I will be away for a few minutes. May I trouble you to wait in the backyard?"

"Can I see Royal?" Buddy said, standing up, too.

The old man put his hand on the door. Elizabeth was holding it open for him. "Shortly," he said. "Now please go to the backyard and wait for us." And then the two of them were inside the house, and I could hear that conversation again, English but not English entirely.

Buddy and I looked at each other. "So let's go around back," I said.

"Damn if I know what's goin' on here," Buddy said quietly. He stopped at the bottom of the steps and I stopped, too, and we looked at each other. "Just some kind of advice? These poor ignorant swamp folks—oh yeah, and some white people from town, too, let's be sure we put that in there—come trooping in here for *advice?* They call him the Rattlesnake Master because he cures snakebite, they tell me he's sanctified of God, and they come here for some talk and some tea and some sympathy? Do you understand all this?"

"No," I said, and now we were walking. "Did you hear him and Elizabeth talking to each other?" The wind had risen a little and was rattling the fronds of the palm trees.

"Uh-huh," Buddy said. "What's that language they're speakin'?"

"English, sort of," I said. "I think it's Bajan—what they speak on Barbados. I've been there. The money's got flying fish and other neat stuff on it. But the road signs aren't worth a shit. Rum's real cheap. It's easy to get drunk and get lost."

"Barbados," Buddy said. "That tray she brought the tea out on.

J. B. Barrett said he come from an island." He looked at me. "Come to think of it, you and this old feller are hittin' it off right easy, dontcha think?"

"I dunno," I said, and then we were in the backyard.

At the far edge was the remains of a vegetable garden—old vines and dried-up bushes and cornstalks. Trellises and wire frames. There had been squash and rows and rows of beans, and okra. Off to the left, between the house and the southern end of the garden but closer to the garden than the house, was a neat wooden outhouse half again as big as any one I'd ever seen.

It was the kind of outhouse that when I saw it I wondered why Mr. Gant had built it or had it built when for not a lot more money he could have had a flush toilet in the house and a septic tank outside in the ground. There was a little pumphouse about thirty feet from the well, which apparently was still being used, too, since it was spick and span and the path leading to it from the house was worn down to dirt in the middle. He had electricity from the REA and water from the ground but he kept his outhouse. Maybe he just liked to look up at the sky.

"Look," Buddy said in a loud whisper. "The goddamned privy has a skylight in it."

But the outstanding thing about the backyard wasn't the vegetable garden or even the outhouse with a skylight in the roof. It was mostly just the backyard itself, or the bulk of it, anyway, all the way out to the clothesline. The whole thing was a network of raised rectangular beds bounded by cross ties, and every bed was planted in something, generally something different. Some of them were still green, and some of them even had plants and bushes that still showed a flower or two, but what there was most of was brown-green stalks and stems and lots and lots of seeds—in pods and balls and tufts and fruit. In one of the larger plots, huge sunflower heads drooped over thick trunks. The effect somehow was lush in spite of the season and the colors.

"Holy mackerel," Buddy said. "I ain't seen nothing like this since Karen dragged me up to South Carolina to the seed company's open house. What you reckon all this stuff is for?"

I hadn't thought about it. "Advice, I 'spect," I said.

Buddy grunted. "I got a feelin' maybe this advice business runs pretty deep," he said.

What wasn't set off by cross ties and planted in whatever it was planted in was covered in grass, St. Augustine or Centipede or something else with runners.

Buddy walked out and stood in the middle of it all, his thumbs hooked in his pants pockets, but I stayed where I was. Euonymus was planted between the windows on the back of the house, and the windows were screened and curtained. A little porch with a roof over it and shelves between the posts was set against the back door, which was also screened and had a pair of bluebirds painted above the lintel. For about six feet on either side of the porch were drying masses of woody stalks about five feet high; from the stalks grew stems crowned by little spiky balls sort of like sweetgum balls. I knew what they were.

I hollered at Buddy, trying to be just loud enough to be sure to get his attention but not so loud as to disturb whatever was going on inside the house. He looked at me, but before I could say anything, the back door opened and Royal Mango—or who I presumed to be Royal Mango, since the scrawny wretch who tottered onto the porch wasn't Leeman Gant or his daughter Elizabeth, either—came out, followed by the old man. The first was blinking into the setting sun, the second was looking at me, then at Buddy.

"Leeman," he said. "Mr. Crittenden. Mr. Mango here is at your disposal."

Royal Mango nodded, belched, and put his right hand on his stomach. He had dark spots like freckles on his deep tan face and frizzy, mud-colored hair above it.

"Hello," I said. Buddy said nothing. Royal Mango nodded again and stood up a little straighter.

"As you know," the old man said pleasantly, "Mr. Mango here needs a ride back to your side of the river. I told him you had come for him and that he is to go with you."

"Ah, sure," Buddy said. "I reckon we're much obliged. You 'bout ready, Leeman?"

"Okay," I said, but I'd have rather stayed to look at the yard some more.

"Is there something you'd like to ask?" the old man said to me. Royal Mango was standing as if confounded, or maybe awestruck. Or maybe even nothing at all.

"Yes sir," I said. "That stuff over there." I pointed. "Did you have hollyhocks?"

"Yes," the old man said. "You know them?"

"I haven't seen many down here," I said. "Maybe I haven't seen any at all down here. But I've seen them up north, mostly in New England."

"They were a favorite of my father's," the old man said. "They are of no use except to look at, but with hollyhocks that seems to be enough, don't you think?"

"Yes," I said.

"What're you people talking about?" Buddy said. He had come up close to the porch and the old man came down the steps and stood between us.

"Hollyhocks," I said, and pointed at the broken stalks. "*Althaea ficifolia* or something like that."

The old man looked at me with delight and surprise, and I tried to pretend I hadn't noticed.

"That stuff in that first bed there," I went on, "next to the primroses sticking up between the ties." Then I looked at the old man.

"*Oenothera biennis,*" he said, "evening primrose," and we both smiled. Buddy looked annoyed.

"It is a pleasure to share a name with you," the old man said to me.

"Yes sir," I said. "Thank you."

"You must come back," he said, and put out his hand for me to shake. I shook it.

"Do I need an appointment?" I said.

The old man grinned and covered our two right hands with his left. "You'll know when to come back," he said. "Come when you will."

"Yes sir," I said. "Thank you. I'll do it."

Then Leeman Gant and Buddy Crittenden shook hands, and we coaxed Royal Mango off the porch and the old man shook his hand as well. We four walked back around past the palm trees—they were cabbage palms, *Sabal palmetto*—to the front of the house and Buddy said, "Thanks for the tea" and for the old man to thank his daughter for serving it to us. Then he said, "So can I come back, too?"

"As the law," the old man said, "or as a man who owns a little less than half interest in a liquor store and so makes enough money to be a deputy sheriff because he wants to be one and not because he is tied to the pittance it pays? Or merely as someone who has a curiosity to satisfy?"

"I don't know," Buddy said, and looked at the ground. I think he was telling the truth.

"Do what you must," the old man said.

Then Buddy said thank you and we said good-bye all around and Buddy and Royal Mango and I got in the Cutlass and Buddy started it and we drove away, leaving the old man standing against a background of his house and a great blazing sunset.

About the time we turned onto the highway, Buddy said, "Royal? You okay?"

"I'm fine as frawg hair," Royal Mango said from the backseat.

"Well, don't go to sleep," Buddy said. "We gone talk in a minute. Looks like I'm doomed to be your guardian angel." I heard him exhale through his nose and then we sped up.

"So," he said to me, "what did *you* think about all that, you're such hot stuff, you and the juju advice man got the same first name and know a lot of the same words."

I decided to let him be angry, or resentful, or whatever he was. "I dunno," I said. "He was a surprise, I mean, finding somebody like that out here in the swamps."

Buddy looked at me to get my attention and then cut his eyes toward the backseat, telling me to be careful what I said in front of our passenger.

"I do know one thing," I said.

"What's that?" Buddy took out a cigarette and punched in the lighter on the dashboard.

"Well," I said, and I didn't have it figured out, really, "maybe all he does is give out advice and such"—Buddy frowned at me and cut his eyes toward the backseat again—"and maybe not." Buddy rolled down his window a few inches, drew out the lighter, and lit his cigarette. At that point Royal Mango asked if he could have a cigarette and got one, too, and lit it himself and leaned up and threw the match out Buddy's window.

"Okay," Buddy said.

"Okay," I said. "But I reckon there might be more to ol' Leeman Gant, maybe, than he told us."

"More like how come he's to be here and not in Barbados?" Buddy said. "Or how come he's got a good-lookin' daughter more than of age but still stayin' at home to look after her daddy? Or how he gets enough money to buy groceries, much less a skylight for his shithouse? Like that?"

"No," I said. "At least not on the surface. I mean, we've been making jokes about him bein' a witch doctor and all"—Buddy made a face and clenched his jaw—"and maybe that's really a joke. But what they call him, the Rattlesnake Master, has got more to do with just him curin' snakebite. I'll bet you that."

Buddy took a drag from his cigarette and blew smoke at the open window.

"You got a feeling?" he said.

"No," I said. "Those plants on both sides of the back porch, all them stalks that were still standin' there with them spiky little balls on them? Every one of those plants had been sprouted in its own pot and then transplanted pot-dirt and all into the ground there. They had been weeded, too, before they began to die off."

"So what?" Buddy said. I saw Royal Mango's hand go past the other side of Buddy's head and the flash of a cigarette being thrown out on the highway.

"So they were what's called *Eryngium yuccifolium*," I said.

"Science marches on," Buddy said derisively. "So what?"

"Otherwise known as rattlesnake master," I said.

"Oh, for Christ's sake," Buddy said, and took a last drag and put his cigarette out in the ashtray.

"It's in the carrot family," I said, and then neither of us said anything until long after we were back across the Ogeechee and could see the lights of town coming at us in the heavy dusk. By that time, Royal Mango was snoring.

I don't know what Buddy did with Royal Mango that night after he took me home, but I know he talked to him in his little cubicle at the sheriff's office sometime in the next couple of days because he told me about it over supper at the Ogeechee Grille.

What Royal Mango said was that he had had those silver dollars for a long time but had never had to spend any of them until now, since they were all the money he had left in the world.

"Maybe you'd better ask J. B. for a raise," Buddy said. "Now let me get this straight—those silver dollars were the only money you had, so what you spent them on was whiskey."

"That's right," Royal Mango said.

"And you know what?" Buddy said. "That's just what Harold Buckminster says he told those guys who broke his nose—that he was spendin' them silver dollars 'cause that was the last money he had."

Royal Mango never even blinked. "Me 'n' Harold think alike, is all," he said.

"Uh-huh," Buddy said. "So how come you went to see Leeman Gant?"

"Who?" Royal Mango said, and looked up from his lap to Buddy.

"The Rattlesnake Master," Buddy said, and ground his teeth.

"Oh," Royal Mango said. "I went to see him about a personal problem I got."

"That problem ain't got nothin' to do with them two guys that jumped Harold, has it?" Buddy said, leaning over and resting his arms on the top of his desk.

"Why should it?" Royal Mango said. "I ain't done nothin' to nobody, and ain't nobody lookin' for me by name, I reckon."

"Yet," Buddy said threateningly. And this time Royal Mango did look a bit uncomfortable.

After a minute, Buddy said, "So what did this, ah, Rattlesnake Master tell you to do?"

Royal Mango looked at Buddy a long time. His eyes were watery and he looked as though he could use a good washing and pressing, but Buddy could see that something was going on behind those eyes, so he just sat there and waited until Royal Mango had finished thinking and had said, "He told me to come back."

"He told you to *come back*?"

"Yes sir," said Royal Mango.

"That's it?"

"Pretty much," Royal Mango said, and Buddy says that here, Royal Mango suddenly seemed to relax, as though he and Buddy might have been playing chess and Royal Mango had just made a move and leaned back and said, "Checkmate."

"Was it worth it?" Buddy said.

"He was free," Royal Mango said.

At that point Buddy was ready to grab Royal Mango by his turkey neck and swing him around the room, but instead he said, "So how come you had to stay down there for the better part of three days?"

And Royal Mango said, "I was sleepin', mostly."

Buddy took a deep breath. "Why were you sleeping?" he said patiently.

"I got there real drunk," Royal Mango said.

"Ain't nobody told me how you got there at all," Buddy said, "other than drunk. How did you?"

"How did I whut?" Royal Mango said.

Buddy pounded his desk and Royal Mango jumped. "How did you get down there, goddammit? What the hell do you think?"

Royal Mango looked at the door. "Sears took me," he said.

"Sears Ellis?" Buddy said. "He took you down there when you were drunk?"

"Yes sir, I was drunk," Royal Mango said.

"Did he come to your house and get you?" Buddy said.

"Yes sir," Royal Mango said.

"Were you drunk when he got there?" Buddy said.

"Yes sir," Royal Mango said. "He come in his sister's car."

Buddy tried to harpoon Royal Mango with a stare, but the little man's gaze slipped away from him. "You were drunk," Buddy said, "even though you were supposed to go see the old man?" He was the one relaxed now, he could tell something was beginning to happen even though he still hadn't figured out what it was.

Royal Mango looked at the door again. "I wadden spoze to go till the next day," he said.

"Wait a second," Buddy said, leaning forward again. "I don't get it. So how come Sears Ellis was to drive out to your place and pick you up the night *before* you were supposed to go to Turleyville? If I've got it right that he was the one that was gone take you down there all the time, how come he didn't wait till the next day?"

"I called him and told him I wadden goin'," Royal Mango said.

"Wait again," Buddy said. "You called up Sears Ellis and told him you weren't gone go down to Turleyville?"

"Yes sir," Royal Mango said. "I walked 'cross the road to Miz Morris's place and called him."

"Why?" Buddy said.

"I was drunk," Royal Mango said wearily. "I didn't know what I was doin'."

Buddy couldn't tell if Royal Mango was being stupid or if he was being clever, but whichever of them he was doing, he was doing it well, because Buddy discovered that his expectations that something was about to happen had suddenly dissipated.

"Okay," Buddy said. "So you got drunk. . . ."

"Drunk as hell," Royal Mango said, and grinned a little.

"You got drunk," Buddy went on, "and you called Sears Ellis, who had probably told you about this old man in the first place"—Royal Mango looked up—"and told him you weren't gone go down there after all, because you were drunk or God knows why, and he drove his sister's car out to your place and picked you up and drove all the way down to Turleyville in what I suppose by then was the middle of the night."

"I reckon so," Royal Mango said.

"What do you mean, you reckon?" Buddy said.

"Well," Royal Mango said, "what I remember is bein' real drunk and walkin' over to Miz Morris's house and givin' her ten cent to use her phone and callin' Sears and then I had some more to drink and when I woke up I was at the old man's house and he gimme some orange juice."

"You don't remember gettin' there?"

"No sir."

"Do you remember havin' the DTs?"

"I remember some really weird shit," Royal Mango said, and giggled.

"Like what?"

"DT shit. Snakes crawlin', birds flyin' around. Swimmin'."

"Swimming?" Buddy said, and sat back.

"Yes sir," Royal Mango said, and Buddy says he relaxed again, as though he had been holding something heavy and had put it down.

"Can I go now?" Royal Mango said.

"No," Buddy said. "Why'd you get drunk?"

"I had a personal problem," Royal Mango said.

"Tell me about it."

"No sir, I cain't," Royal Mango said. His hands were fidgeting in his lap.

"How come?"

Royal Mango didn't look up. "Because it's too personal."

Buddy sat there looking across the desk and the floor at Royal Mango, who was leaning his chair back against the wall and who wouldn't really look back at him, and he could hear a typewriter clicking somewhere and wondered what he would be doing right that minute if he hadn't become a deputy sheriff. But he didn't get to play with that for very long, because Royal Mango said, "Can I go now?" again, and looked at the door.

"No," Buddy said. The typewriter went *clickety-click.*
"Yes," Buddy said. "Get the hell out of here."

     "And that's it," Buddy said, taking a sip of coffee. The waitress brought us the bill. Her name tag had *Brenda* printed on it. She was young enough to be from the college, and while she wasn't especially good-looking she was just the right amalgamation of long legs and dark hair and a noticeable shape to make me think of somebody I had known in another place far away. Somebody in large part responsible for me being where I was now, in fact, since had it not been for certain unhappinesses that had passed between us, I might have been perfectly content to stay where I used to be.

But it got so that I couldn't even stay in the same town with her, so close to the source of my misfortune that I might actually hear somebody say her name or even see her again. The easiest thing was just to run. And so far, so good, too. Some days in Alachua I actually wanted to get out of bed.

"What's the matter with you?" Buddy said, looking at the bill. What he saw made his eyebrows go up.

"Nothing," I said, wishing it were true. "What do you mean, 'That's it'?"

"That's all of it," he said, "at least for now. I'd like to know where Royal Mango really got them silver dollars, and I'd like to go back and ask him if he's got any more where those came from. I'd really like to know who those guys were that beat up Harold Buckminster, but Royal says he ain't got any idea who they were, and I believe him. I don't believe that Harold doesn't know who they were, but what can I do? I'm stuck. And I'd like to talk to this Sears Ellis, too. But I ain't gettin' much help, and right now the only real illegality I got is Harold's busted nose."

"Okay," I said. "So . . ."

"So to hell with it," Buddy said. "It's a waste of my time. Maybe if I just don't mess with it for a while, I'll think of something to do. But this whole business of Harold and Mango—who seems to be pretty good at following directions from somebody, if you ask me—

and somehow even Sears Ellis and that old man down in the swamp besides, I just don't feel good about it, y'know? Somethin' smells funny to me. But I got other fish to fry, and maybe if I just don't do anything at all, somethin' will happen."

Something did happen, too. But for a long time, what happened didn't seem to be pertinent to any of the people Buddy was talking about, but seemed to be only a part of something entirely different that had happened and then was pretty much forgotten.

What happened is that somebody dug some holes. But to get to those holes from here, you've got to go all the way back to last spring and return by another route.

SEVEN

"Of course he left her," Buddy Crittenden said. "And just because he lived with her for thirty-five years before he finally couldn't stand it anymore just means he was incredibly patient, or that he was a simpleton, or maybe even that he loved her. And if he loved that awful woman, he was probably crazy anyway and can't be blamed."

"You don't like Mary Louise very much, do you?" I said.

"I'm ashamed to say it, but I reckon I don't like her at all."

"But you probably have to deal with her once in a while. Ain't she your mama's best friend?"

"My mama is old enough to live with her mistakes," Buddy said, entirely without humor. "Besides, I'm a civilized person. I keep my contempt hidden behind a veneer of manners."

"Cool off," I said. I wished he would, too. I was trying to eat my last mouthful of chicken livers and wanted to enjoy it.

"How can I calm down?" Buddy said, his eyebrows raised to their extremity. "Now I've got to deal with her, and not just as my mama's son who can pay his respects and leave and go straight to the pool room. No, this time I've got to deal with her because I'm a deputy sheriff and it's my bad luck that Mary Louise lives about ten feet outside the city limits where the police won't touch her."

"Huh," I said. "So what's she done?"

Buddy sighed. We were sitting at a little table at Ray's Steak House on Columbia Street, and I could hear Buddy's boots clonging against the metal post the table sat on.

"Nothing," he said. "Unless she's decided to go as batty as her

96

husband was. I mean, what can you do with a sixty-two-year-old woman who says she looked up from her *National Geographic* and saw Richard Nixon staring at her through the window?"

"Wow," I said. "Sounds like she should be put away before she does herself some harm."

"Maybe. But she probably really did see somebody and just thinks it was him."

"Did her husband look like Richard Nixon?"

"Naw. He was a real good-lookin' guy, more like Gregory Peck. Which makes it even more of a mystery why he stayed with her so long."

Buddy took his last bite of biscuit and wiped his mouth. "Anyhow," he went on, "what do you suppose she saw? Or who? Ain't been no Peeping Toms in this town since I been here."

"Well," I said, "maybe Richard Nixon has gone over the edge and is staring at old women reading magazines."

Buddy sighed again. "You ain't bein' much help."

"So what is it you want?" I said, and shrugged. The waitress came over and poured us some more coffee.

"Look," Buddy said, and put his hands out flat on the table in front of him, getting some spilled sugar on a couple of his fingers in the process. "We both know she didn't see Richard Nixon."

"Okay. So who was it?"

"That's the trouble," Buddy said. "That's what bothers me."

So Buddy left me there with the check after asking me to please not tell anybody there might be a Peeping Tom on the loose and drove over to Mary Louise Etheridge's house on Harmon Street and poked around outside under the window where the alleged Richard Nixon had stood, then went inside to talk to Mary Louise. Once inside, he was soon driven to blind fury by what a casual observer might have decided was merely that poor, braying woman's presence on earth, after which he returned to the yard and his investigation of the window to keep from being rude to his mama's best friend.

And what he told me and Sam Campbell the next day while we were watching the Atlanta Braves play a sort of baseball on TV was that he didn't find anything under the window except some flattened ivy and a Salem cigarette butt and didn't learn very much from Mary Louise Etheridge, either.

"In fact," Buddy said, "from what she told me, in between asking me when I was goin' to settle down and get married or start goin' back to church regularly or run for sheriff and get Big Ed Lundquist out of office, I figure this person, whoever he was, must of been something like five-foot-ten, according to where his head was at the window."

"Sounds like Richard Nixon to me," Sam said emphatically.

"Look," I said, pointing at the TV, "Murphy just struck out with the bases loaded."

"So what?" Sam said.

"So that means Horner will hit a pop-up," Buddy said.

We all stopped talking and watched the game, and about the time the shortstop caught Horner's pop-up to end the inning, Buddy's beeper peeped.

"I'll see y'all later," he said when he got back from the hallway, where the telephone was.

"What could possibly have happened on Sunday afternoon?" I said.

"What could possibly happen," Buddy said, "is that it took Sarah Collins since last night to track down Big Ed and tell him that while she and her sister were eatin' supper, she looked up and saw Jimmy Carter watchin' her through the window."

"I didn't know Jimmuh was in town," Sam said.

"Anyway, what have you got to do with Sarah Collins seeing somebody?" I said.

"Well, hell, I've already got one of them, ain't I?" Buddy said testily. "And besides, Big Ed and his kids are all out at their pond house and he ain't comin' back to town for nobody till tonight."

"Mary Louise is right," I said. "Maybe you ought to run for sheriff, if that's how Big Ed got a pond house."

"Seventy-two acres around it, too," Sam said.

"I don't need a pond house," Buddy said. "I'd never get to use it anyway, what with running around after Peeping Toms and stuff.

Besides, Big Ed ain't gone leave that job till they take him out on a board.

"On the other hand," he said, walking over and grabbing the doorknob, "maybe I ought to run for sheriff after all. And if I was to get elected, the first thing I'd do is make it illegal for anybody in this town to look like somebody who used to be president."

And with that, Buddy left. Sam and I figured we wouldn't see him again, but a little while after sundown, when Sam and I were outside and Sam was about to get in his truck and go home, a county cruiser with Buddy in it came up my driveway and stopped and Buddy got out.

"Still associating with perverts, I see," he said to me. Sam laughed.

"That's how I select my friends," I said. "So what happened?"

"Hell, same old thing. Except this time I found two cigarette butts, so this guy—"

"Jimmy Carter," Sam said.

Buddy shot Sam a .30-caliber look. "So this guy must've stood there starin' at them two old biddies for a long time."

"Speaking of perverts," Sam said.

"Maybe," Buddy said. He was leaning against the hood of the cruiser, which was ticking with dissipating heat. "But if we're dealing with the same guy, supposing he can look like Richard Nixon one day and Jimmy Carter a couple days later, how come he ain't been over at the college, where there's some women worth starin' at? How come he's to pick these old ones?"

"I dunno," I said. "If it is the same guy, reckon he's got masks or something?"

"Only thing I can figure," Buddy said.

"So," Sam said, "maybe he's somebody them women would recognize."

"Pretty sharp," Buddy said. "Maybe you could be sheriff yourself."

"No," Sam said. "It doesn't pay much and the uniforms are ugly."

Buddy drummed his fingers on the hood of the cruiser. "Fine," he said. "Anyway, I figure it's got to be masks. Sarah said she'd never seen Jimmy Carter look so puffy and wore out."

"You'd be puffy and wore out, too, if you were him," Sam said.

"What I mean," Buddy said, "is that she could've been describing the way a mask looks."

"Hmm," Sam said. "You call Plains yet to see if Jimmy was at home last night?"

"I'll leave that to Big Ed," Buddy said. "But you guys are supposed to be so damn smart, ain't you got any ideas?"

Sam and I looked at each other. That wasn't as easy as it sounds, because it was dark by then and most of what I could see of Sam was a ghostly ellipse where his head ought to be and under it a ghostly shirt with a tiny blob on it that I knew was a fox. Or maybe it was an alligator.

"Not me," Sam said. "Peeping Jimmies aren't my line."

"I dunno either," I said, "but I'll think about it."

And I did think about it, especially after the *Guardian* came out on Monday with Sarah Collins's picture on the front page with the same picture of Mary Louise Etheridge that had been used the previous Thursday. But I couldn't come up with anything clever and still hadn't by Wednesday, when the radio reported that Miss Rebecca Sawyer, who lives out on highway 49 in the Maple Leaf Senior Citizens Center, went to close the venetian blinds in her room and noticed that a gorilla was standing outside in the shrubbery looking in at her.

"Well," Buddy said when I called him, "two things. First, Miss Rebecca cain't see but about three feet anyhow, and second, it was dark outside and since gorillas are just naturally dark and gorilla masks would be dark, too, there wasn't much for her to see. So if I'd been gone get anything out of my trip out there, that gorilla would have had to've been standing in the window when I drove up."

While Miss Rebecca Sawyer wasn't much help to Buddy's investigation, neither was Betty Young, who got peeped at by what was probably the same gorilla a couple of days later, nor was Alma

Strange, who was temporarily dispossessed of her wits by the sight of Donald Duck peering into her dining room.

All this was duly reported in the *Guardian*, where it was called an insidious form of terrorism against the innocent widows and spinsters of our community and a stench in the nostrils of all decent people. And since both Betty Young and Alma Strange lived inside the city limits, our small and generally undereducated police force was called in to cooperate with the sheriff's department—a circumstance which accomplished only one result, which was to increase Buddy's cynicism about the quality of local law enforcement, himself and maybe the sheriff excepted.

Sometime in early June, Donald Duck got a look at Mary Louise Etheridge in her nightgown, while Earlene Taliaferro's brick bungalow received a visit from Mr. Nixon, and Lucille Abbott, who lived next door to Mary Louise Etheridge, was introduced to the gorilla. By the time we got to Flag Day, just about the entire police force and Buddy Crittenden were on overtime and talk of the Peeping Tom was all over the place.

But the peeper not only didn't get caught, he also got more daring, standing on a Coca-Cola crate to give the gorilla another look at Betty Young, while Mary Louise Etheridge got her third peep, this time from Jimmy Carter, who apparently had crept up on her side porch so as to have a better view of Mary Louise Etheridge making a pimento cheese sandwich at her kitchen table.

Once in a while, largely for purposes of morale, the police would grab someone off the sidewalk at night and take him down to the little office in City Hall next to the jail for the local equivalent of the third degree, but that netted them only some cursing and passionate protestations of innocence and at least one lawsuit, the result of their apprehension of a lawyer for the American Civil Liberties Union who was in town visiting his cousin and had decided to take a walk around the block after dark.

Then, just about the time summer officially came in, Mrs. Walter Tullis's eighty-eight-year-old mama walked into the parlor and scared the daylights out of the widowed Mrs. Tullis, who had begun to nod off, by screaming at what the mama told Buddy Crittenden was a pop-eyed albino with great yellow lips who was looking in the window, but which Buddy said he figured was just Donald Duck taking his turn. And since Betty Young got visit number three the very next day, this time from Jimmy Carter, the pressure on the sheriff's office and the police department was nothing short of ferocious.

So for the next couple of weeks, with the theory that since his quarry had peeped at more women on Harmon Street than any other, Buddy began keeping a lookout from his car near where Harmon Street dead-ended into the Presbyterian Church, or leaving the car and walking up and down Harmon Street searching for somebody who looked like Jimmy Carter or Richard Nixon or maybe even like Donald Duck or a gorilla.

But Jimmy Carter never showed his face in a window again on Harmon Street or anywhere else, and neither did a gorilla or Richard Nixon or Donald Duck.

So after a while people stopped remembering there had been a Peeping Tom in town, or even remembering to be righteously indignant that the local law hadn't been able to catch him. Most elderly women even began not to wonder if they had undergone a violation of sorts when they remembered they hadn't pulled the shades. And by the end of July, unless you read the *Guardian*, which included the story in its midyear roundup of notable events between the sawmill fire and the bus wreck, you'd never have known anything had happened.

Meanwhile, things happened to the ladies who had been peeped on. Mrs. Walter Tullis and her mama announced that they were moving to Boca Raton; Lucille Abbott fell down her front steps and broke her collarbone; Mary Louise Etheridge caused a stir among her friends by actually boarding a plane and allowing it to take off with her in it and land in Buffalo, New York, so she could be present at the second wedding of her son, Oliver; Earlene Taliaferro won fifty dollars in groceries in a contest at the A&P; Betty Young got squired and proposed to by a widower named George Ramsey, who after retiring from the real estate business in Atlanta had returned to the place in which he spent his childhood; Alma Strange sold her house to some newlyweds and moved into an apartment; and Sarah Collins caught a summer cold and then pneumonia and spent an afternoon in the county hospital before quietly going on to Glory. When the congregation sang "Precious Memories" at her funeral, her sister got hysterical and eventually had to be put in a room in the Maple Leaf Senior Citizens Center down the hall from Miss Rebecca Sawyer, to whom nothing happened of any significance whatsoever.

I was among those who mostly forgot the Peeping Tom, and in fact I hadn't given his exploits more than an idle recollection once in a blue moon until I was reminded of them when Betty Young invited me and Sam to her and George Ramsey's engagement party in the backyard of George Ramsey's Hamilton Avenue house in September, just a couple of weeks before Hurricane Harriet came to town.

Earlene Taliaferro and Mary Louise Etheridge, two more of what Sam called our peepees, were there along with thirty or forty other people, and Buddy got invited, too, but I don't know by whom.

But it might have been by George Ramsey himself, whom everyone agreed gave an impression of gentility and polish, since Buddy traveled in a lot of circles unfamiliar to me and since it was him that introduced me to George Ramsey. While we were going through the formalities, Buddy and George Ramsey and Betty Young and I were standing by the dessert table set up among four or five other tables of food in George Ramsey's backyard. The presence of that table and of its attractions, most of which were slowly melting into unrecognizable heaps, meant that Sam Campbell was bound to be close by and so was likely to be introduced to George Ramsey, too.

Betty Young was first to see Sam's back. "Sayum," she said, and reached out and grabbed him lightly by the elbow. Sam turned sharply toward her, grinned broadly, said "hey, there," and turned back to the table and put something red and sticky on his plate.

"Sam," Buddy said. "Look here a minute."

Sam turned around. His left hand was holding a small dish on which were three or four multicolored piles of pie and cake, and his right hand was putting a strawberry into his mouth. He was wearing a pale beige linen suit with a blue shirt and a tie the color of a ripe peach. He was tan and looked happy and confident, both of which he probably was.

Sam smiled. "Hello, everybody," he said. "Hello, Betty." We all smiled. George Ramsey took out a cigarette, and so did Buddy, and Buddy lit them both with a lighter with a picture of an armadillo on it.

"This here's Sam Campbell, honey," Betty Young said, and Sam and George Ramsey shook hands. "He's from, uh . . ."

"The Black Lagoon," Buddy said.

Sam laughed and I smiled and Roy Butts of the hardware store Buttses, who was standing sort of between Sam and Betty Young and a little behind them both, gave Sam such a grin that I could see that most of his back teeth were missing. Betty Young smiled. George Ramsey laughed, hawhawhawhaw.

"Montana," Sam said.

"Montana," Betty Young repeated, but George Ramsey didn't get a chance to say Montana or even "pleased to meet you" because right then a gaggle from the Susannah Wesley Circle of the First United Methodist Church strode up in full cry and ruthlessly seized the conversational ground, from which Buddy, Sam, Roy Butts, and I were quickly routed.

Sam went to find his wife, though I think he was waylaid by the food, while Buddy headed off somewhere on his own. I don't know where Roy Butts went.

Maybe a half hour later, about the time Sam finished a mountain of food from his plate and a hummock of food from his wife April's plate, Buddy came up to where Sam, April, and I were sitting on a bench next to a water spigot with a handle in the shape of a frog. The afternoon was moving on, but even that and an overcast hadn't made it any cooler. At least under the trees it was bearable.

" 'Scuse me," Buddy said. "Hi, April."

"Hi, Buddy," April said cheerily, showing lots of teeth. "What's going on?"

Buddy was smirking and trying not to. "I got an urgent personal matter to talk over with this boy," he said, pointing at me. "Can I borrow him a minute or two?"

"Sure," Sam said. "Maybe if you take him off somewhere, April and I can plan our getaway." April said something to that, but I don't know what it was because Buddy was leading me away to the shade of a big sycamore tree by the side door of George Ramsey's house.

"Come in the house with me a minute," he said.

"What's up?" I said. I had a sliver of chicken between two teeth, and it was driving me crazy.

"Nothing," Buddy said. "Stop doing whatever it is that you're doing with your finger in your mouth and come on."

So we went into the house through the side door, past the kitchen where Betty Young's maid, Hilda, was staring at something in a stainless-steel sink, and down the hall to the utility room, where there was a washing machine, a dryer, another sink, and a closet.

Buddy opened the closet, letting out smells of Ajax, dust, and roach spray. "Look here," he said.

"Brooms," I said. "And a mop. Rags. An old doormat. A plastic rain hat on a wall hanger. Bottles. Cans."

"No, no," Buddy said impatiently. "Look at them boxes."

A half-dozen shoe boxes were stacked against one wall of the closet, and in the middle of the stack was a dark green box a little bigger than the rest.

"Okay," I said. "There's boxes here, too. Want me to guess what's inside them?"

But I didn't have to. After Buddy bent down and pulled the green box out of the stack and opened it so I could see the crude and gaudy likenesses of Richard Nixon, Jimmy Carter, Donald Duck, and a gorilla that were stuffed inside it, I didn't have much of anything to say except what people used to call an oath. I swore, and Buddy looked very pleased with himself.

In a minute or two we were back under the sycamore tree. Betty Young and George Ramsey were across a patch of lawn from us, the center of shrill attention.

"So why him?" I said. Buddy took out a cigarette and lit it with a lighter with an armadillo on it. "What was he doing?"

"He was looking for something," Buddy said, blowing smoke into the branches above him. "The reason he wore them masks is just so nobody could see him and recognize him later."

I could hear Betty Young laughing. "So what was he looking for?"

"What else? A wife." We were both watching George Ramsey, who had removed his blazer and was holding hands with his bride-to-be as they said good-bye to some people I didn't know. "I think he was lonely and for some reason or another didn't have many friends in Atlanta, or the ones he had didn't have time for him or something, and he was starting to get old and didn't really have anywhere to go, so he came back here to get older and die in a place he had some feelings for and one that didn't make him relive any bad memories."

"So you mean he was looking for someone to keep him company."

"Yeah," Buddy said. "I reckon that had to be at least part of it. Though him and Miss Betty seem to have hit it off real well. I figure he was huntin' for somebody about his own age, somebody he thought he could get along with and maybe even somebody he thought he could love a little bit. Maybe he was shy or somethin', or maybe he felt like he didn't have any time to waste."

"Okay," I said. "And you just happened to be in his house looking for . . . what? What was it you were digging for in that closet in the first place?"

"A vase," Buddy said. "Miz Pierce sent over some flowers." A little breeze rocked the branches we were standing under and felt cool on my forehead. "Feel that?" Buddy went on. "Maybe it means we'll get a shower."

"I'm already wet straight through," I said. "But never mind that. So you were looking for a vase in the house of a man maybe you don't know very well but certainly well enough to ask him where he keeps the vases, and you just happened to look in an unmarked box in a stack of boxes in a broom closet in the back of the house."

"Well," Buddy said, and grinned, "looking for a vase works a lot better than tryin' to get a warrant to go through this place." He rolled his cigarette between his fingers until the fire fell off and then took out a piece of Kleenex and wrapped the butt in it and put it in his back pocket. A plume of smoke came up from the grass at Buddy's feet, and he mashed it into the ground.

"So how come you thought it was him? How come you were goin' through his stuff?"

"That's the easiest part. When I lit his cigarette a while ago, it was a Salem, just like them I found on the ground. And right then I knew it had to be him. It was just a matter of thinking it out a little."

"Boy," I said. "I guess if you ever do decide to run for sheriff, this ought to just about propel you into Big Ed's seat. I can't imagine him turning over a case like this probably forever."

"Naw," Buddy said. "I ain't gone tell Big Ed or anybody else about this." We looked at each other. I could hear the faint sound of rattling dishes from the house.

"Yeah? How come?"

Buddy shrugged. "Why would I want to pull the alarm on this guy? I mean, he scared the bejeebers out of some people, but he didn't really hurt nobody. If I was to arrest George Ramsey for being a Peeping Tom, then nothin' good would come of this whole mess. As it is, people had somethin' interesting to talk about for a couple months and Betty and George have got each other. I cain't see anything I oughta go messin' up."

"How about that?" I said, for lack of anything more clever. "So that's why—"

"Sure," Buddy said. "That's why Betty got peeped on three times, and Lord knows how many more times he might've spied on her and she just didn't see him. He kept comin' back because he liked what he saw and had to make sure she was the one to try."

"Yeah, but Mary Louise Etheridge got peeped on three times that we know of, too."

"Uh-huh," Buddy said, and smiled. "All that means is that we'll never know how close maybe it was between her and Betty. I 'spect George Ramsey ain't got any idea how near he came to chasin' after a real piranha."

So I chewed on that awhile, and I was still chewing on it around six o'clock when I went looking for Buddy to ask him something else about it and found him sitting at a table at the edge of the yard with his mama and Mary Louise Etheridge.

Buddy was looking a little cornered and his cheekbones were red, and even before I sat down I knew why.

"What I really want to know," Mary Louise Etheridge was saying, "is when're you and that fatso Ed Lundquist gone put a halt to those young hoodlums racin' their automobiles up and down my street. Myrtle knows what I'm talkin' about, don't you, Myrtle?"

Buddy's mama smiled soothingly at her son and nodded, then along with the rest of us she looked up to see who else was coming over to the table. It was George Ramsey.

"Have a seat," Buddy said, and pointed to the one empty chair. "We're just talkin' traffic." So George Ramsey inclined his head at me and spoke to the women and sat down.

"It's a sin and a shame," Mary Louise Etheridge went on, a little louder now, "that such as that is allowed to go on in this town. All that racket. And what if somebody's dog, no, better than that, what if somebody's innocent young child was to run out into the street while one of them people was racin' by? Then you and Ed Lundquist would have to answer to your consciences, too, and maybe you'd pay more attention to that still small voice than you do to me.

"Mr. Ramsey," Mary Louise Etheridge said, pointing at him across the table, "you won't live in this town much longer before you realize that some people can just about get away with anything and there won't be a thing the sheriff's office or the police department will do about it. I was just tellin' the deputy sheriff here that I'm near about fed up with people drag-racin' or whatever it is they

do up and down my street at all hours of the day and night."
Looking at George Ramsey through her bifocals over her pointy
nose, Mary Louise Etheridge had the demeanor of a great blue
heron about to strike. I instinctively sat back a little.

"Mary Louise," Buddy said evenly, "we've sat there, ol' Tom
Rafshoon at the town end of the street in the police car and me or
Lamar at the other end, and in two weeks we stopped exactly one
guy for speeding, and he was a tourist from Illinois who was lookin'
for I-95."

Mary Louise Etheridge waved a bony hand at him. "I've heard
all the excuses I need to hear," she said hotly, "and if I can't get
any satisfaction from you or that lazy Tom Rafshoon, then maybe
I'll have to take it up with Ed Lundquist or the mayor or somebody
you got to answer to. But I'm not quittin' with you people till I get
those hoodlums off the streets."

"Okay," Buddy said, shrugging, and threw a soft but meaning-
ful glance at his mama, who immediately put her hand on her
pocketbook and stood up.

"C'mon, Mary Louise," Myrtle Crittenden said. "My husband's done got home by now and he's probably starvin' to death.
I've packed a plateful of chicken and collards and stuff in the car
that's gone grow enough bugs on it to kill a moose if I don't get it
there pretty quick."

"You're just lookin' after your boy, Myrtle," Mary Louise
Etheridge said tartly. But she got up, too, and she and Myrtle
Crittenden said good-bye to George Ramsey and then to me, and
Myrtle Crittenden kissed Buddy good-bye and he kissed her good-
bye back, and the two women went off to find Betty Young and tell
her good-bye, too, and that they'd see her at the wedding.

"Whew," I said. George Ramsey took out a Salem. Buddy lit
it with a lighter with an armadillo on it and then took out a cigarette
of his own and lit it in turn.

"Lord have mercy," George Ramsey said, shaking his head. "I
had no idea that woman was such a hellion. Is she always that way?"

Buddy looked quickly at me, then took a puff from his cigarette
and turned to look at George Ramsey. "It's funny," he said. "Some-

times she'll seem to be as sweet as can be, and then somethin' happens and this side of her comes out. The *real* side."

George Ramsey seemed to be thinking.

"You'd never know it just to look at her, would you?" Buddy went on. "But you put that woman up against, uh, Miss Betty Young, and it ain't no contest at all."

George Ramsey nodded, put his Salem to his lips, and gave it a real pull.

And although everybody who was left outside at the party probably still thinks it was just cigarette smoke that George Ramsey choked on till his face got red, and since he didn't contradict us when Buddy and I explained it that way, nobody knew that while it was indeed smoke that George Ramsey choked on, he most likely would have gotten through his cigarette just fine if Buddy Crittenden hadn't grinned hard at him right then and said, "Yeah, George, I got to hand it to you. When it comes to decidin' which woman to marry, you sho got a foolproof method for pickin' 'em."

EIGHT

Regardless of how George Ramsey got his wife, he got her in the form of Betty Young, and after a week's worth of honeymoon in Sarasota the two of them came home and rented out Betty Young's house and settled in at George Ramsey's place on Hamilton Avenue.

And while the newly wed Mr. and Mrs. Ramsey were strolling with random interest and rather less random outrage along the teeming beach, on which there were sights neither of them had expected ever to see, old man Calvin Hutto died and left one hundred acres of trees and broomsedge along the Springfield Road to his daughter, Anita.

George Ramsey got that, too.

He got it mainly because Anita lived in San Diego, California, with her husband, and wanted nothing whatsoever to do with a hundred acres of Georgia woods or in fact with anything that had to do with what she called the thoroughbred son of a bitch that her daddy was. So she listed the place with Don Lucas and Son here in town and George Ramsey and Ricky Lucas went out and walked over it together, then George Ramsey got somebody to cruise the timber and gave a cursory going-over to Calvin Hutto's little frame house, at which point he ponied up what J. B. Barrett says was $40,500 in cash and promises and the hundred acres and the house were his.

Word was out that George Ramsey planned to go in with a developer from Savannah and turn old man Hutto's place into a subdivision with a golf course.

"He says there's holes out there," Buddy Crittenden said. We were sitting in my living room idly watching the Atlanta Falcons play a particularly odious brand of football on TV. Outside it was Sunday afternoon, dark and drizzly. My spirits were about as dim as the daylight.

I made a noncommittal noise.

"Holes?" said Sam Campbell, who was there, too.

"Holes," Buddy said. "He says somebody's been out there diggin' a bunch of holes." Buddy took a sip of hot chocolate and made a face.

"Maybe it's foxes," I said.

"Or giant chipmunks," Sam offered.

Buddy sighed. "George says it ain't animals, he says there's somebody been diggin' with shovels."

"Which we are to presume means that somebody is out there lookin' for something," I said.

"Don't be a show-off," Sam said.

"Uh-huh," Buddy said. "Somebody's lookin'. But what for? And who are they?"

"That's why we have cops," Sam said, still staring at the TV. "Somebody's got to go out and get the answers to questions like that."

Buddy said the holes had begun to appear a couple of weeks before, or at least that's when George Ramsey first noticed them on one of his infrequent visits to make sure nobody had busted into old man Hutto's stripped and boarded-up little house and stolen the glass doorknobs or the mantel or something. Since then George Ramsey had gone back twice and more holes had been dug each time. Most were fairly close to the house, but others popped up at odd intervals within a hundred yards or so of the back steps.

"Maybe there's some kind of treasure buried out there," Sam said.

"I dunno," Buddy said. "I'm gone go out there sometime this week and look at them holes, but it's pretty obvious, ain't it, that somebody's been lookin' for something maybe old man Hutto left behind.

"But what could that old skinflint have had that anybody would want? I cain't think of a thing. If it was money, he'd of spent it himself, I reckon. And if there was something else, something really valuable, why would whoever's out there diggin' holes think he would have buried it?"

Buddy got a handful of potato chips from the bowl in front of him and put some in his mouth. A trail of crumbs ran down the front of his flannel shirt and onto his jeans.

Sam and I were mostly paying attention to the football game, which against all prior expectations was mildly exciting, and we weren't in much of a mood to talk about holes, at least not on a diet of potato chips and hot chocolate. But that's all I had to give them; if they had called first, hadn't just shown up at the door, I'd have had time to go to the grocery store.

There's just one grocery store in town that opens on Sunday afternoon, but some of the others are thinking about it. Sunday used to be different from other days of the week, and not just because you went to church. Once upon a time it was quieter, too, and everybody in these parts thought of it as the one day in the week on which you couldn't run the lawn mower or the tiller under your neighbor's bedroom window at eight o'clock in the morning. But in most of the world Sunday is just another Saturday now, except that you have to go to work the next day. A lot more people have to work on Sundays, too; maybe they need the money, or maybe they just don't care.

Anyhow, Buddy didn't get much of a response from me and Sam except that we agreed that he or somebody ought to go out to George Ramsey's place and lay for the diggers and surprise them in the act of defacing George Ramsey's property and then find out what they were after. Buddy didn't do that, but he did drive out to George Ramsey's place that used to be old man Hutto's place and look at the holes.

He said there was a bunch of them, all right, mostly close to the house, but that three or four were on the periphery of the yard, which was surprisingly kempt and bordered on one side by a line of crape myrtles that needed trimming. The holes were primarily round, the way you'd expect holes to be. The biggest were about two feet deep and two feet wide and there was nothing at all unusual about them except that every one of them was next to something like a tree, a spigot, a light pole, or a shed or something, and two were by a big rock in the backyard. They had been dug with a pointed shovel and most of them had two different kinds of shoe tracks in the dirt around them, which seemed to mean that at least two people were involved in the excavation.

But what Buddy still couldn't figure was what whoever dug those holes was looking for. Finally Sheriff Lundquist went out to George Ramsey's place and looked at the holes himself, and Buddy even took me and Sam to look at them, too, just so he'd have another excuse to stand over some of them and stare into the ground trying to parse it all out.

I had never even met old man Calvin Hutto, but it looked to me as though whoever he was, he didn't leave much of a stamp on his house and yard. When I first looked at them, they seemed to be just a house supported on concrete blocks with a yard around it, the same way the holes had just been holes. Anybody could have lived there, if you didn't notice the bars on the windows.

Calvin Hutto was born and raised here in town, but he got out as soon as he could and moved to Tallahassee, where he got a job in a sawmill and then left that for clerking in a hardware store. Pretty soon, though, he was sent off to fight the Germans, after which he came back home and eventually married a plain but by all accounts reasonable and hardworking woman named Margaret McAfee when she was two months pregnant with their daughter Anita.

He went back to work in a hardware store in Alachua, and in 1947 he and a man named Jeff Moon went in together and opened a hardware store of their own. But Jeff Moon drank, and was a terrible businessman and owned two-thirds of the business to boot, so it wasn't quite eighteen months before Calvin Hutto was flat broke and had to go back to being a clerk in another man's store.

He was for a while the focus of a general sympathetic attention, because it was widely known that Calvin Hutto had worked hard to make his venture with Jeff Moon a success and that he had even paid creditors out of his own shallow pocket in times of crisis.

But Calvin Hutto didn't give a damn for anybody's sympathy, he said, all those people telling him what a bad deal he got and giving him a lot of platitudes when what he needed was cash money. And where were all these confounded people when the store was going under? They were so free with the bullshit, couldn't they have come across with a little business, too?

Even Calvin Hutto must have realized sooner or later that the outpouring of beneficence directed at him had come at exactly the right time, because his aunt Peggy had recently gotten food poisoning after eating at Trueblood's Restaurant and sued old man Marvin Trueblood and his son Bill and subsequently took such a chunk out of their financial substance that the Truebloods had to sell their restaurant to some people from Savannah who tore it down and put up an apartment building.

Calvin Hutto's aunt Peggy had lived with Calvin Hutto's mama and daddy and his brother Ted for most of the years while Calvin Hutto was growing up, and was still there when Calvin Hutto left home the day after graduating from high school. All of which made her a part of the Hutto family as far as most people were concerned, and which meant that the outrage and scorn with which Calvin Hutto's aunt Peggy was generally regarded after she put Trueblood's Restaurant out of business was shared by Calvin Hutto's mama and daddy and his brother Ted, too—all of them except Calvin Hutto, who was apparently felt to have suffered enough already at the hands of Jeff Moon and was thus shielded from the torrent of vituperation that eventually drove Calvin Hutto's brother Ted to move to Folly Beach.

Calvin Hutto's aunt Peggy left town, too, but in her own sweet time and with a lot of money she had squeezed out of old man Marvin Trueblood and his son Bill for giving her food poisoning, and moved to Key West and bought a motel.

It was about this time, when he stopped being an owner and

started being just a clerk again, and now a poorer one even than he was before, that Calvin Hutto began to drink. It was also about this time that he began trying to supplement his income as a clerk by selling door-to-door. But he just wasn't any good at it, didn't have the heart for it, didn't have the drive or the guts to get past the first time his potential customers would say no and start to back into their houses. He didn't really want to sell people brushes or salve or the works of Mark Twain; he wanted people to want to buy those things from him and they almost universally did not.

So he stayed at the hardware store selling nails and paint and tools that people did want to buy, him and Margaret and Anita living in a tiny rented house a few blocks from downtown, and in a couple of years he had managed to save a little money, even though it meant that Anita was frequently wearing other people's clothes and that sometimes breakfast was biscuits and gravy and milk and nothing else. Such as that bothered Calvin Hutto and made him feel small. He had gotten used to having a few beautiful dreams not really so long before, when he was newly married and was going into the hardware business with the man he forever-more called that god damned Jeff Moon, and now he had to adjust to not having very much of anything except failure and shame and want.

He began sitting on his front porch after supper in the dark, silhouetted against the pale rectangle of the curtained window behind him, drinking bourbon whiskey. Sometimes he would grunt a greeting at someone walking by, and sometimes as the night wore on he would begin to clear his throat and spit over his privet hedge and frequently all the way out to the sidewalk. He would hawk and spit until Margaret would put down her sewing or her iron and come outside and ask him to stop, please.

Margaret thought Calvin Hutto would sometimes go into what she called his spitting routine just to bedevil her, just so she would have to stop what she was doing and come outside and ask him to quit doing what he was doing out of spite. But Calvin Hutto knew exactly what he was doing, even though sometimes the buzzing in his head would mix with the shrieking of cicadas and crickets out in the darkness and he would just do it automatically, as though even with all the whiskey there was still a small hot spark somewhere inside him that knew when he needed to spit a few times and get Margaret to the door where he could see her. He knew what he was doing, but he didn't know why he wanted her to come out, and he never knew what to do when she got there—except to feel as though he had forgotten how to do something, maybe even how to get something he desperately wanted someone to give him. And embarrassment, too; he felt that first.

So he would hawk and spit and Margaret would come to the door and ask him not to do that, and he would grunt at her from the profound depths of consternation and stop and pour himself another three fingers of whiskey.

But the Okefenokee of despair into which Calvin Hutto had plunged didn't stop him from being determined to keep saving his pennies, even though Margaret's annual toil and sweat at cultivating a garden was in some months the only thing between them and malnutrition.

Then one January Calvin Hutto took a week off from the hardware store without pay, withdrew his savings from the Exchange Bank, and caught a bus to Las Vegas. He came home with six dollars and ten cents in his pocket and didn't say a word to his wife and daughter for two days. On the following Friday night he went out after supper and sat on his porch with the light turned off and poured himself a Bama jelly glass half-full of whiskey. In the next twenty-four hours he poured himself enough drinks to deliver himself into delirium tremens and get a trip to the asylum in Milledgeville in the sheriff's car to be dried out.

Nobody was surprised when he was fired from the hardware store, and at this particular abyss of his fortunes nobody felt sorry for him, either, but reserved their sympathy and tongue clucking for Margaret and Anita. Anita was turning out to be a hellion, too, which made Margaret's life pretty much of a torment.

So after he got home from Milledgeville and got fired, Calvin Hutto went back to sitting on his porch and stayed up even later now that he didn't have to get up in the morning and go to work.

He went back to drinking whiskey, too, but at his old rate, just enough to get comfortably numb and not enough to make him crazy. Margaret never heard him spit over the privet after he came back.

She took in washing and alterations and began to take little Anita with her to other people's houses to baby-sit for their children, and she also moved out of the bedroom she and her husband had shared and started sleeping in Anita's room on a cot.

Then one day the postman brought Calvin Hutto a letter postmarked from Key West. Margaret opened it for him. Inside was a check for five hundred dollars and one sheet of paper with tight, elegant handwriting on it that said only, *Get out of town. Love, Aunt Peggy.*

Apparently it was not much trouble for Calvin Hutto to decide to take his benefactor's advice, his pride having been bludgeoned into submission if not outright ruin, and he and his two women packed up and moved to Savannah, where after nearly a month of looking, Calvin Hutto got a job as a security guard in a warehouse. Margaret later said that what he had needed was just to get clean of the town he was born in and in which he felt such a stubborn need to be a success or at least have a little money put away.

That might have been some of the reason but it certainly wasn't entirely the reason Calvin Hutto soon quit drinking except for once in a while and even began to be seen on the streets of Savannah with his wife and child. By the time Anita graduated from high school, he was chief of security for a brick company with seven or eight people working for him and everybody in the company who worked in the yards and kilns and on the loading docks calling him Calvin Hitler behind his back.

It was in this time of his life, with a good job and people to boss around and a lot of other people to lord his authority over, that Calvin Hutto indisputably became the thoroughbred son of a bitch that Anita called him after he died. He got cocky and bought himself a .357 Magnum to wear on his hip at the plant, and once he found out what an intoxicating feeling he got by making other people feel second rate, he just got going and couldn't stop. He began to push Margaret around, and he started drinking again, too, but in bars and juke joints instead of on his front porch.

Then one steamy night in July he careened home red-faced and stinking, still in his guard's uniform, and he and Margaret had a fight and Calvin Hutto reached for his pistol. He didn't draw it, but reaching for it was enough for Margaret to see and she was out of the house in twenty minutes with Anita in tow and never came back but one time and that was to get the rest of her belongings.

So now Calvin Hutto was free to do what he pleased, though having to write Margaret an alimony check every month galled and nettled him. Margaret moved to Brunswick and got a job in a dime store, but Anita said to hell with them both and took off for California, where in short order she met and married a used-car salesman and began to have children. Calvin Hutto wrote a letter to her once in a while for a couple of years but never got one back and finally gave up.

The winter in which Anita had her second child but didn't tell her daddy about it any more than she had when he became a granddaddy for the first time, somebody stole a sizable chunk of the brick-company payroll one night after the midnight shift came on.

The theft ruined a personal project of the company's president, whose name was Frank Boyer and who had two other brick companies elsewhere in the South, because Frank Boyer had decided to pay his salaried workers in silver dollars that week since he had always thought silver was a more true and honest kind of money than that which was printed on paper and wanted to see some go back into local circulation.

His bank hadn't been especially pleased about gathering up just over five thousand silver dollars and finally had to appeal to the federal reserve bank in Atlanta. And the bags took up so much room that they wouldn't go into the regular vault at Frank Boyer's brick company and had to be kept in an old painted safe that even Frank Boyer later admitted wouldn't have posed much of a problem for his eleven-year-old daughter, Margie, to get into.

The theft also put Calvin Hutto on the hot seat for a few days because he and the single watchman on duty on that shift that night were the only ones besides the comptroller who had access to the office where the safe was. But since the duty man was from somewhere out of town and didn't have a single friend at the plant, suspicion just naturally began to slide away from the comptroller and Calvin Hutto and more in his direction. He was shiftless and undependable anyway, Calvin Hutto said, and he'd been thinking about firing him even though he, as security chief, had had such high hopes for that feller, too.

The night guard was ultimately arrested even though a search of his house didn't turn up any money, and nobody believed him much when he said he'd never been anywhere near the office where the safe was. The local law couldn't prove anything against him, though, and so after trying as hard to humiliate him as they had to implicate him in the crime, they finally had to let him go. Which is also what the company did, on the recommendation of Calvin Hutto, who said he still figured that skunk had stolen that money despite the fact that so many silver dollars must have been hard not only to get out of that office but also to squirrel away where nobody could find them.

Uh-huh, Calvin would say, and nod for emphasis, he bet that feller couldn't've cared less about getting fired because it meant he could retrieve them dollars at his leisure from whatever hidey-hole he'd put them in once the heat was off and then go somewhere and start spending them. Just watch the liquor stores, he said. Some of 'em'll turn up.

But none of those silver dollars turned up, not a one. What did turn up after about three weeks was a letter addressed to Calvin Hutto telling him that his aunt Peggy had died of cancer of the pancreas in Key West and had left him the deed to her daddy's hundred acres and a house about a mile outside the Alachua city limits, the same land George Ramsey bought after Calvin Hutto died more than fifteen years later.

Everybody who gave any thought to Calvin Hutto figured his inheritance was a windfall of great proportions, since a lot of the hundred acres was covered with young pine trees that eventually would make marketable timber and the house had always been a good rental property. But Calvin Hutto didn't give any of that much of his thinking time, preferring instead to wonder what he'd ever done to his aunt Peggy that she didn't leave him that motel in Key West. Right then, all he saw when he looked at those hundred acres were some trees that he hadn't learned what to do with yet, and besides, he had to pay property taxes on all them trees and that house, and owning a house now meant he was a landlord, too.

After a while he quit brooding and decided to try and make the best of a bad situation, thinking that well, maybe he could find a use for the place sooner or later. The first thing he did was to raise the rent on the house enough so that it not only paid his property taxes but gave him a little extra drinking and womanizing money besides.

In fact, Calvin Hutto had made himself a reputation for spending money about as fast as he got it. And when old man Luther Barnes, with whom Calvin Hutto made friends in hopes of getting at Luther Barnes's daughter Kathy, told him he should be careful or he wouldn't have anything to live on after he retired except the smidgen he'd get from Social Security, Calvin Hutto just laughed and told Luther Barnes that his retirement was already taken care of, thanks.

What Calvin Hutto didn't tell Luther Barnes about his money was that he was also giving Kathy Barnes a pretty fair piece of it at regular intervals. His purpose in doing so was to keep her from telling her daddy that Calvin Hutto had gotten her pregnant and paid for her to go to Jacksonville and have an abortion that time her daddy had thought she was in Charleston looking for a job.

What Kathy Barnes didn't tell Calvin Hutto was that when she went to Jacksonville it was for the second time for the same reason, and that she was also getting regular payments from Terry Kingman, who was assistant pastor at the First Methodist Church, to keep quiet. And perhaps the only thing that saved Calvin Hutto and Terry Kingman from further depredations of this sort was that

Kathy Barnes got pregnant for the third time, this time by the son of a bank president, and decided to trade her secret sources of income for marriage, maternity, a big house with two maids, and a Lincoln Continental.

So if not exactly the pride of Savannah, Calvin Hutto seemed to be doing pretty well for himself. At least that's what some people say, and he certainly thought so. Every year for half of his two weeks' vacation he'd get on the train and go down to Miami and bet on the horse races or the dog races, and while a couple of years, at least, he came home bragging about how well he'd made out, most years he'd come home with considerably less cash than he went with, and that's not even counting his expenses for a room, easy women, and straight bourbon whiskey. When he'd really lose a pile, J. B. Barrett says, people would see him around Alachua for a weekend or two when he came to town to raise the rent on the little house he inherited from his aunt Peggy, and one year he even spent a week of his time off in the little house when it was unten-anted while a few acres of the good hardwoods on the property were timbered off.

When he finally came back to Alachua for good, everything had changed.

It wasn't just that he had left with two legs and came home with one, J. B. Barrett says; it was also as though when Calvin Hutto lost that leg he lost most of his gumption and pretty much all of what he would have exaggerated into calling his congeniality at the same time. It was, J. B. Barrett says, as though when he gave up that leg he figured it meant he had to give up women and going to juke joints or to the dog races and even being civil just the way it meant he had to give up dancing and running and kicking people in the butt.

So Calvin Hutto became a one-legged man living by himself in a frame house on a hundred acres of land on the Springfield Road, with a little disability pension and some Social Security to buy him fatback and whiskey and pay his electric bill. J. B. Barrett says, too, that at one time there was talk about how somebody asked Calvin Hutto why he didn't sell off what few acres of mature timber he had left on the place and buy him some stylish clothes or take a trip or even eat better, and Calvin Hutto had spit and curled his lip and said that if he ever figured out how to get some money it was gone be real money indeed, and there was some money due him and by God he'd have it sooner or later.

He never left his property except to go into town, and that was something he very rarely did. He even paid a retired black postal clerk named Alfred Robbins to come by his house once a week and pick up a grocery list and drive into town and buy his supplies. Alfred Robbins also kept up Calvin Hutto's yard, pruning the crape myrtle and cutting the grass and even one year planting foxglove, which Alfred Robbins loved to look at but which his wife said was bad luck and so wouldn't allow it on their place. People who drove by would see Calvin Hutto stumping around his yard on one real leg and one wooden one and an odd chrome-plated four-footed cane, apparently not doing anything in particular as far as they could tell, just stumping and looking.

A lot of people thought he was crazy, but Alfred Robbins says that instead he was furious, and if being mad all the time was enough to drive a man crazy, well, maybe he was that, too. But he did everything in a fury, slamming each of his back steps with his cane as he held on to the railing Alfred Robbins built for him and heaved himself up toward the house.

What Alfred Robbins and some other people think is that Calvin Hutto was mad at Bucky Wyatt, who was driving the pickup truck that demolished Calvin Hutto's right leg in the parking lot of Frank Boyer's brick company. But Calvin Hutto wasn't angry with Bucky Wyatt, even though everybody agreed that if he hadn't been distracted by the sight of his estranged wife, Diane, standing at the plant gates with her lawyer and a deputy sheriff, Bucky Wyatt probably wouldn't have run into the back of Calvin Hutto's Dodge in such a way as to hit Calvin Hutto, too, as he stood there looking down into the trunk.

He wasn't mad at Bucky Wyatt, though. He *hated* Bucky Wyatt the way some people hate incest or the way some other people hate war. But his hatred was pure and unsullied by anything so ephemeral as anger. Calvin Hutto didn't even want revenge, and he never thought of retribution. All he wanted was his leg back. He believed that without it, nothing would ever work out the way he wanted it to.

Then one day Alfred Robbins found him stretched out on the floor of his living room as cold as yesterday's rice, his wooden leg sticking out cockeyed from his stump, his eyes wide open and staring at the ceiling. He left Anita everything he had, which was pretty much the house and the hundred acres of land and just enough cash money to bury him and pay Anita's fare from San Diego to Savannah and back and for the rented car she drove up here for the funeral.

He also left not quite five thousand dollars in silver dollars hidden in a place he could get to when he stole them, but a place that a one-legged man could only stand and look at and be furious.

NINE

The only reason Calvin Hutto told Jerry Spivey that he had a lot of silver dollars hidden away where nobody could find them was that Jerry Spivey was his godson. And had Jerry Spivey not been his godson, it's likely that Calvin Hutto wouldn't have told anybody at all, that he would just have died with his secret intact. There was nobody else for him to tell.

He didn't have any friends; the one fairly close friend he had ever had was Carl Spivey, Jerry Spivey's father, and Carl was dead. Calvin Hutto was divorced from his wife, his daughter would have nothing to do with him, his parents were dead, and his brother had sent him Christmas cards in some years but that was all. Alfred Robbins was out of the question. And if he was to pick somebody, some stranger, he'd have to get to know them well before he'd know if they might remember his well-publicized but unsolved crime— and if they did remember it, whether they might be the kind of person who would turn him in even after all these years and his many misfortunes.

It got so he couldn't stand it, knowing those silver dollars were out there where he couldn't get at them. Some days he felt as though he might actually die of anger and frustration. So he started wooing Jerry Spivey, first by finally acquiescing to some of that shiftless moron's incessant requests for loans, then by making Jerry Spivey sit down and talk to him so he could hear the larceny in Jerry Spivey's heart coming out through his mouth.

He never did trust Jerry Spivey, and had no reason to think he could, but he wanted to get his hands on those silver dollars and saw Jerry Spivey as his only hope because he couldn't get at them himself. Hell, he thought, he could give Jerry Spivey enough of them to pay him off and keep him quiet, actually making that idiot an accomplice after the fact, too.

Calvin Hutto didn't know precisely what he wanted to do with the dollars he planned to keep for himself, but he had done enough reading to know that his five thousand silver dollars were worth closer to $100,000 now because they had real silver in them and even more value than that in the collector's market. Maybe he'd get himself a better leg, maybe he'd get one of those special vans so he could drive with his left foot, maybe he'd actually go out to Las Vegas and have a good time, find himself a woman to whom money meant more than the man with the money having two legs.

And sometimes he thought that maybe at first he'd just look at those silver dollars for a while, feel them in his hands. It was the bravest thing he'd ever done, stealing them, picking a night on which he'd assigned that smug asshole who didn't have any friends at the plant to be guard, knowing suspicion would just naturally fall first on him, and Calvin Hutto had had all sorts of good stories ready about moving those silver dollars to a safer place if anyone caught him filling his trunk with them, but nobody saw a thing. It was almost too easy.

And it was even easier to bring them dollars up here to the little house and hide them where nobody'd ever know to look, in a place he knew about only by accident. But then, well, then his luck went bad and stayed that way and all he had of those silver dollars he stole was one bag he kept in a paint can in his back room.

Calvin Hutto knew when he showed that sack with ninety-two silver dollars in it to Jerry Spivey that he had hooked himself a real sap, saw how Jerry Spivey's eyes got big as he looked at them coming out of the bag and rattling across the tabletop, knew he had him cold when he promised that boy a lot more than just what he saw on that table if he played his cards right and did as he was told.

But he didn't tell Jerry Spivey where the rest of those dollars were, and he knew Jerry Spivey would leave that bag in the paint can alone because of what it promised him if he was patient.

What Calvin Hutto didn't count on was dying three days after he and Jerry Spivey had sat across the table from one another with ninety-two silver dollars and an empty bag between them and he had played Jerry Spivey's avarice the way he would have played a bass in the lily pads, reeling it into the open with just the proper pull and artifice, hooked and headed for the boat.

When Calvin Hutto died, it was easy enough for Jerry Spivey to get into the old man's house and get that one bag of silver dollars while the funeral was going on in town. But he wished now that he'd never let Sperry Bissell in on his secret, not to mention let Sperry Bissell talk him into heading off out to Brooklet to hide the bag in the woods on some land Sperry Bissell's aunt Melinda owned but never went to now that she was old and feeble. Sure, Jerry Spivey didn't know if maybe somebody had known about that bag and would go looking for it, and he wanted those dollars to be safe where he could get them when he was ready to go to Atlanta and begin selling them off. But now he not only didn't know where the rest of Calvin Hutto's stash was, he didn't even have the ninety-two silver dollars he'd started with.

And maybe Sperry Bissell was right, maybe that goddamned deputy sheriff didn't know they'd had a bag of stolen money in the Pontiac with them, but that didn't make much sense to Jerry Spivey and it didn't matter much now, anyway. He and Sperry Bissell had combed every inch of ground along county road 263 on which that bag of dollars could have landed when Sperry Bissell threw it out the car window, and they'd come up dry. So somebody out that way must've stumbled onto those dollars before he and Sperry Bissell had considered the coast clear enough to go back and look for them.

All Jerry Spivey knew for sure was that he didn't have any silver dollars at all and he wanted that bag with ninety-two of them in it and he wanted to find out where old man Hutto had squirreled away the rest of them, too. He just wasn't quite sure how to go about any of it, but he was hot and determined nonetheless. He and Sperry Bissell had been all through old man Hutto's house, tapping the walls and floors for secret hideaways and rummaging through the insulation in the attic, and then with a splinter of desperation in Jerry Spivey's guts they had started going out there in the early morning and digging holes in what seemed to be the likeliest spots in which Calvin Hutto might have buried those dollars for later retrieval.

But Jerry Spivey knew all that digging was a long shot, since Calvin Hutto had told him those silver dollars were put away somewhere a one-legged man couldn't get at them, and he knew Calvin Hutto would have dug them out with a spoon if he'd had to and they'd just been buried in the ground.

So there was nothing for Jerry Spivey to do but clutch at straws, and the only straw he could see had Harold Buckminster's name on it.

The way Jerry Spivey and Sperry Bissell finally got Royal Mango's name out of Harold Buckminster was not by hitting him—they'd already tried that—and in fact not even by threatening him or any member of his family with personal violence of any sort. Jerry Spivey didn't believe for a minute that Harold Buckminster had been telling him and Sperry Bissell the truth about having been saving those silver dollars they saw him spend at Roberson's Grocery, but he couldn't really bring himself to believe that Harold Buckminster had the bag that Sperry Bissell threw out the window of the Pontiac, either. There just wasn't any reason for that fool to've been out there walking along county road 263 when he had a car that usually worked—and where would he have been going down that way, anyhow?

But Jerry Spivey also figured the appearance of Harold Buckminster with silver dollars in his hands wasn't any coincidence, either. No, Harold Buckminster had got those silver dollars from somebody, and silver dollars didn't just jump out of nowhere and ask to be spent on grits and hog jowls any old day of the week. There had to be a connection between the dollars Harold Buckminster had and those that had found their way out of a paint can at old man Hutto's house and briefly went for a ride in Jerry Spivey's Pontiac.

At least Jerry Spivey hoped so, and he intended to find out.

There was nothing else to do, he'd already tried everything he could think of.

So Jerry Spivey and Sperry Bissell drove out to Brooklet to Harold Buckminster's house one Sunday morning when Doris Buckminster was at church, and decanted Harold Buckminster from his bed and got him into his shoes and clothes and took him for a little walk out behind his house. Harold Buckminster was full of sleep and leftover Saturday night and felt the way he imagined dying people felt, and he didn't know what to do but go along with his antagonists and keep his eyes on the ground. The morning was cool and he wished they had let him put on a jacket and he hoped they wouldn't hit him the way they did the last time.

"Harold," said Jerry Spivey, "I see that this here piece of ground must be where you put in a garden every year."

"Uh-huh," said Harold Buckminster, looking at the little sprigs of grass between his feet. In some places, new green leaves were beginning to peek out. The sun hurt Harold Buckminster's eyes and his head hurt, too. His throat felt as though an avalanche had been down it.

"Little corn, maybe, coupla rows of tomatoes, few peas, and some okra," Jerry Spivey said cheerily. "Ain't that right?"

"Uh-huh," Harold Buckminster said. He could feel Sperry Bissell standing off to his right between him and the house, but Sperry Bissell didn't say anything.

"And maybe over here," Jerry Spivey said, and pointed, and Harold Buckminster looked up and then lowered his eyes again, "maybe over here's where you gone put in them famous watermelons. I b'lieve I even see the remains of some of them vines from last year. You reckon that's about right?"

"Uh-huh," Harold Buckminster said.

"Lord," Jerry Spivey said, "for a poor dumb Cracker you sho do know how to grow a watermelon, Harold. Had a little setback this last year but next time you gone do right, come home with that prize again, biggest watermelon in three counties. Ain't that right?"

"Uh-huh," Harold Buckminster said, and wondered what Jerry Spivey was leading up to.

Jerry Spivey shook his head admiringly. "I swear," he said, and laughed a laugh that Harold Buckminster knew was a fake. "Maybe it'll be a good year for watermelons. Could be."

He paused and Harold Buckminster looked up at him, blinking, but there was a funny something in Jerry Spivey's eyes and Harold Buckminster looked down again.

"Or maybe, well, you never know about these things," Jerry Spivey said. "Somebody might come out here and salt your ground after them melons is planted, or they might pour gasoline all over them new vines, or maybe when them little boogers start to swell up, somebody might come out here and stomp 'em into the ground. There's a lot of really bad shit that can happen before you ever get a watermelon out of this here patch, Harold. You get my drift?"

"Uh-huh," Harold Buckminster said, and he knew he was caught and cornered and that nothing would come out of this Sunday morning that he could look back at and like.

"Now," Jerry Spivey went on, and there was artificial sweetener in his voice, "seems to me that when a man is faced with a crop failure, 'specially when it's a crop he expects to get a whole lot of mileage out of, what he's gotta do is take out some insurance."

"Haw," said Sperry Bissell. Harold Buckminster didn't say anything, but he looked up at Jerry Spivey and saw that the sunlight on his grackle's nest of red hair made it look as though his head was topped with little tongues of flame. Harold Buckminster thought of the devil and wished he had gone to church with Doris.

"Just think of me as your insurance man, Harold," said Jerry Spivey.

"Haw," said Sperry Bissell.

"I can guarantee nothin's gone happen to your watermelons like them things I said, but if you want that kind of insurance, then you got to pay for it," Jerry Spivey said, almost apologetically. "There ain't no such a thing as a free lunch. You with me, Harold?"

"Uh-huh," Harold Buckminster said miserably, and waited for what he now knew was coming.

"But you're lucky," Jerry Spivey said. "Look at me, Harold."

Harold Buckminster didn't look at him, couldn't look at him.

"Okay," Jerry Spivey went on, "have it your way. Y'know, most folks have to pay money for insurance, but all you gotta do is tell me where you got them silver dollars you was spendin' over at Roberson's that time. You remember."

"I tole you," Harold Buckminster said.

"Oh, Harold!" Jerry Spivey said, and put his hands on his hips. "You ain't been listenin' to me! We're talkin' about salt here, and gasoline, and maybe some stompin' where it's gone hurt the most."

Jerry Spivey ground his shoe into the black dirt. "I ain't sellin' insurance for bullshit, Harold. I want a name."

So that's why Harold Buckminster finally told Jerry Spivey and Sperry Bissell that the reason he was spending silver dollars at Roberson's Grocery was because he'd gotten them from this nigger name of Royal Mango, and it didn't take a lot more talk about salt and gasoline and stomping for Jerry Spivey to find out where Royal Mango lived, too, and when he found that out, he felt that all the time and effort he had spent looking for that bag of dollars or the stash they had come out of had been worth it because he finally had the bag, at least, in his sights. Or, he thought sourly, what was left of that bag; God knows how many of what Jerry Spivey regarded as his dollars the little bastard had used up.

Jerry Spivey and Sperry Bissell got back in the Pontiac and sped away from Brooklet after briefly listening to Harold Buckminster beg them not to tell Royal Mango that he was the one who put them onto him, a request to which Jerry Spivey answered that he'd think about it. And since very few cars ever used the track off county road 263 that led to Royal Mango's house, they missed their turn the first time, just the way Buddy Crittenden had missed it, and had to turn around and go back.

But they did find Royal Mango's property, and when they drove up, they could see the house itself squatting on a flat plain of sand and clay, a chicken yard behind it with eight or ten chickens picking idly at some clay of their own, a couple of chinaberry trees, a washtub, and a well. But there wasn't a soul in sight.

Jerry Spivey got halfway out of his side of the Pontiac and blew the horn twice.

In a minute or so, Rita Mango waddled to the door in a sky blue smock with an apron over it, sagging white socks, and tennis shoes that once had been white, too. She didn't say anything, just stood and looked at the two men and the car in the yard.

"Now what?" Sperry Bissell whispered loudly, and Jerry Spivey got the rest of the way out of the Pontiac, shut the door behind him, and walked to a point about fifteen feet from the rickety front steps.

"Royal Mango live here?" Jerry Spivey said civilly.

"Uh-huh," said Rita Mango. Her voice was husky. "What y'all wants wid him?" There was no expression on her face, not even curiosity.

"Tell him, uh, tell him I got a message for him from a friend of his," Jerry Spivey said.

"Fum who?" Rita Mango said, and leaned against the doorpost. There was a screen door, but it was sitting on its side about halfway down the porch from where Rita Mango stood.

"It's personal," said Jerry Spivey.

Rita Mango didn't say anything.

Jerry Spivey shifted his weight to his left leg and put his hands on his hips. "And it's real important, too," he said, a little louder now. "At least that's the way it was tole to me."

Rita Mango still didn't say anything, but pushed herself off the doorpost with her hip and turned and went back into the shadows of the house. Jerry Spivey could hear her and maybe somebody else clomping around in there. His heart had sped up and his hands were sweating. He wiped his palms on his pants legs and turned around to look through the windshield of the Pontiac at Sperry Bissell and said, "Get out," and Sperry Bissell did and came around and stood with his backside against the front of the car.

"That there has got to be one of the ugliest women I ever saw in my life," Sperry Bissell said.

"Yeah, but at least you had your sister to look at for practice," Jerry Spivey said.

"What?" Sperry Bissell said.

"Shut up," Jerry Spivey said, because Royal Mango, or the skinny little runt Jerry Spivey figured must be Royal Mango, was coming through the door and onto the porch. He was wearing an old white undershirt and brown pants rolled up at the cuffs.

"Howdy," Jerry Spivey said.

"Hi do," Royal Mango said. "What y'all want?"

"I got a message for you," Jerry Spivey said, and walked over to the steps. That prompted Royal Mango to walk the two paces from the doorway to the top step and stand there. "Look, whyn't we set down? I been standin' in yo yard ever since I got here."

"Set down, then," Royal Mango said, and he and Jerry Spivey sat down on the steps, Jerry Spivey on the second and Royal Mango one above it and off to the side. That way they could see each other.

"Thanks," Jerry Spivey said, and took a Kool out of the pack in his shirt pocket and lit it with a match.

"Who dis message fum?" Royal Mango said.

"From me," Jerry Spivey said. He took a drag from his cigarette, blew out the smoke, and watched it dissipate. His eyes met those of Sperry Bissell, who was still leaning against the car.

"I ain't studyin' this," Royal Mango said. "You got somethin' to say, you come all the way out here fum somewhere, so say it."

"All right," Jerry Spivey said, looking into the yard. "I got a message for you from me, and this here's it: if you don't tell me where you got them silver dollars you give to Harold Buckminster and where the rest of them are, I'm gone pull your goddamned ugly head off and throw it over this house."

Royal Mango shifted on his step and looked back toward the front door. "I ain't got no silver dollars," he said.

Jerry Spivey blew a smoke ring. "I didn't ask you if you had any," he said contemptuously. "I asked you where you got them and where the rest of them are. That's all I want to know. I already know you got them, I know about where you got them from, but I ain't sure how. You got them, though, and I want them back. They belong to me and I come to get them. There ain't nothing else to discuss."

"I ain't got no silver dollars," Royal Mango said again.

Jerry Spivey flicked his cigarette into the yard and stood up. "Now you listen to me, you scraggly-assed little piece of rat shit," he said, looking mean at Royal Mango. "I ain't come all the way out here to east Jesus to play hide and seek. You found them dollars I lost and now you gone give them back to me or me 'n' this boy yonder"—he nodded toward Sperry Bissell, who was now standing in front of the Pontiac—"are gone do somethin' so bad to you that you'll curse yo mama for givin' you birth."

"I already do that," Royal Mango said, and stood up, too. "And I tole you, I ain't got no silver dollars." He was speaking almost too softly for Jerry Spivey to hear, partly because he was using the bulk of his energy trying to figure out what to do next but mostly because he didn't want Rita to hear them talking about money.

But it was too late to worry about that, because Jerry Spivey was standing on the second step now, which brought him just about eye-to-eye with Royal Mango, and he was pointing a finger at Royal Mango and shouting.

"Listen to me, smut butt!" Jerry Spivey yelled. "You don't get but one chance here, you got them silver dollars and I aim to have them back!" And so saying, he grabbed Royal Mango by the neck of his undershirt and fairly propelled him off the step and into the yard. Royal Mango raised himself on all fours and looked at Sperry Bissell coming toward him, and Jerry Spivey kicked him in the left buttock and rolled him over on his side. "Grab him, Sperry," Jerry Spivey said, and Sperry Bissell grabbed Royal Mango by his shirt with one hand and his wiry hair with the other and pulled him to his feet.

Royal Mango was grimacing, trying to make his hair stop hurting where Sperry Bissell had a handful of it. "Okay," Jerry Spivey said, and showed Royal Mango some of his own teeth in return. "Now tell me."

Royal Mango couldn't help cutting his eyes toward his chicken house, where he put the bagful of silver dollars and where he had been told to leave them, untouched, but he didn't say anything. He'd already used up his ideas.

So Jerry Spivey hit him in the face and yelled "where?" at him again while Sperry Bissell held his arms. Royal Mango thought he was going to cry, his face hurt so bad, and he wondered if Jerry Spivey and Sperry Bissell were going to kill him and he was afraid he'd tell them where the bag of silver dollars was hidden, and he couldn't help wondering, too, if those silver dollars really did belong to Jerry Spivey and if he'd get in trouble for having spent fourteen of them.

While he was thinking all that, he didn't have time to say anything, so Jerry Spivey hit him again, so hard that he saw stars and whirly shapes. "Where?" Jerry Spivey hollered again.

"Wuff," Royal Mango said, and his knees buckled. Sperry Bissell let go of him and he lay down on his back, trying to focus his eyes on a cloud and tasting blood in his mouth.

"Shit," Jerry Spivey said. "Goddamned sissy. Here, let's put him on the porch."

But as Jerry Spivey and Sperry Bissell bent down to pick up Royal Mango there was a terrific noise behind them and they both straightened up as if they'd been goosed. When they turned around and looked, they saw Rita Mango standing on the porch with a twenty-gauge shotgun pointed over their heads at the sky.

"What the hell?" said Jerry Spivey.

Rita Mango pointed the gun at him. He could look straight into the deep black hole at the end of the barrel.

"Leave him alone," Rita Mango said.

"Aw, look," Jerry Spivey said, holding his hands out at his sides. "This, uh, your husband's got some money that belongs to me. He won't tell me where it is, but I come out here to get it."

"What you mean, money?" Rita Mango said, not moving the shotgun.

She hasn't pumped it, Jerry Spivey thought. There ain't no shell in the chamber.

Rita Mango pumped the shotgun. The spent shell flew out and rolled across the porch.

Shit, thought Jerry Spivey. "Uh, a bag of silver dollars my grandma give me," he said. "We was carryin' a bunch of stuff from her house, y'know, she was movin' into a nursin' home and she gimme a lot of her valuable stuff to keep, y'know, and we accidentally left that bag on top of the car and it fell off on the road and I reckon your husband found it. I know he's got them dollars, too. I seen some he give to another fella to buy liquor."

Rita Mango's eyes moved around a little, then came back to rest on Jerry Spivey. "Ain't no money here," she said flatly. Her husband rolled over clumsily and raised himself on all fours and tried to get up but couldn't and lay down again on his stomach and belched loudly into the dirt.

Rita Mango looked at him and then up toward the highway. "Ain't no money here," she said again. "If they was, I'd know about it."

"Lady," Jerry Spivey said, "if you shoot me, you gone be in real trouble, you know that. I come out here all peaceable-like, but yo husband is lyin' to me and I want them silver dollars. If I gotta go away from here without them, next thing I'm gone do is come back with the law and then I'll get 'em sho nuff."

Rita Mango seemed to be thinking. She looked at Jerry Spivey, then at Royal Mango, who was up on his elbows now, then at Sperry Bissell, then through the trees toward the highway. Sperry Bissell turned around once and followed her gaze out to the road, but he didn't see anything and reckoned she didn't, either.

"Now listen here," Jerry Spivey said, and started toward the house. The roar of the shotgun stopped him, made his hair stand on end. Rita Mango pumped the twenty-gauge and lowered the barrel so it pointed at Jerry Spivey again.

"Back off," she said, and Jerry Spivey and Sperry Bissell each took a couple of steps backward.

Jerry Spivey's heart was pounding, but he thought, That's two, and if it's a legal gun there ain't but one more shell in it, and if she shoots the clouds with that one, I'll ram that twenty-gauge up her ass.

Rita Mango took one, then another shell out of her apron pocket and put them into the shotgun, taking her eyes off Jerry Spivey only for an instant.

Sperry Bissell was ready to go home. "Jerry," he said, "I reckon we better leave, uh, and, uh, go get the sheriff."

"God damn it," Jerry Spivey said, spitting his words out. "What's the matter with all you people?" Royal Mango sat up in the dust and looked up at his wife and the shotgun, one of which he usually wished he'd never seen but which today he was thankful for, and the other he was certain he'd never seen before. He wondered where the shotgun had come from and how much it would be worth if he could get it away from Rita someday and go pawn it. Now Jerry Spivey was yelling again. "We're talkin' about my property here! Give to me by my grandma! You people have got my money!"

"Royal," Rita Mango said.

"Honey," Royal Mango said, and wiped flecks of dried blood from his lips with the hem of his undershirt. Flies were circling him, looking for interesting places to land on.

"You got dis man's money?" Rita said.

Royal Mango looked at her past Jerry Spivey's back. "Jest a minute, honey," he said, and stood up groggily. He took a step sideways and almost fell, but caught himself and made his way over to the steps, giving Jerry Spivey a wide berth, then went slowly up the steps past the barrel of the shotgun and stood beside his wife, who never looked at him.

"No, I ain't," Royal Mango said.

"Shit hell goddamn," Jerry Spivey said disgustedly. "You people are in big trouble, I can tell you that."

"Seems to me the onliest ones in trouble 'round here is them what's in front of this here shotgun," Rita Mango said. "He says he ain't got yo money, so you ain't got no mo bidness here. Might do good to go back where you come from."

Jerry Spivey looked at her. "You got the gun," he said.

"I got it," Rita said.

"You got it this time," Jerry Spivey said. They were still looking at each other. "Next time it might be different."

"Uh-huh," Rita Mango said. "Nex' time you be stretched out on de ground bleedin' by now."

Sperry Bissell waited for Jerry Spivey to say something, but Jerry Spivey just stood there and shifted his weight a little, then spat on the ground and turned away and got in the car. Sperry Bissell got in, too, and they scratched off and blew dust all over the place as they pulled out of the yard. Just as Jerry Spivey turned right toward Brooklet, out of the thin dirt track leading to Royal Mango's house, too mad and too confounded to cuss out loud or even to berate himself for not thinking to send Sperry Bissell around to the back of the house when they got there, a black GTO with Sears Ellis at the wheel turned and went in the way they had come out.

It's anybody's guess what Sears Ellis thought when he drove up in front of Royal Mango's house and saw Mr. and Mrs. Mango on the porch, Rita Mango holding a twenty-gauge shotgun still pointed into the yard, which is to say in the general direction of Sears Ellis himself. But whatever he thought, Sears Ellis spent about twenty minutes on the porch in earnest conversation with the two Mangos, and then he and Royal Mango got in the GTO and drove in to Brooklet to Harold Buckminster's place.

When they got there, they didn't do very much in the first half hour or so except to roam around the woods in back of Harold Buckminster's house till they found where Harold Buckminster was hiding. When he saw Royal Mango get out of a GTO in his front yard with a man he didn't know, Harold Buckminster's first and only thought was that Royal Mango had brought somebody over to bust him up a little for ratting on him to Jerry Spivey and Sperry Bissell. And Harold Buckminster was weary with being busted up and pushed around, and so turned and went straight through his house and out the back door and hid in the gully that he and whoever owned his house before he got there used for dumping garbage.

Even so, the two men would have found Harold Buckminster sooner than they did except that Royal Mango was still a little woozy from being busted up and pushed around himself, and when he first got to the gully in which Harold Buckminster was hiding, he just didn't feel like walking up to it and looking over the edge.

Harold Buckminster was so relieved to find out that all this big feller, this Sears Ellis, was interested in was finding out the names of the two guys that had bullied him into giving them Royal Mango's name and directions to his house that he told his two visitors the whole story from the salt through the gasoline all the way to the stomping. In fact, he got so caught up in it that he added a little salt and gas and stomping to what Jerry Spivey had already provided him with.

So Sears Ellis and Royal Mango left Harold Buckminster sitting on his porch, explaining to his wife that when he saw them two fellers drive up, the reason he took off out the back door so fast was to run down into the woods and check on his latest attempt at making whiskey to see if by any chance it was if not quite fit to drink then at least at a point at which he could sell some of it to a pair of thirsty and desperate consumers. Since Doris Buckminster had long ago reached the place in her life at which she figured she had heard just about everything already and so was beyond either surprise or even much real curiosity, that was all Harold Buckminster had to say to her.

But now Sears Ellis had something to say, and he was already obliged to say it to somebody who would want to listen to him say it, so he and Royal Mango rode away in the GTO into the deepening dusk and Sears Ellis drove out down past Turleyville to say it. When they got there, they were made to feel as though they had been expected, which they were.

TEN

Help me, willya?" Buddy Crittenden said.

"Well, hell," I said.

"What else are you gonna do on Saturday afternoon?" Buddy said smartly, as if daring me to name something.

"Well, hell," I said. "If I don't do it, I'll feel bad, and if I do it, I'll be sorry all next week that I didn't just lie around and do nothing. I'm tired."

"Look," Buddy said. "The weather's supposed to be warm, it'll be okay, it'll be a snap. I'll even buy your breakfast."

"Lunch."

"No," Buddy said slowly, drawing out the word. "Then by the time we pick up Aunt Sandy it'd be too late for her to eat lunch and she'll be upset that we couldn't stop for a hamburger. She really looks forward to gettin' a hamburger when I go to see her."

"Lunch," I said, trying to sound firm. "You can call her and tell her you're bringing her hamburger with you."

Buddy looked at me and squirmed on his stool. We were drinking coffee at the bar at the Huddle House, and I had had toast, too. "She won't like it," he said.

"I'm trying to negotiate a compromise."

Buddy took what appeared to be his last sip of coffee and looked in his cup and put it down in the saucer. Now he was watching bacon fry behind the counter. The smell of that bacon made me hungry even after my toast and jelly. I didn't say anything, I was too tired.

"All right," Buddy said. "I'll call her and see what she says. And if she doesn't raise hell about me bringing her hamburger with me instead of us going out and standing at the counter and buying it, then okay, that's what we'll do. You and I'll go somewhere and eat and then get her stuff and go pick her up."

"Let's not let this get to be a habit," I said, and drained the coffee in my cup, too.

"Don't worry about that. I just need some backup. Aunt Sandy and I ain't had a lot of new ground to go over in our conversations in a long time."

"I'll try to be scintillating," I said, and watched the waitress pour us more coffee. I was out of cream, but I didn't care. I'd already had too much coffee. At least with something in my cup I could sit there a little while longer.

"She's a pretty slick old lady," Buddy said, "and smart as a whip. At least she was, once, though I reckon she's been slowing down. But she's gotten on this thing about it being time for me to get married, and sometimes she just won't let it be, even though I've told her a thousand times that Karen and I are gone get married, we just gone do it in our own sweet time." He blew on his coffee, then slurped a little of it. "She's pissed off, too."

"At what?"

"At havin' to be a little old lady and live in a nursing home. At not bein' able to go anywhere she wants to and do what she pleases anymore."

That sounded pretty reasonable to me, and I said so.

"What does?" Buddy said. "Which?"

"The part about her bein' mad. I couldn't care less if you ever get married."

Buddy grunted. "So it's a deal, then," he said.

"Well, hell," I said. "What time do we break her out?"

It was 1:30 in the afternoon when we drove out of the parking lot at the Maple Leaf Senior Citizens Center with Alexandra Porterfield Adams—"but call me Aunt Sandy or I won't answer you"—in the front seat of the Cutlass next to Buddy and with me in the back with two of Buddy's big flashlights, a pair of binoculars in a case, and several months' worth of dust.

Aunt Sandy unwrapped her hamburger, took a bite, and then sipped at her Coke through a straw.

"I sho hope I don't get no crumbs or no ketchup on your car," she said to Buddy, and took another little bite.

"Don't worry about it," Buddy said. He was squinting into the sunlight ahead of us. He'd been right—the day was warm, but too cool to keep the windows open.

"Ain't it about time you got a new car, anyhow?" Aunt Sandy said. "How old's this one?"

"Goin' on four years," Buddy said hesitantly.

" 'Bout time," Aunt Sandy said.

"I ain't ready to spend my money on a new car," Buddy said.

"Believe it or not, I'm glad to hear that," Aunt Sandy said. "You'll need that money for gettin' married on, and for startin' a family."

Buddy's eyebrows constricted.

Aunt Sandy turned around a little and looked at me. Her eyes were dark points of hazy light. Her face was like a landscape of dry riverbeds.

"You know Buddy," she said, peering at me through her glasses. "Don't you think it's time he got married?"

"I dunno," I said. "Hard for me to say."

"Sure you know," Aunt Sandy said. "You're married, aint-cha?"

"No ma'am," I said politely.

Aunt Sandy squinted at me and turned back around. I could hear her crinkling the wrapper her hamburger had come in and putting it in the bag.

"What's the matter with you grown men?" she said to the bag. "And Buddy, I'm ashamed of you, the way you been stringing poor Carla along."

"Karen," Buddy said.

"Karen, then," Aunt Sandy said. "I'm ashamed of the way you been stringing her along. Six years now."

"Four," Buddy said.

"Four, then," Aunt Sandy said. "Just like your car. Time enough for y'all to make up y'all's minds. If it's her that don't want to marry you, then you better let her go and get another one. Men your age ain't got too many productive years left."

"Productive?" Buddy said, and flicked his hand at Lamar Torrance, who passed us going in the opposite direction in a county car, one of the old ones with a single blue light on top.

"You know what I mean," Aunt Sandy said, and looked at him. A thin, pale tongue came a little way out of her mouth and moistened her lips.

Buddy turned and gave her a wry look. "You gone show me where to turn off up here?" he said.

"We got a ways to go," Aunt Sandy said, and looked out her window. I was already looking out mine and had seen us pass the lake and head out into the sparsely peopled countryside southeast of town. Town turns into country in a hurry down there as the land lowers gradually into a series of little creeks surrounded by swamps and bogs overhung with Spanish moss before rising again to a plain of brown and gray woods. We were headed for the part of the county that Aunt Sandy and her sister Myrtle, Buddy's mama, had been raised in and from which everyone in their family had been gone for forty years.

Aunt Sandy hadn't been up to what she called the old home place in almost two years and had been bugging Buddy to take her out there for months. Aunt Sandy was eighty-two years old, fifteen years older than her sister Myrtle, and not particularly confident of being on earth long enough to postpone going out into the farthest extremity of Talmadge County to pay her respects to the ground she was born and raised on and to the people who had raised her there.

Buddy said he hadn't been out to the old Porterfield place himself but a couple of times, and the only time he'd been there when he might have remembered where it was, if he'd tried to, he had mostly just driven his mama and his aunt Sandy around and listened to them tell stories about when they were young.

"Turn here," Aunt Sandy said, so we headed off down a narrow road on sand and loam through pine woods bordered in bayberry, palmetto, and sweetgums.

"Look over there," she said, pointing to what seemed to be nothing in particular. "That's where your granddaddy's first house was, the one that burnt down before I was born."

Buddy slowed down and craned his neck to look through Aunt Sandy's window. "That's where they come to after he decided to leave Savannah," Buddy said. "Right?"

"Sho," Aunt Sandy said. "I'm surprised you remember that story." She turned a little, aiming her face into the backseat.

"Buddy's granddaddy," she said to me, "was a sailor when he was a young man. Ran away from home when he was fourteen years old and stowed away on a fishin' boat. Hid in a barrel till the rest of them found him and put him to work. Haw. He was always crazy about the ocean."

"Uh-huh," I said. "Me too, though I never had any inclination to be a sailor. How come he moved up here, then?"

"Because my mama told him to," Aunt Sandy said, and turned back around. "Buddy, go past the next left, but take the one after that."

"Okay," Buddy said.

"Mama told Daddy she wasn't gone marry no man who was off from home more than he was at home," Aunt Sandy said, and cleared her throat daintily. "It was her or the ocean, I reckon. And he picked her, at least that time."

"Yeah," Buddy said, and looked at me in the rearview mirror. "After all the kids left home, he picked up and went back to the coast and got some kind of job with the harbormaster in Charleston."

Aunt Sandy looked up sharply. "You know about that?" she asked.

"Sure," Buddy said. "You told me yourself. More'n once."

Aunt Sandy sniffed. "It like to have broke Mama's heart to leave this place," she said. "But she came home after all in the end, just like she wanted."

"What?" I said.

"She buried Daddy in the old family cemetery up here," Aunt Sandy said, "and she's buried there, too. We'll be there in a minute."

We were just creeping along now, crunching sand under the tires. I had my window open a little and could smell the woods.

"It's hot as hell for this time of year, ain't it?" Aunt Sandy said.

"I sorta thought it was bearable, maybe just right," Buddy said.

"I'm okay," I said.

"Well, it's hot as hell to me," Aunt Sandy said. "For what ought to be still wintertime, anyhow. Right here, Buddy, right here. Pull off the road."

"Yes'm," Buddy said, and pulled over and stopped the car and we got out in a thin fog of dust. There was nothing to see but trees and underbrush. It was so quiet that we might have stepped out of the car into the forest primeval.

"Now what?" Buddy said.

"Now we gone walk down the hill yonder to the cemetery," Aunt Sandy said, pointing with her cane. She started off briskly through the trees. "Long as it's warm as it is, you men better look out for copperheads. Y'all come clompin' through here with them big feet of yours, if one of them's done woke up early, you're liable to get bit."

"Yes'm," Buddy said, and I said it, too, and we headed off after her.

"There used to be a house over yonder," Aunt Sandy said, pointing her cane like a pistol to her left. "Mama's sister Mary and her husband built it there. This used to be Porterfield land, too, is how come the cemetery's here."

"Were there a lot of people out here then?" I said. So far I hadn't seen any sign of people at all. Aunt Sandy was having a little trouble walking through the brush, but so was I, especially after being reminded about copperheads.

"Lord," Aunt Sandy said, "they was people scattered all over the place around here. Wadden all woods back then, either. Mostly it was woods and fields, too."

She stopped as though to catch her breath, and looked around. "There was even this little town, though I guess it was just a store and some houses. There's a turnoff to it about a mile or so back the way we came in. Somebody still lives up there, or at least they did the last time I was here, me 'n' Myrtle, and you can still see where the little store was. But it's all growed up now, and near 'bout everybody's either done died or moved away and their houses have burnt down or been tore up. Been so long·since I was out here, maybe there ain't even nothin' down there no more."

"Who owns this land now?" I said. I could see Buddy wandering aimlessly through the woods, kicking at clumps and molehills, and I hoped he was watching for copperheads.

"I dunno," Aunt Sandy said. "Some of it's government land, and some Porterfield owns some of it, too, but he lives in Tupelo, Mississippi, or some other godforsaken place, and none of us on this end of the family know him very well."

She lifted up her face as if hunting a scent on the tiny breeze. "We better move on if we're gone see anything," she said.

So we walked on another fifty yards or so down a gentle slope and came to a little grove of cedars so tall and gnarled and branchy that they seemed very nearly as old as the ground itself. Their bark was peeling in wisps and ribbons. The cemetery they shaded was maybe thirty feet square and surrounded by a rusty iron fence with a space where a gate had been. Some of the graves had slabs, some had headstones, and others were marked only by rocks, but all of them were coated with cedar sprinkles and dust. Bits of plastic flowers stuck out of the ground by a few of them. Buddy came up and the three of us stood and looked.

"Here, Buddy," Aunt Sandy said firmly, "help me scrape off some of this stuff. Them's yo people lyin' in here, too." She pulled a couple of little whisk brooms from her pocketbook, which she had refused to leave locked in the trunk of the car, and Buddy and I each took one and went to work. Aunt Sandy moved the larger sticks and pieces of Styrofoam pots around with her cane, keeping up a monologue about the people at our feet and on the other side of our brooms—where they fit in the family and who they married and how long they lived and what they died from, the kind of information that seems to be the one thing everybody manages to leave behind.

Alexander Hamilton Porterfield, Buddy's granddaddy and Aunt Sandy's daddy, the sailor who came home from the sea and then went back, was the only one who had a full-length slab and a headstone, too, though Aunt Sandy said the family was gone get a headstone for her mama to go with the one they got for him. If it hadn't been for her husband, she said, that shiftless Ben Adams, procrastinating over it, they'd have done it, but now it was too late.

"How come it's too late?" Buddy said. He had dead cedar needles all over his jeans. "What'd he do?"

Aunt Sandy sat on her daddy's headstone and cleaned her glasses on the hem of her dress. "He died," she said, "and we used the money to bury him instead of gettin' Mama's stone. He never did have no sense of when to do nothin'."

"Where's he buried?" I said. Chickadees and titmice were working their way through the branches over our heads, buzzing and chuckling at each other.

"In town," Aunt Sandy said. "Where he belongs. He was a town man, didn't know nothin' about the country, didn't want to know nothin', either. I reckon I oughta go by and see him, too, but that's somethin' I can procrastinate over and not worry about very much. I'm sho he ain't expectin' no visit from me."

"Hah," Buddy said, brushing woods debris from his pants legs. "Ain't you gone be buried with him?"

Aunt Sandy jerked her head up and looked at Buddy. "Hellfire," she said. "I'd just as soon be stood straight up and pounded into the ground. Naw. I'm gone be laid in back yonder in Memory Hill in yo mama and daddy's plot. I'd rather be out here with my mama and daddy and these other people"—she looked around, peering over the top of her glasses—"even though I don't even know some of 'em, like whoever that big ol' rock is markin' on the end there. But there ain't no room, y'see?

"And you mean to tell me you didn't know I paid yo mama for a piece of her ground?"

"No'm," Buddy said, drawing it out as though trying to remember.

Aunt Sandy stood up slowly. A few strands of her hair, which was gray but light, the color of the horizon just before the sun comes up, were sticking out over her ears. "Lord," she said, "I reckon if something was to happen to Myrtle, there wouldn't be nobody at all who'd know what to do with me. It's stuff like that that you ought to know."

"Yes'm," Buddy said meekly. The birds had moved on, and the woods around us was still again and quiet except for an airplane droning along somewhere far to the north.

"Huh," Aunt Sandy said. "I reckon I better call yo mama and remind her, too. If she never told you, maybe she's done forgot it herself."

"Naw," Buddy said. "Not Mama. She wouldn't forget somethin' like that."

"Shoot," Aunt Sandy said. "Let's go. We got ground to cover. Just the same, I'll call her anyway."

Now we were walking, and I picked up a little rock and put it in my pocket. "I got to watch what's left of my family like a hawk," Aunt Sandy said. "You're a grown man and didn't even know how to get out here and see where you came from, and maybe yo mama's done forgot that, too."

Buddy looked at me and shrugged. Aunt Sandy made a clucking noise. "Whoever it was said old times ain't long forgotten down here didn't know what he was talkin' about."

So we went back to the Cutlass, where Aunt Sandy served us bananas from a paper bag and poured plastic cups of cool, watery tea from a little thermos.

"I didn't even see you bring that sack of stuff," Buddy said admiringly, peeling a banana.

"There's a whole lot I do that you don't see," Aunt Sandy said tartly. Now we were pulling back onto the narrow road. "Go one mile exactly. There's some big ol' oak trees off to your right. Don't miss that, too."

"Yes'm," Buddy said, and we found the spot all right. There

was even the remains of a little road running from the main road in toward the three giant live oaks that stood high above and arched great branches over the second growth of little pines and water oaks on the hilltop with them. Other people had pulled in here, too, probably in the hunting season, and beer cans and spent shotgun shells were scattered around.

"This here's where your granddaddy's last house was," Aunt Sandy said after we had gotten out. "Be careful, there's a old well somewhere around here. All these old places had a well or two, and sometimes they didn't get filled in all the way and you're liable to fall in one of them and break a leg if you don't look out."

So mostly we just stood in the shade of the oaks, on watch now not just for copperheads but for a bottomless pit, too, and Buddy said, "Did he build a house here, or just move into one?"

"He fixed one up what was here already," Aunt Sandy said, "but he built a barn and a feedlot to go with it. When I was growin' up, all this around here was fields, pretty much, all the way from the house down yonder"—she pointed her cane through the scrubby woods—"to the branch. These here oaks was just as big then as they are now, though, least it seems that way.

"The old well was dry when they got here, and Mama and Daddy had to have water brought up from the branch till they could get somebody out here to dig a new one. Lord, I can still recollect comin' up this hill with a bucket in each hand. . . . I was just a little bitty thing and my legs was short and stubby and I'd have to put down them buckets about every ten feet and rest. Whoo."

She seemed to be listening to something coming to her from far away, not looking at anything in particular except maybe something she could see and Buddy and I couldn't.

"They used to be dances down the road a piece at old Carson Odom's place," she said. "He had three daughters and his wife, her name was Sophie, would play the fiddle, if you can believe that, and somebody else would play the piano, most every family had a couple of people who could play the piano, and we'd just dance and carry on, and then when it was too late to frolic anymore, we'd all get in the wagons and come home."

She smiled, and all her wrinkles turned up and got closer together. Her eyes were bright and her cane poked the air as she talked. "There was some young bucks out here in them days, Lord knows they thought they was somethin', too. One of 'em name of Jack somebody or other even had a Ford car and used to take us girls home in it. Haw, all of us, none of us wanted to be the last one he took home 'cause he'd always want to smooch and none of us was really interested in that, at least not with him. We just wanted to ride in that car.

"Daddy liked him, though, and I can remember he even got up in the middle of the night and took the mules down the road to pull Jack's Ford out of that big gully just this side of what back then was the main road to Savannah. Must've been, oh hell, it's been so long I cain't even remember."

Buddy and I shared a look. Aunt Sandy smiled. "You boys are real nice to bring me out here," she said gently, "and I appreciate it. I guess I sound just like an old woman without much future who's just goin' on and on about the past and won't shut up."

"It ain't that," I said. "We were just listening."

Aunt Sandy sniffed and smiled again and brushed back a few wayward bits of hair from her forehead. "I reckon so," she said, "and I appreciate you sayin' that, too. I've forgot a lot of it, I know, but some parts of them times out here seem just like last week to me when I think about them. Especially when I get to come out here. It's like I can see it all the way it was back then, the house standin' here, and Cousin Ed's little house out yonder across the road, and the Odoms and the Farrars and the Hammersmiths, I used to know 'em all, up and down this road. I've sat on their porches and eaten at their supper tables and now they ain't nothin' to see out here but woods and ghosts."

She put her cane across her lap and held it with both hands. "The colored people, too," she said. "We was all friends out here, or so it seemed like. I dunno what people would say about it now. They worked for Daddy or Mr. Odom and them, all except a couple of them who worked in town. The colored folks was most all po' as rabbits, sho, but none of us was a lot better off."

Aunt Sandy paused as if to catch her breath, then cleared her throat and went on.

" 'Course, by time Ben Adams and I came back to live out here for that little bit, the war was over and some of these colored peoples was doin' okay, at least compared to the way we'd all been doin' just a few years before that. There was even one had a real nice place four, five miles down yonder on the Savannah road. I dunno what he did for a livin', but for some reason all the other colored peoples around here called him the Rattlesnake Master."

Buddy looked up, and he and I looked at each other and then at her.

"The what?" Buddy said.

"Hah?" Aunt Sandy said.

"They called him what?" Buddy said.

"We all called him that," Aunt Sandy said, "though I cain't tell you that I ever saw him much when I was livin' here, and then later on after I moved away, I believe he moved into Savannah, somewhere down that way. Maybe he went to work in town."

"They called him the Rattlesnake Master?" I said, and Buddy and I looked at each other again and then looked back at Aunt Sandy and waited for her to tell us.

"Uh-huh," Aunt Sandy said. "I recollect the colored peoples thought he was like God or somethin'. They'd go troopin' over to his place for first one thing and another and told us he could heal the sick, y'know, stuff like that. Him and his family must've come here from somewhere else, I reckon, 'cause they was all as black as the inside of a coffee can." She grinned. I could hear crows calling, high and far away.

"So tell me more about this feller," Buddy said.

"Well," Aunt Sandy said, "they didn't move in down there till I was nearly 'bout grown, I reckon, but I used to come out here to see Mama and Daddy and then like I say, me 'n Ben come back out here for a bit, y'know. Sometimes we'd run into his chirren at other folks' houses, and they talked funny. I never did see the daddy hisself, though, and that was the one they called the Rattlesnake Master. Daddy said they was just foreign niggers and that a nigger is a nigger no matter where he comes from, but they weren't like the rest of them around here."

Pretty soon we left, and Aunt Sandy looked to be tired out by all the talking and so didn't do very much more of it. Buddy seemed to be thinking hard, and every once in a while he'd give me a peculiar look, like the way he rolled his eyes when we drove up to the place where Aunt Sandy said this long-gone Rattlesnake Master had lived and found the ruins of a house and dried-up stalks of *Eryngium yuccifolium* standing among the remains of last summer's primroses and mullein and other weeds. But Buddy didn't say anything about what he was thinking until we had taken Aunt Sandy home to the Maple Leaf Senior Citizens Center and he had promised to come see her again soon and told her yes, he'd think about what she'd said about settling down and getting married and starting to act like normal folks.

"Jesus," Buddy said to me. "I ain't never heard of a Rattlesnake Master in my life, and now in the space of a few months I've not only heard of two of them, I've even met one, and I know where the other one used to live." He frowned at me, and I shrugged in return.

"What I don't know," he went on, "is what all that means."

"Maybe it was his daddy down there."

"Whose daddy?" Buddy said.

"Leeman Gant's daddy. Maybe being a Rattlesnake Master is something that gets passed on from a father to his son. Something like that."

Buddy grunted, then scratched his left arm and took a deep breath and let it out slowly. We were standing in his kitchen; I was eating grapes and Buddy was drinking a beer. Outside, the day was fading into darkness.

"So ain't this Rattlesnake Master, the one we went way down yonder to meet, supposed to come from an island? Wasn't it Barbados?"

"Yep," I said. "And since your Aunt Sandy says this other one, the one she knew about, had come here from somewhere else, maybe that was Barbados, too."

"And maybe he went back to Barbados from down yonder," Buddy said, "and took his children with him."

"Right so far."

"So why'd he come back? The one we met, I mean. And why'd he come back to the same part of the country his daddy left—if that was his daddy and if he really left?"

"Maybe his daddy told him he'd like it," I said.

"Maybe," Buddy said.

He was staring at the floor, which was covered in linoleum on which there were thousands of tiny hexagons. "I wish I'd had the sense to ask him why he moved here that day you and I went out to see him and bring Royal home, but I reckon I just figured he was an immigrant, y'know, and anyhow that whole afternoon is nothin' but a blur to me. Like it wasn't really there, that house as clean as a whistle and that outhouse with a skylight in it, for God's sake, and them gardens and all out in that poor end of a poor county, and palm trees for lagniappe. And me'n you sittin' on the porch like a couple of Jehovah's Witnesses and you and him shootin' Latin names at each other."

"It was an interesting day," I said.

"Yeah. And too bad we'll never find out whether that was his daddy down yonder and how come he's to be here and all." Buddy took a sip of his beer and looked at the messages on the bottle. I could hear the kitchen clock ticking, and I knew what he was going to say.

"He invited you back," he said.

"Uh-huh," I said, and chewed a grape and swallowed it. There was a bowl of them in the middle of the table, and I picked another one and ate it, too.

"Well," Buddy said after a few seconds, "you could just sort of drop off back down to Turleyville one Saturday afternoon or somethin' and pay the old feller a visit, like he said. You and him could set on the porch and talk about plants and such and wonder when spring's gone come."

"Yes," I said, "and I could ask him about his daddy and if his daddy was called the Rattlesnake Master, too, and if his daddy came from Barbados and if he ever went back there, and how come if all that happened he's to be called the Rattlesnake Master like his daddy was, if that was his daddy down yonder at all. And I could ask him how come he's in Turleyville in the first place so I can drive down there and sit on the porch and ask him this stuff and then come back and tell you about it."

"That's about the way I had it figured," Buddy said, and smiled.

ELEVEN

The day I went to see the Rattlesnake Master was also the day the truckload of rabbits turned over on Hawthorn Street after successfully avoiding a collision with a Chevette driven by Earlene Taliaferro, whom we have met before.

What happened is that Earlene abruptly braked her little tin can of a car to make a left-hand turn into the 7-Eleven and the driver of the rabbit truck, a man whose name was Harley McIntyre and who worked for a rabbit farm in Asheville, North Carolina, had virtually to pulverize his own brakes to keep from chewing the Chevette to pieces. But he had to cut too sharply, and the trailer snapped right off and turned over, dumping rabbit cages down a hill thick with kudzu vines.

The south end of Hawthorn Street was full of rabbits. These were rabbits destined for Miami, but some of them had at least an afternoon of liberty, and some of them may be at large to this day. Harley McIntyre said he reckoned he was dreaming about what he was going to do in Miami and all, and maybe he was following that Chevrolet a little too close, but that woman didn't even put on a turn signal, for God's sake, she didn't even stick out her hand. She just braked and turned in.

But Harley McIntyre was finally judged to be the one at fault, there being if one immutable law of the highway it is that drivers are presumed to be looking out for the cretin in the car ahead of them at all times. But if you don't count Harley and a couple of rabbits who got run over while they and some of their comrades were dispersing to the four winds, everybody had a good time.

Harley McIntyre said it was a miracle none of the rabbits were killed when the trailer turned over, but many of the wooden cages were damaged and many more were busted open. Some of the rabbits got tangled up in the kudzu, what with being farm-bred rabbits and not accustomed to negotiating vines. Those were rather quickly captured one by one by an increasingly numerous group of whooping volunteers. Hawthorn Street was clogged with traffic; everybody wanted to see the rabbits.

But all the rabbits most people got to see were still in cages, because before long the rabbits that didn't get tangled in the kudzu had vanished into the surrounding neighborhoods. Buddy Crittenden said later that you'd have thought a few of these liberated rabbits, out of a cage probably for the first time in their lives, would dawdle around for a while what with the surprise of it all, but the seventeen escapees—by Harley McIntyre's count—knew freedom was a good thing when they saw it and decided to get as much of it as possible.

Two of them were run over by automobiles, thirteen were caught by various means in various parts of town, and two were never bagged at all. Once in a while somebody still says they've seen a white rabbit, but now nobody pays much heed. On the day it happened, though, everyone on the scene became a small center of attention wherever he or she went because everybody who wasn't there wanted to hear the real story of the rabbits from somebody who was.

What happened to Harley McIntyre's truckload of rabbits explains why there was such a crowd at the other end of Hawthorn Street as I crossed it on my way out of town headed south, but I didn't know that then and just figured there had been an accident of some sort, which was correct. It also explains why I saw a white rabbit loping across somebody's yard, and also why I got Coca-Cola on my jeans, which is to say by bending too far to my right to look at the rabbit and thereby tilting the can that was in my lap. There was a cool foam of Coca-Cola between me and the car seat and spots of Coca-Cola arrayed across my lap. You never spill anything where nobody will notice.

But I said to hell with it and drove on down past Turleyville, through land that didn't have anything built on it but a highway, toward Leeman Gant's house. My head was a little thick, maybe because I hadn't been sleeping well, but just as likely because I was getting a cold.

Angela Stallings had just come back to work after three days of dealing with what she said was a cold so bad it felt like the flu, and I was mad at myself for having been unable to stay very far away from her. Maybe I needed the visual comfort or something. Once in a while I'd get up from whatever I was doing at my desk and go out into the reception area and sit down and start talking on some pretext and mostly just look at her. It was like warming myself at a soft, lovely fire that—if I thought about it long enough—could make me break out into a sweat. I don't know how Corey Stallings could keep from burning himself up. And I never understood what Angela saw in Corey Stallings, either, but it didn't matter. He got there first and that was that.

Anyhow, I found the Gants' dirt driveway on the first pass and then there was the house between the pecan tree and the palm trees and the dried-up flower beds in front of it all, some of them sprinkled with green that stood out against the porch behind them, the porch on which Leeman Gant sat and watched me drive into his yard.

Pretty soon I was sitting beside him in a straight-backed chair with a straw bottom. He was sitting in one, too, since he didn't have to bring out a stool this time to make a point to Buddy Crittenden, and we were drinking glasses of well water. We were both wearing sweaters to ward off the little nip in the air, but it was too bright and pretty a day to sit inside. Once in a while the old man would light and puff on a little bone and ivory pipe decorated with scrimshaw. I had already apologized for arriving unannounced and he had already laughed and said he was expecting me, if not today then very soon.

For a little while we talked about woodpeckers, of all things, since we could hear one somewhere in the trees between us and the highway. My nose was beginning to run, so I took out a Kleenex and blew it. Too wetly, I thought. The old man asked if I had a cold and I said I wasn't sure yet. Then he asked if I wanted to go inside, and I said no.

"But we cannot ignore your symptoms," he said kindly, and turned toward the door and called for Elizabeth, who appeared at the screen exactly as I had seen her the first time, all in white. I started to stand, but the old man waved me back into my chair.

Elizabeth and I nodded to each other.

"Yes, Papa?" she said. Her earrings were garnets.

"Please bring our friend Leeman some of the tea for colds," the old man said.

"Hello, Leeman," Elizabeth said pleasantly. Her accent was more musical than her father's. "Don't you feel well?"

"Nice to see you again," I said. "So far, so good, but I think something's drawing a bead on me."

"I'm sorry," she said. "The tea for colds, Papa. Do you want the light or the dark?"

The old man looked at me appraisingly. "The light," he said. "That should do it."

When Elizabeth disappeared into the house, I said, "There's two kinds of tea for colds?"

The old man smiled. "One tea to ward them off and another to make them go away," he said. "You'll be satisfied. This is a good tea for colds."

The tea Elizabeth brought was hot and slightly sweet and tasted of oranges and something else I had smelled somewhere in my life but couldn't put a name to.

"What's in this?" I said.

"Oh," the old man said, shrugging. "A bit of fruit, a bit of herbs, a bit of this and that from my garden . . ." He smiled and took a sip of his water. "And maybe a bit of sorcery, too," he said, and chuckled. "A cold takes some persuading to stay away."

"Sorcery," I said, and took a drink of tea and swallowed it. It was soft in my throat and warm in my stomach.

The old man brushed a string from his pants leg. "So here you are. And what does the deputy sheriff want to know?"

I looked at him, but he seemed to be giving most of his attention to a black squirrel that was crossing the yard in short hops.

"Do you think that's the only reason I'm here?"

Leeman Gant smiled again but kept looking at the squirrel until it reached the trees between the yard and the highway. "No," he said, "but I imagine he has things he would like to ask me and that he thinks I would tell them to you before I would tell them to him."

"Is that true? Would you?"

"Perhaps it is. Perhaps it would depend not on what he wanted to know but on why he wanted to know it."

"His job makes him curious," I said. "Or maybe he's got the job he has because he was curious to begin with."

"And you?"

"I'd like to know some of the things about you that Buddy wants to know, but I don't have to know them and maybe he doesn't really have to know them, either. You seem to be way ahead of us, anyway. And I'd have come back out here sooner or later, just because you invited me."

The old man nodded. "And I didn't invite Mr. Crittenden," he said, "at least not directly."

"No."

"But we are different, you and I. We share a name, and when you want to find out something from me, I don't have to take the time to wonder if you have another purpose in mind besides the simple fact that you want to know something that I know already and perhaps can tell you."

"And with Buddy you think you have to wonder?" My cup was empty and I put it down beside my chair.

"Let me answer you with another question," the old man said. "Do you think you can be sure that you know when he's being a deputy sheriff and when he isn't?" He sounded serious, but there was still a smile on his face.

"I think so. But it doesn't matter. Like I say, I'd sort of like to know more about you, too."

"Why?" the old man asked, and looked at me. Shadows were stretching out across the yard.

"I'm intrigued, I guess." That's not exactly what I felt, but it was all I could think of to say.

"And I'm honored!" the old man cried, and followed with a robust laugh. "So what is it you want to know about me?"

I took a deep breath. The squirrel we had watched cross the yard was now chasing another squirrel up a sweetgum. "Okay. Was your daddy called the Rattlesnake Master, too?"

"He was, indeed," the old man said, and gave me a look that wondered how much I knew and hadn't said yet. He seemed a little taken aback, and for some reason I was surprised at that.

"And he lived down yonder on the road between Alachua and Savannah."

"Yes," the old man said, and nodded. "Yes, he did."

"Did you live there, too?" A little breeze was moving the outer branches of some of the tallest trees.

"When I was quite young," Leeman Gant said. "Well, not precisely." He took off his glasses and rubbed the bridge of his nose. "I suppose you could say I grew up there." He put his glasses back on and looked at me through them, blinking. "How do you know about my father?"

So I told him about Aunt Sandy and Buddy and me, and how Aunt Sandy had told us about the man in her neck of the woods that everybody had called the Rattlesnake Master, and how the three of us had even gone to look at what had been his house.

"Does it surprise you that I remember her?" Leeman Gant asked. "Alexandra, I mean. Though we, of course, called her Miss Alexandra. That was the custom in those days."

"No. I'm not surprised at all." And I wasn't.

The old man showed a few teeth and a pink line of gums. "She had a sister much younger than she was. That would be Mr. Crittenden's mother, am I right?"

"Yes sir."

"Ah," the old man said, and shifted his position a little. "The world is indeed an intricate place, full of patterns, and everything is akin to everything else. Don't you agree? Doesn't that strike you as true?"

"Yes sir," I said again. "Could I please have some more of this tea?"

"Certainly," the old man said, and turned his head toward the door and called for Elizabeth. When she appeared, the old man asked her to bring me more of the tea for colds, and I gave her my empty cup. The backs of Elizabeth's hands were a deep uniform brown, and her fingers and nails were immaculate, as though they had been manicured.

Neither Mr. Gant nor I said anything until she came back with my tea, although at one point he reached out to touch my arm and nod his head to show me a hawk sailing northward in great high circles. As I took my cup from Elizabeth, the old man said, "Leeman has been to your grandfather's house."

Surprise or apprehension or something in between moved around on Elizabeth's face and then was gone, but she replaced it with a look full of questions I couldn't understand. Then she asked me one I could.

"How did you know about it?" she said, and looked at her father, who was already looking placidly at her.

"He and Mr. Crittenden found it quite by accident," Leeman Gant said, answering for me. "Mr. Crittenden's mother's family lived within a few miles of your grandfather's house."

"Mmm," Elizabeth said. "So you have been there?"

"Yes," I said. "Have you?"

She and her father looked at each other. "Yes," she said, "when Papa and I came to America. But not since."

"The tea is wonderful," I said. "Thank you."

"You're welcome," Elizabeth said. "Do you need anything, Papa? I have chores to do."

"No," the old man said. "We won't call you away again." At which point Elizabeth excused herself and went back into the house, but not before the two of them had shared a look.

"Now," the old man said, rubbing his hands together, "the floor is yours again, my friend. Is your tea truly satisfactory?"

"Yes sir. I even feel better."

"Of course you do." He leaned back a little and looked at me. "Now what more may I tell you?"

The yard in front of us was more and more in shadow every time I paid attention to it, and the flower borders in front of us were completely shaded. The air was growing cool.

"Well," I said, "I don't know why your daddy left that place out there."

"He took us home," Leeman Gant said, but he thought about it first.

"To Barbados?"

"Yes. And since you will ask me why, it was because he could no longer make a living here. One day he had employment and the next day he did not, and all he could find after that was day labor—and my father was a man full of pride in himself, and he was ashamed of losing his employment at a mature age, and he was angry at his inability to do anything about it. Digging holes and plowing for people who looked down on him was something he simply could not stand, and that was all that was left to him.

"So he had us pack our belongings. By then we no longer lived in the house you saw, but had moved into Savannah. What we could not take with us was given away, and we went to Jacksonville and took passage on a merchant ship bound for Bridgetown by a circuitous route. And that was that."

"What happened when you got there?" I said. My cup was empty again. I felt light and free, as though I could fly if I tried. Ordinarily, feeling that way, I would have wanted to go home and sit down on my soft, fat sofa and take it easy, but I was taking it easy already and there was no one at home who cared if I came back, anyway. My hands were getting cold, though, so I sat on them.

What happened, Leeman Gant said, was that after their arrival, his family had lived with his father's brother's family in Bridgetown until his father found a job on a sugarcane plantation run by a

British company. Then Leeman Gant went to England and stayed for four years before returning to Barbados.

"And then after two more years, my father died," the old man went on, "and I went to work for the government. What you might call petty officialdom. But I saved money, and my wife and I became parents and lived as ordinary people."

"But you took your father's title," I said, and felt brave for it, and silly.

The old man turned to look at me. "I was given it," he said emphatically. "I earned it."

"I'm sorry I said it that way. I don't even know what being the Rattlesnake Master means."

The old man thought a minute. "People call me that. It means something different to each of them, I suppose. People need to put a name on you when you can accomplish things they cannot and when they think also that you are not only powerful but also to be trusted. And there is magic and imagination in what I am called, wouldn't you say?"

There was pride in his voice, and I thought of the way he had described his father.

"It certainly has some interesting associations."

The old man sniffed derisively and pursed his lips. "Yes," he said. "People have an exaggerated fear of snakes, especially deadly ones. So much the better, I'd say, for someone who has none whatsoever."

"When Buddy and I were out here," I said, "you told us something about people calling you the Rattlesnake Master because you can cure snakebite."

"Yes," he said, and made a cathedral spire with his fingers and rested his chin on it. "I suppose I did say that. Do you have any more questions for me?"

I thought he might be telling me that he had heard enough questions, but in spite of that I said, "Yes sir. Why did you come back to Georgia?"

The old man licked his lips. "My wife died," he said slowly, "and Barbados became a sad place for me. And I had gone all of my life until then having accomplished very little of any substance. I thought perhaps I would come to North America to see what might happen, and I came back to this part of the country because it was a place I remembered and it was a place whose people my father often spoke of with fondness. I have stayed here for many reasons, none of which would be important to you.

"Or," he added after a few seconds, "to Mr. Crittenden."

I thanked him for answering my questions because I couldn't think of anything else to say. I was getting a little cool all over now. There seemed to be a lot of story that he wasn't telling me, but then again, his life wasn't really my business. Or Buddy's either. So I excused myself and went around to the backyard past the plant beds to the outhouse and peed into the hole by the dim light of the skylight. Leeman Gant's privy had a wooden seat over the hole and real toilet paper, two sconces on the wall with candles in them, and a lock on the door.

As I rounded the side of the house past the palm trees I was trying to decide whether to say good-bye and go on home or get my jacket out of the trunk of the car and sit back down on the porch with the old man and watch the night come down. Then I noticed him standing in the doorway, talking with Elizabeth. When I got to the brickwork at the edge of the flower border, they both looked out at me over the porch.

"Leeman," the old man called, "there's a place set for you at supper."

Well, of course I tried to get out of having to stay, particularly since I've always been worried that whoever did the cooking in homes to which I was unexpectedly invited at mealtime wouldn't think that their guest, me, had some definite idiosyncrasies about what was fit to eat, though I do. And very seldom had I ever been invited to sit down to supper with black folks, the world being the way it is. Besides all that, I didn't know enough yet about Leeman Gant to decide whether I should be suspicious about him or what— since I hadn't entirely made up my mind about this Rattlesnake

Master stuff. But I still had curiosity to go on, and above all else I was comfortable at his house.

So I stayed, and we ate pork chops and rice with stewed tomatoes and talked about Barbados and the time Leeman Gant had stood in a line to meet the Queen of England. That's how I found out who Elizabeth was named for.

We ate by candlelight, though an electric lamp was lit in the corner of the room by the door, and there was more electric light, but not very much, farther back in the kitchen by the pantry. We sat at a wooden table that was a few inches too long to be called square; the furniture, what little there was of it, was mostly wooden, too.

In the living room there was an old, overstuffed pale pink sofa with enormous faded green and red flowers on it. There were shelves on all the walls, some holding books, some holding lines and piles of seashells, some holding porcelains and things shaped like birds or turtles or fish. At one end of the room flames popped and flashed in a fireplace. That sofa would have been very noticeable in its heyday, but now it blended quietly into the pervading gentle dimness of the house. Everywhere there were shadows, but none of them were deep. I found myself talking in a way I thought was too soft, but I was always heard.

After supper was cleared away and the dishes were washed, we drank tea in the living room. Again there were candles, but most of our light came from lamps on tiny tables at both ends of the sofa. Leeman Gant sat in an ancient chair with wooden arms and green print cushions, while Elizabeth and I chose opposite ends of the sofa, she knitting and me listening to the old man's stories of the islands, stories he said were handed down from the time his ancestor was brought to Trinidad from across the ocean in Africa. The tea was soothing and my stomach was full and the old man's voice was rich and mesmerizing. When I finally noticed the condition of the candles and looked at my watch, it was after eleven o'clock.

"Holy cats," I said, and sat up. "I've got to go home." Elizabeth looked at me, then at her father.

"Why not stay here?" the old man said. "Spend the night with us. It's a long way back to your side of the river and it's very late. You can have the spare room to yourself—Elizabeth sleeps on a cot in the kitchen."

They were both looking at me—the old man placidly, Elizabeth expectantly.

I didn't know what to say. I felt so peaceful there on that sofa in the shadowy room, and more at ease than I'd been in ages. But I wanted to go home, too. I like being in my own house surrounded by my own stuff.

"Leeman," the old man said gently, "please stay the night with us. We would be honored and delighted to have you here."

The room was warm, sparks were snapping in the fireplace. Who cared where I was? Nobody anywhere was expecting me that night or any other.

"All right," I said, and I saw Elizabeth relax. Maybe it was my imagination.

"I'll go turn down your bed," she said, set her knitting aside, and got up. "Papa, will you have tea before bedtime?"

"Yes," the old man said, sitting back in his chair. "Thank you." Now they were looking at each other again. "And please bring a cup for our guest as well."

When Leeman Gant said "guest," I thought of Royal Mango. He had been a guest in this house, too. He'd probably slept in the bed I had just agreed to occupy.

"I'd better not have any more tea," I said. "It's hard enough for me to get to sleep as it is."

The old man smiled benevolently. "Don't worry," he said. "This is a remarkable tea, one of my—I should say our—own making." Then, to Elizabeth: "The camomile for me, please, and for Leeman the special tea for sleep."

Elizabeth said "Yes, Papa," and went to the kitchen.

"A tea for colds," I said. "No, two of them. And now a tea for sleep. You seem to have a tea for just about everything."

The old man chuckled. "I do have a lot of them," he said, and I felt he was being proud of himself again. "But then God has given us so much to work with, there are so many things from which tea may be made, and as you know"—he smiled broadly—"Elizabeth makes superb tea."

"Yes sir," I said, and in a few minutes Elizabeth was back with our cups. My tea was hot as a volcano and tasted the way honeysuckle smells. It was a deep pink and had millions of tiny specks floating freely in it. I took a big swallow.

The room had begun to cool now that it had been a while since the old man had gotten up to poke the fire. Leeman Gant sipped his own tea and licked his lips, then we complimented Elizabeth on our teas' taste and temperature, and pretty soon I was in a bed in a Spartan little room with my bed and a miniature table and nothing else in it but a blue candle, a candlestick, and a window that looked out onto the backyard. Ruffled curtains the color of katydids hung from a rod halfway up the window; from where I lay I could look over them and see the stars.

One other thing was in my room—a chamber pot under the bed. There was no question but that I would need it sometime before the sun came up, and I already dreaded trying not to be heard throughout the rest of the silent house.

Our ancestors couldn't have been very squeamish, I thought, and then I wasn't just looking at the stars anymore, I was among them.

TWELVE

At first I was afraid to roll over and look over the edge of the bed. But I could feel the same ripply mattress under me and the same hard feather pillow under my head, so I knew that no matter how I had gotten to wherever I had gone, I was still in the bed I had started in, and that gave me some confidence.

I didn't know where I was, but my bed and I seemed to be suspended in purest black space. At respectable distances on all sides, great fiery suns were glowing red and yellow and a fierce pale blue. There was music, too, but I couldn't hear it; I seemed to resonate with it instead.

So this is what it feels like, I thought. I'm dead. Those people must have poisoned me.

But I felt so good, it didn't matter if I was dead. It just can't be helped now, I thought. And apparently God or whoever it was who did metaphysical things hadn't consigned me to a perpetual inferno, either. Everything around me—every pound, jot, tittle, and quark of the universe—seemed to be fairly electric with happiness. Me too. So I took a deep breath and let it out slowly and lay back and closed my eyes.

When I opened them, the glare off the water was so bright that I had to take my sunglasses out of the pocket of my T-shirt and put them on. I got up from the little dune I was sitting on, brushed sand from the seat of my cutoffs, and reconnoitered a little. I was on a beach, maybe even an island beach; I've been on enough of them to know. I recognized the plants—the sea rockets and sea oats and railroad vines—and I knew what the birds were, too, and the sky was full of them. Dead or alive, I figured the odds were that I was somewhere on the coast of the Gulf of Mexico.

That was good enough for me, though, so I did inventory: cap, sunglasses, knife, Kleenex, sunscreen. No question about it, this was me at the beach.

There was just a little surf; puffy white clouds were stacked all the way to the horizon over the sea. I had nowhere to go, nowhere to be, and I wondered again if I was really dead—and again it didn't matter. If I was dead, maybe I had even gone to heaven. I had certainly gone somewhere that I expected heaven to be like, and I felt young and full of life and high expectations.

It didn't take much walking to find out that I was about two hundred and fifty yards from the end of an island, all right, and across a couple of miles of blue channel I could see a bank of dunes and the green of trees behind them, so there was an island next door, too. There were markers in the channel and I wondered if even in heaven there was a danger of running onto sandbars and reefs, but then I realized that heaven wouldn't be heaven for real sailors without something to navigate around or through. If there was a sailor around, I didn't see him.

Since there was only one direction to go in and still stay along the sea, I turned around and headed westward with the breeze in my face. The air was warm and so was the water, which sure looked like the Gulf to me. The only trouble was that I really didn't know anything but that I was me and that something unusual was going on, since the last thing I remembered before this beach was traveling among the stars—and before that, nothing more portentous than going to bed on a ripply mattress in a strange house.

The fact that I had all my seashore paraphernalia made me think maybe I had been somehow involved in getting to wherever I was, though. In particular, only God and I knew that when I'm rambling on the beach I always keep a seashell in my pocket for luck at finding interesting things that have washed up. It was there now, a dark little periwinkle that I picked up long ago in Rhode Island.

It wasn't a perfect enough specimen to be displayed, but it was good enough for luck. A small voice in my head told me that luck was something I might be needing pretty soon, and not just for finding wash-ups, either.

Sanderlings were running ahead of me along the edge of the surf, stopping here and there to poke the ends of their bills into the wet sand as the water retreated. They all took off as I approached, flying in a small, tight flock away from me over the little waves. While I watched them, suddenly they veered slightly out to sea as if being cautious of something. I shifted my gaze from them to the beach and saw that I wasn't dead at all.

I was dreaming.

Two things made me believe I was having a dream. First, my field of vision now had a young woman in a two-piece yellow swimsuit in it. Second, that young woman was a sometime graduate student and full-time waitress at Cook's Restaurant named Donna Calloway.

This Donna Calloway and I had met in Cook's, which was one of the few places in Alachua that I went to after dark, and where she seemed to enjoy razzing me about bringing books to read while I ate supper. For a while she made fun of me often, almost ritually, but I appreciated the attention of a good-looking woman and made a great but very self-conscious effort to sit where she would be my waitress and could razz me to her heart's content.

She knew at least the names of some of the authors whose books I was reading, too, and that got us started in conversation. Then somehow we actually started having coffee together once in a while at the end of her shift; by the time I dreamed her on the beach we'd been doing that for several weeks. I don't even remember whose idea it was, but it gave me something to look forward to after supper besides going home and watching TV. Donna was interesting and inquisitive and funny, and talking to her always gave me as much of a boost as looking at her did. But she was twelve years younger than I was, so I left her alone.

Or maybe that was just an excuse, since not only she but in fact every woman in town was being left alone by me. Even so, Donna was pretty much the only attractive single woman I regularly had anything to do with, so she was just right for dream material. I wasn't too far asleep, or dead, or whatever I was, to realize that.

Some dream, though; even the birdshit on the beach looked real.

If Donna Calloway was attractive in a waitress's uniform, which she certainly was, she was a thermonuclear blast in a two-piece yellow bathing suit. She was waving at me, too. I turned around to make sure no one was behind me. No one was. This, I thought, is really the stuff of which dreams are made.

When I got up to her, she hugged me as though I was either the only other person left in the whole wide world or had just come from circumnavigating that world after being reported lost forever. After I got my breath back and we exchanged a rather less active hello or two, we sat down on a big black and red towel with penguins on it and she asked if I was hungry and I said no. I was busy wondering a lot of things as hard as I could.

But I did manage to feel comfortable, and she must have been at ease, too, because she moved behind me on the towel and began to massage my shoulders. It was as natural as could be and felt terrific, too, but such are dreams. If this was really a dream.

"Am I dead?" I said, not knowing what to hope for.

"No," she said, and giggled. "Don't be silly."

I was almost sorry. Okay, I really was dreaming, and sooner or later it would be over and I would have to wake up. What the hell.

"Dreaming, then," I said.

"Do you feel like you're dreaming?" Her fingers were tender and agile on my neck.

"No. Yes. I don't know. I guess I am."

"Mmm," she said. The air was warm, the wind smelled of salt and ocean, and the sunlight was bright and heavy all over me. I wanted to lie down and go to sleep, and I wondered if I could do that if I was asleep already.

"So I'm asleep," I said, and took my cap off. The top of my head was suddenly cool.

"Why do you care?" she said. "Aren't you happy here?"

"I haven't felt this good since practically forever," I said, telling the truth. "I just need to know what to expect."

"Nobody ever really knows what to expect," she said, and laid her head against my back for a few seconds.

"Besides," she went on, "you might as well call it a dream. You'll wake up, if that's what you mean, and you'll have been asleep."

I had a feeling she knew more than I did about what was going on, but I always get interesting feelings at the beach. Instead of saying that, I said, "But if it's not really a dream, then what is it? How can I be asleep while this is going on and not be dreaming?"

"Sssh," she said. "Maybe someday somebody will explain it to you. We don't have much time. Just relax. Call it a dream if you want to."

"Much time?" I said. "I'm not ready to leave. I just got here. Dream or no dream. I don't want to leave you, either." That sounded awfully funny, coming as it did from my mouth.

"You have to leave eventually," she said. "So do I. But don't worry about that right now, just being here is what's important. Trust me."

"Okay," I said, and leaned backward in her direction and put my arms behind me and as much around her as I could and pulled her against my back. It was good to feel her skin and to have her next to me, but feeling that also called up some pretty raw memories and my arms got tired anyway, so I let her go.

She began rubbing my shoulders again. "I'd like to ask you a couple of questions," she said, "but I just have to ask them, I can't explain them, too."

"Shoot," I said. Willets were high-stepping through the film of water that was sliding up onto the beach in front of us.

I heard her take a breath. "If something bad happened to somebody you didn't know, would you want to help them anyway, if you could?"

"Sure," I said. Funny question.

She rested her hands on my shoulders. "Okay. So what if someone needed your help to make up for something bad that happened a long time ago, only they fixed it so you really did help but never knew you were doing it. How would you feel?"

"If I didn't know I was doing it," I said, "how could it possibly matter?" A line of pelicans flew by over the water. "But do you mean me just helping out a good cause without ever finding out about it, or are we talking about me being sort of somebody's pawn?"

She thought a minute. "Both, I guess."

"Right now," I said, "I don't care a bit. I don't even know what we're talking about and I've already made what sounds to me like an enlistment." What the hell, I thought, saddle me up and ride me into battle. It ain't nothing but a dream.

"All right," she said, but without the enthusiasm I expected. "Thank you."

I didn't know whether to feel confused or wonderful, so I did a little of both. My head was full of the sounds of surf and the feel of the sunlight and the touch of her hands on my shoulders.

"Do you want to take a walk?" she said.

"I just took a walk," I said, and turned halfway around so I could see her face. "That's how I got here."

"Uh-huh," she said with a smirk. "Don't be a smart aleck. What I mean is, do you want to take a walk with me?"

I turned all the way around and put my hand around her ankle. When I looked at her, my stomach filled with butterflies, and I had to swallow to make them settle down.

"West?" I said. But I really wanted to stay right where I was. Something seemed to be happening between us, something I knew I could get high on and never want to come down. Still, if she wanted to walk, I'd walk to Halifax if I had to. Dreams are crazy things.

"You lead," Donna said.

So we stood up and I put on my cap and shook out the towel while she gathered her sun stuff and put it in a net bag with a couple of oranges and a visor and some other things I couldn't make out, and we headed off down the beach. She had asked her two big questions, whatever they were for, and now I had some of my own.

"What's down this way?"

"I'm not sure," she said, squinting a little. I noticed that she was lovely when she did that, but she was lovely even when she didn't. Herring gulls were floating like puddle ducks on the little blue swells offshore.

"Well, then," I said, "how'd we get here?"

"It's sort of a dream," she said teasingly. "Remember?"

"If all of my dreams felt this real," I said, "or made me feel this good, I'd go to bed earlier." The way she smiled, I could tell she knew I was complimenting her and not just the dream. Slow down, I thought, it doesn't matter. This is nothing but air. You breathe it in, you breathe it out.

But the world looked solid enough. And the day was bright and perfect. We were the only people on the beach as far as I could see. I didn't know where we were going, except west; I didn't know where there was to go to except where we were.

Then all of a sudden we weren't just walking, we were walking and holding hands.

"How do you feel?" I said.

"Real good," she said. "I like being with you."

"But you don't even know me." We were sloshing through thin sheets of warm water left by the highest waves, jumping around to dodge the jagged edges of enormous broken cockles, always being sure not to let go of each other's hand.

"Sure I do," she said. "We've had lots of talks about all kinds of stuff. You just haven't been paying as much attention as you should have. I always look forward to you coming into the restaurant. And I'm still getting to know you better, too."

"If this is just a dream," I said, trying not to sound anything but curious, "do you know if there's any sex in it?"

"Of course there isn't," she said. "I don't know you *that* well. We've never even been out. Besides, I'd have to know you had some feelings for me, too, first."

She said "too." I decided to remember to think about that later. Right then I mostly just wondered exactly what kind of dream this was, but I said, "Good for you. I had to ask." I tried to sound apologetic. "I'm still trying to figure this out."

So I figured for a couple of minutes, and I guess that's what she did, too, and then I said, "Have you always been that way?"

"Always," she said, looking at me. "I can't think of a good reason to be any other way. I guess I'm just very choosy."

"Uh-huh," I said. I didn't even know why I had asked, but I'd gotten the answer I wanted. We were passing a thick stand of cabbage palms behind the dunes. "So maybe I ought to let you know that I wouldn't tell you I had any of those feelings for you unless I really did."

"You say it as though you can't have them at all," she said, and it seemed to me that while she might have heard something different from what I meant, she might still be right.

"I've had them before," I said, "but they went away. And they've been a long time coming back."

"Nothing like a little gloom to go with the beach on a beautiful day," she said, but that was the end of this part of our conversation because I noticed a point of shell sticking out of the sand and stopped and let go of her hand and squatted down and began to dig. It was the shell of a lightning whelk and it was big enough to hold a feast of shrimp salad.

"Imagine how that would look all cleaned up and filled with shrimp salad," Donna said.

"Or oyster dressing," I said eagerly. "That's exactly what I'm thinking. Should we take it with us?"

She was splendid standing there on the white sand in her yellow suit with her hands on her hips and her hair blowing across her face. "You'll just have to carry it," she said, squinting at me in the sunlight. "And you can't take it back with you, anyway, when you wake up. You can't keep it."

"I guess not," I said, and put the whelk on the sand. I tried to memorize where it was in case this wasn't a dream after all but was really something else more permanent. If not death, maybe insanity.

As we started walking again Donna must have been thinking about lightning whelks, too, because she said something about wanting to remember what one looked like. Instead of telling her that it didn't matter because she was just acting in my dream and had no need to remember anything, I told her everything I knew about whelks in general and lightning whelks in particular, especially about their single most distinguishing trait—namely that they are sinistral, while practically all other whelks open their shells on the right.

I didn't think that was very exciting, but Donna must have liked it, because she persuaded me to tell her about nearly everything on the beach that I was familiar with. It wasn't hard for her to get me to do that, since I was so pixilated by then that I'd have tried to swim to the horizon if she'd asked me to do that instead. I just like to show off, too.

There was a lot for me to tell her about. Since this was my dream, I guess, the beach on which we were walking was littered with all sorts of things come ashore—coquinas, drills, fighting conchs, quahogs, giant cockles, egg cockles, spiny cockles, tellins, olives, figs, nutmegs, baby's ears, cones, wentletraps, limpets, scallops, pectins, rock crabs, blue crabs, spider crabs and calico crabs, an assortment of sponges, a fat gray sea cucumber, and some cannonball jellyfish.

Terns and gulls were in the air, and turnstones, willets, oyster-catchers, sandpipers, and sanderlings flew up from the waterline as we got close to where they were feeding or sleeping or being patient. There was so much to look at, and so much that Donna wanted to know about, that we weren't making much progress, but then there was nowhere to go, either.

After a while we sat down on a little ledge of sand high on the beach close to the first line of sea oats and she pulled the two oranges out of her net bag and we peeled and ate them, basking like lizards in the sunshine.

"I think we have to go soon," she said. "Have you enjoyed being with me?"

"I thought it was apparent."

She nodded. "It's nice to hear it, though. I like being with you, too. Have you ever thought about falling in love?"

"What?" I said. "Now? Us?"

"Are you making fun of me?" she said.

"No," I said. My hands were sticky with orange juice, so I rubbed them in the sand and then rubbed them together to get some of the sand off. "It's just that the last time I fell *out* of love—or got pushed out of it, whatever it was—I landed so hard that it broke my heart. I reckon it's still sore."

"Oh," she said. "I'm sorry." We weren't looking at each other.

"It'll go away," I said, probably with just a little self-pity.

Now she looked at me; I felt it and looked back at her. "Do you think you could ever fall in love with me?" she said.

Her eyes were the color of rosemary leaves. "You'd have to be different," I said.

"I *am* different!" she cried, and stood up. "I could go out all the time, but what I do is wait for you to come into the restaurant. And I wanted to have a dream with you! I *am* having a dream with you! How different do I have to be?"

"What?" I said, standing, too. "You wanted to do what?"

"I was right," she said, and seemed to be looking around for something. "We have to leave now."

"Why?" I said. "What's going on?" I thought about waking up, which was the same whether this was a dream or something else entirely, and it didn't seem like a very good idea.

"This part is finished," she said. "If you were here for the same reasons I am, you'd know we'd done most of what we came for." She looked away from me and out over the water toward the horizon. "It's beautiful here, isn't it? Everything's so peaceful. This beach must have come from you. I'm glad you like places like this."

"Uh-huh," I said. I couldn't wonder long about what she was saying. I had things to say, too, and maybe she was right, maybe time was running out.

"Will I ever see you again?" I said. "Where are we going?"

"We'll see each other," she said, turning back around to look at me. "But who knows what will happen? Most of it's up to you.

Who knows what we'll even remember about this? And only you know where you're going now, I don't. All I know is that I'm going to be in bed when I wake up, listening to the rain fall. Alone."

"I guess I'm going back to the Rattlesnake Master's house," I said, and held out my hand and she took it. I wanted her to keep it.

"Good-bye," she said, and squeezed my hand.

"Wait," I said. "Why did you ask me those questions? I mean the one about falling in love, the stuff about you and me, and those first two questions way back there, the ones I didn't really understand, that business about if I would mind helping somebody when I didn't know about it."

She looked at me and wrinkled her nose and smiled. "I told you," she said. "Because it's my dream, too."

Then I was in darkness and could hear voices far away.

A woman said, "He is coming back."

A man said, "Yes, I see. We must speak softly."

"He will do it," the woman said.

"Yes," the man said again. "It will be interesting to see how it works between us, between him and me. And her—what was she doing there? Why was it her?"

"It was her dream, too," the woman said. "You had questions and she had questions. She asked them. But only yours were all in words."

"Efficient, very efficient," the man said appreciatively.

"Thank you," the woman said.

Then I heard palm fronds rustling against the house in the wind, scraping the tin roof. That's why I dreamed about the ocean, I thought, but I knew I was still asleep.

I was, too, and didn't think of anything else that I know of until noises from the kitchen woke me and I smelled coffee and bacon in the air in the cool house. I could see through the window that it was overcast and raining.

So I got up and put on my clothes and made my bed, remembering to check the chamber pot, which was empty. I hadn't been up during the night. Except to go to the beach, I thought, and tried briefly to decide what my dream was all about. But I never got past the obvious answer that some of it meant only that I had been too long without the close company of women. Maybe the beach part of it meant I needed a vacation. I figured I did; when I thought of going back to my warm little Sunday-morning house in Alachua, it seemed like being called to the black hole of Calcutta.

For breakfast Elizabeth had fixed sausage gravy and biscuits, thick slabs of bacon, and hot coffee with chicory. There were blackberry jelly and cane syrup for the biscuits we didn't put gravy on.

I had the last piece of biscuit and syrup in my mouth when the old man put down his coffee and said, "So what will you say to Mr. Crittenden?"

I swallowed. "Just what we talked about yesterday," I said. "Your daddy. All that. He'll be curious."

"So I expect," the old man said. He wiped his mouth and laid his napkin on the table. A particularly strong gust of wind shook the little house. "Do you think he will be satisfied?"

"I don't see why not," I said. Elizabeth excused herself, got up, and began clearing the table. "What else could he possibly want to know? And anyhow, what does it matter?"

The old man put his elbows on the table and made a cathedral with his fingers. Instead of answering my questions, he said, "Do you think of Crittenden as an intelligent man?"

"I suppose so," I said, and drank a sip of my coffee and chicory. It was barely warm. "If there's something he can't figure out, he gets real restless until he does. And he's pretty sharp at putting pieces together."

The old man's eyes unfocused a little, and he was quiet for a minute. I wondered what I'd told him to make him think so hard. Elizabeth was running water in the sink, and I heard a pump come on somewhere.

Leeman Gant's eyes drew back in on me. "Well," he said, "I suppose those are good qualities for a deputy sheriff to possess.

Granted, they are not necessarily the same attributes I have generally come to associate with deputy sheriffs around here."

"I think he'd agree," I said, and drained my cup. "Are you worried about what Buddy thinks of you?"

"No," the old man said immediately. "I am deciding what to think of him. Help me for a minute. Would you say that he believes first in the law, or in justice? Do you know what I mean?"

I knew exactly what he meant, and I knew exactly what to say.

"Yes. Yes, I understand you, I mean. And I think Buddy wants law to serve the cause of justice."

"And when it doesn't?" the old man said. He leaned back a little in his chair and put his hands in a heap on the tabletop in front of him.

"Papa," Elizabeth said. She was drying her hands. The old man and I looked at her, but she didn't say anything else.

"I don't know," I said. "I expect he would pick justice."

"Ah," the old man said.

"Papa," Elizabeth said again. "It's getting late."

The old man pulled a bull's-eye watch from his pants pocket and looked at it over his glasses, raising his eyebrows as far as they would go.

"You'll have to excuse us, my boy," he said, looking back at me and returning the watch to his pocket. "Mrs. Tuttle and Mrs. Washington will be here shortly to take us to church. And we also must prepare for visitors coming this afternoon, if the rain doesn't discourage them."

So in a little flurry of conversation about the rain I got up and said my good-byes, remembering to thank them for the tea for colds, which seemed to have done its job. When I turned right at Turleyville and headed back toward the county line and home, I thought to myself that I should have said something to the old man about the tea for sleep, too. I couldn't remember a set of dreams so real or so, well, memorable. If he had made them happen, then I should have said thank you.

THIRTEEN

It was still raining on Tuesday night when I walked into Cook's Restaurant out of a twilight that really didn't seem much darker than the rest of that miserable day had been. Buddy was already sitting in a booth with a cup of coffee in front of him. There was a cigarette butt in the ashtray.

"Looks like you've been here awhile," I said, hanging up my rain jacket and sliding into the seat opposite him.

"I figured we were about to get some more rain," Buddy said, "so I came early. Glad you could make it."

"You must've had the day off, too," I said, looking past his shoulder toward the cash register and down the hall beyond it to the kitchen. I was trying to figure out who our waitress would be.

"Uh-huh," Buddy said. "I'm gone work for Lamar on Saturday so he and his wife can go off somewhere, so we swapped and he worked today. I mostly just piddled around, though."

"Which one is ours?" I said, nodding toward the kitchen.

"The brunette."

"They're all brunette in this place except for that sort-of blonde."

"The one at the coffee urn."

One of them at the coffee urn was Donna Calloway. I remembered my dream about her for the thousandth time since Sunday, and when I did, my stomach made a little leap.

"There's two of them at the coffee urn," I said. "Which is she, the one with the scarf around her head, or"—I put a leer on my face—"the one with the ripe, luscious young body?"

"Ours is the one with the body," Buddy said, and grinned more than I'd have expected. "She'll be over here in a minute. I told her to keep an eye out for you."

So our waitress was Donna, all right, but for some reason I decided against telling Buddy I knew her. In fact, what I thought about most was staying behind after Buddy left to see if she was getting off at a reasonable hour—and, if so, if she was interested in conversation.

She was at our booth in less than a minute with a cup of coffee and cream for me. I wondered if Buddy noticed that she knew what I wanted, but he didn't seem to. I couldn't help looking at her, and I couldn't help thinking of my dream, the one that she said was her dream as well as mine. I was looking at her differently, too, but I couldn't say exactly how. It wasn't just the way she looked, either, though she was more than just pretty, and her eyes were bright and quick. No, there was something else, something new, going on. For some reason I felt I knew her better than I had known her before I spent Saturday night in the Rattlesnake Master's house. But all I had done was have a dream with her in it.

As she put my cup on the table Donna looked straight at me and smiled. My ears got hot. I thought she might have blushed, too, but I couldn't think of a reason for her to do that.

Buddy grinned, then reached out and put his hand on Donna's elbow. She looked at me again and giggled this time. "Donna," he said, "this is my friend Leeman. Leeman, this is Donna Calloway. She's my cousin."

Hells' bells. I suppose that when Buddy said that about her being his cousin my mouth must've dropped open, because Donna's face told me she was waiting for me to say something. But I didn't.

So she said, "We've met," and smiled at us both.

"I'm a regular here," I said quickly. My face was on fire.

Neither Donna nor I got around to telling Buddy that we'd been sitting together sometimes after her shift ended. I didn't think I wanted Buddy to know that, either, since he and Donna were cousins. It would probably make him suspicious of what I was doing, when I wasn't doing anything at all. Good thing, too, that I hadn't told him about my dream.

Donna took out her pad and pencil.

"I can't talk now," she said apologetically. "We're real busy and Miz Cook will chew me out if I'm not hopping around here like a worm on hot ashes. Do y'all know what you want?"

We did, and we placed our orders and Buddy took out a cigarette while I watched Donna walk away and thought novel thoughts. They were novel in that I had never made her the object of them before except overnight at Leeman Gant's house; they were thrilling, too, because I hadn't heard from them in a long time. I was thinking of something she seemed to stand for, maybe something like a way life just might turn out, if you were lucky. Something that was far, far from me.

"Hello," Buddy said. "Where are you?"

"Sorry," I said. "I was thinking."

"Somebody'd better," he said, and had a sip of coffee.

Donna had been back twice and Buddy and I were well into our suppers before I said, "Guess where I went last weekend?"

"Springfield," Buddy said. "Luckenbach, Texas. Rangoon."

"None of the above," I said smugly. "I went out yonder to see the Rattlesnake Master."

"No shit," Buddy said, and wiped his mouth with his napkin. "So tell me about it."

"Well," I said, "there ain't much, but this is it in a nutshell: that *was* his daddy down yonder past your aunt Sandy's old home place. And just like we thought, his daddy came from Barbados and went back there when he lost his job and couldn't find anything else he was satisfied with. Not a long time ago, either, but I didn't ask just when. And Mr. Gant basically says he came back because he liked it here. Amen."

"He *liked* it here," Buddy said theatrically. "Is that what he told you?"

For just a second I tuned him out and listened to the sounds of eating going on around us. Buddy was mocking me just a little and I didn't like it. After all, I was the one who went to Turleyville.

"Uh-huh," I said.

Buddy folded his napkin and put it beside his empty plate. His tongue was busying itself on a couple of his teeth, and through his cheek it looked like a cat playing under the bedclothes.

"He convinced you that's all it was?"

"All what was?"

"That he came back here because he liked it," Buddy said. "What did he like? Ain't much of nothin' out there where they live, and it gets colder here than it does in Barbados."

"Hell," I said. "I don't know, all I know is what he told me, and I told you that already. I didn't go out there just to ask him a lot of pointed questions for you."

"You see anybody else come out there? Maybe some white people?"

"He and Elizabeth said some people were coming out on Sunday afternoon," I said, "if the weather wasn't too bad. But I didn't see anybody, and I dunno who the people coming were. What're you drivin' at?"

Buddy took out a cigarette and lit it with a lighter with an armadillo on it. "Nothin'," he said. "I'm still lookin' for something to drive at. J. B. Barrett was tellin' me there was even some white people from up this way goin' down to see the old feller. For some of that equal opportunity advice or something." Buddy snorted. "Just you there, huh?"

"Yep," I said. I put my knife and fork on my plate and pushed the whole business aside. Maybe Donna would come back if she saw we were finished eating.

"You say anything to him about Mango?" Buddy asked. "Or whether Mango said anything to him about some silver dollars or a couple of peckerwoods that was lookin' for him?"

"No. Should I have?"

Buddy sighed. "I dunno," he said. "I reckon I'd damn sho have asked him if it'd been me."

"Yeah," I said defensively, "but that's nothin' but the cop in you showing through. And besides, I didn't go all the way out there just to get your questions answered, I went out there because he invited me back."

"Why you reckon he did that?" Buddy said, and blew smoke into the air above us. "What is it you got besides his first name?"

"Beats me. But if you want to talk to him about cop stuff, why don't you get one of them Bulloch County bulletheads to go down there with you, so as to make you legal, and ask him yourself?"

"Because I don't think he'd tell me, for one thing," Buddy said. He took a drag from his cigarette and stubbed out what remained in the ashtray. "And besides, I don't want to cause him no trouble. He ain't done nothin' wrong except maybe keep his mouth shut when there was something I wanted to hear. And even more than that, I ain't really got the time to mess with it. If Harold Buckminster gets beat up again over Mango or something else like that happens, then maybe we'll see."

Donna appeared, and the three of us made small talk while she cleared the table. She asked about dessert and we both refused, but I did point out that my cup was empty. I wanted her to come back soon and fill it. It was all right just to watch her work. I was doing a lot of that, too, when I didn't think Buddy was looking.

I had had another cup of coffee and we had seen the bill before Buddy said, "I didn't mean to get onto you about not asking old man Gant about Mango. It's just that something about him sort of bothers me, y'know. Maybe he just intrigues me more than anything else. There's stuff going on down there that I don't understand, and that makes me itchy."

"Maybe this Mango got those dollars from him," I said. "From Mr. Gant, I mean."

"Maybe," Buddy said. "I don't suppose it matters. You think you'll be goin' back out there?"

"Eventually. Probably."

"If you do, lemme know before you go, willya?"

"Sure," I said, "if I go."

When we left the restaurant, Donna smiled at me and said,

"Come back," and I told her I would, but for the first time I considered the possibility that she wasn't just being polite. The rain had stopped, leaving the air cool and fresh. The few cars on Abercrombie Street, where Buddy and I stood on the sidewalk outside Cook's, made hissing noises on the pavement as they went by. I was going left, Buddy right.

"Wait a minute," Buddy said. "I almost forgot, and I promised I'd tell you. George Ramsey, you remember him, he was askin' me about somebody to do somethin' for him out at his place, that house he bought out in the country, and I told him you might be able to help him. You and Campbell, really."

"Out there at that place with the holes?" I said. Mist was beginning to blow through the air. "And what kind of help? I ain't really open to the idea of bein' a night watchman lookin' out for people with shovels or nothing like that. I ain't got enough spare time."

"That ain't it," Buddy said. "I'll wait and let him tell you. Maybe he'll change his mind, even. But it ain't much, maybe you'll have some fun."

"All right," I said. "If he calls, I'll talk to him."

So we said our good nights and I started off down the hill toward Magnolia Street and my quiet little house.

"Hey!" Buddy hollered. "Hey!"

"What?" I hollered back, turning around.

"Call Campbell, willya?"

So I called Sam Campbell later that night and told him he might get a call from George Ramsey.

"I already did," Sam said. "Lots of help you are."

"It's Buddy's fault," I said. "He was supposed to tell you."

Sam made a funny noise. "Anyhow," he said, "your tardiness notwithstanding, what George wants is for you and me to do some digging."

"For what?" I said.

"George has got the notion that there might be something

valuable stashed away out there somewhere on that land he bought. You remember, he kept finding holes dug all over the place where somebody'd been looking for something. He says if there's something worth digging for out there, he wants to find it first."

"Sounds pretty farfetched to me," I said.

"Yeah. But he's willing to pay."

"I like it better now. But what if we run into them other guys out there, the ones that must've been digging those holes? I reckon they and we're looking for the same thing."

"If we see anybody, all we'll do is run like hell," Sam said. "But naw, nobody's going to bother us. Nobody who's up to something would even want us to see them. So whatcha think?"

I could hear Anne, Sam's daughter, screeching in the background.

"If he calls," I said, "I'll talk to him."

"Well, you better hang up," Sam said. "Anne, get off of there! Sorry. George is probably trying to call you right this minute."

He wasn't, though, and pretty soon I went to bed. I was still thinking about Donna.

When George Ramsey called me at the college the next day, he told me pretty much what I already knew from talking to Sam, except that George Ramsey told me what he was willing to pay us by the hour, which wasn't great, but it wasn't bad, either.

"Sam said he'd do it," George Ramsey said, "and who knows— maybe y'all might even find something. And I'd appreciate it. Either way, I could stop worryin' about how maybe there's something out there. Confederate gold. Somebody's family silver." He laughed. "Think of it as a lark."

I didn't say anything right away. I was trying to think of tromping around George Ramsey's hundred acres—that used to be old man Calvin Hutto's hundred acres—as a lark. There wasn't much alive in the woods at that time of year, and certainly no wildflowers. Not much to look at.

"You want more money? Is that it?" George Ramsey said.

"No. Just pay us by the hour and give us each ten percent of whatever we find."

"Okay. It's a deal. And if you don't find anything, I'll throw in supper on me at the Ogeechee Grille."

"A deal," I said.

So we talked it over and I found out the boundaries of George Ramsey's place, and got his telephone number and his assurance that it didn't matter when we went out there to start looking for whatever it was we were looking for, as long as it was soon. I also found out that he didn't mind what we did to look for it except to please not tear up anything or cut down any trees, which I wouldn't have done, anyway. George Ramsey said, too, just to remember that someone else might be trying to beat us to it, whatever it was, heh-heh.

"What if somebody has already beaten us to it?" Sam said. We were standing in George Ramsey's backyard admiring the job Alfred Robbins—though we didn't know his name then, or that he had switched part-time employers practically at the same time the house changed owners from Anita Hutto Scalesi to George Ramsey—had done keeping the place up.

"Then we still get a little money and we eat free at the Ogeechee Grille," I said. "Which way do you want to go?"

"The least he could've done is say he'd take us down to Savannah to the Pirate's House, or something," Sam said. "I've already eaten everything they've got at the Ogeechee Grille. Twice."

"Me too," I said, "except the country fried steak and the onion rings. Which way do you want to go?"

"Toward home," Sam said, looking at the woods in front of us. "But as long as we're here, let's go through these pines first. There's not as much underbrush and briars as on some of the rest of the place."

Maybe two-thirds of George Ramsey's woodlot was in pine trees, and that's where Sam Campbell and I spent most of a partly cloudy Sunday afternoon, walking and looking.

"I wish to God I knew what I was looking for," Sam said. We had been sight-seeing for nearly three hours and had stopped for a few minutes to pee and eat some raisins. The weather was cool; we were both wearing sweaters. Sam had on a brown vest, besides.

Sam took off his cap and scratched the top of his head. I could see his scalp. His hair was too short, had been too short—his wife said—ever since he came home from Vietnam, but Sam professed to like it that way and said it meant he could still go to cheap barbers, too.

"I can't tell any one of these dern trees from any other one," he said. "Every foot of these woods looks alike. Nothing but pine straw and broken limbs and sand and dead weeds and toadstools. Shoot, if anybody ever did hide anything out here, they'd never be able to find it again."

"Maybe we should get a metal detector," I said.

"That's it," Sam said, and he stood up from the pine straw he'd been sitting on, undid his belt, and began to tuck in his shirt. "Depend on you to have a good idea when it's too late for us to do anything about it."

"I'm sorry," I said. "But I don't know anybody who's got one, anyhow."

"As a matter of fact," Sam said, "I know a couple people that have them."

"Well, get one, then," I said. Crows were talking back and forth in the trees between us and the house. "Maybe we'll find an old plow or something General Sherman threw out when he came through on his way to Savannah. It'll beat kicking over every puff-ball and anthill we come across just to see what's under it."

"Suits me," Sam said. "Next time. Maybe next Sunday."

But the next Sunday was cold and rainy, and Sam and I didn't get back to the place George Ramsey bought from Anita Hutto Scalesi for two weeks. We probably wouldn't have gone then, either, since I was feeling particularly indolent, except that George Ramsey called Sam and then me to ask if we couldn't go on back again real soon, even if for just one more time, just to be sure we went over the whole acreage.

So we went back out there, and we had a nice warm day to do it in, too. Sam brought along a metal detector he'd borrowed the week before from somebody else who works at the college, and we both had broad trowels for digging. Before we even got out of George Ramsey's yard the machine beeped up a bolt and a six-inch piece of barbed wire.

Neither of us had any desire to go back over the ground we'd been on the last time, but there was quite enough left to cover. This end of George Ramsey's property had mostly grown up in hardwoods—scrub oaks and sweetgums, with some maples—though the only ones of respectable size were grouped together around what George Ramsey said was the site of a farmhouse that he understood had been built in the nineteenth century and had burned down sometime around 1935.

"Dandy," Sam said, adjusting his cap. "We'll be digging up rusty nails every ten feet around those trees."

But for the first hour and a half or so we didn't do much of anything but increase our acquaintance with the layout of George Ramsey's woods, though the sunlight coming through the branches was pleasant and the understory was home to birds of several pleasantly noisy sorts.

Nothing more exciting than having to stop once in a while and untangle the metal detector from vines and bamboo briars happened until we suddenly came up on an enormous red oak sitting in a stand of smaller trees not a quarter its age. Its branches were nearly as thick and sprawling as a live oak's, and there was nothing growing under them except a few scraggly bayberry bushes.

"How come you reckon this one got left here?" Sam said. I was pleased to hear him say "reckon," just like a native, and pointed it out.

"Never mind that," Sam said, and nodded at the ground. "Look, George's pals have been here ahead of us."

The fat old oak must have had a dozen fairly recent holes dug on all sides of it, as far out as eight feet or so from the trunk. I felt a little uneasy but didn't say so.

"And what's worse," Sam went on, "maybe they beat us to the loot."

Sure enough, one hole was much broader than the rest, though not any deeper than most. I got down on my hands and knees and dug a little dirt from the bottom of the hole with my trowel. My fingers touched something hard and cold.

"It's still in here, whatever it is," I said.

"Hoo boy," Sam said. "Lemme see. What you got?"

"A rock," I said, and stood up. "They were digging along the top of a rock. It must've taken them longer than us to decide that's what it was."

Sam snorted and began scanning the ground around the big tree with the metal detector. A few early honeybees were crawling in and out of a hole about ten feet up the trunk.

But all we found was a couple of empty Budweiser cans that must have been left by our competition, and Sam saw them long before he put the detector over one of them just to hear it squawk.

When we'd finished going over the ground around the tree, we moved off about fifty yards—just in case the people who had dug the holes did decide to come back ("Maybe they want to recycle those beer cans," Sam said)—and sat on a couple of stumps and ate the Vienna sausages and granola bars we had brought to sustain us on our expedition.

"Those guys, whoever they are, had a good idea," Sam said after a while. He had a granola bar in his mouth and sounded like Demosthenes talking around pebbles.

"What?" I said. "Shovels?"

"Shoot," Sam said. "So that's what we forgot." He took the granola bar out of his mouth, set it beside him on the stump, and bent over to retie one of his bootlaces. "But no, not that. We've been up and down this place and haven't seen anything in the ground but a rabbit hole or two, and then lo and behold, we come to a tree bigger than anything else in the vicinity, and there's holes all around it so new they haven't even been rained in yet."

"Landmarks."

"That's right," Sam said, straightening up. "If you had something to bury, wouldn't you pick a spot that'd be easy for you to find when you went back to get whatever it was you hid?"

"Sure. But maybe that's too simple. Even those other guys—and us too—figured that out."

"Maybe," Sam said. "But I bet most people who bury stuff don't figure on a bunch of yahoos trooping around behind them with shovels and plastic mine detectors, either."

"So tell me what you're gettin' at."

"Just that we might make our lives a lot easier if we look around the big stuff, the rocks and the biggest trees, first. It's the logical thing to do."

"Ain't no rocks on the surface out here but little ones," I said. "And as far as I can tell, there aren't any trees like the one we just left till over yonder where George Ramsey says that old house used to be."

"Then I say that's where we go next," Sam said, and belched. "Yagh. Do I really have to taste those sausages twice?"

He wadded up his trash and put it in a little white plastic bag and we both stretched out an arm and he handed the bag to me. I put my trash in it, too, and tied the end of the bag in a knot and stuffed the whole business into my back pocket. It wasn't much, but the two smashed Vienna sausage cans promised to be annoying if I had to sit down again before we reached a dumpster.

"And after that," Sam said, and paused to yawn broadly. "And after that we go home. I'm ready to see my wife."

As soon as I stopped yawning, too, I agreed with him and we got up and tromped through the woods, which was colored in light greens and browns and virtually weedless except for random tangles of bamboo briars, till we came to four more huge red oaks.

Three of them had dark, furrowed trunks and gnarled, spreading branches, but the fourth was in ruins. Most of its main trunk was still standing, but only one short, lean branch stuck out near the top. A broad gash running down the middle of the trunk had been open for years and showed marks of having been worked on by generations of woodpeckers. The ground under our feet was crisp with last summer's leaves.

"I reckon the house was out in here somewhere," Sam said, and pointed the metal detector through a broad arc in front of him.

"Uh-huh, and the fire that got the house must've gotten this tree, too."

"Right. Where do you figure the living room was? Maybe somebody dropped some money behind the sofa cushions and it stayed there when the sofa burned up."

"If anybody was still livin' here," I said. "You see where the old road was?"

"Back that way," Sam said, giving his head a jerk. "It's lower than the rest of the ground, otherwise you might couldn't tell, it's so grown over."

"Where does it come out?" A white-throated sparrow was whistling mournfully somewhere in the distance.

"Damn if I know exactly. George says it leads to some little dirt road about a quarter of a mile away, and then that one runs around and around through people's farms till it hits the back road from Alachua to Swainsboro."

"Wait a minute," I said. Sam was nosing the detector around one of the trees. "What if that's how whoever is diggin' them holes gets in and out of here?"

"Then the next time they come through there, they'll see where two guys with a metal detector smashed down the ground," Sam said. He fiddled with a knob on the detector. "Wonder if this thing's working?" He walked over to me, stuck the head of it onto my belt buckle, and the machine let out an ear-busting shriek. I jumped, and so did Sam.

"Yep," Sam said, and laughed. "I guess it is."

"C'mon," I said. "Let's get to it and get it over with. I ain't going home to a wife, but I was planning to get back in time to go eat supper at Cook's before they close."

"In that case, we'd best be about it. You'll need an extra hour, at least."

"How do you figure that?" I said, and what I thought about was Donna.

"So you'll have time to get your stomach pumped out," Sam said, "and still get to bed at a reasonable hour. Hee-hee."

Instead of laughing, I moved off to what must once have been the periphery of the yard the defunct house had stood in and started looking for something, I wasn't sure what, while Sam strolled around the old oaks with the detector. There wasn't much of a foundation left to mark where the house had been, though there were a couple of piles of rocks that once might have been part of a chimney, and bits of brick were scattered through the litter of leaves.

I had stopped to pull a strand of briars off the leg of my jeans when I heard Sam holler and then say, "shit," followed by a terrific clatter of something breaking. When I turned around, Sam was out of sight.

So I hollered, too, and asked him where he was.

I could barely hear Sam answer, but I still didn't know anything more, so I walked back to where the four oaks were and hollered again.

"Sam!" I shouted. Then a little softer, "What the hell?"

"Leeman!" Sam hollered. "C'mere and help me get out of this thing!"

I followed his voice past the largest oak and then saw a mass of briars with a metal detector in it and the top of Sam's head sticking out of the ground.

"Sam?"

The top of his head swiveled in my direction. "Here, boy," he said, and one of his arms came out of the ground, too. "I think I've found where the well was."

In a few seconds I was standing over the hole Sam was in. He was streaked with dirt and humus.

"Jesus, Sam," I said. "That thing could have been a hundred feet deep."

"Well, it's not," Sam said. "But it stinks in here. I must not've been watching where I stepped. I was trying to get that dang detector untangled from some brambles. . . ."

"Briars," I said. "They got your cap, too."

"Briars, schmiars," Sam said. I could see him down about as far as his knees, where the overhanging debris cut off the sunlight. "When I planted my foot, I guess these old boards just gave way."

He patted a piece of wood at his shoulder. "They were under so many dead leaves and other crap on the ground that I never even saw 'em till I was going through."

Sam's descent had made a jagged hole through four or five rotted planks that apparently had been laid over the hole where the well had been.

"Good thing somebody filled it in, almost," I said. "You need a hand?"

"I'd rather have wings. Help me get these crummy old boards out of the way, though, and I think I can climb out."

So Sam grabbed at a couple of the planks and I squatted down and did the same, and gradually the hole around him got a little bigger and more light went in.

"C'mon," Sam said. "I don't know how steady this stuff is that I'm standing on down here."

"Keep your shirt on," I said. "There's spiders and shit on these planks, and a centipede just fell in there with you."

"Yuck, I hate centipedes," Sam said, and peered apprehensively down at his feet. "Uh, Leeman?" he said.

I was bent around throwing a piece of plank out of the way. "What?" I said.

"Look here," Sam said, and I did. One of Sam's feet was planted on a small pile of dull gray coins. Remains of the bag they had been in unfolded raggedly around them.

"I think we hit pay dirt," Sam said gleefully. He wasn't facing me straight on, but I could see him grin.

"Holy cats," I said. My heart went pitty-pat. "The whole damn hole is full of them! Look at all the bags!"

Sam raised his other foot, the one not surrounded by what I could tell were silver dollars, put it in another spot, and squatted down in the hole. When he stood up again he had a dirty bag in his hand, holding it underneath.

"Some of these bags look pretty rotten," he said, "but this one is just a little decrepit." He raised the bag as if to put it on the ground beside the hole. His shirt sleeves were filthy, and so was his face. I could see where sweat had run down it.

"Here," I said, "give it to me." But as Sam tried to reach up to where I was leaning over the edge, the weight of the bag shifted between his hands and mine and the bag fell back toward him, its top open and silver dollars pouring out. I could hear them rattling and clinking against each other as they fell into the bottom of the hole.

"Shitfire," I said.

Sam looked down. "Puke," he said. "It busted open. There's money all over the place down here."

"Maybe you better hand the next one back this way," said a voice behind me. "I damn sho ain't gone drop it."

FOURTEEN

hat I saw when I turned around to see who had spoken was an ugly redheaded guy in a gray plaid shirt and blue jeans that didn't come down far enough over his boots. Behind him was another guy, a little bit skinnier, with curly black hair. That one was holding a maddock in one hand and a shovel in the other. I had seen them both before. In fact, I had seen Buddy Crittenden hit the redheaded one with his fist.

"That's it, now," said Jerry Spivey. "Both of you just sort of hold your position. That is, unless you want this other feller over here to lay that maddock on yo heads a few times." He laughed.

Sam was looking up expectantly at Jerry Spivey from the hole in the ground. I was trying not to look at anything in particular, but for a second I looked at who I later found out was Sperry Bissell, and he was already looking at me.

"C'mon," Jerry Spivey said. "Hand me one of them sacks. Let's see what you jamokes done discovered." Sam looked down into the hole, toward his feet and the bags of silver dollars.

"Jerry," said Sperry Bissell, "I know one of them." I wondered what good it would do to run. Sam was still in the hole.

"Yeah?" Jerry Spivey said, and turned from Sam to Sperry Bissell. "Which is it?"

"The one there," Sperry Bissell said, and pointed the maddock at me. "He was in the car with that deputy sheriff the day you and me run over that snake. The day we was taking that bag of—"

"Shut up," Jerry Spivey said. "I got it." He grinned, looked at me, and spat on the ground. About the time his spit went *plop* on the dry leaves, I stood up.

"Yeah," Jerry Spivey said. "That sho do make a lot of things clear, don't it?"

I didn't see what it made clear at all, but I still had nothing to say.

"Well, well," Jerry Spivey said. He was still grinning.

"What snake?" Sam said.

"I told you about it," I said. My throat was dry and I didn't know if Sam could hear me or not. "When Buddy and I were coming home from fishing that time and he pulled these two guys over because he said they ran over a snake."

Sam looked up at Jerry Spivey. "Okay," he said. "So who're you and what're you doing out here?" He put his hands on the ground at his shoulders and started to hoist himself out of the hole.

"Whoa, brother," Jerry Spivey said, and motioned for Sperry Bissell to come up beside him, which he did. Sam stopped just as he was flexing his arms and dropped back into the hole. I heard the sound of silver under his feet.

"What we're doin' out here ain't really none of yo damn business," Jerry Spivey said to Sam. "I just might have a little business to discuss with yo friend here before me and Sp—before me and this other feller get through, but that'll wait. Right now you just gone have to live in that hole a little longer."

Sam looked at me and I shrugged.

"I thought I told you to gimme one of them bags," Jerry Spivey said. Sam turned to look at him, then back at me.

"Why not?" I said.

"Back off yonder," Jerry Spivey said to me, "and then don't even move a muscle. Sp—aw, the hell with it. Sperry, you c'mere and watch this 'un. If he so much as flinches, give 'im one with that shovel."

Sperry Bissell stuck the maddock in the ground and moved over between me and Jerry Spivey. "Just blink, motherfucker," he said, looking at me with more dumb meanness than anyone had ever looked at me with before, "and we'll put you in that hole and leave you there forever. Yo pal the big tough deputy is a long way off this time."

"You guys are out of your minds," Sam said.

"Watch yo mouth," Jerry Spivey said, "or maybe you'll never get out that hole atall."

The woods seemed very still, or maybe it's just that I hadn't been listening to anything besides what was right in front of me. Then I heard a car go by on the road past George Ramsey's house and tried stupidly to figure out how far away it was. The next thing I'll do, I thought, is throw up. Then I'll run like hell.

But I couldn't run. Sam was still in that hole.

"Come *on*," Jerry Spivey said to Sam, "get on with it! We ain't come out here to look at your goddamned face starin' up out of the goddamned ground."

Sam turned back and looked at me and I shrugged again. From where I was, all I could see of him was his head and shoulders. Then they disappeared. When they came back, I could see Sam's hands and arms, too, and he had another ratty bag.

Jerry Spivey laughed. "That crazy old Hutto," he said. " 'Scuse me, my dear departed goddaddy. No wonder he couldn't get at them dollars. Gimme that sack, man."

He squatted down at the edge of the old well and took the bag from Sam, holding it with one hand at the top and the other underneath. Then he duckwalked backward a couple of feet, put the bag on the ground, and pulled eagerly at the rotten drawstring.

He fairly tore the bag open and stuck his left hand in it. We were all watching him.

Suddenly Jerry Spivey's mouth dropped open and his eyes got as round as doubloons. Then he was standing up and stumbling backward, his left arm stretched out in front of him. A rattlesnake maybe two feet long was hanging from his wrist.

Jerry Spivey screamed.

Then a lot of things happened at the same time. Jerry Spivey leaped backward some more, yelling in a shrill hysterical voice and shaking his arm. The snake dropped off and I heard it hit the ground, though I didn't see where it went. Jerry Spivey went further backward and sat down on the ground, holding his wrist, his eyes wide and staring. I could see blood on his fingers.

I was also the only one not moving.

When the snake left Jerry Spivey's wrist, Sperry Bissell ran over to him, flinging down the shovel in front of the hole. About the time the shovel hit the ground, Sam Campbell shot out of the well like a rocket and grabbed the shovel and hit Sperry Bissell in the meat of the back as hard as he could. That meant that Sperry Bissell, who was in the process of dropping to one knee beside Jerry Spivey, talking to him, asking him to "stop yellin', c'mon, stop," fell over onto Jerry Spivey and pinned him to the ground.

Then Sam Campbell and Jerry Spivey were talking at the same time.

"Get off me, you goddamned idiot!" Jerry Spivey said, meaning Sperry Bissell. It was a relief to have him stop screeching, even if it meant he hollered instead.

"If you so much as raise up to your knees, fella," Sam Campbell said, also meaning Sperry Bissell, "I'll bash your skull in."

I went over and picked up the maddock and stood beside Sam, trying to look deadly. It would have been nice to brain one of those two goons, certainly.

"Let me up!" Jerry Spivey yelled. Sperry Bissell's left ear was in an ideal position to be yelled into. "Let him get up!"

"Don't either of you move an inch," Sam said. "I'm thinking it over."

"I've got to get to a *doctor*!" Jerry Spivey shouted. His voice was beginning to break. "I been snakebit, god dammit!"

Sam and I reflexively looked around to see where the snake was. I didn't see it, and he didn't say anything.

"Jerry, stop yellin' in my ear," Sperry Bissell said. It was hard to hear him, since he was talking into the ground.

"Oh God, Christ," Jerry Spivey said in a high-pitched voice. "My arm hurts like hell. You got to let me up. *Please.*"

"Okay. Get up real slow," Sam said, "one at a time. Real slow, now. And then both of you run off down that old road. Don't even look back. First one of you so much as looks at me or Leeman gets to stay here and get hurt some more. Don't say anything, either, just get up and go when I tell you to." He planted his feet apart. My hands were sweaty on the maddock, and it was heavy.

But everything happened the way it was supposed to, Sam saying "Now get up and run," and the two men getting up slowly and then loping and running and dodging around little trees on their way away from us down the old road until they were out of sight.

Sam took a deep breath and blew it out all at once. We looked at each other.

"I ain't too sure I like the life of a pirate," he said.

"Me, either," I said. I felt light enough to float away. "Good thing that snake wasn't in that first bag, the one we dropped and broke."

Sam looked at me and made a noise in his mouth. "Lucky, too," he said, "that he was in that second one."

"So let's be careful of him but still get the hell out of here," I said. "I'm all shook up, and we need to call George Ramsey and tell him what we found and then call Buddy and tell him what found us."

"I don't need any excuses at all," Sam said. "I'm ready to go home and sit on April's lap."

So I propped the maddock against one of the big oaks and Sam retrieved his cap and the metal detector. The bag of silver dollars that had had the little rattlesnake in it went back into the well on the blade of the shovel. We figured that was smarter than trying to get the decrepit bag back to George Ramsey's house, given the hurry we were in, and we figured Jerry Spivey and Sperry Bissell wouldn't be coming back any time soon, anyway.

We made fast work of the path to George Ramsey's house and even faster work of the highway to the closest telephone, which was behind the counter of a little Gulf station and fix-it shop about a half mile down the road toward Alachua.

I called Buddy first because I had had a good fright and wanted to talk to the law as well as a friend who hadn't been there, and because what Sam and I had found was silver dollars and silver dollars were something Buddy seemed prepared to be interested in hearing about. Calling Buddy first saved me a quarter, too, because he volunteered to call George Ramsey.

"Go back out there," Buddy said when I asked him what Sam and I should do, "and wait for me. Them dollars ain't going nowhere, and what's important right now is gettin' hold of Spivey and that other feller. I'll see if I cain't get some help and we'll do what we can and I'll meet you and Sam in a little while."

It took Buddy an hour and a half to get out to George Ramsey's place, to which George Ramsey hadn't yet come, either, and that was long enough for me to drive into the outskirts of town and buy me and Sam a six-pack of Beck's Beer and for us to drink most of it. The Beck's was expensive, but I figured we'd earned it.

We could hear Buddy coming long before he got to George Ramsey's house. There must have been traffic of some sort, because he was using the siren, which also meant he was driving one of the county cruisers. We also knew he was driving one because down the last straightaway he had it cranked up and was roaring like a Messerschmitt before he slowed to make the turn into George Ramsey's yard.

"God, I hate sirens," Buddy said as he got out of the car. "Sorry it took me so long to get here, but I had to help hunt for Spivey and then for George Ramsey. We got Spivey easy enough, but George still don't know you struck it rich out here unless Lamar or somebody's found him by now. Whew. You guys okay?"

"We won, but we had help," Sam said, and put down his third empty bottle of Beck's.

Buddy looked at us, his hands on his hips. "Yeah," he said. "Leeman told me. Funny thing about those two fellers. Every time you—Leeman, I mean—and them are in the same place, there's a snake around, too."

"Funny," I said. "And every time they and I are in the same place, I get the shit scared out of me."

Sam and I weren't smiling. Buddy smiled at us, though. "Lamar and I got 'em both at the emergency room," he said. "Actually we just got Bissell, they're gone keep Spivey in a room tonight. We'll

get 'em for somethin', criminal trespass or intimidation or somethin', and then I got a lot of things to talk to them about—like if
it was them that went after Harold Buckminster that time, for
instance. Them guys and all them silver dollars are mixed up together somehow, don't you reckon?"

He looked at me. "And I still wouldn't be surprised if your pal
the juju man didn't figure in there somewhere, too."

"What are you talking about?" Sam said, and leaned back
against the top step.

"It's a long story," Buddy said. "Wait till I get done sortin' it
all out. Now y'all want to show me this mess of money y'all done
stumbled over in the woods?"

It was late afternoon now, and though the sun hadn't
set, it had fallen below the tops of the trees in George Ramsey's
woods, so we quickstepped through the briars and the gathering
shadows out to where Calvin Hutto had hidden a mound of silver
dollars on the filled-in floor of an old well between two ancient trees.

The shovel and the maddock were propped where we had left
them. Buddy volunteered to be the one to go down into the hole,
but only on the stipulation that we tear off the rest of the boards
covering it so as to let in as much of the remaining light of day as
we could and thereby scout out the possibility of another snake
being down there.

Since we were all working together, it didn't take us long to deal
with the old boards, and since Buddy had a flashlight, it also didn't
take us long to confirm that there were a couple of rotten bags and
seven or eight silver dollars and nothing else but what is normal and
natural in a hole of that depth in a temperate deciduous woods.

"Where are them damn hell dollars you guys were yammerin'
about?" Buddy said hotly. "What the hell do you mean?"

"The bottom of that hole was paved in money when I got out
of it," Sam said. "It was lumpy all over down there with those bags."

"Well, it ain't now," Buddy said, and stood up. Sam and I stood
up, too.

"Wait here for me," Buddy snarled, "and try not to lose anything else." He started off at a trot in the direction we had seen Jerry Spivey and Sperry Bissell go.

"Where're you goin'?" I called.

Buddy stopped and turned around. "Down this damn road to try to get those damn silver dollars back," he said. Buddy was steaming with anger, or it might have been frustration. Now he was looking at me.

"It's that old man," he said, "that Gant. I know it is."

"You want us to come?" I said.

"No!" Buddy shouted. "You guys stand right there and try not to fall into that hole and wait'll I get back."

But we didn't. We said to hell with Buddy Crittenden and walked back to George Ramsey's house and sat on the front porch and drank a can of orange juice we found in the back of Buddy's cruiser while I told Sam some of what I knew about silver dollars being loose in the county. It was almost pitch-black dark when we finally saw Buddy's light coming at us through the woods.

"I don't want to talk," he said darkly. "I'm too busy thinking."

But he did tell me and Sam not to worry about anything because he'd take care of all of it, for us just to go home and wait till he had something to tell us besides what we already knew.

So, while driving Sam home, I got back on the subject of silver dollars and told him what I knew about Harold Buckminster having some of them that he got from Royal Mango and about how I figured the two guys that broke Harold Buckminster's nose must have been Jerry Spivey and Sperry Bissell. What I didn't know and so couldn't tell him was how any or all of the four of them connected to the silver dollars we found that afternoon except that Jerry Spivey and Sperry Bissell had tried to take them away from us.

"What's this stuff about a juju man?" Sam said.

So I also told him about Royal Mango going to see the Rattlesnake Master and how Buddy really didn't have anything to make him think the old man was mixed up with those silver dollars except that he got visited by or was delivered Royal Mango, who had some silver dollars but whose visit or even whose delivery to the old man's house didn't have an obvious silver dollar anywhere near it.

But the thing that puzzled Sam and me most, all the way to his house and into his kitchen, where he hugged his wife and his daughter and where we both had another beer even though I was driving, was what had in fact happened to those silver dollars in the two hours or so between the time he and I left them in that hole and the time we got back with Buddy Crittenden.

"I wonder where those suckers are," Sam said, putting his elbow on the table and his chin in his hand. Anne was pulling furiously at his pants leg.

"Who knows?" I said. "Who else besides Spivey and Bissell and you and me knew they were out there?"

"Hah," Sam said, and picked Anne off the floor and sat her on his knee. "Maybe that's what Buddy meant when he was talking about the juju man—that whatchacallit, that Rattlesnake Master."

"Maybe," I said. But I knew Sam was right.

"I reckon I can keep the old man out of it," Buddy said, "even though it rankles the shit out of me."

"What?" I said. "Oh. I didn't even know he was in it for sure."

"Got to be," Buddy said. "Wait a minute, I've got a bite."

Sure enough, his cork was bouncing around on the green water. Then it went under and Buddy pulled up a bream about four inches long.

"Dern little pipsqueaks," Buddy growled. "Reckon ain't nothin' else got an appetite for crickets today. " 'Course, if we'd kept 'em all, we'd probably have five pounds of fish by now."

We were in a boat in the middle of Percy Akers's pond, which was swamp on one side and had a field of broomsedge and scrubby little trees on the other. Buddy's Cutlass was parked where the field began an easy slope to the water's edge. We'd been there about an hour, maybe a little more, paddling around and pulling in tiny bream and watching the clouds go by. Most of what we'd been talking about was the fact that Buddy and Karen had decided to get married.

They weren't going to waste any time now that they had resolved to go ahead and do it, either. The wedding wasn't but three weeks away—to give Buddy's mama and Karen's mama just enough time to do what they had to do to get a church wedding and a reception and God knows what else put together, but also not quite enough time to get themselves and everyone else so frazzled from preparations as to be glad when the thing was over and done with. I had agreed to be an usher.

Buddy put a cricket on his hook, adjusted his bobber a little, and flipped his line toward the bank, which was lined with reeds. His bait and sinker went *ploont* and settled into the pond.

"Now we'll see," Buddy said menacingly.

I moved slightly, trying to find a soft spot on my seat. Frogs, just a few of them, began honking loudly from the other side of the pond.

"You were saying," I reminded him.

"Yeah," Buddy said, and took out a cigarette and lit it with a match.

"You lose your lighter?"

"No," Buddy said. "I forgot it. Anyhow, you know it wasn't Spivey or Bissell went back out there and got them bags of money out of that hole. And as far as I know, it wasn't you or Campbell, either."

The frogs stopped, one by one. There were four of them. I didn't say anything.

"And it wasn't even George Ramsey," Buddy went on, "though I 'spect he'll end up with the seventy-six of them that we took out of the junk in that well."

I already knew about George Ramsey, about how he'd been pretty upset that Buddy hadn't gotten in touch with him until long after Sam and I had found those silver dollars and lost them again. He demanded and got a meeting with Buddy and Sheriff Lundquist in the sheriff's office on Camellia Street. George Ramsey came in wearing a blue coat, a red tie, gray pants, and black and white shoes. He was perfectly happy to sign anything that would bring difficulty and possibly time in jail to Jerry Spivey and Sperry Bissell, but he was stridently unsatisfied that all he had to show for the discovery of a substantial cache of silver dollars on his property was a measly seventy-six of them. Those dollars rightly belonged to his wife, George Ramsey said, to his wife whose daddy was old man Marvin Trueblood, God rest his soul, because one of Calvin Hutto's relatives—the same aunt, in fact, who died and left Calvin Hutto the property George Ramsey bought—had robbed her family of its restaurant and ruined them besides with some half-assed lawsuit.

Sheriff Lundquist just sat there, with Buddy in a chair behind him a little and to his left, and listened to George Ramsey until his eyes began to glaze over and George Ramsey noticed and began to direct himself to Buddy instead. What he said to Buddy then was that he took a lot of pleasure in buying Calvin Hutto's hundred acres—"got them cheap, too," he said, "and that house"—because it made Betty Trueblood Young Ramsey feel better and appealed to his sense of justice, too.

Every once in a while during his speech George Ramsey would throw a glance at the sheriff to see if he was listening yet, and the depth of the sheriff's reverie meant that George Ramsey had to do an awful lot of talking before he was allowed to turn and make straight for his point. But the sheriff finally flinched, Buddy says, and George Ramsey looked at him and immediately said, "I can make a good case for them silver dollars belonging to Betty and me, and I think if your deputy here had been a bit more conscientious, we might still have them."

Then Sheriff Lundquist flinched again, and Buddy realized that Big Ed had the hiccups.

Sheriff Lundquist took a mouthful of air and swallowed it. "Look, George," he said. "I done been through *hic* excuse me this with you before. Buddy's priority was to find and catch a couple men who it looked like had committed *hic* a criminal act. And we followed them two sets of wheelbarrow tracks somebody left out there as far as we could, all the way down to the dirt road. What else you want us to do? We *hic* got our eyes open for them dollars, and if one shows up at any pawnshop inside of fifty miles in any direction, I'll know about it."

He shrugged, then sat forward and put his thick hands palms-down on the desk in front of him. "And if we *hic* think of something else, we'll do that, too."

Then George Ramsey got out of his chair and started waving his arms and talking in a loud voice about how it wasn't enough that those two hoodlums had come out and dug all those holes on his property with absolute impunity—no, he said, now that we not only know what they were looking for but Sam Campbell and Leeman Truesdale had found it, even, somebody had just traipsed out to his place and hauled it away in a couple of wheelbarrows.

"It took him nearly two hours to get out there," George Ramsey said to the sheriff, though he was pointing a finger at Buddy. "I want to know how you can tolerate that."

So the sheriff sighed and picked at an earlobe and asked Buddy if he had any kind of response to make, and Buddy said, "Not really, I was just sittin' here thinkin' about a green shoe box in somebody's broom closet."

George Ramsey stared at Buddy. The veins in his neck looked like rods holding his head to his shoulders.

"All right," George Ramsey said, and looked down at the floor. "Perhaps you're doing the best you can." And then he thanked them for their time and got up and walked out, leaving the door open.

The sheriff sighed again and rubbed his eyes. "Buddy," he said, without turning around, "I ain't even sure I heard what you said, but what I want to know is, do I want to know what you said and how come you said it, or do I just want to go on about my business and leave it be? Do you want to tell me?"

"No sir," Buddy said.

"Fine," the sheriff said. "Thank you. Lemme know if you figure out where them dollars might of got off to."

I was getting a nibble but then I wasn't anymore, so I checked my bait and found I didn't have any. Buddy watched me put a cricket on my hook and throw the line back into the water.

"He can prove it wasn't him, then," I said.

"Who?" Buddy said. "George? Sho. He's airtight. And I'm pretty sure it wasn't Mango on his own, and I'm positive it wasn't Harold Buckminster, and there ain't nobody else ever seen them dollars or even knows about them except a coupla grocery-store cashiers."

"So why him?" I said. "Why Mr. Gant? And how does he know, unless maybe that Mango told him? And besides that, just how do you figure them other silver dollars and those out yonder on Calvin Hutto's place came out of the same pot?"

"All right," Buddy said. "I been waitin' to tell you this." He took up his rod, reeled in a little slack in the line, and set it down again, pointing over the side of the boat.

"The first thing I had to do was figure out how Calvin Hutto could get hold of a pile of silver dollars like that. I knew he was the one had them, I got that from Spivey, who got the one bag the old man had hid in his house when he died. And y'know, those fellers threw that bag out the window of their car that day I, we, ran them down about runnin' over that snake last year when we were on the way home from fishin'.

"That must've been how Mango got them, some way or another, too. Can you believe it? They thought that's how come we were chasin' them! Because they had them dollars in the car!

"And it didn't take me but four phone calls to find out: the place where he, old man Hutto, used to work years ago in Savannah, when he had both his legs, had five thousand silver dollars stolen from it—*boom!*—out of some old safe that just a few people knew about. The night guard lost his job over it, though they never could prove anything, and Hutto was his supervisor. He had a key, too, but he also had some sort of bullshit alibi. The night guard was black and from out of town to boot, so people weren't about to think about Calvin Hutto very long when he was available for them to point at. But like I say, didn't nobody ever find nothin'."

"Hah," I said. I had a fish on my line only slightly smaller than Buddy's last catch. I threw him back and did the same thing with my hook after impaling a new cricket on it. I always wonder if it hurts them, but I still use them for bait.

"I'm with you so far."

"What do you mean?" Buddy said. "There ain't no so far—that's it. That's all there is. The night guard's name was Augustus Gant. Pretty soon after he got fired, he left the country."

"Wow," I said. "The Rattlesnake Master."

"The Rattlesnake Master's daddy is what you mean," Buddy said. "I know that old man Gant has got them silver dollars as sho as there's Christmas, and I'd be willin' to bet a dollar to a doughnut that this county won't ever see hide nor hair of him or that money ever again.

"But if he's going back to Barbados like I think he is, I could still make some trouble for him, I reckon, and I reckon he knows it."

I stifled a yawn at just about the same time some little frogs began singing in the reeds behind us. "Well," I said, "he should figure you're smart enough to find out about his daddy being set up by Calvin Hutto. Is that sort of what you mean?"

"Yeah. That's to his good, too, though, 'cause it means his daddy's name is cleared, I guess, though now it don't mean doodledy-squat to anybody but him."

"And his daughter," I said. Now all kinds of frogs were beginning to sing around us. Red-winged blackbirds were screeching from the willows on the dam.

"Her too," Buddy said. "But I'm not gonna do nothin', see? Let 'em have 'em, that's what I say. Have you got a bite?"

"No. What you mean is that you think he got those dollars but you really don't have any proof or even any evidence at hand and so can't do a thing without raising a bigger stink than Ed Lundquist is gonna want to mess with or pay for."

Buddy laughed. "That's right," he said. "So the hell with it. Let's paddle over to the other side and catch some real fish."

Later, as the sun was just about down, we pulled the boat up on the bank and unloaded our stuff and carried it to the car. The sky was pink in the west and the cool evening air smelled wonderfully of mud and pond water. Chorus frogs and leopard frogs were peeping and clacking away to beat the band. It was a lovely moment to be alive in.

"Listen to them things out there," Buddy said, meaning the frogs. I heard him take a deep breath and let it out. "The thing that still bothers me most is that I just can't manage to figure out how he did it. And Jesus, how could he have known you and Sam had found that money?"

"Listen," Buddy said, "and tell me what you think about this."

We were in my kitchen, me washing blood and other fishy fluids off my hands into the sink while Buddy lounged against the counter. We'd ended up with five bream of sufficient size for Buddy to take to his mother, who loved bream so much that she expected to be served them straightway when she arrived in heaven.

"Shoot," I said, turning off the water and grabbing a couple of paper towels.

"Okay," Buddy said. "So we know old man Gant knew, or probably figured he knew, that Calvin Hutto had them dollars stashed away someplace. He knew his daddy didn't steal them, and there wasn't really nobody else. Maybe he even came back here from Barbados to get them, I dunno. But if he did, why would he wait so long?"

"Well," I said, but Buddy held up his hand.

"Hold on a minute," he said. "We're still assuming it was him that got them dollars the other day, even though I can't imagine how he . . . Did *you* tell him?"

"No," I said. "And he never said anything to me about silver dollars, either."

"Thank you," Buddy said self-consciously. "I reckon you know it's somethin' I had to ask."

"Uh-huh. Don't worry about it."

"All right," Buddy said. "So let's suppose it was him that got them. But he had to have had some help. Mango, maybe. It was Mango got hold of some of them dollars first, anyway, after Bissell chunked them out the window. I dunno, maybe it was Ellis, that Sears Ellis who paddled J. B. Barrett out of the swamp that time and toted Mango down to see Gant the night he was drunk—the night, you remember, before he was supposed to go down there anyway.

"And by God!" Buddy said, clapping his hands. "That old scoundrel would never've known Mango had them dollars if Ellis hadn't of took him down there. That's got to be it!"

I had finished wrapping the bream in aluminum foil.

"Uh, look," Buddy said. "I'm gone go ahead and leave, I just thought of somethin' I'd better do."

"A pity," I said. "Engaged less than a week and already she's got you watchin' your time."

Buddy gave me a funny look, then frowned. "Nah," he said. "It ain't that. I'm gone put on my uniform and drive out to that place Sears Ellis rented in Brooklet and pay him a call. I got some questions I figure maybe he can answer."

FIFTEEN

At 10:30 Sunday morning the god damned phone rang. I hadn't been up very long—in fact, no longer than it took to get out of bed and pick up the phone and bark hello at it. I'd stayed up too late the night before, mostly just by thinking up excuses not to go to bed. After Buddy left to go see Sears Ellis I had walked over to Cook's for supper, a little anticipatory adrenaline added to my hunger, but Donna wasn't there to wait on me and listen to my smooth talk. Then maybe I had too much wine after I got home.

"Hey, it's Buddy. Did I wake you up?"

"No," I said, but my voice was thick and full of gristle.

"Uh, okay," Buddy said. "Uh, listen, Sears Ellis wasn't at home last night when I went out there and he wasn't there a half hour ago, either. And J. B. Barrett doesn't know where he is, he took Friday off and wasn't supposed to work yesterday."

"How about that," I said. So far I was not impressed. The only thing in the world I wanted was to go back to bed.

"Yeah," Buddy said, "I reckon I was right about him bein' in with old man Gant. He's probably halfway to Barbados with them other two right now."

"How about that," I said. I wanted to sit down, but my telephone was in the hall and all my chairs were elsewhere.

"You sure I didn't get you up?" Buddy said.

"Yes!" I said.

"Well, okay," Buddy said. "Look, you wanna ride with me out to Gant's place this afternoon? Karen and I are gone take Mama to

213

church in a little while, but I'd sho like to go out there and nose around some later on. I don't expect nobody to be there, but maybe there's something for me to see if I look hard enough."

I thought about it.

"Leeman?" Buddy said.

"I'm thinking," I said.

"Well, don't think I got any intentions of tryin' to drag the bunch of them back here from wherever they are," Buddy said, "because I don't. If the old man's got them silver dollars, that's just fine. It's better'n Calvin Hutto and Jerry Spivey havin' them, and it's better'n them bein' out yonder in a hole in the ground. I just don't understand some of what's been goin' on around here, and it's about to drive me crazy."

I thought about it some more.

After a minute, Buddy said, "Leeman?"

"Okay," I said. "I'll go with you." And then I went back to bed.

When we drove up into the yard of Leeman Gant's house, Sears Ellis's GTO was parked at the end of the little rock walkway that led to the steps. Buddy parked the Cutlass beside it. As he and I started up the walk Sears Ellis came out of the house and sat down in the one chair that remained on the porch. The flower beds along the porch were showing splotches of green where things were coming up, and here and there little clumps of daffodils were blooming.

Except for the flowers, everything looked pretty much the same as it had the last time I was there, but the way Sears Ellis came through the screen door and sat down in that chair, I could tell that the house behind him was empty of life.

"Good evenin'," Buddy said.

"Yeah," said Sears Ellis, and waved a hand.

"Howdy," I said.

Buddy walked up and put one foot on the first step.

"You by yourself?" he said.

"Uh-huh," Sears Ellis said.

"Where's the rest of 'em?" Buddy said.

"Gone," Sears Ellis said flatly. "Long gone."

Buddy nodded. "I figured as much," he said. "Y'know, you and me never met officially, but I know who you are and I reckon you know who I am." He turned and nodded at me. "I reckon maybe you know Leeman, too."

Sears Ellis looked at me and one corner of his mouth went up. "No, we ain't never really met," he said, "even if I done seen y'all out at Barrett's a coupla times." He looked back at Buddy. "And yeah, I know you, but I know *of* him. I know of him real well."

Sears Ellis smiled tightly. I wasn't sure exactly what he meant, but Buddy was already talking again.

"I was 'spectin' you'd be gone, too," he said. "But I'm mighty pleased that you ain't. We need to have a little confabulation."

"You ain't wearin' no badge," Sears Ellis said.

"That's right," Buddy said. "I'm just a private citizen makin' a visit."

"Uh-huh," Sears Ellis said, with no conviction whatsoever.

Buddy wasn't put off, though. "And maybe you look to me like a man who could use a talk," he said, as friendly as could be. "Maybe there's something we could do for each other."

Sears Ellis looked at Buddy as if he thought Buddy just might be crazy, and then turned his head a little and squinted into the yard.

"What if I ain't got nothin' to say?"

"Sears, look," Buddy said. "I've done made up my mind to leave Mr. Gant alone"—Sears did look at Buddy now, and even seemed to be paying attention—"and to forget about them silver dollars, too, but it's gettin' to be sort of a personal matter to me to understand what's been goin' on out here, and I think maybe you know what that is."

Buddy took his foot off the step. His hands moved through the air in front of him as he talked.

"I mean, Sears, let's face it. You know about them silver dollars, and God knows what else you were doin', like with Mango, and I can drag that old man and that daughter of his back here eventually and drag you through some stuff, too, and just generally cause all kinds of shit to fall on them and you. But I ain't gone do that, y'all can all clear out as far as I'm concerned, dollars and all, and to hell with the lot of you."

Sears Ellis didn't say anything, but he and Buddy were looking at each other. Buddy folded his arms.

"But *you* didn't clear out," Buddy said. "*You* stayed here."

Sears Ellis sat forward a little in his chair. "Why I'm gone go anywhere?" he said.

"More than just that," Buddy said. "Since you stayed here, one way or another you are gone tell me what all this is about."

"All what?" Sears Ellis said. "You threatenin' me with somethin'?"

Buddy threw up his hands. "Sears," he said, "be reasonable with me. Both of us know that old man took off from here with a lot of silver dollars or the proceeds from them, at least. All I want to do is to understand how he, how y'all did it."

Sears sat up, but seemed to relax a little. "Haw," he said, "You and me, we got somethin' in common. I don't understand it all, either." He gave Buddy a quizzical look, and Buddy looked back at him. Nobody looked at me, and nobody said anything for a minute.

Finally Sears said, "All right. At least y'all come on up here on the porch and we'll see."

So we did, and Buddy sat on the porch rail on the other side of the steps from me. He was closer to Sears than I was. I leaned against the rail on my side of the steps and had a long, slow look at the yard, and I thought of the Sunday morning I came into the rain out of Leeman Gant's little house, full of biscuits and gravy, and went home. The morning after I'd had the dream with Donna Calloway in it. By that afternoon with Buddy and Sears I'd just as soon have stopped thinking about it, but there it was again.

"Okay," Buddy said, "let me start it off. What began all this was Royal Mango gettin' them silver dollars somehow or another after what's-his-name, Sperry Bissell, threw them out the window of that Pontiac. Then he gives a few of them to Harold Buckminster, and—"

"Wait a minute," I said, and turned around. "No, forget it, it's stupid." Both of them were looking at me, and Sears Ellis was rocking back and forth in his seat.

"Okay, listen," I said, and sat on the porch rail. "What really started this whole thing was you"—I pointed at Buddy—"seein' those two guys run over that snake, or look like they did, anyway." Buddy cocked his head a little and threw me a look I couldn't read.

"What I mean is, do you reckon anything can be made of the fact that it was a rattlesnake?"

Sears Ellis laughed and grasped the arms of his chair. "Man," he said, "how do I know? Who's gone tell you now? And anyhow, that ain't when nothin' got started 'cept for you and him"—he nodded at Buddy—"gettin' involved in somethin' I reckon was already goin' on."

"Unless maybe he wanted us to get mixed up in it," Buddy said. I could hear sparrows chattering somewhere behind the house.

"Uh-huh," Sears Ellis said. "And because of you and that snake and all, them dollars in that bag went on to Royal. Then I go over there and carry him out here drunk in the middle of the night and pretty soon Mr. Gant starts to know for sure that he can get his hands on what it was that he came after. I mean, on what it was he left Barbados for."

"Okay," Buddy said. "And he was already sitting down here dispensing tea and advice and maybe even a genuine miracle or two, and workin' in his garden for eight or ten years waitin' for Calvin Hutto to die. That the way you see it?"

"Uh-huh," Sears Ellis said. "And then he couldn't wait no longer."

"Wait a minute," I said. "What do you mean?"

"All I mean is that he couldn't wait around no more for that Hutto man to die," Sears Ellis said. He looked from Buddy to me and then back to Buddy, who was picking at a tooth with his thumbnail. "Don't y'see? Because couldn't none of this other stuff get started till that Hutto man was dead and out of the way. That's how I sees it."

"That doesn't mean he started it," I said. "Mr. Gant, I mean."

"Man," Sears Ellis said, and gave me an exasperated look. "Listen. He's out here and he's waitin', and waitin', and just incidentally some people come to see him and go home cured if they was sick. Or maybe they come to see him when they in a tight spot, and when they go home, or soon after it, they ain't in that spot no more, or at least they knows how to get out of it. And all that time he ain't never heard a peep out of them silver dollars, ain't never even seen one of them, but he knowed they was out there on that Hutto man's place sho as they's Christmas. And here he was, waitin' for a chance to get them from that man what stole them."

"But he didn't have any way to find them, even, much less get them away from Calvin Hutto," Buddy said.

"No," Sears Ellis said. "There wasn't no way for him to get at them or get them away from that Hutto man, at least not while that Hutto man was alive."

Buddy took a cigarette out of the pack in his shirt pocket and put fire to it with a lighter with an armadillo on it. I wondered how many of those things he had left.

"Okay," he said, "so . . ."

"So he went out there to see him," Sears Ellis said, and crossed and uncrossed his legs. "He went out to that Hutto man's place, and he told me he knew for sho that them silver dollars was somewhere close as soon as he got there. He just didn't know where."

"How'd he get there?" I said.

"I took him," Sears Ellis said. "In my sister's car. That was before I went to work for Mr. J. B. and got that GTO." Sears Ellis smiled a little.

"All right," Buddy said, and took a long drag from his cigarette and let the smoke out slowly. "So he got tired of waitin' for Calvin Hutto to die, and he persuaded you or asked you or told you to take him out there so he could see the man who ruint his daddy face-to-face."

"That's about it," Sears Ellis said, nodding.

"No," Buddy said. "Like you already said—that was just the beginning. Maybe he decided it was time for Calvin Hutto to die, maybe he figured that was the only way even a juju man was gone get at them silver dollars. And maybe he just wanted to talk to him, y'know? But if anybody around here knows why he went out there besides him, that's gotta be you. You was out there, too."

Sears Ellis quit rocking and leaned forward in his chair. "Yeah," he said. "But I don't know what went on for sure, 'cause I never got out of the car."

"How come?" Buddy said, raising an eyebrow.

"He told me not to," Sears Ellis said. "And it was his show, wadden it? I didn't know that Hutto man from Lester Maddox, and *he* knew everything about that Hutto man that there was to know. Like he'd been studyin' him." Sears grinned broadly. "An' ain't no way that Hutto man was gone open the door to two of us, nohow."

"All right," Buddy said. He was holding the stub of his cigarette, fidgeting with it, and finally balanced it straight up on its filter end on the two-by-four that was the porch railing. His breath came out all at once, *shoo!* "So there ain't but one person alive who knows what went on in that house. He say anything to you about it? You mind tellin' me?"

"I don't care," Sears Ellis said. "I ain't studyin' this nohow, tryin' not to. He said he just told that Hutto man who he was and that he had come back to this country to see justice done and them silver dollars got away from where they were. He said he told that Hutto man he wanted to see his daddy's name cleared, as if anybody but him cared. And he told that Hutto man he wouldn't rest till that Hutto man was exposed for the criminal he was and them silver dollars got back, though I spoze he didn't tell that Hutto man he wanted them dollars himself.

"Anyhow, he said that as he kept talkin', that Hutto man got redder and redder and his jaws got all crunched together and you could see the veins runnin' in his forehead. And when he was tellin' him some stuff about his daddy, the one that called himself the Rattlesnake Master, too, he said that Hutto man just got up off the sofa and said 'awp' and fell on the floor and died with his eyes wide open."

"Awp?" Buddy said.

"Uh-huh," Sears Ellis said. "Then Mr. Gant looked hard at me and said, 'Drive,' and we got the hell out of there."

"Lemme see if I got this," Buddy said, and leaned closer to Sears Ellis. Past Buddy, a pair of sparrows lit on the rail at the end of the porch and nuzzled each other. "When y'all left out there, the only obstacle to old man Gant gettin' hold of them dollars, if only because that obstacle spent most of his time frowning out the windows and wandering around the yard, was gone"—Buddy snapped his fingers—"just like *that*."

"Hey," Sears Ellis said appreciatively.

"Thank you," Buddy said, and grinned, and leaned back till he was sitting more or less straight. "See how you like this part. Then it ain't much time until Royal Mango, who likes you and trusts you, is tellin' you there's these two white guys lookin' for him because, uh, he's come into some silver. And let's say that you don't know what to say to that, but that you know somebody who might, so you haul ol' Mango down here and him drunk as a skunk, too. Besides that, I'd almost be willing to bet somebody told you to be sure to get Mango down here one way or another."

Sears Ellis smiled a little. I could hear palm fronds rustling against the house and thought of the ocean and wanted to see it.

"I hear you," Sears Ellis said.

"Yeah," Buddy said. "But I ain't finished decidin' about it yet. That part, what you said about him tellin' Calvin Hutto somethin' about his daddy, the one that was the Rattlesnake Master, too. You got any idea what that means? What he was tellin' him?"

Sears Ellis leaned back in his chair. "Man, gimme one them cigarettes," he said, and held out his hand. Buddy gave him the pack and Sears made his selection and Buddy lit it with his lighter. Sears Ellis took a drag and dealt with it. "Yeah," he said.

Something didn't sound right. "Did he tell you?" I said.

Sears looked at me. "No," he said.

"Elizabeth," Buddy said.

Sears looked at him, now. "You got it," he said.

"They talked then, him and her," I said.

"Yeah," Sears Ellis said. "Sho they did." He had another hit from his cigarette and smoke came out of his mouth and nose and lifted up above his head until a breeze caught it and took it away.

"Okay," Buddy said. "He told Calvin Hutto something about his daddy, the sap on the late shift."

Sears Ellis looked at Buddy. So did I, and noticed that the two sparrows were no longer on the railing at the end of the porch. They and other birds were singing to beat the band from the yard, though.

"It ain't nothin' you can believe," Sears Ellis said to Buddy. "It ain't nothin' you can prove, either. And I ain't sure I'd even *want* to believe it, and sometimes I think I believe it already and I can't believe I'm really believin' it, y'know?"

"Not yet," Buddy said.

"Listen," Sears Ellis said, "you got to put it together." He leaned up again and started poking the palm of his hand with a finger. "All us know that Hutto man stole them dollars and that he hid them out there on his place, the one he didn't live at yet. Now, man, he ain't just stole them dollars, he'd done brought down some real heat on another man, one that half the upper end of Chatham County could have told him was a man you didn't mess with even on yo best day."

"The Rattlesnake Master," I said. The prospects for what was to come were thrilling.

"The man himself," Sears Ellis said. He flicked his cigarette over the steps and into the yard. Buddy looked down at his stub still balanced on the porch rail and brushed it off into the flower bed.

"Wait," Buddy said. "Let me try it again. Old man Hutto steals them silver dollars and hides them in the woods except for one bag that he kept God-knows-where until he was livin' in that house and put it in a paint can. But he never got nothin' out of those silver dollars, he never got to spend a one of them or sell any, either. He just had a bagful of them to remind him of all the others he couldn't get his hands on anymore. And he didn't have but one leg, so there he was: a smelly old bastard livin' alone in a little house until somethin' from out of his past came to the door and killed him."

"Are you guys talkin' about revenge?" I said, and Buddy nodded.

"I'd have said somethin' else, maybe like a curse," Sears Ellis said.

"They go together," Buddy said, and now Sears Ellis nodded. "But I dunno."

"I tole you you wasn't gone believe it," Sears Ellis said. He looked over at me. "Do you?"

"I dunno," I said, and what they were getting at was hard to swallow, but so was the idea of a rattlesnake in a bag and how it was in the second bag Sam picked up and not in the first one, the one we dropped. "There's an awful lot of coincidences goin' on here if there ain't something behind them."

"Uh-huh," Sears Ellis said. "Coincidences. Mr. Gant goes out to see that Hutto man and he dies. Then here comes Mango with them dollars." He paused. I didn't recognize the look on his face. "And then for a while, nothin' happened."

"How come?" I said.

"Wait," Buddy said. "Who killed old man Hutto?"

Sears Ellis shrugged. "You pick," he said. "But whoever you pick, didn't neither one of 'em do it. One of them left the country, and the other one didn't do nothin' but sit on that Hutto man's sofa and talk."

"Didn't neither of them do it directly, you mean," Buddy said wryly. He stood up, walked a few steps down the porch, and turned around and came back. Standing beside me and in front of Sears Ellis, he put out his right hand, looked at it, then folded his arms.

Buddy looked down at Sears, as if to give him a cue.

"Uh-huh," Sears Ellis said. "Maybe that first one, the one that was a Rattlesnake Master sometimes and a security guard some other times, maybe he left somethin' behind him. That's what I mean."

"That's why you mean a curse," I said, and Sears Ellis looked at me. Buddy snorted softly.

"You say it," Sears Ellis said. "I ain't. But just spozin' it was possible, yeah. Or you could say it another way. You could say Mr.

Gant killed that Hutto man by tellin' him that his daddy had made sure that Hutto man wouldn't never get no good out of them dollars he stole."

Buddy sat down on the railing. "Or," he said, "maybe you could say both of 'em did it."

"Maybe I could," Sears Ellis said. "Maybe I could say the first one started somethin' and the second one just finished it by showing up at the door and bein' who he was."

"And then the show was on the road," Buddy said.

"What show?" I said.

"Oh, man," Sears Ellis said. "And him always talkin' 'bout how he liked you, too. Ain't you been listenin' to me? Once that Hutto man was gone, then he could get them dollars."

"Look," I said, and stood up into a cool breeze coming across the steps and onto the porch. "Even if we suppose it was him all along, curse or no curse, even if we suppose he had a hand in tracking down them silver dollars and getting them off old man Hutto's place, how come he picked the time he picked to go out there?"

"What?" Sears said.

"How come you and him went out there when you did," I said.

"He couldn't wait anymore," Buddy said. "Sears already said that, sort of. But there's somethin' here I ain't entirely sure about."

I sat down. Buddy stood up again and took a few steps around the porch while Sears Ellis and I watched him. Then he sat back down on the rail and put his hands on his thighs. I heard a low rumble of thunder a long way away.

"What I reckon," Buddy said, "is that he had to hurry because Calvin Hutto was gone get at them dollars himself if he didn't. Him and Spivey." The wind had picked up and was blowing little cyclones of dust around the yard.

"So?" Sears Ellis said.

"So," Buddy said. "I can say it and maybe I can live with it, but I got a feelin' there's somethin' we ain't got around to talkin' about yet."

"Like what?" Sears Ellis said, and shifted in his seat.

"Wait a minute," Buddy said, his eyebrows scrunched in toward one another. "I got to go back and try to catch up. Did you know old man Gant before you went to work for J. B. Barrett?"

Sears squinted at him.

"Yeah," he said.

"How'd you meet him?" Buddy said. "Old man Gant, I mean."

"I just met him around somewhere," Sears Ellis said. "Look here, man—you askin' questions, well, I been askin' questions, too. Like what if I hadn't never gone to work for J. B. Barrett? You tell me, you been to college, I bet. And what if Mr. J. B. ain't got stuck out in a shack in a god-dern hurricane and this here fool hadn't tried to ride a god-dern bicycle down the road past it?" His voice rose and fell, and sometimes he was almost shouting. "Go on," he said. "You want to take it back that far?"

"All right," Buddy said. "What you're wonderin' is—"

"What I'm wonderin'," Sears Ellis said, "is if all that time I was doin' what I wanted to do or what he wanted me to do. Whenever I'd see him, pretty soon he'd have me doin' somethin' I ain't real sure he didn't have me doin' for him even when I was twenty miles away."

Buddy scratched the back of his neck, *scritch scritch scritch.* "I see what you mean," he said. "But I'm in there, too. I'm the one made those two peckerwoods heave that bag of dollars down that bank. Shit. Now I know I don't believe it. I don't believe *any* of it."

"At the risk of repeating myself," I said, "it was a rattlesnake that got you and me mixed up in this, and got that bag out of that car."

"Nuts," Buddy said. "It's crazy."

Sears Ellis blew a little laugh out his nose. "Sho," he said, "but it happened. You was even around for some of it."

"But that don't go for everything," Buddy said. I could hear thunder again, but farther away. Cool fingers of wind were still coming around the corners of the house. "Like, it had to just be chance that George Ramsey got involved. I mean, marryin' Betty Trueblood Young and then buyin' old man Hutto's place. I reckon it just made Betty feel good to own the place Calvin Hutto got out of what his aunt Peggy did to the Truebloods.

"But look here—despite the fact that it was me George came to about them holes, all that really came to nothing. He was operatin' on his own. You can't draw no link between him and the old man and say that one of them was on a leash and the other one was holdin' it."

"I got a answer for you," Sears Ellis said brightly. "First, you got another cigarette?"

Buddy and Sears both lit cigarettes and I stood up a minute to relieve my sore behind. I had just sat down again when Sears Ellis exhaled his first smoke.

"Okay," he said. "Maybe they ain't no link"—he looked at me, then back to Buddy—"but what it was, was more like a set of lines, like them lines between people in a footrace."

"They both wanted the same thing," I said. Buddy was pulling at his chin.

"Man, you get the prize," Sears said with exaggerated ceremony. "Old Mr. Ramsey, he was just competition, just like that Hutto."

"I'm beginning to like this," Buddy said, and rubbed his hands together. "So when Spivey and Bissell started goin' out there and diggin' holes, George figured he better look for whatever old man Hutto must've left out there. And I was perfectly happy to recommend Leeman, here. And Sam Campbell."

"He's the one who found them," I said. "Sam, I mean." Sears looked quickly at me, then back at Buddy.

"Meaning," Buddy said, "that it was George Ramsey's hired representatives who found them dollars. So by all rights, he should've got them; he beat Mr. Gant to the prize."

Sears Ellis smiled and shook his head. "You're almost there," he said. "But you ain't. Y'see, Mr. Ramsey thought Leeman here was workin' for him, but he was wrong. And Mr. Ramsey may have looked like he was competition to Mr. Gant, but it wasn't never a fair fight."

"Come again," Buddy said.

Sears turned to look at me. "Hell," he said, "it wadden fair 'cause it was *you* out there lookin'. Maybe it was directly 'cause yo pal the deputy sheriff told Mr. Ramsey you could help him out, and maybe it was somethin' else. I dunno exactly.

"But what I figure," Sears said, pointing a finger at me, "is that you and that Sam feller was really lookin' for them dollars for somebody else besides George Ramsey."

"Hellfire," Buddy said, and stood up and sat back down. "Leeman," he said, "are you goin' along with all this? I done bought a lot of stuff that makes my brain hurt, but maybe I ain't sure I think much of where we're headed."

Sears Ellis leaned over and picked a piece of fuzz from his jeans. When he sat back up, he looked at me again. "You come out here," he said conspiratorially. "You spent the night." (I felt Buddy look up.) "He give you some sleepy tea, too, didn't he?"

"Yes," I said. I figured that Sears of all people didn't need me to elaborate, and to hell with Buddy for the moment.

"Tea?" Buddy said. "You spent the night?"

"Yeah, sleepy tea," Sears Ellis said. He was smirking.

"I don't get it," Buddy said.

"Shit, man," Sears Ellis said. "It ain't no damn tea what matters nohow. All you got to understand is that when this feller"—he jerked his head in my direction—"left from out here, if he'd of put his finger on one of them silver dollars or even heard a couple of them clink together, Mr. Gant would of knowed about it."

Buddy stood up quickly and walked down to the end of the porch, most of which was now splotched with shadows. I heard him spit into the dirt. Then he turned around and looked at me and Sears.

"I've come all the way out here to the butt end of Jerusalem," he said, "just to sit here on this porch in front of an empty house and let you two just about convince me that one of you has had some sort of spell put on him or something."

"Ain't nobody talkin' 'bout no spells this time," Sears Ellis said. "We're jest talkin' about how all three of us got took up by somethin' we didn't know nothin' about—and all the time it was too big for us to figure out, anyway."

Buddy grunted. "Okay," he said. "I spoze I'm to believe that when Leeman and Sam found them dollars, the old man knew about it."

"Believe it if you want to," Sears Ellis said. "Ain't nobody sayin' you got to."

Buddy walked slowly back up to us and sat on the railing again. "Who was it got them bags out of that hole?" he said. "Was it you?"

Sears Ellis didn't say anything, just sat slumped in his chair, rubbing the fingers of his right hand together.

"Sho it was," Buddy said. "And maybe Mango, too. Alfred Robbins, even. I dunno how many people got mixed up in this in some way or another. But I do know that somebody went back out there between the time Leeman and Sam called me and the time we all got back to that hole. And listen, don't you reckon that whoever it was, they stole them silver dollars just as sure as Calvin Hutto did?"

"You callin' me a thief, right?" Sears Ellis said, looking Buddy in the eye. Buddy looked back.

"Not necessarily," he said. "What I'm doin' is tellin' you one way to look at what happened. And I'm thinkin' that if I do that, maybe you'll tell me another way."

"You talkin' 'bout the *law* way," Sears Ellis said.

"Yeah," Buddy said. "Did they leave anything to drink in this house?"

"Naw," Sears said. "But I got a six-pack of beer in the bucket in the well. You want one?"

"I want somethin'," Buddy said. "Let's go see."

So we all got up and went around to the back of the house and Sears Ellis fished the beer out of the well and we sat down on the steps to the little back porch, close together, and looked out into what had been Leeman Gant's garden. Some of the woodier plants had tiny leaves, and daffodils and a few tulips were up in the corners and surrounding the outhouse. In most of the raised plant beds there was a lot of green, but none of it was far enough along for me to tell if it was weeds or something he might have seeded in.

Nobody spoke for a while until Buddy said, "Which one of them did you do it for?"

And Sears Ellis said softly, "I put that there skylight in that outhouse for him, but after that, I don't know."

"You want another cigarette?" Buddy said, and Sears said "sho," so they lit up and we just sat there. I hadn't heard any thunder for a while, but great gray and white thunderheads were boiling up out of the southwest. When I leaned back against the porch post, I could see that where the previous year's border of rattlesnake master had been planted, there were now rows of peat pots stuck in the ground. The pots had fresh green shoots poking out of them, as if they had been recently put in.

"I just don't know what the hell," Buddy said. "Look here, Sears."

Sears Ellis took a draw from his beer. "I'm listenin'," he said.

"You done told me, I mean told us," Buddy said, "about how Mr. Gant figured he couldn't wait no longer for Calvin Hutto to die. I got that. But you also told me he wasn't prepared to worry much about Jerry Spivey. Maybe George Ramsey made him worry a little at first, but what I'm wonderin' goes back a lot farther than that. I figure Hutto tellin' Spivey about them dollars was bad enough, but I'm ready to bet that Mr. Gant probably had an even better reason he couldn't wait no longer. You still listenin'?"

"I'm settin' here in front of yo mouth," Sears Ellis said.

Buddy took a swallow of beer and his cheeks puffed out.

" 'Scuse me," he said. "You want tell me how you got mixed up in all this stuff?"

"No," Sears Ellis said.

"It was Elizabeth, wasn't it?" Buddy said softly.

Sears Ellis's head went down so he was looking at his feet.

"Sears?" Buddy said.

Sears blew out his breath and looked up into the yard.

"I reckon it was," he said.

Buddy pursed his lips. "Uh-huh. Sure. That's how come you started comin' out here, and pretty soon you were doin' stuff all the time for somebody, though whichever one of them it was is beyond me to say."

"Man," Sears Ellis said, "if she was to tell me to dig a hole to China, I'd of asked her where the shovel was. She'd say, 'Sears, do this for Papa and me,' and I'd fall right to it like I was the hired help." He drained his beer. "And then 'fore long it wasn't even her askin' no more, it was him sayin', 'Sears, go out yonder and pick up Mango for me.' Or 'Sears, carry me out to so-and-so's place.' Onliest thing couldn't neither of them get me to do was handle them snakes."

"What snakes?" I said.

"Ones used to live sometimes in them hutches out yonder," Sears Ellis said. "Two of 'em, both of 'em more'n six feet long and big around as a post."

Buddy and I whistled at the same time.

"Yeah," Sears Ellis said. "Don't let that fool you none—they was out free most of the time. I've seen him come to this door and clap his hands twice and here they'd come out of the bushes somewhere, scarin' hell out of the chickens, just like a couple ol' hound dogs."

"Wait," Buddy said, and reached out and touched Sears Ellis on the shoulder. "Hold on a minute. We're gettin' away from it."

"Maybe you can," Sears Ellis said. "That ain't sayin' I can."

"That's what I mean," Buddy said. "You 'n' Elizabeth."

Sears laughed a short, sharp laugh that didn't seem to have anything amusing behind it. "Yeah," he said, "me 'n' Elizabeth."

"Well?" Buddy said.

"You cain't see it?" Sears said with real annoyance. "You the big, smart deputy sheriff? I got to draw you a picture? Me 'n' Elizabeth, we was in love, man. Or at least one of us was, I was. That part didn't have no tea behind it, either. And it scared him, I b'lieve. Got to look to me like she was gone have to make a choice, and I b'lieve it scared the ol' Rattlesnake Master just a little bit."

"I don't see it," I said. "It ain't like he was going to lose her if she, uh, went off with you and got married or something."

"Uh-huh," Sears Ellis said. "That would of been all right, I reckon. But he wasn't ready for her to do it, wasn't ready for her to leave."

Buddy opened his mouth, but nothing came out.

Sears Ellis was still staring past the garden and the outhouse and the clothesline, deep into the woods behind them all.

"The thing about it," he said, "was that she wasn't ready, either."

"You mean she wasn't in love with you, really?" Buddy said.

"No," I said. "That's not it. I think I get it. Elizabeth wasn't just his daughter, she was his heir, too. Ain't that it?"

Sears Ellis's face moved a little and was still. "I wish I had a nickel," he said slowly, "for ever' time I've set on these here steps in the black dark of night, settin' here watchin' them out there in the yard, makin' circles out of candles and mixin' up shit in that ol' washpot with a fire under it and all, just like a coupla damn witches in the damn movies. Him standin' there stirrin' it, her sayin', 'Do you use the young shoots, Papa, or the stems?' Shit like that. Learnin' her trade. And her singin'—Lord God, it gimme a chill to set here and hear her singin' out there in the night some-where. Got to where I finally had to move around to the front of the house."

"So Leeman's right," Buddy said. "If you were her, what would you do? There was his daddy, and maybe even his daddy's daddy, and there was him, and there's her."

"You got it, brother," Sears said flatly. "She's gone be the next one. She's gone be the Rattlesnake Master."

"Far out," Buddy said.

"Ain't it," Sears Ellis said. "He even started gettin' some of the people who came down here to see him to see her instead. But what with her startin' in helpin' him do his work and him and her both worryin' over them silver dollars and gettin' ready to get out of here, me 'n' Elizabeth ain't had much time lately. And now she's gone."

So we sat there and gnawed on our own thoughts for a while,

and Sears and Buddy each opened another beer. I could hear robins squawking petulantly at each other in the woods.

Finally Buddy said, "How'd they leave?"

"Somebody come and got 'em," Sears Ellis said.

"Somebody," Buddy said. "What happened to all their stuff?"

"Took it or give it away," Sears said. "What ain't left in the house."

"Did either one of them say how he planned to get them dollars out of the country?" Buddy said. "Or had he already got rid of them somehow, sellin' them or somethin'?"

"Man, make up yo mind which end of this story you wanta listen to," Sears said.

"I'm sorry," Buddy said, and shifted his feet. "I reckon I'm just actin' like the law again."

"I 'spect you're excused," Sears said. "She didn't say nothin' about that, noway. We didn't get to talk much. And I ain't well acquainted enough with either of you to be tellin' you the things we did talk about. It was between me and her."

"That's all right with me," Buddy said. "Did she say she was gone come back?"

Sears Ellis seemed to be thinking. "Yeah," he said after a minute. "She said she's gone come back, but she didn't know just when and it might be a little time and it might be a long time."

Buddy grunted.

"So what're you gonna do?" I said.

"I reckon I'm doin' it," Sears Ellis said. "Looks to me like I'm waitin' around for somethin'. Maybe she won't be gone long."

We all seemed to think that was as good a time as any to stop talking, so we did, and nobody said a word until the sun was in the treetops. Mourning doves were calling, and I could hear the evening breeze rattling Leeman Gant's palm trees.

"Well," Buddy said, "I reckon till she gets back I've seen the end of it." He stood up. I did, too, and stepped onto the ground. Buddy followed me and we stood in the yard and looked at Sears Ellis and the house with a pair of bluebirds painted over the back door.

"Y'all leavin', I see," said Sears Ellis.

"Yeah," Buddy said. "We got to be back in town before too late, somebody's puttin' on a big to-do for me and my girlfriend."

"They're about to get married," I said.

"How about that?" Sears Ellis said. "One of 'em got you, huh?"

"Yeah," Buddy said, "I reckon."

"It was a long struggle," I said. Sears chuckled. Buddy and I were smiling. It was a good moment to leave on.

"If y'all really are goin'," Sears Ellis said, "hold on a minute. I got to get somethin' out of the house. I'll meet y'all round yonder."

So Buddy and I walked around to the front of the house, though he got there ahead of me since I stopped to look at Leeman Gant's backyard for the last time and stopped again under the palm trees and closed my eyes and listened to the wind blow through them above my head. When I got to the front yard, Buddy and Sears Ellis were standing beside the Cutlass, each of them holding a small package wrapped in brown paper.

"Here," Sears Ellis said, and handed me his package. It fit in my hand.

"What's this?" I said.

"Somethin' he wanted me to give you," Sears Ellis said. "He said it was somethin' for you to remember him by. He said to tell you it was a present from the Rattlesnake Master."

The one Buddy got was made in 1921 at the mint in Philadelphia. It was in pretty good shape, and Buddy got it cleaned up and encased in Lucite and still uses it as a paperweight, I guess.

The one Leeman Gant left for me was made in 1889 at the mint in Carson City, Nevada. When I last looked, it was worth something like $675. Or $1,350 if you're in Barbados.

SIXTEEN

When Karen told me she and Buddy were going to Barbados on their honeymoon, the first thing I thought was that I should have figured on that to begin with.

I didn't hear about it from Buddy himself until three days later. It was a Thursday, and he and I were sitting in my little office at the college. This time he had managed to come by when Angela Stallings was at her desk, and I finally had to get up from my own desk and go out into the reception area and invite him in, or he would have shortly run out of relatives of hers that he knew and could ask her about.

Buddy shut the door behind him, then went and sat in the big armchair by the window.

"Whew," he said, and grinned. A lock of hair had fallen across his forehead, and his hand went up and put it back in place.

"Did you get your fill of coveting your neighbor's wife?" I said.

Buddy made a clicking noise with his tongue. "Wasn't that," he said. "Well, not entirely. She's too good-lookin' to be real. Tell me she's stupid or somethin'."

"Sharp as a tack. She could be governor."

"Nuts," Buddy said. "There's got to be something the matter with her."

"Yes," I said smugly. "Morning sickness. She's pregnant. You can come in here and watch her swell up for the next few months, then she'll go on maternity leave, and who knows if she'll ever come back?"

"Damn that Corey Stallings," Buddy said.

"Why? She's his wife, they're young and in love, they're going to have a lovely, screaming, shitting little baby."

Buddy scrunched up his mouth. "Yeah, yeah," he said. "It's sour grapes, is all."

"Anyhow," I said, "you've got one of your own that most men would kill for."

"Sure," Buddy said defensively. "But that's not the point. I mean, well, I dunno. I reckon you never can stop lookin' at them."

"Especially when they look like Angela Stallings."

Buddy laughed. "Okay, okay," he said. "Enough of that. So how're you?"

"Annoyed. How come you didn't tell me you and Karen were going to Barbados on your honeymoon? Is it because you thought I'd make fun of you—since I know how come you're really going down there?"

"Karen told me she spilled the beans," Buddy said, "and I figured I should say something, but I been real busy. And besides, I wanted some time to think about it before I sat down in front of you and got bombarded with questions."

"You're really gone do it, then," I said, and smirked at him.

"Yep. Might as well. It got Karen all excited."

"Uh-huh. And she doesn't even know the real reason you're springing for a trip to the West Indies. She probably thinks you're going to a tropical island to be with her."

"Aw," Buddy said, "I'm going on my honeymoon. Really. We're gone sit in the sun, drink rum, eat lots of fish, dance under the stars, go to bed early, and sleep late—just like we'd do if we was goin' to Bermuda or Jamaica or one of them other places."

"Except."

"Except that one day while we're there I'm gone turn Karen loose in town with her credit cards and go out and explore the countryside a little bit. Talk to some of the people, y'know. . . ."

"Two people in particular," I said. I envied him for a minute. I wanted to go somewhere, too. His trip to Barbados was going to have a little intrigue in it besides the natural romance, and it was easy for me to want some of both. Or either.

"Uh-huh," Buddy said.

"You better have a good map," I said knowingly, and backed up my chair and put my feet on my desk. "There ain't a whole lot of signs on the roads. And how do you expect to find them people, anyway? Look in the yellow pages under Rattlesnake Masters?"

Buddy laughed. "In case you ain't had a chance to notice lately, I'm a deputy sheriff. And they've got law in Barbados, too. Ol' Pete Markowitz down yonder at the Law Enforcement Training Center got me hooked up with some people in whatchacallit, Bridgetown, and it just so happens that I know exactly where our friends the Gants are livin'—and all their silver dollars, too, I reckon." He pulled at his nose with his thumb and forefinger.

"It ain't been all that long since they left," I said. "Maybe they're still lookin' out for something like this. I mean, they got to know that you know it was them that got that money."

"And if they do," Buddy said, "I bet they also know I ain't gone try and get it back."

Neither of us said anything for maybe thirty seconds. I could hear Grace Teal's typewriter clicking and dinging in the next room. I gave Buddy what I hoped was a piercing look and he cocked a questioning eyebrow back at me.

"So what's this really all about?" I said. "If that's the way you feel, I'm happy about it, but I got to admit I'm not real sure what you want to accomplish by going down there."

Buddy felt in his shirt pocket for a cigarette, then seemed to change his mind. I wondered if it had anything to do with Angela Stallings's condition or the sign on her desk that said *Please Don't Smoke Here.*

"I ain't all that sure myself," he said. "Maybe it's because I feel like I got fooled just a little bit, and I ain't as docile about that as you are. Or maybe it's because I still can't make myself believe that a lot of mumbo jumbo was really behind what happened."

I raised an eyebrow of my own.

"Yeah, I know," Buddy said. "I'm like you and Sears Ellis, I cain't explain it any other way, either. But man, this is the twentieth century! Shit like that ain't supposed to happen."

"If you go down there and they turn you into a frog, I reckon you'll finally be content," I said.

Buddy grinned. "Then I could get your secretary to kiss me and turn me into a prince," he said happily.

"Jesus," I said, and took my feet off the desk and sat up relatively straight in my chair. "What's the matter with you?"

Buddy's face fell a little. "I dunno," he said, and looked at the closed door. "I love Karen more'n anything else in the world, but God oughta stop makin' women like Angela Stallings. They burrow down into your brain."

"I knew it had something to do with your brain," I said, just to be mean. Outside the window beside my desk, the campus was filling with people, so I knew without looking at my watch that it was nearly five o'clock.

"Listen," I said, "I'm thinking a couple of things. First, it's not just that Sears Ellis and I were prepared to stand being taken to the cleaners and you weren't. I bet pride's got something to do with it. Ain't no way you could be very happy about that old man coming into your county and pullin' off something like that right under your nose. And second, maybe you're still a little put out that it was me they invited down there to their place and not you."

Buddy thought a minute. He was looking out his window at the people going by, too. "Maybe they did hurt my pride a little," he said, "by doin' just about whatever they damn well pleased right here in my backyard, but I wasn't ever put out by them makin' up to you like that. I just puzzled over it.

"But now I understand. Why should they have bothered with me? It was you they had plans for."

"Now you're getting back to the mumbo jumbo part," I said.

Buddy reached for his cigarettes again, and this time he got one and took it out of the pack and put the pack back in his pocket.

"Okay," he said. "Maybe that's it. Maybe that's really what I want to find out about. Maybe I want the two of them to tell me straight out exactly how they did all that stuff." He shrugged. "And as long as I can get down there to where they are and have an even better reason than them to be there, then why the hell not see if I can get them to talk to me?"

"Sure," I said. "So this time it'll be you that's coming back to tell me what you found out from the old man and not the other way around."

"Who else gives a damn but you?"

"Okay, I'll send Karen a terrarium to bring you home in."

"Haw," Buddy said. He sat back in his chair, crossed his legs, and stuck his cigarette in his mouth. His right hand went to his pants pocket to get his lighter.

Before he got it, there was a knock on the door. I said, "Come in," and Angela Stallings did. Buddy's right hand came slowly out of his pocket, but his left hand came up off the arm of his chair in a hurry and snatched the cigarette out of his mouth. Angela said she was sorry to interrupt and I said she wasn't interrupting, and she sat down in the straight-backed chair next to Buddy.

"I'm just about to leave," she said with obvious satisfaction, "and just wanted to know if there was something else you wanted me to do before I go. I got all those fliers ready to go off in tomorrow morning's mail."

"Thanks," I said. She had a beautiful mouth, and I looked at it. "I reckon that's about all there is for today. I'm just sitting here killing time with the deputy myself."

Buddy threw me a hurt look, but then he turned toward Angela and the look he had sent me was replaced by the sort of gaze with which some people regard the Sistine Chapel or the Taj Mahal.

"Uh, Angela," Buddy said, and got her to look back at him. "Leeman here tells me you're, uh, you're goin' to have a baby."

Angela Stallings's face bloomed into a smile of considerable brilliance. "Yes," she said happily. "Isn't it something? I'm so excited about it!"

"Yeah, well, congratulations," Buddy said lamely. "Congratulations to Corey, too."

Angela beamed rapturously. "It's a dream come true."

Buddy looked at me. "Yeah, I know what you mean," he said, not quite suppressing a silly grin. I scowled at him.

So Angela Stallings made some more sounds of joy and then excused herself and went back to her desk and made some noise there and at the coatrack, too, and in a minute she and Grace Teal both hollered " 'bye!" and went through the glass doors into the hall.

Buddy retrieved his cigarette, took out a lighter with an armadillo on it, and lit up.

"Hunh," he said, shaking his head. "A baby. Lord have mercy. Let's just hope it looks like its mama."

"That does it," I said. "You're definitely coming home as a frog."

Before Buddy and Karen could go to Barbados they had to get married, and they did that just over two weeks from the afternoon Buddy and I sat in my office with Angela Stallings.

On the Friday night before the Sunday they got married, Lamar Torrance and Sheriff Lundquist and a bunch of people I didn't know very well had a big party for Buddy in the back room of the Red Hot Saloon, a brand-new gaudy bar and grill out on highway 301 across from the mall.

When Sam Campbell and I got there, the front of the place was jam-packed with college kids, but we both recognized people we knew, too. Some of them should have been at home with their wives or their husbands.

There was one particular person I knew: Donna Calloway was sitting in a booth near the bar with two other women. One of them was named Christine Smock and was a registered nurse at the college health center; she didn't know me, but I had read her nameplate once. I don't know who the other woman was, but she and Christine Smock didn't get much of my attention, anyway. Mostly what I wondered when I wasn't just looking at Donna or replaying my dream at the Rattlesnake Master's house was whether this trio was out cruising for love.

I decided to find out, hoping they weren't. As if it was any of my business.

Donna saw me and smiled and waved as I made my way over to her booth through the loud mass of people standing around the bar. She had on jeans and a white blouse with a lightweight denim jacket over it, and she was clean-scrubbed and shampooed and looked vigorous and supple and daring.

She seemed genuinely glad to see me, too, or so I said to myself, and she introduced me to Christine Smock and to the other woman I still don't know, and told them both about how she'd been waiting on me at Cook's for months now—"he's gotten to be a regular," she said, throwing me a little glance that might have been conspiracy—and about how sometimes we'd sit together when her shift ended and talk about books, mostly. When she said "books," the woman whose name I can't remember looked at me as though I was some sort of curio.

But since my dream with her in it, I had been less and less inclined to talk to Donna about books, and in fact we seemed to be able to talk about pretty much anything at all—sitting there in my usual booth at Cook's while the other waitresses, the ones still working, stole glances at us and wondered what the hell was really going on—except romance, which I avoided entirely. I thought long and hard about it, true; but she was still a lot younger than I was and she was Buddy Crittenden's cousin, to boot. Besides, my heart was still wary from having had somebody give it the kind of treatment generally reserved for cockroaches and scorpions. And Donna Calloway looked pretty dangerous to me. So whatever other talk I might otherwise have had, or wanted to have, with her never got out of my mouth.

I explained to the three women why Sam and I were there—by then Sam had come up, too, and I had introduced him around, though I forgot that other woman's name and she had to say it herself—and Donna said she was not only going to be at the wedding, she was also going to represent Buddy's side of the family in Karen's entourage as a bridesmaid. So I assumed she was going to be at the rehearsal on Saturday night, and by great force of will managed to volunteer to pick her up. But she had another wedding, one of the formal evening variety, to go to instead.

"Oh," I said, and, thus rejected, tried to think of a conversational smoke screen under the cover of which I could beat a dignified retreat and sulk a little bit.

"What about the wedding?" she said. "We could go to that together. You can show me what I've got to do since I'll miss the rehearsal."

That sounded good to me, so Donna and I agreed that I would pick her up and that we'd go to Buddy and Karen's wedding together, and even be in it together, too, and Sam and I excused ourselves and went to find the room in which Buddy's pals and colleagues were drinking beer and smoking and telling dirty stories.

Buddy was trying conscientiously to have a good time, though Sam said it seemed pretty obvious that if Buddy had really had a choice about how to spend the penultimate night of his life as a single man, he would not have chosen to spend it pretending to pay attention to Lamar Torrance's recitation of the extraordinary sexual habits of Empress Catherine the Great of Russia, about which he had read in a skin magazine loaned to him by his brother-in-law.

Things started to get tough when Sheriff Lundquist said good night and wished Buddy the best of luck and said he'd see him after the ceremony and went home. But I think Buddy didn't decide to start drinking in earnest until the crew from the local law enforcement contingent revealed that it had arranged a surprise—which turned out to be a stripper with a big nose and too much eye shadow who thoroughly embarrassed Buddy by flinging parts of her body at him and who refused to remove her one remaining piece of clothing even after Rusty Cooper of the police department offered her a twenty-dollar bill.

When Sam and I went home, which was early relative to the run of celebrants, Donna and her friends and a lot of other people had already left the place ahead of us. I didn't have to worry until Sunday about the circumstances under which she had left, though, because on the way to Buddy and Karen's wedding at the First United Methodist Church she told me that she and Christine Smock and the other woman, whose name I can't remember, had gone to Christine Smock's apartment and played gin rummy. For some reason I was relieved. As if it was any of my business.

Then when I escorted her down the aisle of the church while the organ played, I remembered how it felt to walk with her on the beach in my dream in the little bedroom at Leeman Gant's house, and how well it seemed that I knew her then, and she was perfect, she was different from anyone I had ever known. Different enough, anyway. As we made our way, me looking straight ahead and trying to be dignified even though I knew not one soul in that congregation was watching me when Donna was next to me to be looked at instead, for just an instant it seemed not only that it hadn't been a dream at all but also that when the wedding was over, it would be utterly plausible for us to go home to the same place and stay there.

But that was stupid. I knew I couldn't do anything, I couldn't even decide how to approach her, even if I ever decided to approach her in the first place.

I didn't even want to be interested in her, but I was, anyway, and didn't know what to do about it. I felt like some sort of invalid that she was helping to get past the rows of pews and all the faces in them so we could separate and join Buddy and the preacher and Buddy's daddy at the altar.

The wedding went off about as smoothly as weddings go, though Buddy's daddy, who was best man, had a cold and kept punctuating the service with sniffles of the sort that locomotives made when there were locomotives around to make them.

If I stood just right at the altar, then anyone in the pews choosing to look at me for whatever reason would have thought I was watching Karen and Buddy. But except for one time when I was watching Buddy's aunt Sandy, who was scribbling something and paying absolutely no attention to the ceremony, I was watching Donna. She was stupefyingly lovely in a long, pale yellow dress. The same yellow as her bathing suit, the one in my dream.

At first I tried just watching parts of her, but it got so that I didn't know which part to watch, the various parts from which she was assembled being as eye-catching as they were. So I tried just to watch her in general, thinking also that she might catch me looking at one particularly attractive part or another and be offended.

Once in a while she did catch me looking at her, but only once in a while, and it was disgruntling to me to think she wasn't paying the same attention to me that I was paying to her—until I remembered that we were there to see a wedding, after all, and that it's the men who do the looking and the women who wait while the men look and decide what to do. When our eyes did meet, one of us, usually me, would look away, except for one time when the preacher was giving a little lecture on the meaning of marriage or some such and our eyes stayed locked together for a few seconds. She seemed to be trying to tell me something, too, something that felt as though it might even be encouragement, but I couldn't be sure and so what I did was blush and turn away.

When the preacher told us that Buddy and Karen had suddenly become husband and wife, everyone audibly relaxed and Buddy and Karen kissed. Buddy's daddy took out a handkerchief and blew his nose so loudly that at first I thought the organ had begun to play. Then when the organ did begin to play an instant later, I jumped. I looked at Donna and she was looking at me and obviously she had seen me jump, but she just smiled and wrinkled her nose and I thought again of her in my dream. I decided to stop doing that. And then we were walking toward each other and locking arms and following Buddy's daddy and Karen's best friend, the maid of honor, back up the aisle and out of the church into the sunlight.

We all went to a reception out at the Holiday Inn and drank champagne and ate cake and finger food, and then Buddy and Karen left for Savannah to spend the night at the Hilton before catching a plane to Miami and on to Bridgetown the next day. I took Donna home and didn't say anything to her about going out or any of the other things a loud part of me wanted to say. I decided that she had actually expected me to say something besides good night, but I did that only after I had gotten home and sat down in the dark and was wondering what to do next. And by then it was too late to do anything but get the Sunday-night blues.

SEVENTEEN

The thing about Jerry Spivey was that once something started to bother him, he couldn't rest until he had done something about it.

And what was bothering him most was that no matter how close he got to them, those silver dollars stayed just out of his grasp. First that little asshole Mango getting that bag of them, a bag Jerry Spivey had actually had in his own hands, a bag with silver dollars in it that he had even touched. Gone now.

Then there was the rest of those five thousand dollars old man Hutto hid in that filled-in well on his place in the country. Jerry Spivey remembered how he had reached into the bag that guy had handed him out of that hole and shuddered. Two days in the goddamn hospital. Just the worst damn luck. At least those two fellers, the one that handed him the bag and who had hit Sperry Bissell with the shovel, and that other one, the one who had been with that god damned deputy sheriff on the Saturday afternoon Sperry threw the sack of dollars out the car window, hadn't pressed any charges. So even with what he called that bastard Ramsey doing everything he could against him, Jerry Spivey didn't spend but thirty-three days in the lockup.

And now he'd been out for three weeks, spending most of his productive time loading trucks at the sock factory, and he was already tired of scrabbling for nickels and dimes and was thinking hard about what could have happened to that real money. He didn't know where Sperry Bissell was, and Sperry's daddy said he didn't know, either, just that Sperry's mama had thrown him out of the house after his run-in with the law. Maybe he had gone to Savannah or Atlanta.

Jerry Spivey wasn't even sure he wanted to find Sperry Bissell, anyhow. He still thought that fool took his time about getting him to the emergency room on purpose.

Dorothy Spivey had thrown her son out of the house, too, and Jerry Spivey had been forced to rent half of a run-down and filthy duplex on Yucca Terrace, a place Dorothy Spivey said a pig would turn up his nose at, which meant that it ought to be just the place for the son God gave her as punishment for her adultery with Hoyt Flowers the furnace man.

"Trash from trash," Dorothy Spivey said. "That dern furnace never did work right, either."

But Jerry Spivey didn't care what his mama thought, all he really wanted was to find out where those silver dollars had gone to. He didn't know yet, but as far as he was able to tell, nobody else had figured out where they were, either, so maybe he still had a shot.

He made a point of checking out Harold Buckminster just to see if he showed any evidence of a sudden increase in affluence. In fact, Jerry Spivey went so far as to go to Harold Buckminster's house in Brooklet and stand in the front yard and tell Harold Buckminster, who was behind the locked screen door, that he was sorry he had threatened him that time and how he'd turned over a new leaf and found Jesus and wanted to let bygones be bygones and buy a pint of Harold Buckminster's whiskey.

It wasn't bad whiskey, Jerry Spivey admitted to himself, and took another swallow from the jar. He couldn't have known that while Harold Buckminster showed no overt signs of having bettered his station in life, his whiskey-making operation had in fact had its physical plant drastically improved, and thereby also had begun to turn out a product of unquestionably higher quality and safety. Harold Buckminster was confident that he had used what came to him in such a way as to make an investment in his future, and that made him feel good.

After they left Harold Buckminster's place, Jerry Spivey and his

jar of whiskey parked in Jerry Spivey's Pontiac on the side of Putnam Street, which runs along behind J. B. Barrett's store in Brooklet. That meant Jerry Spivey was in a good position to see Royal
Mango come out of J. B. Barrett's parking lot at 6:15 P.M. and turn
right and head in a direction more or less out of town.

Jerry Spivey was no fool; he knew Royal Mango hadn't had a
vehicle of any kind the last time he saw the scruffy little twerp, and
now he could see plain as day that Royal Mango left J. B. Barrett's
store in a '79 Chevy truck.

This is too easy, Jerry Spivey thought. All I've got to do is follow
him out of here and see where he goes. As long as it ain't home to
that bitch and that shotgun, then we'll see.

But Royal Mango did go home, and Jerry Spivey had to get off
an hour early from the sock factory the next day to go back down
to Brooklet and sit on the side of Putnam Street and watch him
leave J. B. Barrett's store in his truck again.

And this time it was easy indeed, because Royal Mango's truck
was carrying three large plastic bags of trash that J. B. Barrett had
asked him to take by the dump on his way home. So when Royal
Mango got out of his truck at the dump and went around to unload
the bags, he was treated to the sight of Jerry Spivey driving in
behind him and pulling up in a half circle and turning off the
Pontiac and getting out and saying "Remember me?" as though in
one grand motion.

"Sho," Royal Mango said, and took a quick inventory of safe
places he could run to.

"Don't think nothin' about goin' anywhere," Jerry Spivey said.
"Last time I made you and that horse's butt you married a promise
that this time I'd have the metal, and this time I got it."

What Royal Mango saw in Jerry Spivey's right hand was Jerry
Spivey's daddy's .32 automatic. It was too little and too far away for
him to see if the safety catch was on, however.

"Put up the gun," Royal Mango said. "If'n you shoot me, you
ain't gone fine out nothin'. If you puts the gun back in yo pocket,
I'll tell you whatever it is that you wants to know."

For just a second, Jerry Spivey didn't know what to say. He'd expected deceit, denial, even pleading, maybe; but cooperation, capitulation, was far down the list.

"You swear to God?" he said.

"Sho," Royal Mango said. "Whatever you wants to know."

"Okay," Jerry Spivey said, pocketing the .32. "Look, I'm doin' it. Now come over here nice and easy."

So Jerry Spivey leaned back against his car and Royal Mango walked over to him nice and easy, careful to stay out of reach, and Jerry Spivey said, "I ain't gone beat around the bush. Who got all them silver dollars what was in that well out yonder on Calvin Hutto's place?"

"Whose place?" Royal Mango said.

"All right, god damn it," Jerry Spivey said, standing up straight now. "Don't play stupid with me. It ain't the place that matters noway, it's them dollars and I saw them with my own eyes and somebody came out there and stole them. And I b'lieve you was in on it, or know about it, anyway."

"Oh," Royal Mango said. "Uh-huh."

"Uh-huh what?" Jerry Spivey said. He felt his ears getting warm.

"What is it you wants to know?" Royal Mango said.

"Jesus at the rodeo," Jerry Spivey said. "Maybe you really are that stupid. Them silver dollars you got on the side of the road down yonder—I don't know how you got 'em, but you can have 'em, for all I care. If there's any of them you ain't circled behind that shotgun and spent yet.

"You listenin' to me?"

"Sho," Royal Mango said, and nodded.

"There was a lot more of them buried on Calvin Hutto's place back up here on the Springfield Road. They all come out of the same pile. Somebody got them what was buried, they come in and stole 'em. You hearin' me?"

"Sho," said Royal Mango. He didn't know where to look, but he didn't want to look at Jerry Spivey.

"All right, then," Jerry Spivey said, and Royal Mango looked at him, anyway. "You know what I'm talkin' about. Tell me where the rest of them dollars are at."

"What you gone do if I does?" Royal Mango said.

"I'm gone negotiate for their return," Jerry Spivey said, and grinned, thinking of the help he would get from the arbitrator in his jacket. His hand went into the pocket where the gun was and bounced the ugly little machine around where Royal Mango could see it.

Royal Mango saw it. He didn't know the .32 wasn't loaded, but it wasn't, since Jerry Spivey had gone through everything his father left behind without finding a clip with cartridges in it.

Even if Royal Mango had known about the empty clip, he probably still would have said, "What about me?"

"What about you?" Jerry Spivey said derisively.

"What gone happen to me after I tell you?" Royal Mango said.

"Nothing," Jerry Spivey said.

Neither of them said anything for a minute, they just stood there as the sun inched its way down toward the piles of debris. The air around the two men stank of rotting food. Jerry Spivey could look past Royal Mango's left shoulder and see a rat gnawing furiously at something, but he tried not to watch it.

To get his mind off the rat, Jerry Spivey said, "Well?"

"You got to follow me to Turleyville," Royal Mango said.

"Turleyville?" Jerry Spivey said, and laughed. "Man, what the hell's down there?"

"Silver dollars, I reckon," Royal Mango said. He could feel sweat running from his armpits down his sides.

"Then you and me sho gone have to go down there," Jerry Spivey said.

"You gone follow me?" Royal Mango said hopefully.

"Shit, no," Jerry Spivey said. "And have you drive up to the police station or somethin'? You gone ride down there *with* me, and that's all there is to it."

Royal Mango thought about the gun in Jerry Spivey's jacket

pocket. "You let me off at Brewster's Grocery there in Turleyville?" he said. "They locks it up at eight o'clock and the telephone's inside."

"Maybe," Jerry Spivey said. "After we drive by the place where them dollars are at and you show it to me. But don't get no ideas about tellin' any them other niggers about this, you understand?" His hand, still in his jacket pocket, dandled the gun some more.

"I ain't tellin' nobody nothin'," Royal Mango said.

So they got into Jerry Spivey's Pontiac, Jerry Spivey telling Royal Mango he sho hoped that ugly pickup of his was still there when he finally got back to the dump, and drove down to Turleyville in absolute silence except for Royal Mango saying turn right or turn left or go straight.

By and by after the sun had been down for a while, Royal Mango said, "That there's it," and Jerry Spivey stopped in the middle of the dark road and backed up and looked and could see a light at the end of a narrow dirt track, meaning there was a house somewhere back in behind the trees that bordered the road.

"Them silver dollars are back there?" Jerry Spivey said.

"I reckon so," Royal Mango said.

"Well, tallyho," Jerry Spivey said, beginning to feel adrenaline sizzle through him like electricity. He took the Pontiac through a U-turn and headed back toward Turleyville. But instead of taking Royal Mango all the way to Brewster's Grocery, where there were always a couple of people sitting around outside and where there might be a telephone that Royal Mango had lied to him about, Jerry Spivey let his passenger out about a mile and a half short of Turleyville, warning him again to keep his mouth shut.

Royal Mango stood and watched while Jerry Spivey made another U-turn and accelerated into the darkness. Then he grinned and turned his back on the Pontiac's retreating taillights and began walking toward the intersection that was Turleyville. The great black woods loomed up around him.

"No sir," Royal Mango said, and grinned again. "I ain't sayin' nothin' to nobody. Not for a couple hours, anyway." And then he laughed loud and long, the sound careening ahead of him down the corridor of trees.

Jerry Spivey turned off the paved road and drove on dirt past a thin line of woods and underbrush into the yard of Leeman Gant's house. One window was lit. Jerry Spivey wasn't particularly happy to be out there at night, principally because it meant he couldn't try to pass himself off as a salesman or somebody from the REA and would have to come up with something more direct.

He stopped the Pontiac close to the house and got out and walked softly up the little path to the porch steps. He had seen the palm trees, but the night was too dark for him to tell what they were, or even to wonder.

"Hello!" he called. "Anybody home in there?"

Elizabeth Gant came to the screen door. Jerry Spivey could see her silhouette, but he couldn't tell much about it.

"Yes," she said. "What is it?"

" 'Scuse me," Jerry Spivey said. "Is the man of the house at home?"

"No," Elizabeth said. "What do you want?"

So far, Jerry Spivey had heard nothing but good news. "Well, frankly," he said, "what I want is to talk. I hear tell you folks may have come into some money that not a whole lot of other people know you got. But I know about it, and I even got a claim on it. We need to talk it over before I do something drastic, like go to the law."

"Step up into the light," Elizabeth said, and her hand went to the wall beside her and a bare bulb lit up on the ceiling of the porch.

Jerry Spivey did as she asked. He figured he could tie this gal up or something and go through the place if he had to, but he didn't want to get ugly unless there wasn't any other way. First he'd see how reasonable she was, and then he'd know what to do.

"I don't think you will go to the law," Elizabeth said. Her voice was soft, its inflection barely changing.

"Maybe," Jerry Spivey said, and smiled, "and maybe not. But as long as you got them silver dollars—and that's what we're talkin' about, ain't it?—then you cain't never rest over them as long as I know you got them."

Elizabeth stood in the doorway behind the screen and didn't say anything at all.

"Well?" Jerry Spivey said, after a minute. He could feel the lump the .32 made in his jacket pocket. "We gone talk, or what?"

"Come into the house," Elizabeth said, and unlocked the screen door and held it open wide.

Hot dog, Jerry Spivey thought. He wasn't used to spending time in nigger houses, but this was for a good cause. And he could probably talk this weird nigger gal right out of her shoes if he had to. He'd find out where them silver dollars was put away, and he'd let on that all he wanted was a fair cut of them, and then he'd figure what to do from there. But once he found out where they were, these people had better look out.

So Jerry Spivey clomped up the steps and Elizabeth backed up until he had his hand on the screen door and then led him into the house to the table in the kitchen, where Jerry Spivey sat down on one side and she sat down on the other.

No sooner were they both seated than Elizabeth said, "Please excuse me for a minute," and stood up and left the room.

What now? Jerry Spivey thought, and as he put his hand in his jacket pocket to feel the gun he heard the back door open and Elizabeth clap her hands hard, twice, and then the door closed again.

When Elizabeth returned to the kitchen, she got a little kettle from a shelf and filled it with water from the tap and put it on the stove. Jerry Spivey heard a pump come on somewhere.

"Um, where's the rest of your people?" Jerry Spivey said.

"They are away," Elizabeth said, not looking at him, and took a match out of her apron pocket and lit a pale blue candle standing in a cockle shell in the middle of the table. Then she sat down.

At least she's clean, Jerry Spivey thought, and this house is pretty neat, maybe she's got some sense and I can get somewhere if I just be cool.

"Uh, okay," he said. "Then I reckon it's just us two got to negotiate this thing."

"Apparently," Elizabeth said. She was dressed all in white, and Jerry Spivey thought to himself that if the light was any dimmer he'd probably feel as though he was sitting across the table from a ghost. Nah, he thought, niggers are afraid of ghosts, none of them would ever be one.

"Okay," Jerry Spivey said again. "Who's gone be first?"

"You," Elizabeth said, and met his gaze. "You are the one who wants to negotiate."

Jerry Spivey chuckled and took a Kool and a pack of matches out of his shirt pocket.

"Would you like an ashtray?" Elizabeth said, standing up.

"Much obliged," Jerry Spivey said, and she went to a drawer by the sink and got another cockle shell and handed it to him and sat down again. Jerry Spivey lit his cigarette and put his dead match in the cockle. The night was black and featureless through the kitchen window, but he could hear crickets.

"All right," Elizabeth said.

"Well, um," Jerry Spivey said, blowing smoke. He felt remarkably relaxed. Maybe all the trouble he'd been through was worth it. Looked like he'd get them dollars yet if this was all that was left in his way. Then he'd be able to get out of this godforsaken south Georgia shitpile, go to California or something. Maybe to Miami. Live it up a little.

"Um, I know about them silver dollars what was buried in that old well out yonder on Calvin Hutto's place," Jerry Spivey went on, "and I got it on good report that somebody who lives in this house has got 'em or knows where they are. I know the law didn't find them, at least they said they didn't. All I want is to be included in the deal."

Elizabeth didn't say anything right away, but there was a bump at the back door and Jerry Spivey saw her eyes move in that direction.

"You sure there ain't nobody else here?" he said suspiciously.

"Yes," Elizabeth said. "No one else is here. Please continue."

"Look," Jerry Spivey said, "what else can I say? Either you gone tell me where them silver dollars have got off to, or you ain't."

"Your interest in them is personal," Elizabeth said.

She *does* know, Jerry Spivey thought. He wanted to shout it. *She knows where they are!*

"You might say that," he said matter-of-factly. "Mr. Hutto was my goddaddy and he promised them to me."

"But he stole them," Elizabeth said patiently, as if correcting a child. The kettle was beginning to hum.

Jerry Spivey took a drag from his cigarette. There was another bump at the back door, but Elizabeth ignored it, or seemed to. Smoke was hanging low over the table, swirling crazily where it rose with heat from the candle.

"I heard tell of that," Jerry Spivey said. "But I ain't seen no proof of it yet. All I know is that they was promised to me and I ain't got 'em, I ain't got a single one of 'em.

"And lady," he said, and smiled mockingly across the table at Elizabeth, "I do mean to have my cut."

Elizabeth looked at him. "What if I tell you they are spent?" she said.

Jerry Spivey shrugged. "Then I wouldn't believe you," he said. "You don't spend real silver dollars no more, nohow. You smart, you sell 'em first, then you spend what you get. I ain't ready to believe you done sold 'em all. I believe they're somewhere on this place."

"Who told you that?" Elizabeth said. The kettle began to sing, and she got up and turned down the fire under it.

"A little bird," Jerry Spivey said.

"Did you do anything to Mr. Mango?" Elizabeth said. She was pulling tiny jars from a cupboard, arranging them on the counter, watching her work and not looking at Jerry Spivey.

"What do you mean?" Jerry Spivey said, and put out his cigarette in the cockle shell.

"Did you hurt him?" Elizabeth said. She was reaching into a drawer, and Jerry Spivey stiffened a little and put his hand in his jacket pocket again in case hers reappeared with a knife in it. But when Elizabeth closed the drawer she had a pair of tea balls in her hand, and she laid them on the counter with the jars. Jerry Spivey wondered what they were.

"Naw," he said. "Why would I want to do that?"

"What if I refuse to talk to you anymore about silver dollars?" Elizabeth said, and came back to the table and sat primly on the edge of her chair.

"Then I reckon I go out of here and come back with the law," Jerry Spivey said. Even he could tell there wasn't much conviction behind it.

Elizabeth smiled, and it infuriated him.

"Mr. Spivey," Elizabeth said, "for that's who you are, isn't it? We both know you have no intention of going to the law about this. If you had a legitimate claim to those silver dollars, you'd be there now instead of here."

Jerry Spivey nodded slowly. For a nigger gal, he thought, this one had something on the ball. She was making him just a little bit uncomfortable, too, being so laid-back about the whole thing. Maybe he'd have to change his approach.

But not yet.

"Look," he said, "maybe you're right. But maybe, too, if you ain't willin' to let me in on some of the action, could be that ain't neither one of us gone end up with that money. All I want to do is work out an arrangement with you where you people get some and I get some and then everybody's happy."

"I'm happy now," Elizabeth said.

"Good for you," Jerry Spivey said, and took out another Marlboro and lit it with a match. Smoke slithered through the air over the candle. "I reckon you don't think I'm serious about this."

"On the contrary," Elizabeth said, and stood up again and went back to the counter and the little jars and began opening them. Jerry Spivey felt the gun in his pocket. "I consider you to be very serious."

"Good," Jerry Spivey said. "I don't want to have to make no trouble for nobody."

Elizabeth filled one of the tea balls from the largest jar, set it aside, then filled the other from three of the tiny jars and set it beside the first one.

"Perhaps there is something we can discuss," she said, and walked past the table at which Jerry Spivey sat with one hand holding a cigarette and the other in the pocket of his jacket, and went into the hallway and to the back door. Jerry Spivey heard the door open and stood up, putting his cigarette into the cockle.

But Elizabeth came back looking the same as when she left, so Jerry Spivey sat back down and picked up his cigarette.

"What's out there you keep goin' to see?" he asked as Elizabeth took two thick white mugs from the cupboard.

"Just checking on the animals," she said, "calling them to the house."

"Hunh," Jerry Spivey said. "I'm waitin'."

"So are we all, for something," Elizabeth said, and wiped the mugs with a dish towel.

Jerry Spivey sighed. First she says we got something to talk about, he thought, then she's stalling me again.

"You gone let me see them silver dollars, or what?" he said. "I ain't got all night to mess around out here in the boondocks."

Elizabeth put a tea ball in each mug and poured hot water over them from the kettle.

"Presuming they are here," she said, "how do you propose to take some of them with you?"

"I got a car," Jerry Spivey said.

"Yes," Elizabeth said. "And what if they aren't here?"

Jerry Spivey shifted in his seat. He was getting pretty tired of all this. "Then you gone have to take me to wherever they're at, I reckon."

"Perhaps I would do that," Elizabeth said, looking down into the mugs of tea, "but how do I know you wouldn't want them all? What assurance do I have that you would simply take a cut, as you say, and leave us alone?"

"You got my word on it," Jerry Spivey said, and smiled, mostly to himself. He put the butt of his cigarette into the cockle with the first one.

"Ah," Elizabeth said. "Is Mr. Mango safe?"

"You already asked me that," Jerry Spivey said. "I reckon he is, if he's walked back to Turleyville by now." He tried to laugh, but sniffed loudly instead. "So how 'bout it? Are we partners, or not?"

"Your tea is ready," Elizabeth said, and brought the two mugs to the table and put one of them down beside Jerry Spivey's hand. He saw that the tea in his cup was as brown as swamp water, the kind that's full of tannin, and had a tiny fog of steam on its surface.

"Why, that's mighty nice of you," he said with exaggerated politeness, "but I ain't studyin' no tea. In fact, I'm gettin' a bit tired of all this foolin' around." He looked at Elizabeth, who was seated again and looking at him, too.

"Drink your tea," she said, "and we'll talk some more." She took a sip from her own mug.

"Shit," Jerry Spivey said. "To hell with this damn tea and to hell with all this talk, too. Are you gone show me where them dollars are?"

"No," Elizabeth said softly, and took a sip from her cup.

"Well, lady," Jerry Spivey said, "then you are about to have more trouble than you can stand."

His right hand went into the pocket of his jacket and came out with the .32 and put it down on the edge of the table in front of him.

"I'm sorry," he said, "but you don't leave me no choice. And I reckon when it's all done, I ain't gone leave you with no dollars, either. All this conversation has made me greedy."

Elizabeth looked at the gun, then at Jerry Spivey, who had one corner of his mouth turned up. "Are you sure this is what you want to do?" she said.

"Lady," Jerry Spivey said, "I'm gone clean you out and there ain't nothin' you can do about it."

Elizabeth clapped her hands twice.

"What the hell?" Jerry Spivey said. He reached for the gun but didn't touch it, and suddenly his whole body was in motion and very soon he was standing on his chair.

"Ow!" Jerry Spivey said, bumping his head on the ceiling.

Elizabeth reached across the table between the cockle ashtray and the cockle with the blue candle in it, picked up the .32, and ejected the empty clip. She smiled then, but Jerry Spivey wasn't looking at her and didn't see it.

"Don't make a lot of commotion," she said. "They know me but they don't know you, and it's a good idea not to get them excited."

Jerry Spivey's mouth was open, but nothing came out. His eyes were wide open, too, staring at the floor.

Elizabeth clapped her hands softly and one of the two rattlesnakes slid over to her and raised part of itself into the air and worked its way into Elizabeth's lap and put its head on the table. Its tongue flicked out, then in, then out and in again.

"Sit down, Mr. Spivey," Elizabeth said, "and drink your tea."

Jerry Spivey was still looking down at the floor. "Ah, ah, there's another snake over here," he said hoarsely.

There was, indeed, a black and green eastern diamondback rattler as thick as Jerry Spivey's arm and all of seven feet long. The floor was covered, Jerry Spivey thought, covered with a snake.

"Yes," Elizabeth said. "But he probably won't bite you unless I tell him to. And then this one"—she ran a hand tenderly over the thick mass of snake in her lap—"will bite you, too."

"I done been snakebit once," Jerry Spivey said. He was sweating and his neck was beginning to cramp from holding his head bent under the ceiling.

"Yes," Elizabeth said again. "But that was a little one."

Jerry Spivey looked down at her. He remembered reaching into that bag of silver dollars by the old well on Calvin Hutto's place and feeling the snake inside it strike him and hold on and the poison burning in his arm.

"How d'you know that?" he said. There was something in his voice that he didn't like to hear.

"Mr. Spivey," Elizabeth said, as though talking to a child,

"you'd be surprised at what I know about you. Now sit down at the table and drink your tea before it gets cold."

"Get that bastard down there out of the way first," Jerry Spivey croaked.

"Certainly," Elizabeth said, and snapped her fingers lightly. The snake in her lap lifted its head from the table and looked at her hand, which she was holding in the air over the kitchen floor. The second snake slid over to her chair and raised its head to be rubbed and Elizabeth obliged. The snake rattled softly.

"Jesus," Jerry Spivey said, thinking it was a wonder he hadn't had a blowout in his pants, he'd never had a scare like that when he wasn't expecting one at all. And it wasn't just that he had already been bitten by one rattlesnake in his life, although it was that, too; it was more that these were the biggest god damned rattlesnakes he had ever seen up close, and these were too close. He sat back down in his chair very slowly, then took out another cigarette and lit it, pulling the cockle shell over to the edge of the table in front of him.

"All right," he said. "I guess we do this on your terms."

Elizabeth smiled and took her hand from the larger snake, which lowered itself back to the floor and disappeared under the table.

"I suppose we do," she said, and smiled. "If you try to leave, you will be bitten. You are much farther from assistance than you were the last time, and my friend under the table is full of venom."

"I ain't movin', bitch," Jerry Spivey snarled. "Just tell me what you want me to do."

"Drink your tea," Elizabeth said politely. "Then, if you still wish to talk, we will do so. But if you move too quickly, or even if you stand up, chances are that you will soon be dead."

"Who the hell are you?" Jerry Spivey said.

"My name is Elizabeth Gant," Elizabeth said.

"No," Jerry Spivey said, and took a deep drag from his cigarette. He was thinking fast, thinking what he could do. "That ain't what I mean." He flicked an ash into the cockle shell. Across the table from him the rattlesnake's tongue came out of its mouth, trembled, and returned.

"Some things are not for you to know," Elizabeth said. "Such as who I am, besides my name, and where the silver dollars are. They are no longer with the man who stole them long ago. Their theft caused another man, an innocent man, a lot of trouble and sorrow, but now they are going to make up for that. No one will ever tell you where they are."

"Well," Jerry Spivey said, stubbing out his cigarette, "why don't you and these two fellers let me waltz on out of here and we'll just forget the whole thing. Know what I mean?"

The snake with its head on the table seemed to be staring at him.

"How about it? Let's just forget I ever come out here, and I won't bother you, uh, people no more." He drummed his fingertips on the table, causing the snake, the one he could see, to put out its tongue again.

"No," Elizabeth said. "It's too late for that." The two of them looked at each other. "But drink your tea, and then perhaps you can go home."

Jerry Spivey picked up his cup.

"And supposin' I just sling this shit all over your kitchen?" he said. "What about that?"

Elizabeth tapped the table with the knuckles of her right hand and the two snakes rattled loudly. Jerry Spivey's feet retreated as far as they could under his chair.

"Please, Mr. Spivey," she said. "You will gain nothing by being difficult. Drink it."

Jerry Spivey's shoulders sagged. "You ain't gone poison me, are you?"

"No," Elizabeth said. "But you must drink it."

Jerry Spivey looked at her, then at the snake in her lap. Its head was still resting on the table, and Jerry Spivey thought for an instant about turning the table over and making a run for it, but there was still that other snake, the biggest one, somewhere around his feet.

"Now, Mr. Spivey," Elizabeth said, and the snake in her lap raised its head from the table and showed Jerry Spivey the inside of its mouth for a few seconds and then lay back down.

"All right," Jerry Spivey said angrily. "You got me. But I promise you I ain't forgettin' this." He brought the mug to his lips and took a swallow. The tea on his tongue was sweet and tasted the way flowers smell at a funeral.

"Just another promise you are unable to keep," Elizabeth said. "Drink it all."

Four eyes stared at Jerry Spivey. There was a fire in his stomach.

"Now," Elizabeth said, and Jerry Spivey tipped the cup and the warm tea went down his throat.

"Shit," he said, and looked at the blue candle. The flame seemed to dance and grow taller. The snake across from him raised its head from the table again and Jerry Spivey tried to look at it, but his eyes wouldn't move and his head was too heavy to turn. Now the candle roared in front of him like a bonfire.

And then Jerry Spivey went to hell.

It was well after midnight by the time Sears Ellis and Royal Mango arranged Jerry Spivey in the front seat of his car outside his duplex on Yucca Terrace. They put him behind the wheel of the Pontiac, his head thrown back and his mouth open, and closed the door.

"Man," Royal Mango said softly, "he sho went somewhere far off."

"Yeah," Sears Ellis said, "and somewhere neither you or me ever wants to go to, I reckon. Too bad he's still breathin'. If she'd left it up to me, we'd of just thowed him in the river."

"Haw," Royal Mango said. "What you reckon he's gone do when he wakes up?"

"Nothin'," Sears Ellis said. "She says he'll prob'ly wonder where he's been to and how he got home, and he'll have a hangover big as his head. But he won't remember nothin', 'cept maybe a dream, and if he does that, he's liable to wish he didn't."

"Haw," Royal Mango said again, and they walked back down Yucca Terrace to Sears Ellis's GTO, hearing nothing but their own footsteps, keeping a lookout for headlights.

They had gotten almost to the city limits when Royal Mango said, "Wonder what she'll do if'n he shows up back out there again wantin' to get him some silver dollars?"

Sears Ellis shifted down and made the turn off Hawthorn Street and headed toward Brooklet. "She ain't gone have to worry with that one anymore," he said. "Come tomorrow mornin', he ain't gone never even heard of them silver dollars."

Royal Mango looked at him. In the pale light from the dashboard he could barely see Sears Ellis's face.

"You swear," he said.

"Uh-huh," Sears Ellis said. "And don't you worry none about him, either. She fixed him up real good."

EIGHTEEN

The third day Buddy and Karen were in Barbados, they rented a little Ford at the Hilton in Bridgetown and went for what Karen thought was a look at the countryside but which Buddy also intended as an opportunity to get his bearings.

But after they had driven out of and back into Bridgetown for ninety minutes on roads that never seemed to go anywhere but back to where they started, Buddy gave up trying to find Leeman Gant's house and settled for finding the district it was in when he and Karen were finally able to get out of the city.

It didn't take Buddy long to decide that he didn't like driving in Barbados, mostly because he had to stay on the wrong side of the roads and often didn't remember to. Karen didn't like Buddy driving in Barbados, either, because he couldn't remember which side of the roads to drive on and because it was impossible to tell on which blind curves the sugarcane trucks would come around on no side at all but squarely in the middle.

The fifth day Buddy and Karen were in Barbados, Buddy took the little Ford and headed for the village of Bathsheba on the Atlantic side of the island. After miles of cane fields the land began to rise and then finally rounded off into steep grassy hills and smaller, rounder hills thick with vegetation. This time Buddy had a map given to him by the constabulary in Bridgetown, and he knew exactly where to go.

In fact, when he pulled over on the side of the winding road as it topped a hill and looked down and saw the little pink house among the deep green trees below him and the great blue ocean

261

beyond it, he knew at once that he had only to follow the road halfway down the hill and that when he went up and knocked on the door of the house, he would soon see people he last saw in Talmadge County, Georgia more than two months before.

He also realized he had no earthly idea what he would say to the old man. And God only knew what he'd say if it was Elizabeth who met him. Nor did he really know why he thought he could get her or the old man to talk to him and tell him the truth, either. It bothered him, and made him feel silly, that so far he had devoted himself to getting to the Rattlesnake Master's house to the exclusion of figuring out precisely what he would do when he got there.

So he got out of the little car and lit a cigarette and leaned back against the closed door on the driver's side and tried to come up with a plan.

The air was warm and there was wind, but in Barbados, he'd noticed, wind was always blowing some way or another. Enormous white clouds were strewn across the sky over the ocean in front of him. Behind him over the hills and over his head were more clouds, but these were the color of asphalt and looked full of rain. Straight down the hill from him a little boy was climbing the steep grade, picking his way through the brush.

He probably wants to sell me some pot or get me to give him a tip for something I didn't even ask for, Buddy thought, what a pain in the ass, and went back to his cigarette and his plan.

The wind was picking up, and he could hear palm fronds and banana leaves rustling on the slopes around him. The boy was almost to the top of the hill; Buddy could see all of him down to his bare legs and feet.

To hell, Buddy thought, I'll wing it, and broke the fire from his cigarette and smashed it underfoot and got back into the car and put the butt in the ashtray.

"Hey, mistah!" the boy yelled, and waved both arms.

Hell, Buddy thought again.

The boy reached the edge of the road. He was very deep brown except his teeth, which were marvelously white, and his hair, which was black. He was out of breath.

"Excuse me, sah," the boy said, panting.

Buddy rolled down the window and wind came through it.

"What can I do for you, son?" he said.

"Excuse me, sah," the boy said. "Mistah Gant say for you to come on down to the house."

"What?" Buddy said.

"He say come on down," the boy said, and pointed back the way he had come. "It be about to rain, you get wet."

Buddy looked at the boy for a few seconds, then down the hill at the house, and started the car.

He was rolling up the window when the boy said, "Excuse me, sah," again, only louder.

Buddy rolled the window down.

"Now what?" he said.

"Excuse me, sah," the boy said. "Can I ride with you?"

"Aw, shoot. Excuse me," Buddy said. "Come on round here and get in."

So Buddy and the little boy, who said his name was Vincent, drove the winding road down the hill to the pink house under the manchineel trees. When they pulled up into the yard, the little boy jumped out and said, "Thank you, sah," and vanished around the corner of the house. Children were making noise somewhere close by, their voices mingling with a grumble of thunder.

Leeman Gant came through a screen door onto a tiny uncovered porch as Buddy was getting out of the car. He was wearing blue pants and a collarless white shirt, and raised his hand in a greeting.

"Mr. Crittenden," he said, smiling, "what an intriguing circumstance!" There was no surprise in his voice. "Welcome to Barbados." Buddy wondered if there was any welcome in there, either.

They went into the house, which was as full of shadows as Leeman Gant's house in Turleyville because the manchineels were tall and dense and kept most of the sunlight, what there was of it, away from the windows. Buddy sat on a pale green sofa, the shell of a loggerhead turtle hanging on the wall behind him. Most of the other walls were fairly covered with watercolor scenes of the island.

Everywhere there were seashells—in jars, on tables, inside great thick water jugs that had been made into lamps. A row of queen conchs sat on a shelf. Against the wall between the front door and the entrance to the kitchen was an old wooden console radio, topped by a jar of spotted volutes.

The only piece of furniture Buddy could see with no seashells on it was a long narrow sideboard against the wall across the room in front of him. On the sideboard a single blue candle stood in a holder that might have been silver.

The old man was still standing. "Would you like something to drink?" he asked pleasantly.

"No, thanks," Buddy said, "Unless you have a beer." He felt a little jumpy, and thought the air was full of electricity from the approaching storm.

"No beer," the old man said. "Lime juice, guava juice, orange juice, papaya juice, milk, rum. And tea."

"All right," Buddy said. "Orange juice. Straight."

"How else?" the old man said, and went into the kitchen. When he returned with Buddy's orange juice, he had a glass of water and lime juice for himself.

Leeman Gant sat down in a dark fuzzy armchair across from Buddy. "You've come a long way to see me," he said, and lifted his glass.

Buddy lifted his glass, too. "I got married, and we wanted to go somewhere nice on our honeymoon. This looked like as good a place as any."

"A place where you could take time to look up some old friends?"

"Call it that," Buddy said, "or call it coincidence." He took a sip of his juice. It was delicious, with just the right amount of pulp.

"And now that you're here?"

"I'm not sure," Buddy said. Large drops of rain began to hit the roof, and the two men looked at the ceiling. "First of all, you're safe from me, you understand that."

"Mr. Crittenden," the old man said with a shrug, "while I

thank you for your thoughtfulness, I can assure you that at no time have I been in danger from anything you might do. Except perhaps hurry, and that was on but one occasion."

Buddy looked at him dumbfoundedly.

"There were obstacles between me and my goal, but they were surmountable. You were never truly between us, but if you had been, I would have found a way to get around you, too."

"I didn't mean . . ." Buddy said.

"Please," the old man said, and lifted a hand. "If we are to speak frankly, for I suspect that is why you are here, then you must know what you are dealing with. I owe you that, you having come so far."

"But it ain't that," Buddy said. "Isn't that. As long as I'm here on my honeymoon—"

"With the former Miss Wheeler," the old man interrupted.

"Right," Buddy said. "How d'you know?"

"Mr. Crittenden," the old man said, and sighed. "You come thousands of miles to my house and tell me I don't have to worry about you, when I *know* I don't. It is my habit to know as much as I can about people I may have to deal with."

"Especially when the stakes are high," Buddy said.

"Ah, you see, then. Yes. I have previously sought to become acquainted with you from afar, in case—"

"In case you ever had to deal with me up close," Buddy said.

"Yes," the old man said, and smiled benignly at him.

Buddy cocked his head a little. "But you said you never, uh . . ."

"I never had anything to fear from you, no. Even if you had been belligerent and pigheaded, which you were not."

"Thank you," Buddy said.

"You're welcome," the old man said, still smiling. "Now. Here you are. How do you like the island?"

"It's beautiful," Buddy said. Rain was clattering on the roof above them. "We're having a good time. I like it over on this side, too—being able to hear the ocean and all. When it's not raining, I mean."

"I understand," the old man said. "I was happy to come back."

"Do you plan to stay?" Buddy said, and had another sip of juice.

The old man took a sip from his glass, too. "That remains to be seen," he said. "I am an American citizen, but when I am on Barbados I am Bajan. I am happy here, but I was happy there, so who can tell?"

"It's a little hard for me to believe that you can't tell," Buddy said. "But maybe that's neither here nor there. What I really want you to tell me straight out is how you managed to get hold of those silver dollars in the first place, and then what you did with them."

The old man chuckled. "Of course," he said. Through the window Buddy could see the whole world turned silver-gray by falling water. "I have had good reason not to underestimate you, Mr. Crittenden. But then, I appreciate a man driven by his curiosity. Do you wish to smoke?"

"Only if you do."

The old man got up and went into the kitchen, from where he called back to Buddy, offering more juice or a glass of rum. When Buddy declined both, he came back, stuffing tobacco into a small, white pipe. "The cockles are our ashtrays," he said, sitting down.

While Leeman Gant lit his pipe, Buddy took out a cigarette and lit it with his lighter. The old man took a few short puffs, blew out smoke, and leaned back in the fuzzy chair.

"Mr. Gant," Buddy said, "did you bring those silver dollars to Barbados?"

"No," the old man said immediately.

"Then why did you come back?"

Suddenly the rain was very loud, and the old man looked up at it, then at Buddy, and the two of them smiled and waited.

When the rain let up, Leeman Gant said, "First of all, simply to make you think the silver dollars were here as well, or to assume that they had been disposed of prior to our departure. That way there was no reason for you to look for them." He took a puff from his pipe.

"Second, it would have been easy to confirm that we had left America by ship for Barbados. So obviously we were making our getaway; we had a lot of baggage. What reason could you possibly have had to expect one of us to come back?"

Buddy sat up. "What?" he said. "Elizabeth?"

The old man took another pull from his pipe. "She has been there for a week," he said, smoke coming from his mouth. There was no triumph, or anything else, in his voice.

"She's back there," Buddy said wonderingly. "Jesus. I suppose that by the time I get home, them dollars will be long gone."

"I expect so," the old man said. "The purchases should be completed this week."

"She's back there," Buddy said again, shaking his head. "And in the most critical time of all—who knows, maybe I'd get an urge to ride back out to your house just to have another look, or maybe I'd run into Sears Ellis and catch him tellin' me a lie—when them dollars are honest to God bein' toted off, I'm sittin' here talkin' to you in a place three thousand miles away. I can't believe it."

"What?" the old man said. "That I would take advantage of your being away to rid myself of those silver dollars? That sounds like simple good sense to me."

Suddenly the rain stopped. The house was very quiet.

"But that you are here at this particular time is mere happenstance," the old man went on. "It was your choice, certainly not my doing. You cannot possibly think I would want to reveal Elizabeth's presence back there to you so soon as this."

"You could have lied to me just now," Buddy said.

"No," the old man said, and shook his head. "I have spent some time navigating around you for convenience's sake, but I have no wish to tell you a lie. Not anymore."

"Thank you."

"Wait," the old man said. "But what you do with the truth is your business. And if you take the truth and try to work against me, then I might use deceit to thwart you. Do you see what I mean?"

"Yes," Buddy said. "All I want to do with the truth is hear it."

"Well, then, if you see her when you get back, please tell her we spoke and that I am well."

Buddy grunted. "I suspect she'll already know," he said.

"Perhaps you're right," Leeman Gant said blandly.

At this point Buddy said he was sorry, but he had to go to the bathroom and the old man gave him directions down the hall to what proved to be a spotlessly white little room with a toilet with a chain and a tank above it and a lavatory and a tub with feet. A mirror flanked by sconces hung over the sink. Buddy pulled the chain once for hygiene and again just to watch it make the toilet work.

When he got back, he stood for a while in front of the sideboard with the blue candle on it, looking through the window at the dripping trees. Past the highest branches he could see a break in the clouds and blue sky.

"All right," he said, "let's say you sold them dollars in lots."

"You may say that," the old man said, not looking at him. He was still smoking his pipe, and Buddy took out another cigarette and lit it and sat down on the sofa.

"And they've been hidden somewhere out on your place."

"Yes and no. Some of them went straight to market, some of them were put away at my house—"

"Presided over by a snake, I bet," Buddy said dryly.

"Two. And some of them were at the home of Sears Ellis's family."

"Ah," Buddy said. "Out there near to where Sears and J. B. Barrett got caught in that hurricane. I reckon you know about that, too."

"Yes. Do you need anything?"

"No, thanks. Just for us to keep talking till I get a hold on all this."

"As you wish." The old man took off his glasses and massaged the bridge of his nose. Down the hall a clock chimed three times.

"Well," Buddy said, "tell me this, then. Can you make people do things they might not otherwise do?"

The old man put his pipe in a cockle shell on the table beside his chair and cleared his throat. "I'm not certain this is the answer you wish," he said, "but wouldn't you say that the actions of people are made up of infinite possibilities?"

"I reckon."

"Well, then, let us say that I offer people certain opportunities, or alternatives, perhaps, but alternatives to which they may respond in many ways. But let us also say that I have the ability to create situations in which the desired outcome is probable, but not always definite."

"And if something doesn't work," Buddy said, "you try something else."

The old man nodded.

Buddy sat up straight and brushed a dusting of ashes from his shirt. "Mango and them dollars," he said. "Spivey. Jerry Spivey."

"I know of Mr. Spivey."

"Yeah," Buddy said, "I reckon you do. And Leeman, too. Sears says you knew when Leeman found them silver dollars."

"Sam Campbell found them," the old man said with a tiny smile.

"Yeah, but Leeman was right there. And if I can believe Sears, that's how you knew."

The old man nodded. "Yes," he said, "that's true."

"You ain't gone tell me how you did that, are you?"

"I'm afraid not," the old man said softly. "You still might not believe me if I did."

"Well, hell," Buddy said, and sat back. "Excuse me. Then what did I come all this way for?"

The old man uncrossed his legs and shifted in his seat. "Are you disappointed that there are things you don't understand? Is it not enough to acknowledge that particular things happened, and that together they produced a specific result?"

"I just want to understand it," Buddy said glumly.

"You cannot understand it. I could tell you how I knew what some people were doing and when they were doing it, I could tell you also how I knew those silver dollars had been found in that well. And what would you know then? It would mean nothing to you. What matters is what happened and what resulted."

Buddy sighed. "Tell me true—are you the devil?"

The old man's head went back and a laugh of substance and beauty came out of his mouth.

"No, no, no," he said, still laughing but trying to stop. "I suppose I should be flattered; they say the devil is a very powerful fellow.

"But at the same time, you disappoint me, Mr. Crittenden. The devil, whoever he may be, and I are not on the same side."

Buddy looked down at the floor for a minute, then back up at the old man. "Okay. Just whose side are you really on?"

"My family's. My own. The side of light against darkness. Order against chaos. Good against evil. Your side. We are on the same side. I'm surprised you have to ask."

"But you use people to get what you want."

"So it seems to you."

Buddy waited a few seconds. "That's all you got to say about that? So it seems to me? You got another way of looking at it?"

"Yes," the old man said, "but you would not be able to see it."

Buddy sighed again and sat back. The old man excused himself, got up, and went down the hall.

What the hell am I doing here? Buddy thought. Not only am I a long way from home, but I'm sittin' here on this sofa under a turtle shell big enough to sleep in and this man is tellin' me that things I want to know about and even things that I have been a part of are things I didn't really understand when they happened and probably won't ever be able to understand, anyway.

He looked around the room, which was now brighter with sunlight making its way through the trees, and he thought about his and Karen's brick house in Georgia and how he wished he were with her and they were home and he could go back to doing his job five days a week like everybody else. He heard the chain being pulled in the bathroom and the sound of the toilet flushing, and then the old man was coming back into the room.

Leeman Gant opened the window over the sideboard with the candle on it and sat back down in the fuzzy chair.

"Now, then," he said. "I do not mean to evade your questions, Mr. Crittenden, but there are things that are simply past your understanding. Not to say that you could not come eventually to understand them, of course, but it would take you many years."

"Have it your way," Buddy said. "But at least tell me this: you knew when Leeman and Sam found them dollars, but what if Spivey had found them? Hell, what if *I* had been jukin' around old man Hutto's place for some reason and found them myself?"

The old man smiled. He was rubbing his fingers together, and he looked at them in his lap. "Simple. We would still be sitting here, you asking me questions."

"How do you figure that?"

"Because if Mr. Spivey had found them, or even if you had found them, I would still have them now and I would have come here. And probably you would have followed me, just as you did."

"You're a very confident man."

"Oh yes. I have been at work for a long time."

"That's right," Buddy said. "I guess you have. But what about Elizabeth? Ain't you just a little worried about her bein' back there all by herself? Spivey's still kickin' around, maybe he'll lean on Mango or somethin' and go out to your house. And she and Sears may be sweet on each other, but he can't be there all the time."

"Elizabeth can take care of herself," the old man said matter-of-factly. "She is a resourceful young woman."

"Carefully taught, too, I bet."

Leeman Gant ignored the sarcasm in Buddy's voice. "Yes," he said. "That's the tradition, and she has learned very well."

"But a guy like Spivey don't mess around. And somebody like Mango or even Sears could get hurt if Spivey was to go lookin' for information and didn't get it right away."

The old man smiled thinly, showing no teeth. "If Mr. Spivey goes looking for information, it will be forthcoming. All he has to do is ask. He will have no reason to get upset."

Buddy looked up. "Mango would tell him?"

"Unquestionably," the old man said.

"And Sears Ellis, if Spivey got to him somehow?"

"He would tell Mr. Spivey whatever he wants to know."

"Wait a minute," Buddy said. "You want him to go out there! You want Spivey to go see Elizabeth!"

The old man said nothing. Buddy's mouth was dry and his glass was empty.

"You're going to let that redheaded fool go out there," he said quickly, "and God knows what he'll think he's doing, but whatever it is won't really be what he's doing at all. And then, uh, well, I dunno. Then what?"

"They will talk and have tea and Mr. Spivey will go home, I imagine," the old man said flatly.

"God Almighty," Buddy said. "He'll think he's goin' in there dealin' with what to him won't be nothin' but a woman, and a black woman at that, even if he grants that she's pretty good at thievery. And what he's really gonna do is go head-to-head with, uh, with the Rattlesnake Master's daughter."

The old man nodded. "I'm sure it will happen while you are away. It may already have happened. But Mr. Spivey will certainly see Elizabeth."

"And then he'll go home, right?"

"Yes, certainly. After a while, he will go home."

Buddy stood up and began pacing around the room.

"And then he won't ever bother you again, is that right, too?"

"Never."

"Jesus," Buddy said, and stuck his fingers in his pants pockets and leaned back against the sideboard. The candle rocked in its holder.

"Please, not there," the old man said, and Buddy stood up again and did some more pacing, looking.

He stopped in front of the old man and glowered down at him. "Look," he said, "it seems to me you didn't give Jerry Spivey none of them famous alternatives of yours. He's just gone be picked up and put out of your way."

The old man raised his eyes to meet Buddy's. "Mr. Spivey could have chosen to leave us alone," he said, "but he won't. He has the itch of greed to scratch. And what would you have had me do? I could have killed him a long time ago, squashed him like an insect. Would you have preferred that?"

"No," Buddy said. "I don't know. It's just . . ."

"Mr. Crittenden, please," the old man said gently. "Sit down. I am sorry to make you so uncomfortable."

Buddy sat on the edge of the sofa. "I'm about ready for some of that tea of yours myself. Sears was gettin' on to Leeman about drinkin' your tea; he seemed to believe that's one way Leeman got to be uh, workin' for you. And just now you said Elizabeth and Spivey will or might have already had some tea, too. Whatever you want to do, you got a tea for it?"

The old man chuckled. "No, it's not so simple as that, although tea may be brewed for many purposes."

"You make 'em all yourself?" Buddy asked. It wasn't what he wanted to talk about, but he didn't really know what to say.

"Of course. Before you leave, we can go to the kitchen and I will show you some of the blends, some of the ingredients. You may be surprised."

Now Buddy laughed a little and felt himself relax. "I'm getting used to surprises. Tell me: is Elizabeth comin' back down here when she's through disposin' of them dollars and makin' a kittycat out of Jerry Spivey?"

"Why do you ask?"

"Just curious."

Leeman Gant seemed to be thinking.

"Not immediately," he said. "She will come later, if she wishes."

"And stay?"

"No," the old man said. "When she comes to Barbados again, I do not imagine it will be for long. Then she will return to America."

"And leave you behind."

The old man reached over and knocked the ashes out of his pipe into the cockle. He held the pipe in the air. "Do you mind?" he said.

"No," Buddy said. "Go ahead. I'll have another cigarette."

So the old man went to the kitchen and filled his pipe and came back and opened the front door, leaving the screen door closed. Then he sat down and lit his pipe with a match and put the dead match into the cockle beside him.

"Leave me behind," he said reflectively. "I suppose so, in a manner of speaking. Perhaps I could follow her to America, but it isn't likely."

"Um," Buddy said. "Her and Sears, are they gone get married?"

"Who knows?" the old man said, shrugging. "It's them, not me."

"Yeah."

They sat and smoked in silence until the clock struck four times.

"Just what is it you Rattlesnake Masters do, then," Buddy said, "when you ain't arrangin' for half of south Georgia to deliver silver dollars to you?"

"Mr. Crittenden," the old man said patiently. "How can I tell you? I could tell you of people healed from sickness, sorrow, and loneliness. Or I can tell you of lovers brought together, the good rewarded and the evil punished. Or peace of mind restored, or revenge. And what would you know? Only the what and not the why. And to the people I serve, only the what matters."

"Uh-huh," Buddy said. "And it's only people like me that might have to deal with bits and pieces of them Whats from the outside, like me worryin' over who beat up Harold Buckminster and who stole them dollars out of that well, who waste time worryin' about the Hows and Whys.

"I got a need to know the reason things happen. I always thought Leeman was that way, too, but he seems to have just gone right along with this whole business, and all he got from it was a lot of trouble and runnin' around."

"Leeman," the old man said, and took a couple of puffs from

his pipe. "Yes, he was a great help to me. Let's just say Leeman has not yet chosen to take advantage of his recompense."

"Does he know about it?"

"He may figure it out. Or he may choose to ignore it. I create opportunities, remember? I could not have given Leeman a truck or cash money outright; he was not my employee."

"Not that he knew about, anyway," Buddy said, a bit snidely.

"He was not my employee," the old man repeated. "But I have a high regard for Leeman, perhaps not the least because we share a name. So for his help he has been given an opportunity."

"At least tell me what you did for him," Buddy said. "I figured out that you were how Mango got his truck, y'know."

"I didn't decide about Leeman," the old man said. "Elizabeth did."

"I don't reckon you gone tell me what it is, though."

"Of course not."

"Hunh," Buddy said. "Just as long as he don't have to step over no rattlesnakes to get it."

The old man laughed softly. "No, no rattlesnakes! Did you know that there are no rattlesnakes in Barbados? Here they call me the Doctor. But a name is only that.

"And I will tell you this about Leeman: Elizabeth said it, that if he is brave enough to try for the good himself, then out of it will come something good for two."

"Somebody else is mixed up in it," Buddy said.

"Correct," the old man said wryly. He made a cathedral with his fingers, his elbows on the arms of his chair. "Quite astute."

"Leeman had better look out," Buddy said. He looked at his watch. "And I've got to get out of here."

"I'm sorry," the old man said. "You are good company. And provocative, though pleasantly so."

Buddy twisted up his mouth and then opened it to talk. "Well, there's one more thing I want to know, and I suppose I should give you a chance to give me some reason why you can't give me a straight answer."

The old man put his pipe in the cockle beside him. "Go on."

Buddy took a deep breath and let it out slowly. "All right," he said. "I want to know why Calvin Hutto had to die. Why'd you wait so long and then suddenly go after them silver dollars like a house afire? What was your hurry? I've had answers, but it's yours I want."

The old man took out a handkerchief and wiped his glasses. "Two questions," he said, replacing his glasses and blinking rapidly. "Two answers.

"I had no idea Calvin Hutto would die when I went to see him. Long ago my father had said, 'Wait until he dies,' but I could wait no longer. I decided to confront him, to see my enemy face-to-face. When I told him about my father, and who my father was, at first he laughed. He was a terrible, bitter man. He stank of sweat and liquor. Him sitting there laughing at me, when my father had . . . Well, anyway, when I told him how my father had made sure he would never enjoy a single one of those dollars, and told him about myself, what I would do to him, what was yet to come, then he began to believe, then to get angry, then afraid. And then he simply stood up and fell down and died." The old man shook his head.

"Uh-huh," Buddy said. "That poor old bastard didn't have any idea who he had been dealin' with all along, until you went out there. I figure maybe your daddy really killed Calvin Hutto a long time ago and it just took seeing you to make him fall over."

"A novel way of expressing it," the old man said. "My father was very powerful. Perhaps you are right."

Buddy sat on the edge of the sofa and put on what he hoped was a shrewd face. "Was he powerful enough to keep his son dancing on the end of a string for most of his life? Who was it contrived to get them dollars away from Calvin Hutto? You? Or was it really him?"

"My father asked me only to grant a wish," Leeman Gant said. "I am carrying out his request." He pointed a finger at Buddy. "At any time I *could* have abandoned my waiting, or abandoned my search. But I *would* not. Such was my promise to my father."

The old man drew back his finger and folded his hands in his lap. "Are you satisfied so far?"

"Yes."

"A promise to my father. I am an old man, Mr. Crittenden, and I have seen and done strange and wonderful things, but none of them has ever made me any younger.

"I have a problem with my heart," he went on, patting the center of his chest. "I may live a year, I may die sitting here looking at you. My time was growing short and my promise was still unkept."

"There was Elizabeth. Your heir."

"It was not her promise," the old man said tenderly. "But she has helped me greatly."

Buddy looked at his watch again, then sat back on the sofa. "Lemme see if I got this," he said. "It's part of what I come a long way to get. So your daddy the Rattlesnake Master put the whammy on Calvin Hutto. Then your daddy the Rattlesnake Master and his son the Rattlesnake Master conspired to get them silver dollars from wherever the old weasel had stashed them."

The old man nodded. "In effect, yes."

"Okay. So when you come to find you got a bad heart, you figured you had to hurry sho nuff, so you did this and that and got them and then you run off down here. And Elizabeth goes back to sell them off."

"That's fairly accurate," the old man said. He was watching Buddy intently.

"I dunno," Buddy said. "Something still don't fit. What was the use of gettin' them dollars in the first place? Revenge?"

The old man leaned forward in the fuzzy chair. Buddy could hear children's voices again, coming through the open front door.

"No. The taste of revenge is unquestionably sweet, but a terrible revenge had already been exacted on Mr. Hutto. And I have told you—I went in search of those silver dollars in order to keep a promise to my father."

"But it wasn't just to get the dollars away from Hutto," Buddy said. "Or to clean up your daddy's name in the eyes of maybe the two or three people, if that many, who would remember him. I don't think I'd believe that now."

"No," the old man said. "Both of those things, but not them only." He sat back and put his hands on the arms of his chair.

"When my father brought us back to Barbados, he lost the house we lived in and the few acres surrounding it. Now I have arranged to buy them back. In a few days Elizabeth will have the money in hand to do that."

"But why?"

Leeman Gant turned to face Buddy and his gaze made Buddy uneasy, because the old man's eyes were merry behind his glasses.

"Because it was my father's wish to be buried there," he said.

"In South Georgia? Where is he now?"

"Here in Barbados," the old man said, as though it were obvious. "Where he died."

"Well," Buddy said, and sighed. "I just hope your daddy's satisfied." He stood up and adjusted his belt.

"I'm sure he will be," the old man said, standing, too. "Before you leave, come to the kitchen and I'll give you a short lesson in the magic of tea making."

"Or the tea of magic making."

The old man laughed. Buddy thought his host was in remarkable spirits and wondered if it was because he was leaving and they'd probably never see each other again.

"Mr. Crittenden," the old man said, "your wit is of such keenness that it deserves a reward. Would you like to see my father?"

"Sure," Buddy said, and he followed Leeman Gant over to the sideboard with the blue candle on it. The old man picked up the candle in one hand and lifted the top of the sideboard with the other to get a photograph, or so Buddy thought until he saw the body of an old, very black man lying in the narrow box with his eyes closed and his hands clasped across his chest. He was dressed in a black suit and a white shirt with a black bow tie; a silver snake with ruby eyes was entwined among his fingers.

"Mother of God," Buddy said.

"Mr. Crittenden," Leeman Gant said, "this is my father."

"What the hell," Buddy said hoarsely, staring down at the corpse in the sideboard. "He doesn't even look dead."

"But he is," the old man said. "We've made him wait a long time, but as soon as I have the deed to the land that was once his, I will ship his body to Elizabeth and she will take care of the rest."

"Jesus," Buddy said. His heart was racing. "Him lyin' over here in this box all the time. You do this yourself?" Nodding at Augustus Gant below him.

"Yes. You could, too, if you knew how."

"I'll pass," Buddy said, looking up. "Uh, listen—it's against the law just to go out and bury somebody. You can't do that anymore."

The old man smiled broadly. "Have us arrested."

He knows he gave me a jolt, the old scoundrel, Buddy thought, but he said, "No, thanks, I don't think I could stand the strain. I'm already sort of an accomplice to these shenanigans anyhow."

The old man closed the lid. "Now you know what you need to know," he said, "which is that those silver dollars will provide a harvest that will be well spent. Are you ready to learn about tea?"

Buddy's throat felt funny. "In a minute, thanks," he said. "Are you still willin' to make good on that offer of rum?"

"So that's it in a nutshell," Buddy said. "He got them dollars that Calvin Hutto stole so he could buy that place his daddy used to live on and send his body back there where he wanted to be buried."

Karen tilted her empty wineglass back and forth. A little breeze carried the smell of frangipani around and past their table. "I can believe that, all right," she said, "but all the other stuff—there's got to be another explanation."

"I'll grant that it's hard to believe," Buddy said. "But believin' it is better than me wearin' myself out tryin' to figure out logical reasons for some of the things that happened. The old man says they've even cooked up something good for Leeman, though somehow it's supposed to be good for somebody else, too."

"What is it?" Karen said, pulling at an eyelash.

"I dunno," Buddy said. "I reckon we'll just have to wait and see."

Only a few couples were still lingering over dinner on the terrace. The sun had gone down in a broad splotch of red and purple, and now the stars were brilliant in a clear dark sky. Buddy looked across the table at Karen, who was now his wife. She was wearing a pale blue sleeveless dress, cut fairly low in front. Her hair was shining and falling onto her shoulders. Buddy was so happy that he wanted to sing, but he knew that if he did, she'd laugh.

"And then there was the tea!" he said, still excited from looking at her. "Jars and jars and jars of all kinds of stuff, and all of it makes different kinds of tea. The old man says they all have, ah, special uses and functions, and if he says it, I believe they do." Buddy grinned.

"Like what?" Karen said. Steel-band music was coming faintly from somewhere out of sight. Buddy signaled a waiter and ordered two cups, hot water, and two tea balls.

"Did you see him give you that funny look when you asked for tea balls?" Karen said. "Are we having tea?"

"Yes and yes. Maybe he'll have to ask somebody what they are, but I know they've got 'em. What else was it you asked me?"

"What kinds of tea."

"Oh, yeah," Buddy said. "Tea to make you feel good, tea to cure colds and flu and other stuff, tea to make you remember something, and tea to make you forget; and tea that can make you dream all sorts of things.

"Mr. Gant says there's a tea out there for just about anything you want to feel or stop feeling—and, I imagine, for just about anything *he* wants somebody to feel, or do or not do."

"Oh, come on," Karen said teasingly.

"No, really. There were a lot of little jars he wouldn't tell me about, either, and I believe I'd just as soon not know what kind of brew they make."

"Spare me," Karen said, and then the waiter was back with two cups and two porcelain pitchers of hot water and two small, silver, egg-shaped, perforated tea balls dangling tiny chains.

"There's also this," Buddy said as the waiter retreated. He took a tiny bottle out of his pants pocket and began to pour its contents into the two tea balls.

"Wouldn't you rather just roll it and smoke it?"

"Cut it out. This was made especially for us. This is tea for honeymooners." He leered at her and dropped a tea ball into each cup, then poured hot water over them.

"Oh yeah? What's it do?" Karen raised her cup and sniffed it.

"I don't know," Buddy said, "or at least I'm not sure. He said we'd appreciate the gift, that this was a rare and popular tea."

"And you trust him?" Karen said, still looking into her cup.

"Absolutely. I think it's part of my reward."

"Reward for what?"

"For being such a good sport. And for not showing him but a little of how much it blew me away when he opened the top of that fake sideboard."

Karen looked at Buddy and smiled. He took the dripping ball out of his cup and put it in a saucer, then did the same with the ball in her cup.

"What the heck," Karen said. "Maybe I'll drink half a cup. Or maybe I'll just watch you drink yours and stand back out of the way." She giggled. "Buddy? Are you listening?"

"Drink your tea, honey," Buddy said, and lifted his cup to his lips.

NINETEEN

Oh, no," Buddy said, "probably not by now. They ain't had the time, I reckon. I don't even know if the sale's been closed yet."

"You could ride out there and have a look," I said. "See if there's a fresh grave somewhere on the place. I'd go, too."

"Uh-huh," Buddy said, biting a fingernail. "Maybe. But let's give it a couple of weeks, make sure we give them time to do it. I do want to see it, though, and be sure that whole business is over with."

It was raining in torrents, the wind blowing splashes of water against the windows. I could hear the gutters overflowing onto the driveway. We were sitting in my kitchen at six o'clock on Saturday evening with the lights turned on because there was so much water between us and the sun.

For more than an hour Buddy had talked up a blue streak, leading me around Barbados in general and Leeman Gant's house in particular. We'd gone from a hotel shaped like loaves of bread to the warm Caribbean and the roaring Atlantic through good food and drink to a roadside on a hilltop and a little boy who bummed a ride.

Then we went through Buddy's afternoon with the old man, inch by inch, and emerged whole on the hotel terrace with him and Karen having the Rattlesnake Master's tea.

"Pretty good tea, huh?" I said.

"Man," Buddy said. "I wish I could tell you."

"Is that why y'all stayed an extra three days?" I said sweetly.

"Hah," Buddy said, and grinned, and his cheekbones turned red.

"Anyway," I said, "it sounds like a rousing trip."

"Yep," Buddy said, "it was sho that. Uh, can I smoke another cigarette here?"

"Sure," I said. "I didn't figure you could stop at one, anyway."

"I'm indulging myself," Buddy said defensively. He took out a cigarette and lit it with a lighter with an armadillo on it. "Karen's after me to quit."

"Good luck," I said, and Buddy grunted and blew smoke.

I had already had a Coca-Cola and a Yoo-Hoo, sitting there listening to Buddy talk about his trip, so at this point I got up and went to the other end of my house to the little green bathroom and stood over the toilet and peed and stared at the row of shampoos and lotions and dust on the shelf on the wall behind it. Then after that I stood over the sink for a minute and looked in the mirror. Maybe I was looking for new lines on my face, or maybe I was just studying myself, looking for something different from the last time. Sometimes I do that.

When I got back to the kitchen, Buddy had poured himself another glass of milk.

"All right," I said, and sat down. "Now what?"

"How're you doin'?" Buddy said cheerfully. "You okay?"

"Sure," I said. "In fact, I'm doing just fine. Why?"

"Nothin'," Buddy said, "just curious."

"Yeah," I said, "but why? Did the old man say anything about me to you?" The windows were rattling in the rain and wind.

"Well, uh," Buddy said, "he asked about you and, uh, sends you his regards."

I saw Buddy's shoulders relax.

"Nothing else?" I said.

"Uh, no," Buddy said. He was lying, unquestionably an irritating pastime for him, but it didn't matter. "Sorry."

"That's okay," I said. "He sent me a message by somebody else."

"Sears?" Buddy said.

"Elizabeth," I said, and bared my teeth at him without meaning to.

"Well, god damn," Buddy said. "It ain't enough that she was back here unloadin' them silver dollars while I was talkin' to her daddy a zillion miles away with a corpse in the room with us listenin' in. No, I got to go way down yonder—"

"It was your honeymoon," I said. "Remember?"

"Yes," Buddy said. "I got to go way off down yonder to the doggone West Indies to talk to one of these people, and then the other one just strolls up and rings your doorbell."

"Actually, she knocked," I said.

"What was the message?" Buddy said.

"That he would not see me again in this life," I said, "but that he remembered me fondly and hoped that I would do the same for him."

"Pretty heavy stuff," Buddy said, and took a sip of milk. Lightning flashed and we both flinched. The thunderclap was terrific.

"Jesus," Buddy said. "Maybe that's him now."

"Cute," I said, "but there's more." Buddy raised an eyebrow at me. Because of that and the crescent of milk on his upper lip, his face seemed to be decorated with quarter moons. "There's a message for you, too."

"Yeah?" Buddy said, and sat up straight.

"He said to thank you for the visit. . . ."

"Which I probably hadn't even made yet," Buddy grumbled.

"And he advises you to learn to stop listening with your head so much and learn to listen with your heart. As you must have, he reminds you, after drinking the tea for honeymooners."

Buddy blushed magnificently. He looked like a boiled crab. "Hah," he gasped. "I hope you said thank you to Elizabeth for me."

"I did," I said, and got up and went to the refrigerator.

Elizabeth had asked if she could come in, but she had to ask me again before I was able to get over the surprise of seeing her enough to tell her yes and bring her inside and offer her a seat on the sofa. I sat in a monstrosity of two-by-fours and cushions—something I had bought but never quite got accustomed to owning, much less using—by the fireplace.

She was willing to tell me just about everything I wanted to know—why she was back in town, where her father was, and what happened to those silver dollars Sam and I had found. She even told me why she and Leeman Gant went after those dollars in the first place and what the money they got from selling them would do. But I didn't say anything about that to Buddy when he was telling me about his trip. Until then I didn't know that he knew, or that it was all right for me to tell him if he didn't.

She did not, however, tell me that her grandfather's corpse was in a sideboard in the living room of her father's house in Barbados, but I don't mind that; it gave Buddy a good story to bring home with him and something he could tell me that I didn't already know.

Elizabeth was dressed in white, as I'd always seen her. Her earrings were pearls, and once in a while she would touch one as if to see that it was still there.

"I have another matter," she said.

"Shoot," I said, and took a deep breath.

Elizabeth straightened the hem of her dress. "Do you remember," she said, "when you slept at our house in Turleyville, did you have a dream?"

"Don't think I'm trying to be rude," I said, "but I'm willing to bet you know good and well that I had a dream."

Elizabeth smiled. "Do you remember it very well?" she said.

"Vividly," I said.

"You met a young woman on a beach," Elizabeth said. "She asked you questions."

"Yes," I said. My heart was speeding up, but I couldn't have said exactly why.

"Do you remember her?"

"Vividly," I said. "In my dream, anyway, she was somebody

who goes to graduate school and works evenings in a restaurant about a block and a half from here. Her name's Donna Calloway."

"I know her name," Elizabeth said, and smiled again.

"You do?" I said, but then I thought it over and wasn't surprised anymore.

"Of course," Elizabeth said, and reached up to touch an earring. "It was her dream, too."

I had heard that before, and it seemed worth thinking about, so I didn't say anything right away.

Elizabeth sat back on the sofa and crossed her legs. I thought she looked like a graduate student herself. She even had a purse with her. A graduate student whose friends were rattlesnakes.

Finally I said, "She told me that. The girl in my dream, I mean. Donna. It was all part of my dream, though, the substance of which I'm not surprised that you know."

"No," Elizabeth said, and the corners of her graduate student's mouth turned up. "She was in your dream, but you were in hers, too."

"Oh, for Pete's sake," I said, trying my best to sound skeptical.

"Have you known my father and me for nothing?" Elizabeth said. "Think about it. You must believe me. She told you, too. It's true. Just don't ask me how it happened."

Okay, I thought, maybe so. After everything else, the least I could do was believe that two people could have the same dream. As for the how, I didn't care. And then I remembered, and knew I wasn't dreaming at all when I had heard a man and a woman—Elizabeth and her father, I supposed—talking about the girl on the beach in my dream as I lay in bed in the little house in the woods down below Turleyville.

"Let's say I do believe you," I said. "Then what?"

"Do you not have a woman of your own?" she said.

"No," I said.

"You wanted the young woman in your dream," she said. "It was Donna you wanted then."

"Yes," I said. I did, no doubt about it. "But . . ."

"Do you mind telling me why?"

"Because I felt as though I could see into her heart," I said, "or that I could feel what she was like in her heart, and I liked it." It sounded silly, but it was true.

"Papa was right about you," Elizabeth said. "What are dreams but a way to see into one's heart? And you had a dream in which you were allowed a vision of someone else's! Do you see now?"

"It was still a dream," I said, "no matter who was having it." My pulse, which had begun to race, began to slow down.

"No," she said. "Then you don't see at all. No wonder you haven't done anything about her."

"Like what?" I said defensively. "It's never, until now, at least, been anything more than a dream to me. And as far as doing anything, I have a broken heart." Somehow, when I said it then, it seemed to be a pretty lame excuse.

"With enough time gone by for it to heal," Elizabeth said firmly. "There's not much nourishment in loneliness. Your dream should have told you that, too."

"It would be nice to believe you," I said.

"Then what reason have you not to believe me?" she said with a bit of impatience in her voice. "I can tell you this, that it was really your friend Donna that you met in your dream, and she was as real as you and I are now."

Elizabeth paused as if she was considering something. Then she said, "I don't know why I should have to tell you this, but she is yours for the asking, as well."

My mouth was dry and I swallowed. It didn't work, so I swallowed again. "How do you figure that?" I said.

"I will say it again," Elizabeth said. "It was her dream, too."

She uncrossed her legs, smoothed her dress, touched an earring, and sat back.

"Which means," I said.

"All right," she said, "I will say it for you since you cannot say it for yourself. It is irrelevant how she and I met, this young woman in your dream and in whose dream you were. It does matter that she, too, has had a broken heart, but she is at least a little bit brave and I offered her a chance to find out about you—so she would know if you are perhaps worth the trouble and hazards."

"Then it was really Donna," I said.

"Of course," Elizabeth said. "Haven't you been listening to me?"

"I suppose she had a good look at me, then, too," I said. I seemed to be getting a fever, and the room was smaller than I remembered it.

"Oh, yes," Elizabeth said.

"What did she think?" I said. "What do you think?"

"Thank you for asking two questions," Elizabeth said, "because I cannot answer the first one. But I will answer the second one by saying that I think you would have done better to have approached her before now. I'm sure you have thought of her since your dream, unless my ability to brew the tea for sleep is not what it used to be."

"Sure, I've thought of her," I said. "But none of the women in my dreams has ever turned out to be the woman of my dreams, if you know what I mean."

"I know," Elizabeth said, and smiled broadly. She sat forward, clasped her hands in front of her, looked me in the eye, and said, "But this one is."

"You reckon so?" I said.

"If you try."

"I've tried before."

"Try again!" she cried. "This time may be different."

"What the hell," I said, and then we sat there for a minute or so, not saying anything. Finally Elizabeth stood up, so I stood up, too.

"I have to go," she said. "Sears will be waiting, and we have many things to do."

"You mean it about that dream," I said. "About Donna, I mean."

"Of course," she said. "What are you going to do?"

"Think about it some more," I said.

"Men are idiots," Elizabeth said, and sighed. "Do what you will. But before I go, I have something for you."

She opened her purse and reached in, and when her hand came out it had a periwinkle in it. It was dark, and a little worn. It could have been the same one I always carried with me on the beach, the one I had with me in my dream in Elizabeth's house. In her daddy's house.

Elizabeth held out the periwinkle and I took it. It shone on one side from the soft afternoon light coming through the curtains.

"Thank you," I said. "What's this for?"

"You already know that," Elizabeth said, and began to turn toward the door. "It's for luck."

EPILOGUE

I poured myself a glass of lemonade, put the jug back in the refrigerator, shut the door, and sat down again. The rain had just about stopped, and the thunder was retreating.

"There's something you need to know," I said, and Buddy looked at me. "I've got a girlfriend. In the twelve days you were gone, we've been out six, maybe seven times, and she's coming over here tonight, too, when she gets off work. And then next Friday we're both going to take the day off and drive to Brunswick and spend a long weekend at the beach."

"Good Lord," Buddy said, grinning. "Let me shake your hand!" And he sat up and did it. Mine was a little damp, I guess. I still had one more thing I wanted to say.

But Buddy wasn't finished yet. "Sounds like y'all been goin' pretty hot and heavy, huh? Are you about to fall in love or somethin'?"

"Could be," I said cagily.

"Oooweee," Buddy said. He looked genuinely happy. "No sooner do I get married than you start spendin' weekends at the beach with, uh, is she good-lookin'?"

"A knockout," I said, and found that I was trying not to smile at him with what felt like a sort of triumph.

Buddy clapped his hands. "Well," he said, "now I reckon I ought to tell you. Old man Gant told me somethin' good was gone come your way and that if you were up to it, it'd be somethin' good for somebody else, too. My, my. If what we're talkin' about is that, I reckon we gotta score another one for the old buzzard."

290

I didn't have to wonder.

"A toast," I said, and Buddy raised his glass of milk and I raised my lemonade.

"To the Rattlesnake Master," I said.

"All right," Buddy said. "Might as well. Here's to the dam blam Rattlesnake Master."

We clinked our glasses together over the middle of the table and brought them back and drank.

"Okay," Buddy said, "don't keep this good news to yourself. Who's this woman? Who's this sweet thing that's gone spend a weekend of sin with you at some seaside hideaway?"

"Your cousin Donna," I said, and showed him some teeth.

"You're kidding," Buddy said, and I could see him stiffen just a little bit, as though he thought he might need to pounce.

"No," I said. "It's the truth." He could pounce if he wanted to, I didn't care.

"Really?" he said. "Donna." The first part was a question, but the second part wasn't. He seemed to be thinking about something.

"Really," I said. Then I lied: "I thought you'd be happy about it."

"Uh, yeah," Buddy said, and tried to smile, but he didn't get far. "Yeah. It was just a surprise, y'know?"

"Look," I said, "you're my friend and she's your cousin. So what?"

"So you're my friend and she's my cousin," Buddy said. "And she's a lot younger than you are."

"Believe me, it's okay," I said. "My intentions are as honorable as can be, if that's what's got your hackles up. We like each other. After you think it over a little bit, you'll feel better. Talk to her if you want to, if this ain't enough."

"I already thought it over," Buddy said, running his hand over his chin. "Just now. And what I've been thinking about is this: old man Gant and that stuff about how somethin' good was gone happen to you and to somebody else. Jesus, to think that somebody was my cousin."

"If it was her, it was supposed to be something good for her, too," I said. "So don't worry about it."

Buddy tried to smile again and had a little more success than the last time. We sat there for a few minutes drinking our drinks and listening to the whole world dripping water outside, and then I got up and took a can of peanuts out of the pantry and we ate some of them.

"Look here," Buddy said finally.

I had a mouthful of peanuts and couldn't say anything, but I waved at him to continue.

"There's something you ain't told me, isn't there?"

I swallowed. "What do you mean?" I said, but I already knew.

"I shoulda known Gant was in this," Buddy said, and sighed. "Your reward for helpin' him and all. She's your reward. It just sounds sort of peculiar, sort of strange, y'know, not like somethin' you'd go along with, knowin' you the way I do, or reckon I do. Unless . . ."

He looked at me. The windows rattled a little from thunder so far away that I could barely hear it.

"Unless what?" I said.

"Unless she knew about it," he said. "Unless . . . Aw, hell, this is makin' my head hurt. There's got to be more to it, something else I don't know, something else ain't nobody told me yet."

I didn't say anything right away. What I did first was to reach into my left-hand jeans pocket, past my knife and my comb, and put my fingers around the little black periwinkle Elizabeth had given me and pull it out and show it to Buddy.

"You know what this is?" I said.

Buddy squinted. "Some kind of seashell, looks like."

"Right," I said, "it's a periwinkle." I put it in my left hand and picked up my lemonade in my right and drained everything, pulp and little pieces of ice, too, all the way to the bottom of the glass.

"I don't get it," Buddy said. "But I guess I'm going to, and probably right between the eyes."

"You should be used to it by now," I said, and leaned back in my chair. "Besides, this is probably the last part of the whole business that you haven't heard about."

Buddy leaned back and crossed his arms. "Shoot," he said. "I'm at your mercy."

I held the periwinkle up into the light where he could see it. "Let me tell you a story," I said.